Born on April 1st,  to her auspicious natal day class and might have brou d she written in that ancien ed to the stage and became first successful summer m ....vine, New Jersey. She studied music for .... years and, during that time, became intensely interested in the stage direction of opera and operetta, ending that phase of her experience with the stage direction of the American première of Carl Orff's *Ludus De Nato Infante Mirificus*, in which she also played a witch.

By the time the three children of her marriage were comfortably in school most of the day, she had already achieved enough success with short stories to devote herself full time to writing. Her first novel, *Restoree*, was written in protest against the absurd and unrealistic portrayals of women in the science fiction novels of the Fifties. It is, however, in the handling of broader themes and the worlds of her imagination, particularly the two series (*Helva, The Ship Who Sang*, and the fourteen novels about the Dragonriders of Pern) that Ms McCaffrey's talents as a story-teller are best displayed. One of the world's leading science fiction writers, she has won both the Hugo and Nebula Awards, the E.E. 'Doc' Smith, the Golden Pen, and has been seven times winner of the Science Fiction Book Club Award.

Between her appearances in the States, England, Europe, Australia, New Zealand and Alaska as a lecturer in secondary schools and universities, and guest-of-honour at science fiction conventions, Ms McCaffrey lives in a house of her own design, Dragonhold-Underhill (because she had to dig out a hill on her farm to build it) in County Wicklow, Ireland. She runs a private livery stable and her three-day-event horses have been successful in international competitions. She does not do the competition riding, she hastens to add, but enjoys the success of horse and rider and the occasional canter on her favourite mount, a black and white mare named Pi.

Of herself, Ms McCaffrey warns: 'My eyes are green, my hair is silver and I freckle; the rest is still subject to change without notice.'

Ms Mcaffrey graduated *cum laude* from Radcliffe College, majoring in the Slavonic Languages and Literatures.

Anne McCaffrey's books can be read individually or as series. However, for greatest enjoyment the following sequences are recommended:

FREEDOM'S CHOICE

Anne McCaffrey

CORGI BOOKS

FREEDOM'S CHOICE
A CORGI BOOK : 0 552 14273 5

Originally published in Great Britain by Bantam Press
a division of Transworld Publishers Ltd

PRINTING HISTORY
Bantam Press edition published 1997
Corgi edition published 1997
Corgi edition reprinted 1997

Set in Plantin
by Phoenix Typesetting, Ilkley, West Yorkshire.

Corgi Books are published by Transworld Publishers Ltd,
61–63 Uxbridge Road, London W5 5SA,
in Australia by Transworld Publishers (Australia) Pty Ltd,
15–25 Helles Avenue, Moorebank, NSW 2170
and in New Zealand by Transworld Publishers (NZ) Ltd,
3 William Pickering Drive, Albany, Auckland.

Printed and bound in Great Britain by
Cox & Wyman Ltd, Reading, Berkshire.

*This book is affectionately
dedicated
to
Jan Regan
Who is more like Lessa than Lessa was*

*Exercising racehorses is the nearest
thing to riding dragons on this good
earth.*

List of Characters

Kris Bjornsen
Zainal – Emassi captain
Chuck Mitford – marine sergeant
Dick Aarens – mechanical genius
Dowdall – Mitford aide
Jay Greene
Patti Sue – victim
Matt Su – oriental engineer
Bart – cook
Sandy Areson – cook/potter/manager
Lenny Doyle (ex-Chicago) – plumber
Ninety Doyle (Lenny's brother) – useful type
Joe Latore
Mack Dargle
Anna Bollinger – pregnant
Janet

First Drop
Pess – a Deski
Coo – Deski
Murn – pregnant Deski female
Slav – Rugarian
Annie
Bass
Tesco
Murphy
Case Oliver
Taglione
Bob the Herb

Second Drop
Capstan
Macy
Leon Dane – medic
Astrid
Ole
Oskar
Jan
Bjorn
Peter
Sarah McDouall
(Francis) Joe Marley – Aussie medic/botanist
Worrell ('Worry') – Aussie
Bert Put – mission specialist
Raisha Simonova – mission specialist

Since Second Drop
Peter Easley – publicist, management type
Yuri Palit – resettlement UN man
Ray Scott – ex-Admiral
Jim Rastancil – ex-Maj. General
Bob Reidenbacker – ex-General
Bull Fetterman – ex-General
John Beverly – black ex-General
Gino Marrucci – test pilot
Sev Balenquah – test pilot
Boris Slavinkovin – Russian pilot
Salvinato – ex-Colonel
Geoffrey Ainger – British naval officer
Beggs – ex-Lieutenant, aide to Ray Scott
Peter Snyder – engineer
Ayckburn – ex-governor

Francois Chavell – Catteni speaker
Irene Palcos
Iri Bempechat – judge
Walter Duxie – mining engineer
Fek – Deski female
Tul – Deski
Mic Rowland – stunt-man, useful type
Basil Whitby – geologist/climber
Leila Massuri – Maltese-French
Baxter – ex-film cameraman
Mavis Belton – nurse
Hassan Moussa – late of Israeli forces
Mayock – medic and hooch-maker
Laughrey – Concorde pilot
Beth Isbell – Catteni speaker/reader
Sally Stoffers – Catteni speaker/reader
Sheila – cartographer
Lex Kariatin
Zane Bjornsen
Anthony Marley } new babies

Catteni
Perizec – Zainal's father
Lenvec – Zainal's younger brother
Clern – Lenvec's life-mate
Kubitai – Zainal's alias
Bulent – High Emassi commander on Earth
Eosi – Ix Mentat, senior
    Co, junior
    Se, junior

Preface

When the Catteni, mercenaries for a race called the Eosi, invaded Earth, they used their standard tactic of domination by landing in fifty cities across the planet and removing entire urban populations. These were distributed throughout the Catteni worlds and sold as slaves along with other conquered species.

Since slavery did not sit well with many of the first-world countries, the conquerors met with considerably more resistance than had been anticipated. The size and general brutality of the Catteni soldier generally inculcated sufficient fear and obedience to inhibit active resistance on many of their previous invasions. However, since many M-type planets had been discovered by the Eosi, the Catteni were advised to round up sufficient dissidents and felons alike, deposit them on whatever M-type planet was currently available for occupation and let them fend for themselves.

Not all M-type worlds are suitable for colonization but, since the Catteni had quantities of expendable personnel, they could utilize an empirical method of discovering which was fertile and friendly, and which contained dangers making them inimical. A check was kept on the survival rate of such inadvertent settlers. If few remained alive, the world was abandoned. If the survival rate was high, more deliveries were made. When the imposed population had made the world tenable, the Catteni would install an overlord and exact a percentage of the gross planetary product. Any dissenters to this procedure were then rounded up and deposited on yet another potential colonial world.

Botany was one such colonial world on which the Catteni, emptying holding cells on Barevi and Earth, dropped several species to see how they survived – each other as well as the peculiar, but as yet unidentified, denizens.

The Catteni outfitted each of the unsuspecting colonists with durable clothing, a blanket and a packet of dry rations. The 'shipment' spent the voyage in a form of suspended animation and were deposited on the planet where knives, hatchets and rudimentary medical kits were left for their use, or abuse.

On Botany, however, a former staff sergeant took charge of those dropped with him and, warned by one of the alien species, the Deski, managed to avoid one of the local avian predators.

Zainal, the one Catteni who had been shanghaied in that shipment, remembered other vague problems about this planet from a cursory reading of the original exploration report. Although some of the stranded people wanted to revenge themselves by taking the Catteni's life, Kris Bjornsen forestalled the attempt, suggesting that he knew more than anyone else did about this planet and they'd better keep him alive for a while. Sergeant Chuck Mitford saw the wisdom in that – and also in the Catteni's advice to seek higher, stonier ground if they wished to survive. In a forced march to the safety of the nearby hills, Mitford realized that Zainal could be useful for quite a few reasons.

Establishing a base camp, hunting for edible life forms and foods, occupied every one of the survivors under Mitford's command. The settlers discovered that this planet was not as unoccupied as the Catteni report suggested. In fact, it seemed to be a planet extensively farmed by mechanized, highly sophisticated machinery, operating without any 'live' supervision. On a scouting mission, Kris Bjornsen and Zainal encountered more humans, as well as representatives of the other four races also dumped on Botany.

In order to save the Deski from dying of malnutrition, since Botany did not produce a basic dietary requirement, Zainal forced a confrontation with the Catteni captain of a second transport which was dumping a new load of people. He also sent back the message that this planet was obviously an agricultural subsidiary of a heretofore undiscovered sophisticated race.

Then he was summoned to a covert meeting with another Emassi high-ranking official, with an offer to be returned to his rank and duties: an offer he summarily rejected.

By then, there were sufficient technicians and engineers available to redesign some of the available equipment into useful appliances and machines, supplying communications and useful equipment to assist the settlers.

Using the aerial maps reluctantly supplied him,

Zainal led a group to what might be a command centre on the planet. However although it had obviously not been occupied for a very long time, a garage held several aerial devices and smaller missiles of a homing device design. One of these was deliberately launched by Dick Aarens.

The launch is observed by interested agencies – and so begins the second part of the Catteni story.

Prologue

Part One

The satellite logged the departure of a missile from the surface of the planet under observation. It analysed the components and attempted to correlate the information within its memory banks, but found no match. The unusual speed and approximate direction of the device was also noted as it headed galactically north and east towards the furthest edge of the Milky Way. Just as the missile reached the heliopause of the system, it disappeared. A scan produced no debris; no ion or any other trace of what had powered its drive could be detected. It had vanished: a fact that was unacceptable to the monitoring program and caused a functional error which required internal investigation and repair. Although its earlier tracking was recorded, the satellite did not – due to the anomalies – immediately forward the data to its servor.

Consequently, without a requisite emergency code, the information went through several processings before the anomalies were noticed. It was then immediately reported to the proper authority. A team was despatched to correct the malfunction, but none was found even after a complete overhaul and maintenance check of the satellite. The data were therefore suspect as a malfunction in themselves, rather than the recording of an event. The planet was, after all, a penal colony; the exiles equipped with the barest essentials for survival and no technological equipment whatever. It was only by chance that the report was ever seen by persons with the essential information to realize the significance of the sighting, and the mysterious disappearance of the homing device.

Part Two

'You say that he *refused* to answer the summons?' The speaker scowled at the Emassi captain.

As they were also father and son, the son was accustomed to his sire's scowls; he almost enjoyed the reaction, knowing that Zainal's refusal to return and accept the duty imposed on his rank and family would blacken his brother's previously spotless reputation in their father's estimation.

'He was chosen,' Perizec continued, bashing one huge fist onto the pervalloy worktop. 'He cannot refuse the summons.'

'He did,' Lenvec said, with an imperturbable shrug of one shoulder. ' "I'm dropped, I stay." You know the convention.'

Perizec crashed both fists onto the worktop, bouncing everything on it, and scattering the files from the desk rack. 'An Eosi matter has precedence over any Catteni convention! You know that!' The scowl deepened, pulling down the heavy mouth and jaw, darkening the grey-toned skin. 'He has known of this duty since he was presented to the Eosi. Dropped or not, he is to return to accept that duty.' The fists banged emphatically again. Then Perizec's eyes narrowed to slits through which his yellow pupils flashed with anger. 'How did he come to be dropped on that felon planet?'

Lenvec shrugged. He knew that his father was well aware of the whole circumstance, but he repeated the report.

'Zainal engaged in a fatal brawl with a minor transport officer. The crew sought vengeance and Zainal escaped in a flitter, which was hit and crashed in the western hunting grounds. No trace was found of him then, but he was discovered later that night among dissidents who had been gassed during a riot. Because it was within the twenty-four hours, one of the crewmen made certain that he remained in the transport facility and was included in the shipment. He made his presence known to a second Drop crew. Your office was alerted and I made the run to retrieve him. He refused—'

'I know, I know,' and Perizec flicked thick fingers to end the recital. 'He must return. The duty is required of him. We cannot avoid the choosing.' He frowned, deep in thought. 'See to it that the crew who arranged his deportation are sent to the same destination. They will ensure that he is ready to be collected when next you land there.'

'A thought, sir,' Lenvec began. 'Catteni would

not be popular on the planet and may even be prevented from finding Zainal.'

Perizec regarded him with a direct anger. 'Zainal survived. You said yourself that he was the member of some sort of team.'

Lenvec shrugged. 'Zainal is, after all, Emassi, sir, and as clever a man as you yourself . . .'

Perizec grunted at the filial compliment. 'He is also Catteni and would resist attempts to eliminate members of his own race.'

'He might not be in a position to do so. He may also wish to eliminate the crew for having put him on that planet in the first instance.'

'They will have to be "rewarded",' and Perizec's smile was unpleasant, 'for their part in his exile. See to that. And let us find among the Emassi two or three of Zainal's hunting friends. Them he would certainly protect, would he not?' Lenvec nodded. 'They will see to it that he is willing to leave when next you land.'

'Am I to transport them there?'

'By no means. That would put Zainal on his guard. When is the next mass transportation scheduled?'

Lenvec consulted his wrist unit. 'In twenty-two days.'

'Choose the men . . .'

'A female, too, sir, if I may suggest it. He's been a long time without . . . companionship.'

'An excellent notion,' and Perizec grinned back at his son. 'You have someone in mind?' Lenvec nodded. 'They will all be rewarded.' He reached to

18

the files and methodically began stacking them in order as he continued speaking. 'This must be completed as expeditiously as possible. I have told the Eosi that Zainal was sent on a special assignment and is unaware of their need of him. We have been granted a respite, but their anger will fall on us all if we do not present him within a reasonable period of time.'

Lenvec nodded. Since Zainal had been acceptable to the Eosi, there had been no need for Lenvec to be presented. Nor would he wish to be accorded such an Eosi 'honour' since he knew exactly what that entailed. However, he might yet find himself the substitute, if Zainal did not present himself. The honour of the family was at stake. Failure to comply with an Eosi demand brought disaster and disgrace to every blood relation.

'Keep me informed, Lenvec,' Perizec told his son by way of dismissal.

As Lenvec saluted formally, pivoted smartly and left the office, Perizec began to consider how to punish the stupidity of a mere freighter crew who had presumed to place an Emassi among transported dissidents. He enjoyed deciding on the exact and perfect punishment for their presumption and shortly was able to issue the necessary orders. Once the rumour was circulated, few Tudo or Drassi would dare to repeat such treatment, no matter what the cause. That this abrogated one of the main tenets of Catteni discipline did not bother Perizec. But then his rank had some privileges, and he exercised all frequently.

Chapter One

As he was supposed to do, the Deski immediately informed the camp leader what he had heard on the height above Camp Rock.

'You heard a ship come down?' Worrell asked, rubbing his face hard in an effort to comprehend what Coo was telling him.

'Come down,' Coo said, nodding vigorously, 'not big. Not you-zoo-al,' he added, struggling with the syllables.

'Not usual?' Worrell repeated, while Coo nodded with a Deski-style grin which Worrell was now accustomed to. 'You mean, not a Drop?' Coo shook his head and then nodded, to be sure he was understood.

Worrell sighed with relief. The damned Catteni had speeded up their deposits of 'colonists' over the past month to the point where there was barely time to assimilate each new delivery.

'No Drop. No long down. Come,' and Coo gestured with his thin, oddly-knuckled digits, swooping them down to close with his other hand, then pausing briefly before elevating it again. 'Go. Soft.' And now he put a hand to his ear and pretended to listen hard.

Instantly Worrell began to fret. His nickname 'Worry' was less a contraction of his surname and more a description of his chief trait.

'A quick Drop, then. A few people at the most. Only what kind?' he asked himself more than Coo. 'Nearby?'

'Not near-near.' Coo dropped his head, orienting himself, then shifted his feet slightly to the right so that he was facing due north. The Deski ability to know where they were was an extremely useful trait on Botany. They could get themselves back to the main settlements, like Camp Ayres Rock, from any point so that it had become practice to include at least one Deski in every scouting expedition.

Now Coo extended both long, double-jointed arms, kept the right one facing due north and angled his left arm almost due west. 'There. Not near-near.'

'Really?' Worry rose and patted Coo's bony shoulder. 'Real good, Coo. Thanks.'

'Good job done?'

'Beaut job, Coo.' Worrell turned up the light so that he could see the map hung on his wall. Much of the continent it represented was still blank but, over the past few wintry months, details had been added by scouting teams. 'If we're here, Coo,' and Worrell put his finger on the cave system of Camp Rock, 'how far west?'

Coo extended his head towards the map on a neck that seemed elastic, put one digit on the Camp and then slid it in the appropriate direction. 'No more far.'

'Really?' Worrell felt anxiety bloom in his gut. The point Coo had indicated was where Zainal and his team had met the scout ship: the one sent to take him back to his duties as a Catteni Emassi. 'Thanks, Coo. You'd best get back on duty.'

'I go.' And the Deski slipped quietly from the room.

Worrell glanced briefly at his timepiece. Dawn was too far away for him to send a squad to check the landing site. The night-crawlers would be all too eager to catch anything that travelled above ground. Not even a large team, stamping heavily, would escape those winter-hungry denizens.

Then Worrell chuckled to himself. If Catteni had indeed landed someone for some purpose . . . like getting in touch with Zainal again . . . they'd have had a welcome they didn't expect.

'Serve 'em right, too,' Worrell said to himself, though he was not by nature a vindictive man. In a considerably more cheerful mood, he returned to his bed and went soundly back to sleep.

Worrell would like to have had Zainal to send down to investigate the reported landing, but he and Kris Bjornsen were out with their team on another long scouting trip: looking for more caves, barns or rocky terrain to house the settlers continuously supplied them by the Catteni. So he sent for Mic Rowland, one of the Fifth Drop group. He'd been a stunt-man for the movies and could be trusted to observe, be discreet and get himself and a team out of trouble.

Worry told him about the late-night landing, and where Coo had thought the ship had touched down.

'If a Deski said it landed there, we'll find some signs.' Mic was far too accustomed to working with all-sorts, as he called them, not to appreciate talent wherever it was found.

'Even scoutships leave a stench behind them,' Worrell agreed. 'Take a party of those newbies with you. Give 'em a chance to hunt.'

'Sure thing,' Mic said with a businesslike nod.

Worrell grinned when he saw Rowland tag the first five people in the breakfast line whose new-looking coveralls marked them as the latest Drop. He did let them eat first before he took them off.

Worrell knew the trip would do them good. So many got to Botany still full of their Earthside sabotage activities, and how many Cats they'd injured or killed and other kinds of derring-do, so that they needed to be taken down a few pegs to the realities of Botany. Fortunately, more were adapting well to the new world than Worry would have expected.

What caused the Australian – and the other Camp managers – concern, was the indisputable fact that the Catteni were making more frequent deposits of dissidents. Zainal had been surprised too and had suggested, slyly, that it was because Earth was showing far more rebellion than any other race the Catteni had subjugated. So there were more rebels to be exiled. So far the colony had been able to absorb both quantities and alien species, though they had followed Zainal's suggestion to let the belligerent and unco-operative Turs go off on their own in the small groups in which they arrived. However, the population of Botany had risen from the original Drop of 572 to nearly 9,000.

Worrell worried all day over what Mic Rowland would find. He also widened the perimeter guard in case of infiltration, warning them vaguely that someone had seen Turs prowling about. It was possible, in Worrell's view of human frailties, that even some specimens of Mankind could have been brainwashed into co-operating with their Catteni masters and would try to slip into the colony to cause trouble. That actually made more sense to him than a secret landing of Catteni, since they would be instantly noticed. So far Zainal remained the only one of his race resident on Botany. And he had barely escaped being killed that first day – which was fortunate since he had proved so helpful in the early Drop, and ever since: even to rejecting a chance to leave.

Mic Rowland returned with enough game to justify the hunt. Dismissing his weary group, he caught Worrell's glance, jerked his head towards Worrell's office on the height and moved quickly to join the Camp manager there. He dropped the rock-squats with the cooks, but not the sack in his right hand.

Once they were private, Mic upended the sack on the table and grinned at Worrell's surprise.

'Boots?'

'That was all that was left. And not the same sort

they issued us,' Mic said, 'much better made. And this.' He took from his chest pocket a very thin plate about seven centimetres long and maybe two thick. 'I'd say it was a comunit, or some sort of call device. Maybe even an implant. I rubbed the gore off.' Then he picked up one of the boots which was scored as if something hot, or very strong, had twined around it, leaving deep grooves. He twisted the heel and the whole lower part of the shoe swivelled free, showing a compact kit of small tools, embedded in the material of the thick sole. 'There's something in each boot.' He picked up the smallest pair and opened the sole of one, revealing its contents to Worrell. 'This looks like a drug injector.' He opened the other, which contained two small vials. 'And the drugs.'

'Drugs? Yes, well, I'll give that stuff to Dane.' Worrell counted eight boots in an effort to defuse his mounting anxiety. 'Dropped a team, did they? To do what?' Though he had an awful suspicion his first guess might prove correct. Would Mic know?

Mic shrugged. 'You been here longer. An educated guess would be they were after Zainal.' When he caught Worrell's sharp look, he grinned. 'I heard. Damn few would have stayed if they had a chance to leave.'

'Hmmm. No other . . . remains?'

Mic shook his head. 'Some bits of metal, probably from whatever they were wearing, but even Catteni material is edible to the crawlers. Boots are just a touch too tough for 'em.' And he flicked his fingers at one. 'Big mothers wore 'em. Big even for Catteni. They have goon squads, too.'

'One pair is much smaller. *Would* they have sent a woman with them?'

Mic shrugged. 'Who knows what Catteni will do?' He closed his lips on whatever he had been about to add and shrugged again.

Worrell could very well imagine what had been left unsaid. Before his deportation, he had seen enough of the higher-ranking Catteni women to know that Kris Bjornsen was a lot better-looking than the best of them. Many disapproved of her liaison with Zainal but no-one, other than Dick Aarens, had the gall to complain or dispute it.

'Thanks, Mic. Did the others notice?'

'Couldn't fail to, not with those empty boots scattered around. I don't think the newbies noticed that the footwear isn't the same stuff we have. So I'm reporting a missing patrol to you. Right?'

'Too right,' Worrell said, 'and I trust you rammed home the lesson?'

'Never miss an opportunity like that, Worry.' And Mic left with a big grin on his face.

Worrell made a mental note that Mic was ready for more responsibility. First he dialled Zainal's team number for them to report in, then he got in touch with Chuck Mitford.

'Well, put 'em in a safe place, Worry,' Mitford said, 'until either Zainal or I can have a look-see. Just give the medical junk to Dane; he might know what it is and maybe have a use for it. I suppose you better send those tools down here to Narrow for the engineering types. They could use some high-quality stuff despite some of the new items they've been able to turn out recently. I'll have to figure out a way to explain their . . . ah . . . acquisition.' He contradicted himself a moment later. 'I don't have to explain anything, do I?'

'Sure don't, sarge.'

Worrell grinned at the comment. In one of the recent Drops there had been several ex-admirals, ex-generals and assorted other brass, most of whom – when they had had a chance to recover from the trials of their journey – were quite willing to refer respectfully to Mitford as 'Sergeant'. Most . . . and those who didn't soon learned how much was owed that 'sergeant', or found themselves settling into perhaps less amenable camp sites. No-one – except someone on sick call – shirked assigned duties, and everyone took a turn at hunting, preparing food, sentry and whatever other duty they were thought capable of managing. When he hadn't anything else to fuss about, though, Worrell worried that some sort of high-level executive-type consortium might try to bounce Mitford out of his current eminence. Of course, if Mitford decided on his own hook to step down, that had to be entirely his option. So far, Mitford's management – and he had listened to suggestions from just about everyone in the first couple of Drops – had worked pretty damn well.

'Sarge, should we worry about human infil-trators?' he asked, hoping to have such a notion knocked down.

Mitford's snort made the diaphragm of the

portable phone vibrate and Worrell began to relax.

'Not unless they can run faster than a crawler can grab. And if there were four Catteni, they'd have been heavy enough on those big feet of theirs to have alerted every scavenger four fields over.' There was a brief pause. 'Worry, you don't actually believe any human being would work *with* the Catteni, do you?'

'There've been traitors, renegades, spies, quislings in every war, sarge. Why not this one?'

Mitford cursed briefly, but colourfully. 'You could be right. Damn it! Only why send in infiltrators by special delivery? You could as easily send 'em in a regular Drop. Anyway, why mess us up? Zainal says the Catteni prefer colonies to prosper so they can come in and take over when one gets going well.' Pause. 'Furthermore,' and Mitford's tone was adamant, 'they'll have their work cut out for them if they try that tactic on *my* planet.'

Nor would anyone dispute Mitford's use of the possessive pronoun.

'We'd be with you four hundred per cent, sarge.'

Another brief pause. 'I'll tell Easley we'd better be double careful checking IDs on the next Drops. Right?'

With that he cut off, leaving Worrell not quite as anxious as he had been: no-one was going to take over 'my planet'. He grinned at the outrage in Mitford's voice. Scouts had come across the remains of several rough camps in the hills, above the level the night scavengers inhabited, and the skeletons of those who hadn't survived. But everything was much better organized now, especially the Drops. Peter Easley, former personnel manager of a huge international firm, had been responsible for that. His second morning on Botany, he sought Mitford out and made suggestions on how to simplify, speed up in-flow, and how to catch the signs of those still in trauma and needing counselling. He'd deferentially organized additional men and women experienced in crowd control and personnel handling, and passed on recommendations of other specialists that Mitford might want to interview himself. Mitford turned the whole problem of Drops over to Easley and the complexity of Resettlement – another of Easley's sensible recommendations – to Yuri Palit, previously a UN resettlement manager for displaced persons. There were now enough degree engineers, aviation and production line mechanics and inventor-types to keep Aarens from getting cocky while speeding up their output.

With enough hand-held communication units available, scouting teams could report in to Mitford on any unusual occurrences, as Worrell had just done, and the sergeant had actually been able to keep 'business hours'.

'I'll get enough time yet', Mitford had recently confided to Worrell on a trip through Camp Rock to Camp Silo, 'to lead a recon group myself.'

'Is that what you'd really like to do?' Worrell had asked, since it was the first time he'd ever heard something akin to a complaint from the man.

'All this brand-new world, and everyone else is

getting to see it first!' Mitford had flung up his hand in frustration. 'Well, I get closer to it all the time.' Then he'd grinned. 'And I get less and less paperwork to do.'

So now Mitford had more time to spend on organizing the teams and sending expeditions in every direction, trying to locate more bases, especially to replace Camp Rock which was established just above a deep gorge that showed the scars from centuries of spring flooding. Zainal and Kris Bjornsen were on just such a scouting mission now, hoping to find a site that was not an installation of the 'Mech Makers' or the 'Farmers', as many people were beginning to call them because of the agricultural emphasis of the planet.

Worrell packed the boots back into the sack, but he peered more closely at the plate. There did seem to be round indentations on one end: possibly touch points. He counted nine – as many as a numeric pad, and was sorely tempted, but decided against any whimsical experimentation. He'd sent out the recall sequence and Zainal and Kris should be back in a few days.

The team were at that time in a state of exultation, for they had managed to complete a difficult ascent up an irregular cliff mass and now looked down into a long valley that bore no traces of the neatness which typified the land the Mech Makers farmed. Their ascent had been a quick decision, prompted by certain anomalies that both Zainal and Whitby, the mountaineering expert of the team, had noticed. The first was a stream bubbling vigorously from what seemed like a solid rock-face. Investigating, they found the stream had bored a channel through the stony barrier.

'That's not the kind of rock that water erodes,' Whitby said. 'It was carved somehow.'

The second curiosity was that, in Whitby's estimation, the high mound of rubble that barred their way could not have been caused by a natural landslide or depression, and he called their attention to the top of the cliffs which did look shorn.

'Could have been an earthquake,' Kris had suggested.

'We've seen no other subsidence on our way here,' Basil Whitby had said, shaking his head and glancing along the cliffs on either side. 'Not a landslide, not with that kind of stone.' Then he grimaced at the tumbled rocks of the barrier.

'Don't see any kind of a road leading up here,' said Sarah, swinging around to be sure.

'As if mechanicals left any tracks with those air cushions,' Joe Marley reminded her, and she made a face at him. 'Not even a mark where a big mother would have parked for a time.'

'Animals do leave tracks,' she replied.

'And we haven't seen many of them lately, now have we?' he said in good-natured sparring.

'There have to be other animals than loo-cows, rocksquats, night-crawlers and those vicious avians. Even I know that much about ecological balance.'

'Maybe', and Leila Massuri's tone was cautious,

'that barrier's there for a good reason.' She and Whitby were the new members of the Kris-Zainal team. Leila contributed more to the pot with her crossbow prowess than to discussions.

'Keeping something in? Or out?' Joe asked, accepting the premise.

'We find out,' said Zainal, and began to pass out appropriate equipment for scaling the barrier. Though the air cushion of their all-terrain vehicle allowed it to traverse very rough ground, the gradient of the rocky obstacle in front of them was too acute.

They were far better equipped now for explorations than they had been in the initial days after being dumped on Botany. Leila slung her crossbow across her back and made sure the quarrel pouch was fastened, while Kris loaded her pouch with pebbles for her sling and slung the rope coil Zainal handed her over one shoulder. Whitby had fashioned himself a proper climbing pick which he slid into the loop at his belt, then stuffed pitons into thigh pockets and secured the short compound bow and quiver of arrows to the harness on his back. Sarah and Joe had slings as well as boomerangs, a type of equipment that was becoming more popular; Fek and Slav armed themselves with lances and hatchets. They all carried blanket rolls and a small sack with food and water.

The climb up the irregular and often shifting cliffside had taken most of the morning, but the view at the top was more than worth the effort. Below them lay a peaceful valley, obviously undisturbed by the agricultural mechanicals that dominated the slopes behind them. At the narrow end of the valley they could see a distant waterfall, its descent a murmur as it fell into a small lake. The stream leading from it meandered down the far, lower side of the valley and blundered into the cliff, answering the question of its origin. The valley floor was interspersed with flat grasslands and some of the odd-looking thickets that in their season would bear edible berries. But the most unusual feature was the little groves of what Kris called lodge-pole trees: straight tall trunks that flattened at the very top into a thick, flat crest of narrow branches fanning out, that were covered in needles during the warmer weather. Specimens did grow in some of the hedgerows that lined the mechanicals' fields but only as single trees, not in copses like these, and certainly not as many groves as could be seen from their vantage point. A cool, pungently scented breeze cooled their sweaty faces.

'It's as good as Shangri-la,' Sarah McDouall said, beaming down at the valley. 'It's lovely. So peaceful, so . . .'

'Secret?' Joe supplied. 'I wonder what else we'll find down there.'

'Why, there's space for hundreds here,' she said, ignoring his implicit pessimism.

'Hmmmm,' Zainal murmured, obviously sharing Joe's caution. 'Slav?' he asked the Rugarian, who was shielding his eyes as he surveyed the valley.

Slav shrugged.

'Fek?' Zainal turned to the Deski, the only one who showed no exertion from the difficult ascent, but the Deskis were such natural climbers that Kris had wondered if their home planet was nothing but perpendicular surfaces. Actually, their oddly-shaped hands and the soles of their feet became slick with a sort of adhesive substance which gave them purchase on sheer surfaces, and their unusually jointed arms and legs permitted them to assume postures that would have broken human limbs.

Fek had assumed her intensive listening posture, almost as if her hearing organs were extending themselves from the side of her head, wide open to experience the slightest of sounds.

'Wind. Water. Small noises,' she said, shaking her head to indicate a lack of obvious danger. 'No livings.' Without waiting for Zainal's signal, she started to descend. He shifted the heavy coil of rope he carried, rubbed the sweat off his face and followed.

Fek found the easiest descent for the rest of the party, zig-zagging down some of the sheerer boulders which she would have managed quite easily with her natural advantages. But she, too, stopped where sheer-sided stone angled sharply outward.

'I'd say that looks like something was meant to stay in there,' Kris said.

'Twenty-five metres slanted at fifteen degrees or more,' said Whitby. 'So we rappel down.' He unloosed his pick, found a piton and started hammering it in while Zainal removed the coil from his shoulder to rig it for the drop.

Once again, Kris thought as she took her turn at the descent, that silly survival course comes in handy in my new life on Botany. All of them, even Fek, grinning for all she was worth as she rappelled, made it safely to the floor of the valley.

'Leave,' Zainal said when Whitby would have released one of the three ropes used. He grinned. 'If something is kept in, we can leave quickly.'

Leila immediately armed herself with her crossbow and looked around warily.

'It's full daylight, Lee,' Kris said reassuringly. 'So even if our thudding on the ground here aroused anything, we're safe as long as the sun shines. Me, I'm for that stream.'

One bend of the meandering water was not far from them and, though Leila did not put up her crossbow, they all approached the stream. Sarah, as team medic, used one of the testing strips on a cupfull.

'Potable,' she said and dipped her cup back in to bring it full to her mouth, though she sipped carefully.

The other humans did likewise, then rinsed their sweaty faces in the cooling water. Fek and Slav, who never seemed to need much water, remained alert, listening and looking for any dangers unseen from the height. Then both knelt to take a sample mouthful directly from the stream, as they preferred to drink.

'This place looks almost too good to be true,' Sarah said, breaking off a branch from a nearby shrub and smelling it. 'One of the burnables, and growing all over the place,' she said with an expansive gesture of her hand up the length of the valley.

They could just make out the waterfall through the copses of lodge-pole trees. 'Plenty of stone, too, ready to build from,' she added, jerking her thumb over her shoulder at the rocks behind them.

'Not bad at all,' said Joe Marley, already closely examining a handful of the ground vegetation and discarding the varieties he recognized. He was the team's botanist and medic.

'It is very pretty place here,' Leila Massuri said in her careful English, her contralto voice making inflections which were almost musical. She gazed around her with an almost dreamy smile on her unusual face. Maltese by birth, but with both parents of mixed blood, she had been corralled by the Catteni in a demonstration raid in Marseille. 'So why was it blocked off?'

'We look closer,' Zainal said, pointing at Joe, Sarah and Whitby. 'You go right with Slav,' he said. 'Rest of us go left and meet at falls.'

Zainal gestured for Fek and the rest to accompany him as he waded across the stream, not more than knee-height at this point. Once on the other side, they spread out in a loose line, checking the ground, noting which of the low bushes would bear fruit in season and generally sizing up the environment.

'No rocksquats. That's odd,' Kris said when they had been travelling a few moments. She pointed to rocky projections where the stupid creatures would be likely to perch, since they enjoyed the sun.

'There were some,' Zainal said, and pointed to a little heap of bones just visible through the branches of a low shrub.

'No night-crawlers then,' Leila Massuri said with a shudder. She was a Fourth Drop, and remembered all too keenly that the person next to her had been absorbed by a night-crawler before her horrified eyes just as she was waking up.

'I'm not sure I like the possibility of more omnivores,' Kris said although, in truth, they hadn't seen much in the way of any other hostile creatures in their considerable travels, except for the aerial marauders which either Slav or Fek warned them about. They now camped in the vehicle or on rock heights to avoid earth-bound scavengers.

'Things do die of old age or of falling off high places,' suggested Leila.

'This stream gets swollen, to judge by the height of these banks,' Kris said, pointing to them.

'Spring melt,' Whitby said. They could not see the higher ranges, now hidden by the unbroken line of cliff surrounding this valley; mountains which were snow-clad all year round. Sarah McDouall had quipped that it must have annoyed the mechanicals to have so much unusable uphill land. Whitby's face had had a hungry look on it as he surveyed the towering peaks.

'Never did get to the Himalayas,' he had murmured, 'but those buggers'd be great fun.'

'Later,' Zainal had said, but grinned as if he understood the mountaineer's yearning.

Now the Catteni stopped to squat beside dried dung, partially covered by dirt. Grooves did suggest the claw-marks of a considerable-size animal.

'Old,' Zainal said, finding a stick and poking the droppings.

'Big,' Kris remarked, and looked around the glade.

Zainal picked up the desiccated patty and dropped it into the sack he kept for fire makings. Then they all continued on their sweep, more vigilant now. More dried dung was found, but all examples seemed to be old and Kris was somewhat reassured.

'Reminds me of a place I went to once in Yellowstone Park,' she said when they reached the far side of the valley and its stony barrier. Craning her head she peered upward, looking for cave entrances, but saw nothing, not even a ledge to give access to even the most agile creature. 'We could use this wall for backing and build outward,' she said. 'If we could get one of the vehicles to manoeuvre through the pass, so we could transport all that stone someone dumped across it.'

'We'd need explosives to move the lower rank,' Whitby said. 'They were planted there to stay.'

'To keep *what* in?' asked Kris with a shiver for whatever that might be.

Zainal shrugged but, by the way he was examining everything, Kris rather thought he could see the valley as a human settlement too; it could accommodate several hundred folk, leaving plenty of elbow room. Of course, first they had to find out why the valley had been so tightly sealed.

Despite that consideration, she found herself

looking for likely home sites. Imagine, a proper house at ground level . . . maybe even steps to a sleeping loft . . . one with plenty of head room. She glanced over at Zainal's large figure quartering the ground ahead, searching, searching. Considering how much time he'd spent in space, he seemed completely at ease on planetary surfaces. He looked over his shoulder and beckoned for her to join him.

More bones, larger ones this time.

'A six-footed animal. Too small for loo-cow,' and he held up what looked like a handful of thigh bones, then a smaller one that fitted neatly into a clean socket. He rubbed his fingers across the bones. 'Chewed, too.' He pointed to obvious tooth-marks. 'Wouldn't want to meet that on a dark night!'

Kris grinned, as much for his use of the slang expression as for a sentiment she could immediately share. He fiddled with the bones, making her hold the front set of legs, trying to get a size on the animal. The skull had been smashed into fragments, including the jawbone, although a scattering of molars and pointed teeth did not suggest to Kris that this had been a herbivore.

'That should please the biologists,' Whitby said, joining them. Leila and Fek peered over his shoulder. 'They said there had to be other carnivores for ecological balance.' He picked up a fragment of the cranium and tapped it. 'Hmmm. Thick. And yet crushed like a melon. Wouldn't like to meet what did it.'

'A sentiment we all share,' Kris remarked dryly,

letting the bones fall out of her hands. Several smaller ones shattered. 'Been here a long time if they're that brittle.'

'Hmmmm,' was the response from Zainal and Whitby.

'Caves, possibly?' Zainal added.

'Haven't seen any yet,' Kris said cheerfully, and then Zainal had them spread out again to search.

Though they came across more scattered bones, some in advanced states of decay, nothing else came to light. They reached the lake first, as the other scouts were finishing their explorations of the other side which was wider at the point.

Suddenly Joe let out one of his ear-splitting Australian howls and gestured broadly for them to come on the double to the cliff wall where he was standing. Zainal strode into the stream without a second thought, but Whitby pointed to a convenient scatter of rocks and boulders to get the rest of them across the water. Zainal was up to his chest in the centre of the stream, but he was already running towards Joe and the others before the rest of them managed to cross.

'I don't like the look of this,' Joe said, holding aside branches so that the skeleton grotesquely draped on the scattering of rocks could be seen.

'It's human,' Sarah said. 'Or was.' She was pale under her tan.

Kris peered briefly, enough to see that the skull was human but not all the rest of it. No leg- or arm-bones, just the torso. Slav and Fek looked and nodded.

'Bird,' Fek suggested, gesturing the swoop of the predatory avians.

'Could be.' Joe cleared his throat and let the bushes fall back.

Suddenly everyone was craning their necks back to scan the top of the precipice.

'Ah, they'd have attacked before now if they were nearby,' Joe said. 'You haven't heard anything, have you, Fek?' he asked.

Fek shook her head and pointed above her head. 'I hear high.'

'We do know that the avians always come down from the mountains when they attack,' Sarah said, her colour returning as she and the others moved towards the cover of the nearest copse of trees.

'I listen good,' Fek added, touching both ear holes.

'We found lots of other bones, all old, some even partially embedded in the dirt,' said Joe. He sighed as he let his gaze rove across the valley. 'Too bad. It'd be a great place to set up a permanent head-quarters.'

Zainal was shading his eyes from the now noon-high sun to look at the straight cliffs that formed the boundaries. He shook his head. 'We must know why,' and he pointed back to the barred pass. He clapped his big hands together, startling everyone so that he grinned. 'There are fish in stream. Let's catch and eat. We have time.'

So far all the brook and lake denizens had been edible, with the one exception of a multi-legged bottom-hugging worm that appeared only in stiller water and was toxic.

The dung that had been collected gave off such a stench that they doused the fire with water and started a new one in a fresh place, using windfall branches. Whitby rivalled everyone else by catching the orange-grey scaled fish with his bare hands. Everyone ate their fill, and there was enough cooked left over to save for the next day.

Worrell and Chuck Mitford were enjoying a few pints of beer by the fire when they both heard a growling bark. With no dogs on Botany, the unexpected noise had both of them reaching for their daggers while Mitford roared for a sentry's report.

'Nothing's moving, sarge,' the call came back. 'And First Moon's bright enough to see klicks in all directions.'

A second bark, which had at least three syllables to it, sounded again, this time with a hint of impatience. Instantly Worrell reached for the pouch in which he had put the thin plate that Mic Rowland had discovered.

'How did Leon say you operated one of these things?' Worrell whispered to Chuck.

Chuck took the object from his second-in-command and depressed the first button. 'Tikso damt. Chouma,' he said in a guttural voice as if he were expectorating rather than speaking. He put the unit down on the table beside them and glared at it.

'Didn't know you spoke any Catten, sarge,' said Worrell, impressed.

'Whoever it is wants a report. I told him later. And to be quiet,' said Chuck Mitford. 'At least, I hope that's what he'll understand I said. Where's Zainal?'

'Still hunting safe places up in the hills.'

'I'll see can I reach him,' Mitford said and connected his unit to the aerial socket that served Camp Rock, high up on the cliff. He let it ring awhile. 'Asleep or out of range. Well, let's keep after him until he does answer. Come to think of it, Leon Dane knows more Catten that I do. At least enough to stall them until Zainal gets back.'

Leon Dane was on duty, but not occupied, when Mitford and Worrell went to the infirmary caverns. He had already been given the injector and drugs, but had put them aside until Zainal could tell him what he might know about the contents of the vials.

'So someone's looking for those the midnight beasties ate up for us,' Leon said with a faint grin. 'Someone forgot to brief the landing party about Botanical life-forms. And Zainal went to such trouble to give 'em a demonstration. Served 'em right. D'you think they were here to collect Zainal?'

'Only reason I can think of for them to send four,' Chuck Mitford said with a snort. 'That wouldn't have been enough of a guerrilla gang to do doodly against us, but sufficient to snatch a man. Zainal did mention that he was wanted back home for a duty of some sort he'd rather avoid. Maybe they want him badly enough to come after him.'

'Lemme see the unit,' Dane asked and Chuck

handed it over. 'Oh, that's the idiot kind. Already pre-set to its destination. So what do you want me to report?'

'Do they give a damn if the team landed safely?' Chuck asked.

'I doubt it.'

'Then let's say that they're hiding out. Haven't located Zainal . . . no, make that target personnel.'

'Emassi?' Worrell suggested and Chuck nodded agreement to the change.

Leon scribbled what looked like hieroglyphics on a sheet of paper.

'You can write it, too?' Worrell asked, impressed.

'A little,' Leon said with a wry grin. In his professional capacity as a surgeon working on injured Catteni under the eyes of their medics, he had been in a very good position to pick up the language as well as aid the subversive elements in Sydney. 'Most of what I learned is either medical or military. I can't ask for my aunt's pen on the table or order a meal. But I can spout real good Emassi-like orders.' He scribbled something else, this time in English. 'How does this sound, sarge? "Emassi not here. Moving to find. Report tomorrow this time. Do not contact."'

'That sounds about right. They'd hide from our people during the day,' Chuck said thoughtfully. 'That'll give us some time at any rate. You can say that much?'

'Too right,' Leon said, grinning broadly. 'Most fun I've had all week.'

They went outside and up to the top of the Rock

45

for a clearer message. The moon shone down on the trio.

'Right out in the bright light, too,' Leon said, shaking his head and grinning. Then he sobered, depressed the appropriate 'send' stud and, with his free hand clutching at his throat, growled out the message in a hoarse whisper.

He released the stud, counting. Then he shrugged, depressed the stud and repeated the message. This time a single word answered his effort.

'What was that?' Chuck asked.

Leon gave them a conspiratorial grin. '"Kotik". Means "Accept". Nothing about doing a good job or anything, but Catteni don't expect thanks, do they?' He handed the unit back to Chuck Mitford, and they were starting back down when he had a sudden thought. 'Hey, maybe I should have sounded feminine. You did say you think one of the victims was a female?'

'One set of boots was much smaller,' Worrell said. 'But', and he scrubbed his head, 'I don't think women lead many Catteni commando units.'

'No,' and now Chuck's tone was smug, 'though they might just have sent along someone Zainal might be glad to see about now . . . as bait.'

'Guessed wrong, didn't they?' Leon remarked in a level tone.

It was when Kris, Sarah and Leila decided to have an afternoon swim that more skeletons were found, gleaming white bones in the shallows among the thick water reeds that grew there.

'That does it,' Sarah announced, refastening her coverall. 'Makes me wonder what the fish we ate had for lunch.'

Leila looked slightly nauseous.

'Sarah!' Kris exclaimed. Medics often displayed a ghoulish sense of humour. She did have to swallow before she added, 'We'd better see what kind these are.'

Zainal waded in to fetch some of the nearer skeletons which were identified as loo-cow, rocksquat, Turs and another human skull, still partly attached to its neck. It was Leila who found the odd scales and quills. No-one had taken any more than a glancing look skywards for any hovering avian predators, but everyone agreed they didn't seem to be feathered so perhaps they used the lake for bathing or removing damaged parts in a grooming ritual.

'But they could just fly in and out. That barrier wasn't for them,' Sarah said, frowning over the puzzle.

'It must have been something real bad for the Farmers to want to keep it contained,' Kris said, trying not to shiver. She glanced up to see the position of the sun. 'I move we get back to the vehicle and out of here. I don't want my next place of residence to be that lake.'

So they put out the fire and retraced their steps to the barrier.

'Start up,' Zainal told the others. 'Whitby, with me. I look closer at stream . . .'

The two trotted down to the other end of the valley. Kris, Leila and Slav made the first ascent on the ropes. When Kris gratefully reached the top, she could see Zainal and Whitby having quite a gawk where the stream went through the bluff. The water boiled up over whatever outlet there was, for its flow made a wide pond at cliff base. She wondered what Zainal had hoped to learn from this scrutiny. As soon as Fek, Sarah and Joe joined them, they continued on up the cliff, reaching the top just as Zainal and Whitby surmounted the slanted barrier and began to unhitch the rappel equipment. The others started down to the vehicle, but Kris waited for Zainal and Whitby.

'Well?' she asked as Zainal pulled himself up beside her.

'Something could swim through underneath,' he said.

'Have to have been damned desperate to take such a risk,' Whitby added, 'unless you've some amphibious species here you haven't told me about yet.'

'On Earth large carnivores will swim,' said Kris.

'On Earth,' Whitby agreed, nodding as he mopped his forehead and face. He looked back down at the daunting rock-face. 'If whatever it was had nothing left to eat, even the fish, possibly it would take such a risk. But I would still rather not meet whatever it was. Let's take a look at that aerial—'

His words were broken off by the loud buzz of Zainal's portable.

'Worrell here. You guys all right?' The Aussie was shouting into the speaker.

'Yes, all right. Deep in a valley all day,' Zainal explained.

'Oh. Well, a problem dropped in here the other night,' he said. 'And you're needed back as fast as you can make it, Zainal.'

'What sort of problem?' Zainal asked, but Kris thought from the twinkle in his eyes that he had some idea. 'They look for me?'

'We think so. Only they weren't briefed proper.'

'Night-crawlers?' Zainal asked, and grinned when Kris shuddered.

'You bet,' and Worrell sounded pleased. 'Only someone's asking questions over the portable that was about all that was left of them . . . bar the shoes. Leon told whoever called that you weren't here and they were still looking.'

'You want me to give myself up?'

If Zainal hadn't been grinning like a loon, Kris would have gasped.

'Hell no, Zainal,' and Worrell's tone was indignant. 'Chuck's got an idea.'

'I wonder if we have same one,' Zainal said, winking at Kris. 'We come as fast as possible.'

'Find anything good?'

'Tell you when we get there.'

Worrell disconnected and Zainal replaced the unit in its pouch, fastening the flap.

'Should I know what I just heard?' Whitby asked respectfully, but his curiosity was apparent.

'Why not?' Zainal said with a shrug and nodded

to Kris to explain. Whitby had breath for a good chuckle over 'I drop, I stay,' and Zainal's demonstration about the night-crawlers and showing the hand unit that proved the planet possibly had another owner.

The question which Whitby did not ask, nor did Kris volunteer to answer since she didn't know it, was what duty was so important that Zainal had to be abducted by stealth. They had reached the ground now.

'We go back to Camp as fast as we can,' Zainal said.

'We're five days away,' Joe protested.

'We took side trips up here,' Zainal reminded him. 'We take turns. Drive all night.'

'Hey, it sounds important.'

'Dirty work with cross feet?' asked Zainal.

'Cross roads,' Kris corrected, in spite of realizing that he was being deliberately obtuse.

'Sticky wicket, huh?' Joe said and neatly finished re-coiling the ropes. 'Let's move out. I'll drive first. I've had a breather.'

Both Slav and Fek liked to stand up in the front of the load bed of the vehicle, hanging on to the frame, staying alert and watchful. Sarah and Leila sat in the wide front seat with Joe. Kris, Whitby and Zainal arranged themselves on the bedrolls in the back. Zainal then slid down until he could put his head on Kris's shoulder, then folded his arms and promptly went to sleep in the smooth-riding air-cushioned ground machine.

Chapter Two

They arrived back in Camp Rock by sunset of the next day, having pushed the vehicle to the limits of its panel-supplied power. Joe was of the opinion that the two full moons had been bright enough to keep the power levels high, but Whitby and Leila had argued the point. It made an interesting discussion during the long hours of the trek, when they halted only long enough for natural requirements and to bag a few rocksquats. Joe turned out to be correct about additional power, though the vehicle had slowed down considerably.

The sentry hailed them on their approach and rang the bell so that Worrell and Mitford were awaiting them in the parking area, one of Camp Rock's newer amenities. A big haulier and a small runabout, reserved for Mitford's use, occupied the space.

'We heard the transport,' Zainal said as he swung down from the driver's seat. 'Another Drop?'

'Yeah, another thirteen hundred reluctant colonists,' Mitford said with a grimace.

'Your species shouldn't be so difficult to manage,' said Zainal with a grin.

'We also had to answer another message,' Mitford said, showing his teeth.

'Tell me,' Zainal invited.

'We'll just unpack,' Joe said tactfully and gestured to the others.

Zainal caught Kris's arm as Mitford and Worrell started up the stone steps that led to the height's office. The two-roomed stone building had been built on a levelled-off area, well above any spring flood that might rampage down the gorge that split Camp Rock. Aerials and solar panels were attached to the slated roof of the good-sized facility. A desk, occupied as much by Mitford as Worrell in his capacity as Rock's manager, commanded a view down the length of the camp from the main window. From the other, smaller one, the view was across sloping stone to the first of the Farmers' fields.

Mitford gestured for all to sit on the stools and benches provided. 'Leon's coming,' he added. 'Lemme fill you in.'

Zainal nodded.

'The unit buzzed off shortly before we heard the transport angling in for a landing.'

'Usual field?' Zainal asked.

Mitford nodded. 'They've got that much right at any rate. Leon got a message that suggested the commando group was to meet with the transport and deliver your unconscious body. Certainly there was a group hanging around near the hedges doing nothing, apart from peering around and listening to their wrists a lot.'

'What did you say back?'

'Leon told them the search continued.'

Zainal frowned slightly. 'What words did he use?'

'I knew the right ones,' Leon said, entering just then and leaning against the door frame to catch his breath from the climb. 'I always had a team watching me operate on any wounded Catteni. I got used to some of the distinctions Emassi made. So I adopted a hoarse whisper in case it was the female who was to report.' Zainal shook his head, his expression inscrutable. 'I said,' and he put one hand on his windpipe to alter the sounds he made: ' "Mektichak Zainal obli. Tik escag eridi. Tikso taq".' He removed his hand to speak less growlingly. 'Which, I think, translates into "Moves Zainal much. Hear returns soon. Report then." ' Leon raised an eyebrow at Zainal.

It wasn't often that the big Catteni burst out laughing as he did now, grinning broadly and obviously also enjoying some sort of a personally satisfying private joke.

'You don't know it, Leon, but I am always moving a lot. You said exactly what they will believe. Where is the unit?'

Leon slid it out of a chest pocket. 'Since I'm the only one who knows enough Catten to answer, I've been in charge of it.'

The communicator looked much smaller in Zainal's large hands and could be slipped into a pocket or down a boot. He examined it carefully, his smile broadening again.

'This is very good. Very good,' and Zainal's eyes sparkled with amused triumph.

'These were found in a boot,' and Dane very carefully laid the other three items on the table.

Zainal held one vial up to the light and snorted. 'Vikso. In very small doses, it will be useful to you, Dane. Makes muscles weak,' and he pretended to sag like a limp string puppet before he handed it back to the surgeon.

'So, they knew they'd have to knock you out,' said Chuck Mitford, tipping back in his chair and folding his arms across his chest. 'Care to tell us why they'd go to this much trouble over you?'

Zainal chuckled again, still very pleased, and seeming to ignore the question. 'This will be useful,' he said and waggled the unit before replacing it carefully on the stone slab that was the sergeant's worktop. 'Now we can set traps. Two would be the most we could get.'

'Two ships?' Kris caught on first, though Mitford's chair returned to all four legs as he leaned across the desk, looking so eager and hopeful that Kris caught her breath.

'Two?' Worrell exclaimed, amazed at the audacious prospect.

Zainal nodded, leaning across the table towards the sergeant. 'You have captured me. You, Kris, will speak this in a message, but I have fought hard and killed two. You need fast scout before vikso', and he tapped the vial, 'wears off. They must land where Emassi scout met us. They must land silent,' and he dropped his voice to a dramatic whisper, 'with no lights, and walk to edge of field to help you move captured Zainal.'

'But I don't know enough Catten.'

'You will when you send message,' Zainal said, and the look he gave her told her she was in for it now, but she managed a grin. After all, she'd been teaching him English: turnabout was fair play. '*You* will have made my capture.'

'Me?' Kris looked around the room at the others, grinning at her almost maliciously. 'Cut it out, you guys,' she said with an edge to her voice.

'At ease, Kris,' Mitford said, understanding her flare of resentment, and then focused his attention back on Zainal. There was no question that the sergeant would do much to possess a useful space-ship, but he was not totally reassured by such sketchy details. 'So you get them out of the scout, and preferably disposed of by the night-crawlers, and then what?'

'We have one scout vessel.'

'And no reprisals?' Mitford was extremely sceptical.

'No reason because the ship will take off . . .' and everyone exclaimed at that and Zainal glanced about, grinning again. 'It leaves to make them believe what will happen next.' He turned to Kris. 'You will manage to make one more message . . . and then . . .' He slid one finger across his throat and grinned.

'You overpower us again?' Kris rolled her eyes incredulously. 'Boy, will they buy that?'

'Buy it?' Zainal asked. His command of idiom and grammar was increasing, but was not yet as good as his accent.

'Believe it,' she substituted, and Zainal grinned.

'On Barevi I showed you I am difficult to catch.'

Kris laughed. 'All right. So I manage a message out before you kill me . . .'

'And I alter course . . .'

'YOU alter course?' Mitford asked, suspicious, narrowing his eyes and staring hard at Zainal.

'Certainly, so that moon hides ship to get back here.' Then Zainal grinned again. 'I will bring Kris with me . . .' and Mitford glowered more deeply, 'and Bert Put and the woman, Raisha Simonova – who flew in space from your planet. They learn to use the ship. It is very simple to fly. You may come, too,' he added with a grin and a bow to Mitford.

'Thanks, but no thanks,' Mitford said with a wave of his hand and a fleeting expression of distaste. 'I'll stick to good ol' Terra Firma. But taking the spacers is a damned good idea.'

'I'll go in your place, sarge,' said Worrell, raising his hand, his expression avid for the experience. 'If I could . . .' he added hopefully. 'We don't want too many people in on this, do we?'

Mitford shook his head, fretting over flaws in the plan, then caught Zainal's eyes again. 'Your guys won't come looking here for the scout?'

'Scout does not leave much trail, and they will not be quick to look around here,' and he circled his finger in the air, meaning Botany. 'They will start looking where I have friends to hide me. If they come back, the scout will be hidden with other metallic stuff at Camp Narrow. It will not be noticed in a scan.' Then, after a moment of silence when the others were thinking the plan over, he added, 'The last place they will look for me is here!' He pointed an emphatic finger at the ground as he grinned at them.

'Well, I'll buy that,' Mitford agreed in a droll tone, with the beginning of a smile on his lips.

'It will work,' Zainal said with such conviction that Mitford began to straighten up from his crouch across the table. The Catteni paused, a smile tugging at his mouth. 'Then . . .' and he had everyone's attention, 'the next transport ship to arrive will be surprised and we will have two to use.'

There was a long moment of surprised reflection, but Mitford broke it. 'Your people can't be that stupid—' he began.

'No?' Zainal said, raising his eyebrows with a sarcastic expression. 'The transport uses only Drassi. Not Emassi. The transports that come here are all in bad condition.' He grinned again. 'Used over often. So if the ship explodes after take-off . . .' and he spread his hands at such a simple ruse.

'The ship will explode?' Mitford asked, jutting out his chin.

'An explosion can be made with metal left in space to prove accident. That is why it is very necessary to get the scoutship first. It can dump garbage into space. Then, we have two ships.'

'Only one of them is not in good shape,' Mitford pointed out.

Zainal shook his head in denial. 'Many people here are trained to work with machinery. I am not

57

just pilot. I know how to . . .' He tapped an impatient finger on the worktop as he searched for a word, 'to . . . repair as well.' He grinned. 'I have faith in your people, Mitford. Have faith in me.'

'Jesus, Zainal, I do, believe me,' Mitford said forcefully, slamming both palms flat on the table. 'And I think that goes for all here.' That vote of confidence was immediately seconded. 'And it would be great to know we're not stuck any more on . . .' He paused, looked surprised and then laughed. 'You know, I'm not as eager to leave Botany as I used to be.' He brushed away that candid remark. 'Won't the Emassi retaliate on Earth when they've lost both a scout and a transport here on Botany?'

'I don't think they would,' Leon Dane spoke up with a wry grin. 'The Catteni I met considered us a short step above aborigines. Our sabotage and revolts are annoyances that will stop when the leaders are all rounded up and dropped here.'

'Or elsewhere.' Zainal disconcerted them all by that qualification. 'There are other planets that need to be . . . tested for occupation. Not this one alone. I do have one worry,' and he glanced at Worrell.

'I'm almost glad to hear that,' Mitford answered drolly. 'What?'

'That Lenvec, who came in the first scoutship, speaks to a higher commander that we have technology not sent with us. That this planet is in use. That is another reason to capture me again.'

'How big are the odds he's done that?'

Zainal looked dubious. 'He can be persuasive but', and now he gave a snort, 'many Catteni believe only what they like to believe.'

'Just like some humans I know,' Leon said in a caustic tone.

'So, we might even have something to defend ourselves with if the Farmers come looking for us,' said Worrell, looking relieved.

Zainal shook his head. 'Only scout has weapons. But two is better than nothing, and there are other uses for a scout.'

'Our own exploratory missions?' Mitford asked.

'I myself will like to know who the other owners are. Don't you?' and Zainal dropped yet another startling proposal. He grinned. 'Also, it is not the Catteni who are your real enemy. It is the Eosi. Who farms this planet, who left that command tower, may be stronger, wiser and better than Eosi.' He leaned back then, watching Mitford's expression changing as he absorbed this concept. 'I do not want Eosi controlling my people any more. Or yours. This is the first time I think there is the chance to end Eosi.'

'Well, I'll be fucked,' Mitford murmured, dropping his shoulders as he relaxed in complete surprise at Zainal. He began to grin and a laugh started in his belly, a laugh that was joined by Leon Dane's yowl of approval and Worrell's expression of sheer incredulous delight.

'So that's what you hatched up on the way back here last night,' Kris said, eyeing him drolly.

'Isn't that taking on one helluva lot?' Mitford

asked, but the gleam in his eye and the jut of his jaw suggested a measure of approval.

'Yes,' and Zainal shrugged. 'Why not?'

Mitford slapped the table again and gave another burst of laughter. 'Yeah, why not?'

'We can *try* . . .' Leon said, swatting his thigh with one hand in emphasis. 'By God, I want to!'

'Do you think we should?' asked Worrell, hitching his pants with his elbows. 'I mean, they may be mad enough at *us* for what we've already done to their neat agricultural enterprise . . .'

'But who put us here in the first place?' asked Kris. 'Only why do you have to pretend the transport explodes? And why do you have to be careful returning the scout to Botany?'

'We must joke the satellite.'

'Joke?' Mitford raised his eyebrows. 'Oh, fool.'

'Satellite?' Worrell exclaimed, anxiously.

Zainal held up the slim unit. 'They have one because this relays the messages. A satellite is standard for any colony planet. It sends in reports. It must send in the right ones so we . . . ah . . . fool it.'

'Clarify one point for me, will you, Zainal?' Mitford asked and when Zainal nodded, he went on, 'Why do they want you so bad for that duty you don't want any part of?'

Zainal gave a harsh laugh. 'I was chosen for it by Eosi. They can choose someone else now.'

'Just what *is* that duty?' Mitford asked, at his bluntest.

The change in Zainal's posture and face, though

subtle, sent chills down Kris's spine and caused Mitford to recoil slightly.

'Eosi use your body.' Then, with a second almost imperceptible change which emphatically told Kris that he would not elaborate on that subject, he went on, 'So, do we take the scoutship?' His expression altered back to his usual bland one as he looked around at the expectant expressions of Kris, Dane and Worrell before settling his gaze on Mitford. 'That much is possible, but we must act tonight. Kris must learn what to say. I need Bert Put and woman. Is that possible?'

'Can do,' Mitford said and reached for the hand-held com, tapping out the code for Camp Narrow. 'Yo, Latore? Send Bert Put and Raisha Simonova up here on the double, will ya? Something's come up. We need them before . . .' he glanced at Zainal who held up two fingers, 'second moonrise. Okay?' Then he paused, his eyes flickering with rapid thoughts. 'We'll call this Phase One, and all of it stays among us.' The others nodded. 'Phase Two we'll talk about if Phase One works.'

'It will work,' Zainal said with absolute confidence.

'Phase Three . . .' and Mitford pointed a finger at Zainal, 'is going to need a lot more thinking.'

Zainal was in total agreement.

'Dammit, sarge,' said Leon Dane staunchly, 'even the mere notion of . . . Phase Three . . . puts heart in me. Think what it can do to the general morale?'

'I do,' and Mitford's voice had dropped to a

growl, 'and I don't want even a whisper of a happy smile on your faces when you leave here. We're doing well enough right now, better all the time, and I don't want to have to deal with false hopes. Let's take it a step at a time.'

'Don't you mean a phase at a time?' Kris asked, stifling a desire to giggle.

Actually she wanted to cheer wildly for the surge of hope that Zainal's master-plan had personally given her. Securing the first ship would be a big enough coup. Hijacking a transport would prove to everyone on Botany that they could get their own back on the Catteni. She wasn't at all sure about Phase Three, but having two space-going ships gave them a positive advantage in finding whoever did own Botany. Would a Catteni scout ship be able to keep up with the monstrous leviathans sent by the Farmers to collect the harvests of Botany? *First*, she told herself firmly, *get it, then dream*. And, if *they* were a species that resented having their supply planets taken over by another space-faring power, maybe Phase Three would happen. And both Earth and Catten might get free of Eosian domination.

'Right,' and Mitford gave her an odd smile, 'hijacking spaceships sure beats sitting around waiting for the next Drop-ins.' He caught Zainal's eyes and began ticking off details on his fingers. 'You teach Kris what to say to get the scout down here by second moonrise?' Zainal nodded. 'So, if the scout buys it, they come down, leave the ship . . . only how'll they know you're there to be picked up? I can't volunteer anyone at night out on a field . . .'

'Air-cushioned vehicles attract no night-crawlers,' Zainal said, grinning.

'On the way back', Kris added, 'we found out that the full moon's enough to keep power up.'

'Good point,' and Mitford went on, 'So we've got stand-ins far enough up the field . . .'

'Vehicle will move towards Catteni,' Zainal said, nodding. 'But not fast because they carry heavy load.' He thumbed his chest. 'Me.'

'Good . . . so there's enough time for the night-crawlers to attack. What about the Catteni shooting 'em? That Lenvec Emassi saw what night-crawlers do.'

Zainal shrugged. 'Winter night-crawlers are very hungry, very fast and grab feet. Or we can be humane,' and he grinned as he saw the reaction to the word, 'and kill before they know. We have fast and silent weapons. Lance, crossbow, slingshot.'

'Won't they leave a man on board?' asked Mitford.

Zainal shrugged. 'I am drugged. It will take two-three to carry me. If is one, once we open hatch, it is over for him.' He tapped the knife at his belt.

Mitford made an approving sort of grimace. 'All right . . . Everything goes according to plan and you, with your crew, take off and do your disappearing act. One small detail. Kris might be useful to lure the pick-up squad down but if you are overcoming a crew, would you not kill off the female first, the one who drugged you?'

Zainal slowly nodded his head, perceptive enough to know what Mitford did not spell out. 'Leon speaks Catteni. I cannot talk because they have record of my voice. Leon can give final message.'

'Point,' and Mitford looked at Kris. 'You understand, don't you?'

Kris did, and did not bother to hide the bitterness she felt for such a suggestion.

'You will go to space another time,' Zainal told her, looking from Mitford to her.

'Now, wait a minute, Mitford,' Dane began to protest.

'Leon will speak the necessary dying words,' Zainal said firmly, his eyes still holding Kris's. 'It reassures.'

'It had better,' and Kris glared fiercely at Mitford for his insulting contingency.

'Why do you need Bert and Raisha?' Worrell asked.

'They need to have a first lesson in flying a scout. More people who know is better.' Zainal put an odd smile on his face. 'And soon.'

'I'll buy that,' said Mitford, shifting his eyes anywhere but in Kris's direction. 'Phase One is green for go . . . and definitely top security. Use your team, Zainal, for the driving and . . . the executions. Slav and Fek see well in the dark. I'll send Bert and Raisha to you as soon as they get here.' Then, in a complete change of voice and manner, 'Did your patrol find anything interesting before you were recalled for this?'

Astonished by that 'business-as-usual' switch, even in Mitford, Kris glared at him.

'A very interesting valley,' Zainal said, rising and

popping the unit into his pocket before he picked up the sack of empty boots. Leon took charge of the medical items. 'Let Joe and others debrief.' Then he held out his free hand to Kris. 'Now, you must to learn to speak like Catten female.'

'I thought I'd already done that well enough to fool a Catten,' she said, cocking her head at him and reminding him of the episode when 'she' had suddenly become his 'leader' in front of the Emassi.

'We will improve the fool,' he said and gestured for her to precede him.

'No, joke is the right word in that context,' she murmured, still trying to defuse the anger she felt over Mitford's show of distrust. The trouble was, she could see his point and that made her madder still. Surely he couldn't doubt Zainal's integrity?

'After all you've done,' Leon Dane muttered, exiting behind them.

'Not to worry, Leon,' Zainal said.

'I do all the worrying,' said Worrell, but his tone made it obvious that he felt Mitford's precaution of keeping Kris out of space unnecessary.

'Don't worry about tonight,' Zainal said – sounding, to Kris's ears, far too cheerful considering what he had just set into motion.

Then Kris found her mind going back to the echo of his colourless voice saying, 'Eosi use your body.' Small wonder he wanted to avoid that duty. She knew without a doubt that he would have hated possession. And yet, his original comment on 'that duty' had indicated that it was considered an honour for an Emassi, and one they undertook with some pride. Had Botany wrought a great change in him, or was it simply that he now had an escape from such a hideous future? Then she began to wonder how deeply the possession went: was just the body used as a vehicle for these mysterious Eosi? Or did they subsume the entire personality, leaving nothing of the original man? Or . . . what?

'Don't think about it,' Zainal said softly, touching her elbow as they reached ground level. 'I do not mean Mitford.' Then he hailed the other members of their team, obviously waiting a turn to report to Mitford. 'Go on up. He's waiting to debrief you.'

'We're in our usual abode,' Sarah told them as she followed Joe up the steps. 'We've already put your gear there.'

'Good. We have a small job to do at second moonrise. I tell you later.'

Kris knew Sarah was dying to ask what that was about, or why had Dane and Worrell also been in Mitford's office for an ordinary scout debriefing.

'We swim first?' Zainal asked as they made their way to their quarters in Michelstown cave.

'You bet. I think better cleaner,' Kris said and besides, not only could she use the immersion in the cold waters of the lake to reduce her anger but she also needed the privacy with Zainal . . . if they had the lake to themselves.

They did, and there had been clean coveralls in their quarters to change into. Zainal put the Catteni communicator carefully in the pouch with his portable unit in his fresh clothing before they left for their wash.

He seemed as eager to make this a special occasion, too. They spent time soaping each other and then swimming exuberant lengths against the lake's deep current within the roped safety area before emerging to dry each other off. That led to a chance to release tension. In moments like these, Kris wondered just how much Zainal really did deviate – no, differ – from other Catteni and even Emassi. She knew that her association with Zainal was not universally accepted. There were incidents of spitefulness with each new Drop but gradually, over the past months, that had altered – with very few exceptions – when most Botany settlers learned just how much they owed to Zainal's presence on the planet. Xenophobia was not encouraged by Mitford or Easley, or any of those involved in introducing the new world to its whilom residents.

Her pleasurable ruminations were rudely interrupted the moment they started back up the stairs to the main cavern, as Zainal barked sounds at her.

'We're starting already?'

'Second moon rises soon. You must be ready.'

'I gotta know what the sounds mean, Zainal,' she complained.

'Get the sound right and then I tell you meanings,' he said, and repeated the four staccato syllables which she did her best to imitate . . . though the combination of fricatives was enough to choke her. She'd already noticed that characteristic of the Catten language. Sort of like German with a French accent . . . or maybe guttural French with a very bad German accent, and a little Chinese for seasoning.

She managed to get the first set of syllables to his satisfaction by the time they reached the main cavern. Food was still being served, and they stood in line for their portions which they took to the privacy of one of the look-out levels, out of earshot from those who were enjoying their meal outside in the mild evening. Botany's primary had not yet set but the first moon was already above the eastern hills, a pale ghost in what was left of sunlight. That reminded Kris that time was a constraint.

Because she had always learned better using visual aids, Kris took a sharp pebble and scratched out the phonetics of what Zainal coached her to say . . . as well as she could. Just when she thought her mimicry was accurate, Zainal would shake his head.

'What's the matter with that?'

He shook his head again but patted her shoulder. 'You don't sound . . . mean.'

'Mean?'

He growled out the words she now knew meant, 'Report. Found Zainal. He fought hard. Two dead. He is drugged. Land where Lenvec did. No lights. Meet in field.'

She tried again, as deep in her throat as she could, still realizing that even that wasn't perfect.

'Look, I'll growl a whisper. How'll they know the difference?'

'They might.' Then he held up his hand. 'What was it that Leon did to sound hoarse?'

'Grabbed his throat,' and doing that, she repeated the phrases once again, hoping she wouldn't accidentally strangle herself.

'That's it,' Zainal said, bringing both his hands together in a clap of approval. 'Now, listen . . .' and he rattled off a sentence of which she understood three words: 'Report' 'dead' and 'land'.

She told him what she understood.

'You may be asked. You must know what to answer to any question.'

'What about "I don't know?"'

'You must sound as if you do know all. So, say first "Chouma" – quiet – as if you can be overheard. Then "Schkelk" . . .' and Kris sat upright with surprise because she knew what that meant.

'Listen?'

Zainal grinned with surprise as he nodded. 'Say as harsh as you can because you are dealing with a stupid person.'

'I heard it said that way often enough on Barevi,' Kris said in a rueful tone, and then spat out the word with appropriate venom. Zainal laughed and gave her hand an approving squeeze.

'Just use that tone with all the words and they will not argue with you. You sound almost Emassi. After "Schkelk", you repeat the original message to be sure they heard you right the first time. Next you say "Kotik?" in the way which means they are not to question you again?'

'Got it.'

He drilled her and drilled her until her voice became hoarse enough without the need to strangle herself. She was surprised to see that first moon was bright and high when he finally said she was good enough.

He took out the unit and held it up. 'Now!'

'Now? You mean, we do it tonight?' She panicked; she wasn't ready yet. 'But Bert and Raisha—'

'They are here. I saw them drive in. I brief them, too. So we send message now. All is fresh in your mind. And mouth.'

He pressed the finger pad and, much too quickly for Kris's peace of mind, a voice responded. Kris gulped and began her well-rehearsed message: over-riding one question with as harsh a 'Schkelk' as she had ever been given. Zainal nodded assurance, wagging his hand to reassure that the interruption meant nothing. She said 'Chouma' as nastily as she could and went right into the prepared speech again. By this time she was so scared that her final 'Kotik?' came out every bit as savage as the worst Catten guard.

An almost meek 'Kotik' plus two syllables she didn't understand was the response, and Zainal depressed the disconnect button.

'Baby, you were great!' And Zainal tousled her hair and pressed his cheek against hers with great affection. That had become his special caress for her.

'But what was that last bit?'

'Your name. You are, or were, Arvonk.'

Kris made a face. 'Awful name.'

'Useful to know.'

'They answered awful fast.'

Zainal considered that. 'They want Zainal bad. They are there till they get me.'

'In a bigger ship?'

'The scout is ship enough for this errand.'

'They're NOT getting you!' she said, jumping to her feet.

'No, they are not,' he agreed equably and took her hand as they made their way down and across to Mitford's office.

Mitford must have been watching because the group he had been speaking to were abruptly dismissed. Surprised, they passed Zainal and Kris on the way up the steps. Bert Put, his lean face alight with anticipation, and Raisha Simonova raced across the gorge to catch up. They didn't until Zainal and Kris entered Mitford's office.

'You got the message through?' Mitford asked.

'They come. Kris spoke like good Emassi.' Zainal was grinning with obvious pride as he held the door open for her.

'I had to say it often enough to get it right,' she said gruffly and, with instant solicitude, Mitford offered her a cup of the herbal tea that everyone had come to enjoy.

Bert and Raisha came in and took seats, but sitting so tentatively that Kris knew they had no idea why they had been summoned.

'Have you spoken to your team yet, Zainal?' Mitford asked.

'Not yet. They will do what needs to be done with no problems.'

Mitford grunted and scratched the back of his head. He still did not look Kris in the eye, which somewhat appeased her.

'May I have paper?' Zainal asked and Mitford quickly supplied him with sheets and a pencil. With his usual quick, sure strokes, Zainal sketched what had to be the interior of the scout. Bert's eyes grew rounder and wider, while Raisha watched with avid fascination.

'The interior of a Catteni scout?' Bert asked, incredulous eyes on Zainal's face. 'How?' he demanded, and Raisha sat right on the edge of her stool.

'You said nothing to them about Phase One, sergeant?' Zainal asked as he continued to detail the layout.

Kris covered her grin with her hand because Zainal had suddenly turned pure-Emassi and Mitford reacted by sitting straight up, exactly as a subordinate should. He did spare one droll but respectful look in Zainal's direction before he spoke.

'Bert, Raisha, we mean to catch us a scoutship tonight,' he said, and both gawked in disbelief. 'A few nights ago a Catteni ship landed four commando types on a field.'

'Oho!' Raisha said and turned pale.

'That would have been their first mistake,' Bert said with a smug grin.

'Their second was in thinking it would be easy to find Zainal,' Mitford said. 'Fortunately night-crawlers left boots and some other inedible pieces of equipment. So we can lure the scout back down.'

'You mean, like tonight?' Raisha shifted forward on her chair, inhaling with deep delight.

Kris couldn't resist jumping in then. 'I told them to land silently, with no lights, to meet me and an unconscious Zainal. That I needed help moving him as he'd killed two others trying to escape before I could zap him.' Raisha looked slightly confused. 'One pair of boots was a lot smaller. Cherchez la femme.'

'Oh, gotcha!' Raisha said. 'Only how do *we* avoid the night-crawlers?'

Mitford went through the rest of Phase One and the two gave a small round of applause when he finished.

'Look, I did a lot of training but only one short shuttle flight,' Raisha began anxiously.

'I only had two, but one as navigator,' Bert said, though both were clearly dying to go on despite admitting their inexperience.

'You'll do good,' Zainal said, so convincingly that both demurred. 'A scout can carry six at most. Four were set down. I think only two remain. Both can be told to come help Arvonk, the contact,' and he pointed at Kris. 'Maybe not. So, if we have to get in fast and kill, inside is like this.'

He walked them through the tight passageways of the scout ship and then, using the drawings he had also made of the control panels, talked them through the short pre-flight sequences. He mentioned the colours of the relevant toggles and drew diagrams of the icons above other controls. They concentrated so hard that Kris could almost see them absorb words and drawings into their heads.

'We take Leon who speaks Catten to give last warning of trick by Zainal and then . . .' Once again he used his finger across his throat and grinned. 'I will show you how to circle moon and glide to land.' He turned to Mitford. 'We hide scout and then I work you hard to learn how to pilot Catten vessel.'

'You will?' Bert's eyes were nearly popping out of their sockets, but Raisha assumed an aura of complete calm confidence and gave a little sigh.

Zainal had certainly made two people very happy. 'Study hard now. Kris and I prepare our team.'

Chapter Three

For a plan that had been so hastily put together, it could not have gone more smoothly. Kris was shaking badly when the comunit buzzed, but Zainal had rehearsed her in two more phrases.

'Arvonk,' she said, hand on her windpipe, and added in harsh Catteni, 'See you. Glide in. Chouma.' Which she added on her own.

They could just make out the ship in the gleam of the rising moon as it settled silently in the corner of the field. A brief glint of muted light was cut off as the hatch closed.

Zainal was pretending to be one of his own captors, Kris the other, while Leon, being tall, was plainly leaning against Zainal as if unconscious. Joe Marley, face blackened, hunched over the controls of Mitford's usual air-cushion machine and eased it forward at a slow walking pace.

The first surprised burst from the Catteni was the signal for Fek and Slav to rise from their crouching positions and despatch both with silent lances. Then Joe increased the power of the vehicle and they whizzed down the field to the scout. Zainal hit the exterior release and Bert and Raisha bolted through as soon as the hatch was wide enough. It was Leon's turn now.

'Stolix Zainal,' he called out, trying to sound triumphant but listening to be sure there was no sound of another person on board.

Zainal pushed past, knife at the ready, and strode with no stealth at all towards the bridge in the prow of the small spaceship. Those listening outside heard him slide a panel.

'Were only two,' he called back.

'Permission to come aboard, sir?' asked Bert, not quite facetiously, as he adhered to protocol.

'Permission given,' Zainal replied and Kris heard the relief in his voice.

'I just want a quick look,' she said and followed Raisha and Bert down the passageway. She wondered if scout crews were chosen because they were physically small enough to manoeuvre in such enclosed spaces. Zainal certainly had to walk sideways.

Raisha was already seated in one position, with Bert running his fingers lightly across this and that panel as if confirming the briefing Zainal had given them. The look on his face made Kris gulp. He was having a hard time believing that he was actually preparing to go into space again – not as an unconscious passenger this time. She envied them.

'Kris, one last message,' Zainal said, turning her towards the controls. 'Say "Arvonk icts, stolix Zainal. Escag. Klotink."'

She muttered them over to herself and then Zainal pointed to the speaker grille and threw up a toggle. She almost forgot to grab her throat, but the fact that she could say the words with authority lent a certain vibrant triumph to her tone. 'What did I say?'

Zainal ruffled her hair. 'Arvonk here, have Zainal. Return. Out.'

'Out sounds too much like Kotik, accept.'

'Not to Catteni listener. Now, out. The satellite must record the take-off.' He escorted her down the cramped aisle to the hatch, one large hand on her shoulder. At the hatch, he put his cheek against hers, pressing hard against it before he hit the 'open' button.

Dazed as she was by the night's success and the prospect of being without him for a day or two, she remembered to step carefully down onto the air-cushion platform. She lifted one hand to her cheek, feeling his against hers.

Joe drove off, and was picking up speed when Fek abruptly shouted, 'Stop!' Surprised, Joe braked so quickly his passengers had to grab at each other to remain upright and in the vehicle. Fek leaned over the side, peering down at something Kris was very glad she could not see as clearly as the Deski could. With a grab as deft as Whitby's fishing, Fek wrenched aboard something that clattered as it fell. She reached down again, arm at full stretch and her other hand clutching Joe, and got hold of something else. A ray of light illuminated a field that writhed and seethed, for it was a hand beam she had retrieved. Kris groaned and turned her face away. The night-crawlers

77

bumped in futile search at the floor of the vehicle.

'You see, Slav?' Fek asked, grinning the triangular Deski smile as she focused light on the other side of the vehicle, and the other victim.

'I see. I get.' And Slav made two equally speedy retrievals. One he held up for Kris to see in the light, and his smile was the broadest she'd yet seen on a Rugarian face. 'Stunner.' And in a sudden, unexpectedly juvenile manner, he leaned the barrel across his arm and made the hissing sound of a stunner blast.

'Can we leave now?' Joe Marley asked in an edged voice. He didn't wait for an answer, pushing the control bar hard over. 'We could have waited until morning. Crawlers can't digest metal.'

'I want tonight,' Fek said with uncharacteristic firmness.

'And stop shining that thing around,' Joe added testily as they sped up a field which writhed and glistened.

Mitford was waiting in the parking area, as if he didn't quite trust the participants to keep the night's event to themselves. Kris knew herself to be on an adrenalin high, so his presence had a certain sobering effect on her. He gestured for them all to go through the silent Camp and up to his office, where he had thoughtfully provided beer and the salty pretzel-like snacks. Rugarians and Deskis rather liked beer now and then but they were careful not to drink much or often. It had some sort of an effect on their metabolism – not a hangover, according to Leon Dane, but something similar – that they did not cope well with.

Kris took a long pull on her beer, to settle her stomach, and noticed that Joe did too. Mitford just waited, knowing from the looks of their faces that the hijack had been successful.

'I'd say by now I've been killed and Leon is dying,' she began. 'Otherwise it all worked out just as we planned . . . with a little diversion from Fek and Slav.' She shuddered as the two now dropped the retrieved equipment on Mitford's desk.

He only glanced at the hand beams, which Kris thought would have been more useful than stunners. But, of course, weapons would come first with a military man. He picked up the stunner, turning it over in his hand, checking the controls and snapping something shut. 'That's the safety on – now – but you guys wouldn't have known.' He almost patted it when he put it down and took up the other to render it harmless.

'Bert and Raisha looked as if they were having Christmas,' she went on. 'I had a peek around once Zainal said the coast was clear.' Mitford nodded, and she went on. 'Rather cramped. Good thing Leon isn't an inch taller.' Mitford nodded again. 'He will be back, you know.' Mitford nodded once more.

She finished off the beer, took a handful of the pretzels and stood up. 'I'm knackered,' she said. 'Good night – and thanks, Joe, Fek, Slav. We're the best team on Botany!'

Mitford nodded.

It was only when she turned over in her bed that Kris realized she still had the comunit. A lot of good it did her, even if it was a link with Zainal up in the scout ship, faking the next step of Phase One. She slipped it up onto her shelf and then let herself fall deeply asleep.

Mitford took her and the unit down to Drop Field the second day, when Zainal could be expected to return. Camp Rock had vibrated with rumours, although everyone connected with Phase One had done their best to act in a normal fashion. To keep out of the way and not unintentionally give something away, Kris had to pretend she'd sprained her ankle, so Sarah kept getting hot or cold water to reduce the swelling. Joe, Fek and Slav worked on servicing their big exploratory vehicle or writing reports. Leon Dane was reported to have gone off with Zainal, Bert and Raisha for some emergency at Shutdown Camp. But the rumours persisted.

'We'll still surprise them,' Mitford said as he pulled the little air-cushion runabout up against the hedge. They'd seen a few of the avian predators on their way there, so he took what cover there was. 'I hope.'

'We're alone, sarge, so I'll give you a piece of my mind on that stunt you pulled . . .' Kris had the satisfaction of seeing Mitford flush with embarrassment. 'You had no right to insult Zainal that way . . . and even less right to use *me* as his surety. I came awful close to hitting you . . .' She cocked her fist in demonstration.

'Goddamitall to hell'n'gone, Kris Bjornsen,' and Mitford recovered sufficiently to snarl at her, 'I had to! I do trust Zainal, quite likely more than I've ever trusted another human being . . . and he is human to me . . .' Mitford's response was as fervent as hers had been, and his eyes were sparking. 'But I can't take any chances. With him or you.' He let out a deep snort, rubbing his hands through his close-cropped hair in a gesture of exasperation and, oddly, impotence. 'And I need *him* more. *We*', and he meant the colony, 'need him more.' Then, in one of his swift mood changes, he grinned at her, impudent and oddly melancholy. 'I would have liked to be where he is now with you . . .' He held up both hands quickly in defence. 'Don't take me up wrong, Kris. But you're a fine woman and Zainal's the only man I wouldn't try to muscle out.'

It was Kris's turn to be embarrassed. She had vaguely known that Mitford fancied her, though, after he kept sending her out with Zainal, she had to decide that she had imagined it.

'I'm sorry, Chuck,' she said, all her previous aggravation dissipating. 'It sort of happened and you kept throwing me at him . . . more or less.'

'More,' and Mitford let a wry expression touch his rough features, 'because I shouldn't. And you were the only one *I* could trust to keep him alive until the rest of them figured out he was far more valuable alive than dead.'

'We owe you a lot, sarge,' she said and touched

81

his arm lightly and gratefully. 'But you still made me real mad yesterday.'

Mitford laughed, stretching his legs out of the side of the parked vehicle.

'Yeah, well, sometimes I gotta do what I gotta do, and there was no time really to call in some of the brass we got around here now.'

'Ha!' Kris grinned back at him. 'You wanted this one to yourself without any brass involved. But I strongly suspect you'd really better let the others in on planning Phase Two . . .'

'And Phase Three,' said Mitford, turning his head slightly to gaze off down the field – its ground cover matted down by the frequent landings of the transport ship and unconscious bodies. He scratched at his head again and looked back at her. 'I'd be stupid, real stupid, not to get the strategists in on Phase Two. But this first one . . . that,' and he jabbed his thumb into his chest, 'was for me! And you,' he added magnanimously. 'In fact, I'm sort of phasing me out.'

'Oh, come now, Chuck . . .'

'No, I mean it, Kris. We've getting on to eight thousand here now. I knew what I was doing for five hundred and seventy-two, even two thousand, but . . . goddammit all, I want to be the one finding the good stuff, not leave it up to you and Zainal, or the Doyles or that Scandinavian crowd. Me, Chuck Mitford, wants to have some of the fun.'

'Who'll you have on your team?' she asked, as much to cope with his surprising announcement. She knew very well that the colony had trained men like Easley and Rastancil, and governors like Ayckburn and Chavell, but Mitford had made the colony *work*.

'It won't be the same without you in charge. Not at all,' she said with deep regret.

Now he touched her arm lightly and winked. 'You won't know I've been gone until I get back. Frankly, my dear, I'd rather someone else who really knows how to plan big pushes carried the can on Phase Two and Phase Three. But you can bet your last nickel, I'll wangle some part in it.'

'You wouldn't be you if you didn't.'

'Hell, Kris,' and he was serious again, 'I made a promise to the folks when I took command Day One that somehow we'd get free.' He looked off into the distance of morning-mist-shrouded fields. 'Free, yes. Leave? I'm not so sure about that now.' He looked around him at a landscape that no longer seemed alien and unreal.

'I wondered,' she said, encouragingly.

'If we could come to some sort of an agreement with the landlords, either or both, this'd be a great place to build up without all those damned minorities on Earth messing up their own landscapes. It'd be a fresh start for everyone.'

'We've already made one, you know.'

He nodded and knuckled his nose. 'That I do. But free. I promised that, and now we've got a chance to deliver.'

'Phase Three might mean leaving here if the brass does buy Zainal's master plan and free Earth, and Catten, from those Eosi.'

He gave her a narrow-eyed look of pure devilment.

'Hell, gal, there's at least one more war in this marine. I'm not at all sure of the combat zone or the weapons and you better believe', he waggled his finger at her sternly, 'that I'm not going to be the only one to debrief that Zainal, article, clause and all the fine print. There's an awful lot we don't know about the Catteni, not to mention the Eosi.'

'And our landlords, the Farmers.'

They both heard the faint rumbling sound from above, followed by a more vigorous rustling as Slav, Fek, Joe, Sarah, Whitby and Leila pushed through the hedgerows just beyond them.

Kris managed one startled glance at Mitford, wondering if their very private conversation had been overheard. He winked and pointed to the team, who were panting as if they'd been running a good distance.

'Fek hear,' the Deski said, grinning. 'Scout comes.'

Slav pointed and they could see the speck in the sky that rapidly increased in size. The noise became not louder but clearer. Suddenly more avians that anyone watching had ever seen at one time swarmed around it: some bodies dropped as oak seeds might, flittering and twisting ground-ward: some dropped more quickly as disparate sections, while those left alive did astonishing aerial manoeuvres and flew away as fast as they could.

'That's handy to know,' said Mitford with an approving grunt, and climbed out of the runabout.

He stood, arms crossed on his chest, his eyes narrowing as he watched the ship's steady approach.

Was Zainal piloting, Kris wondered, or had he let Bert? Whoever it was made a very neat touchdown about twenty yards from the onlookers, with a final burst of steamy exhaust from the portside thruster. The hatch moved open and Raisha jumped down, grinning radiantly. She snapped a salute to Mitford, which he returned.

'Mission accomplished, sir. All present and accounted for.' Then she thrust her right arm in the air and let out an exceedingly unmilitary yell.

With everyone else, Kris moved towards her, trying to peer around for a sight of Zainal, and Bert too.

'That Zainal . . . he even let Bert land her,' Raisha cried, shaking hands with everyone, including Fek and Slav who were now accustomed to that odd human habit. 'You should see this place from outer space, sarge. It's even more beautiful than Earth. I know that sounds like heresy, but it's true! And we know where the satellite is, so Zainal says there'll be an easy way to avoid it by taking different windows out because it's positioned geo-synchronously for this area. No way of telling how long it's been up so it's possible that, even if it was in geo-synch with this landing area, it might not have seen the Farmers' ships.'

Kris grinned at Raisha, recognizing the high she was on, but she also kept looking for Zainal.

'Oh, he's still explaining some of the finer points

to Bert. You'll have to drag them out of there,' Raisha said. 'Sarge, we got good views of the other continents during our landing orbit. It looks like only one other one is being farmed as intensively as this. It'd be smart to have a look and see if it isn't wiser to transfer everything to an unoccupied continent and just put the Farms back to the way they were before we got here. Just think how that'd confuse the Catteni.'

'Easy, now, Raisha,' said Mitford, grinning at her babble.

'Oh!' She looked over to the others. 'I should just debrief to you, shouldn't I? But they all know about Phase One, don't they? It's . . .' and she stopped, took a deep breath, brushed sudden tears out of her eyes, '. . . it's just that once the Catteni took over, I never thought I'd make space in a real ship.' She dashed the tears from her eyes and made an obvious effort to control herself. 'One helluvan astronaut I'm making!'

'You did just great, ma'am,' Mitford said in military tones, and that did the trick.

'Thank you, sergeant. I appreciate having had the honour to go.'

'"Where no human has gone before",' Kris heard herself repeating the Star Trek phrase.

Mitford inched closer to the open hatch, but Kris reached it first.

'Zainal?' she called, damning herself for acting like a possessive female.

'On the bridge!' He sounded elated, too.

As Raisha had said, he was still explaining to

86

Bert about yaw and roll procedures and which toggles and handles were used in which situations.

'You landed her on a dime,' Kris said, looking from one to the other, and it was Bert who smiled proudly back at her.

'Zainal insisted. Damn near wet myself,' he said, but Kris only laughed at him. 'There seem to be only so many ways to arrange controls and panels that it wasn't actually that hard. Not that Zainal wouldn't have taken over if I glitched . . .' He pointed to the right-hand position at the bridge. 'Mind you, those predators coming at me like F-88s were scary . . .'

'I don't think they'll be back any time soon,' Kris said. 'Those that lived to fly away.'

'They don't appear when transports do,' Zainal said thoughtfully.

'The scout makes a sort of whistle . . .' Kris suggested and he nodded. She wanted to do something more than stand there with both hands at her sides, something to show Zainal how very, very glad she was to see him. She wished Bert anywhere but on the bridge.

Then Zainal stepped to her side, pulled her so that their cheeks touched and his lips brushed her ear before he stepped back. 'I go debrief to Mitford.' He turned back to Bert. 'Go through the sequences. We must put her out of sight before we close her down.' Then he pushed Kris around and down the narrow passageway. 'We now know much more about Botany that is useful to know.'

All Kris could think of was that he was back and Phase One complete and Mitford was willing to go to Phase Two. As she stepped out onto the field where she had lain unconscious and vulnerable nine months ago, she could scarcely believe the change in fortune. And all because she'd rescued a fugitive Catteni.

As Kris discovered, while the curious – and they came in droves down from Camp Narrow – inspected the scoutship, Zainal's debriefing with Mitford dealt more with the details of what he had observed of the rest of the planet during the landing orbit than the flight. He had piloted in the initial stages, past the satellite, given the scout some rolls and yaws.

'To look out of control,' Zainal said with a grin, 'and then I went behind the moon and out of the satellite's range.' Of Bert and Raisha, he said, 'They know more than they think they do. Well trained. Able to drive while I looked. The scout makes fast . . . sketches . . .' He looked enquiringly at Kris who supplied 'photos'. 'Yes, photos, details of other continents. Got very close on last pass.' Zainal grinned. 'Much better than what we were given.' And he paused, twitching one eyebrow in irritation over the earlier reluctant handouts.

'Raisha said something about only two continents being farmed.'

Zainal nodded. 'One is empty but greening. Other not too good, I think. But I am not farmer.'

'You want us to shift our living space?' and Mitford waved over his head to mean the campsites the colonists now occupied, 'and keep us out of trouble with the real landlords?'

'Land . . .' and Zainal separated the two words in puzzlement, 'lords?'

'The race which first claimed this planet.'

'Ah, landlords. Yes. This is considerable. A people who could make a prison of that valley we explored do not act as Catteni or Eosi do. They kept something in there, or kept something from getting in. That is not how Catteni or Eosi work.'

'Nor even humans, if you look at history,' said Mitford in a droll tone, crossing his arms on his chest again.

Then, out of the corner of his eye, Zainal gave Mitford a long look.

'Phase Two, sarge?'

Mitford chuckled, dropped his arms to slap his hands on his knees. 'You found weapons?'

'Enough to overpower stupid Drassi,' Zainal said almost contemptuously.

'Things are getting more and more interesting, aren't they?' Mitford said to no-one in particular.

Someone nearby cleared his throat and Kris looked over her shoulder at a group of men she vaguely remembered were formerly military and naval brass. Instantly she was alarmed for Mitford's sake. She didn't want him summarily replaced by newcomers who figured they knew more about running this world than Mitford. It was Peter Easley who had cleared his throat.

'Sergeant, when you have a chance, we'd like a few words with you?'

'More than a few, and your being here saves me sending for you,' Mitford said, stepping down from the driver's seat. 'Have you met Emassi Zainal and Kris Bjornsen yet?'

There was a formal shaking of hands all round, hands which Kris noticed were calloused and hardened by 'civilian' labours. She noticed that everyone was respectful to both her and Zainal and told herself that she was imagining 'hostile take-overs'. The cordiality of all nine did not seem forced. Their comments ranged from 'Well done' to 'A terrific boost to morale here'.

'What Earth rank is "Emassi" equal to, Zainal?' Mitford asked and winked at Kris.

' "Emassi" is captain,' Zainal informed Mitford, regarding him blandly. 'Emassi outranks sergeant,' he added and grinned.

'Beg pardon,' Peter Easley said, leaning forward politely, as if he thought he had missed something.

'Old joke,' Mitford said. 'Have you been in the ship yet, gentlemen?'

They all nodded and grins widened.

'Might we get filled in on the details?' asked one silver-haired man – one of the generals, Kris thought. His eyes travelled from Zainal to Kris to Mitford and then Easley. 'The implications of such a capture are staggering. Rastancil, Major General,' and he added with a rueful expression, 'retired.'

'As I said,' Mitford began, 'I was going to send

for you as soon as I could report that Phase One was successful.' He gestured towards the ship, frowning briefly as there was a scuffle at the hatch. Cupping his hands over his mouth, he let out his parade-ground voice. 'EASY DOWN THERE! OR NO-ONE GOES IN! LATORE, DOYLE, MAKE 'EM FORM A PROPER LINE. Sorry about that,' as he turned back to the brass. 'It is successful, and I think it's time I turned the matter over to Tactics or Strategy or whatever you want to call an appropriate body.'

'Sergeant, if you got this much done,' Rastancil said, 'you've more than earned the right to sit in on a Phase Two, if that's what I think you mean.'

Mitford nodded sharply. 'A Phase Two and a Phase Three.' He gestured to Zainal again. 'Yeah, we do need to talk.' More sharp yells of protest from the spaceship. 'Lemme handle this first,' he said and, slipping back in the runabout, his expression ominous, he circled down to the crowd around the hatch.

'Just what had you in mind for Phase Two, Emassi Zainal?' one of the naval men asked. He had a definite British accent, so Kris placed him as Geoffrey Ainger.

'I am Zainal, no more Emassi,' he said. 'I will tell you about Phase One.'

'Then do it up at Narrow, why don't you?' Kris suggested as yet more people swarmed across the field to set eyes on the space vehicle. 'I'll wait here for the sergeant.'

'We will all wait for the sergeant,' said Easley,

but he gestured to a point further up the field, well out of the traffic from Camp to the parked ship, where there was a slope up to the hedgerow providing seating.

If there were one or two men who cleared their throats or raised eyebrows of surprise at that firmly delivered order, Easley was so deft at easing them the way he wanted them to go that they all complied. When they got to the spot, Zainal crossed his ankles and sank gracefully to the ground. Kris sat beside him and Easley on Zainal's other side, facing the others as they made themselves comfortable. Zainal gave a concise report of Phase One, from the first report by Coo to the moment it landed. Kris was particularly proud of his English, maybe not couched in perfect grammatical English but concise.

When he was finished, a balding, stockily built man with a weather-beaten face and a fine scar from jaw to temple held up his hand. 'Why would you have been the object of such a concerted kidnap attempt, Zainal?'

'How much do you know of Eosi?'

'More than I like, but not enough to understand why they'd hunt out one man,' was the reply.

'You are the American general, Bull Fetterman?' A nod answered Zainal's question and Kris gave him full marks for having sorted out names and ranks. But then Zainal kept himself informed of what sort of people had been dropped and knew from Mitford's report of the presence of military and naval officers. 'Then you will know that Eosi command Catteni manoeuvres.' Fetterman wasn't the only one who nodded. 'They pick Emassi to make longer their lives.'

'Say what?' Bull Fetterman assumed a posture and expression that had undoubtedly given him his nickname.

'They subsume the Catteni totally,' Kris said. 'Zainal would have become a zombie . . . or worse . . . he wouldn't be dead, but he wouldn't have any personality left. Like Heinlein's *Puppet Masters'* yarn.'

'And the first scout came to take you back because you'd been chosen?' Easley asked.

Zainal nodded.

'I heard it was some sort of honour,' Rastancil said, though his expression suggested he didn't consider it so.

'It is.' And then Zainal grinned. 'But I was dropped. I stay.' He made a scissors motion with his big hands. 'I am off the honours list.'

Easley blinked and grinned. Rastancil did, too.

'But it was duty?' Fetterman said.

'Not once I was dropped here.' And Zainal pointed emphatically at the ground.

'Someone has to take your place?' asked a black officer, late-forties Kris judged his age.

'Another male of my line. There are several,' Zainal said with a shrug.

'What about reprisals here?' another man asked. Kris thought he was Reidenbacker. She'd been reviewing in her mind all the names and occupations on Drop lists and was putting them now to faces.

'The last place they will look is here,' Zainal said.

'You're sure of that?' Admiral Scott asked, his tone barely civil.

'He's got a point, Ray,' Rastancil replied. 'If you were deserting, the last place you'd go to is the place you deserted from.'

'I do not desert,' Zainal said with a slight frown. 'I was dropped. I stay.'

'Then that's some kind of duty or just a personal preference?' Scott wanted to know.

'Zainal is referring to the fact that no-one placed on one of these trial planetary occupations is ever released,' Kris said firmly, trying not to glare at Scott. 'This is essentially a penal colony, you know. Which is why we called it Botany. Zainal *refused* the option to leave because that would break another rule: only because it suited his superiors. If they'd retrieved him before he was sent off with us dissenters, it'd have been another matter entirely. But they let him get sent.' She added that, whether it was true or not, just to make sure Scott wasn't going to call Zainal a deserter or coward or anything like that.

'We concede the issue,' Rastancil said, smiling.

'So we can be sure we won't be in for any reprisals because you brought the scout here,' Scott added.

'I think we've established that that is unlikely,' said Easley, trying to end that topic, 'since Zainal deliberately took a course that would take him out of this system on his departure. Ah, here's the sergeant.'

Mitford cleared the look of irritation from his face as he stepped down from his runabout.

'Damn Aarens claiming he had rights . . .' he muttered to Kris as he hunkered down beside her. 'Finished discussing Phase One?'

'Indeed we have . . .' Easley began.

'Could we have a written report for the record?' Scott asked.

'One's all we got paper for, sir,' said Mitford with no apology. 'Kris, can you do it for me? So, Zainal, if you'll describe Phase Two just as you told it to me three nights ago . . .'

Zainal suddenly rose to his feet. Even though most of the brass were sitting on a slope, his new position required them all to look up at him, as neat a bit of strategy as Kris had ever seen.

'The transports that make the Drops come more often. Your planet is giving Catteni trouble they did not expect. The ships are not in good repair. We have weapons now. We can take a second ship.' He held up one hand to forestall questions that goal provoked. The gesture was one of such dignified command that even Scott subsided, scowling. 'We take transport. Then scout takes load of metals from mechs and bomb and explode in space far enough up there . . .' He extended his hand upward. 'Satellite is geo-syn-chron-ous,' and if he sounded out the syllables, he had them in the right order. 'Can only see this side. Will see explosion.' He made the scissors gesture again.

'Now don't try to tell me the Catteni will let that go without some sort of an in-depth investigation!'

95

Scott said, making no attempt to disguise his scepticism and disapproval.

'Not if crew's last message tells of . . . system's failure.' Zainal had had to find the words, but he also found the right ones.

'Two famous last messages, and each time a ship disappears?' Scott said, openly scoffing.

'Only Drassi are on transport ship. No big loss,' Zainal said coldly. 'Catteni . . .' and he laid an emphasis on the word, 'do not worry over small casualties. Ship or Drassi. You should know that by now.'

'Does that mean you, a Catteni officer, are willing to let *us* kill Catteni?' Scott demanded, watching Zainal with narrowed eyes.

Zainal gave a shrug. 'War makes casualties. You know that. I know that. Or,' and he let a wry smile play on his lips, 'do as Catteni do. Let crew go free, those that remain alive. If they are not found in one whole day,' and he lifted a finger, 'they live and join us. They are dropped. They stay.'

Kris hastily covered her mouth with her hand, but she scanned faces to see who understood Zainal's wit. More got it than didn't. These guys were sharp enough. Scott seemed the only hard critic.

'You did know about that Catteni rule, didn't you, Admiral?' Mitford asked very politely.

Scott gave him a curt nod.

'With respect, sir, in case no-one mentioned it,' the sergeant went on, 'Zainal was shanghaied aboard that ship in a contradiction to that rule. Just in case any of you wondered why he didn't feel he had to comply with any further orders from Emassi.'

'Thank you for explaining that, sergeant,' Easley said. 'I think it should clear up any lingering doubts about where Zainal's loyalties now lie. To return to Phase Two, what good does it do us to have a ship that may not be useful? Even if Zainal believes we can disregard reprisals.'

'I think of the Farmers,' Zainal said, and all eyes were on him again. 'With two ships, we can send one with their transport . . .'

Scott dismissed that notion with a snort and looked away.

'Now, wait a minute, Scott,' said Fetterman. 'I'm not entirely clear on these Farmers or Mech Makers or whatever you want to call them.' Then he turned back to Zainal. 'You *want* them to know we're squatting on their land?'

'Squatting?' Puzzled, Zainal looked down at Kris for an explanation.

'Slang for taking over lands or a place that you don't own,' she said quickly. 'Actually, that's Phase Three.' Before they started arguing over Phase Two, Kris wanted them to have some grasp of the scope of Zainal's plans. 'Forming an alliance with the Farmers against the Eosi because if they can farm a planet without any sentient being in charge, Zainal thinks they may have a sufficiently sophisticated technology to help the Catteni get out from under the domination of the Eosi – and stop being made into zombies and do things because the Eosi order them to be done. Like take over Earth.'

'Whoa, there, young lady,' Fetterman said, but he was grinning and so was Rastancil, while Scott looked more annoyed than ever. 'Pretty ambitious, if you ask me.'

'The longest journey starts with the first step,' she said in a firm but clear voice and gestured back over her shoulder at the spaceship. 'Step number one.'

'Kris has a point,' Easley said, once again taking charge as he seemed able to do almost effortlessly. 'Until this morning none of us would have remotely considered the possibility of hijacking a Catteni ship . . .'

'Having a damaged transport's no damned good . . . for going after Catteni or Eosi or these Farmers,' Scott said, standing up.

'But transport allows us to shift a lot of people to one of the other continents that the Farmers are not using.' Mitford said, beginning to let his irritation show. 'It's another step to owning ourselves instead of being a goddamned Catteni colony they think they could just walk into and take over when it gets on its feet. That's the usual plan, isn't it, Zainal?'

Kris watched Mitford winding himself up and looked anxiously in Easley's direction, but the man was watching eagerly as if he wanted Mitford to sound off.

'Well, a scout's a start on our Botany Defence Initiative, and I'll back Phase Two with every man and woman that's been following me the past nine months.' Then Mitford caught hold of himself, took a deep breath. 'If we pull that off, too, then we can re-evaluate the situation. And there's more than just the Catteni to worry about. There're the Farmers, and how they'll take to us being dropped here on their prime real estate without their say-so. Now I know I've mentioned to you that most of us are beginning to think we ought to leave the Farmers' installations alone and find our own. That's why I have scout parties out all over the continent.'

'Hold it there a minute, sergeant,' Rastancil said, getting to his feet. 'Thought you dismantled all those Mechanicals so that the Farmers would come and see who was vandalizing their planet?'

'That was the only option open to us *then*, sir. But we've been having discussions about that,' and Mitford gestured to Easley, Fetterman and up the hill towards Camp Narrow. 'I wasn't the only one who wanted to get off this planet *then*.' He paused. 'I'm not so sure I want to leave now. And I know a lot of others have had second thoughts like me. But that', and he pointed back towards the scout-ship, 'alters everything. Or . . . hell, you should see that as well as I can.' And he ended with his arms at his sides, waiting for reaction.

'Definitely the situation has changed,' Easley said and heard murmurs seconding that. He seemed to be appraising the moods around him. 'Phase Two seems feasible but, as Sergeant Mitford says, it's going to need some intense planning and good timing . . . even with weapons at our disposal. I suggest that we adjourn and discuss ways and means.'

'Scout hides,' Zainal said and pointed towards Camp Narrow.

'You're going to fly it in?' asked a man with a rather rakish moustache as he got to his feet, brushing off the seat of his coverall. 'I'd like permission to be aboard, sir. I was mission control on the last shuttle project. Trained as a test pilot. Gino Marrucci.'

Zainal looked to Mitford who nodded. Then Zainal looked at Scott. 'You come too?'

Someone stifled a chuckle but Scott, controlling his expression, stood up. 'I would like to.'

'Ship only holds eight at the most,' Kris said, though she'd hoped to be one. 'You have to go, sergeant.'

'Then you do, too,' said Mitford, jutting out his chin.

'One more,' Zainal said. 'Air force man?'

'I was air force,' the black general said and he stood, grinning. 'John Beverly.'

'That's settled then,' said Peter Easley. 'Shall I drive your runabout back to Camp Narrow, sarge? And be sure the garage's . . . or should I say, hangar's ready.'

'Good idea,' Mitford said.

Zainal pivoted and, without looking back to see who followed, led the way back down the field.

'Always meant to go see the display at Houston but never found the time,' Mitford said conversationally to no-one in particular in the group walking in step with him. He grinned as Kris made a hasty leg change to match strides with the others. 'Happens all the time with us military types.'

*   *   *

'Okay, okay,' Joe Latore was saying when he saw the phalanx moving in on the spaceship, and gestured for those in line to make way. Grumbling started from those next to go until Mitford swung into view, when it was replaced by cheers for Zainal and Mitford.

'We're gonna fly this baby up to Narrow now,' Mitford said. 'You'll get a chance to look inside later.'

'You mean, the Catteni are goin' to be lookin' for it?' a man asked in a nervous tone.

'Naw,' said Bert, appearing in the open hatch. He grinned when he saw the delegation and jumped to the ground, waving those behind him from the last tour to make a quick exit. 'Why would a Catteni in his right mind want to live on Botany if he could get off?'

There was good-natured laughter at that sally, as those still hoping to see inside the prize began to drift back up the hill.

'Gentlemen,' Bert waved the new group in. 'Shall I . . .?' he began to Zainal, as if he anticipated being replaced.

'You must watch me do it,' Zainal said. 'These watch, too.'

'I'll bet they do,' Bert murmured low enough for only Kris and Zainal to hear as they passed him.

Kris stepped up, into the hatch, ahead of the brass. She wasn't going to be left behind this time. Mitford gave precedence to Scott, Beverly and

Gino Marrucci. When they reached the bridge, Raisha was in the second seat and hastily got to her feet.

Zainal gave her a nod and then pointed to Bert to take her place while he folded himself into the pilot's chair.

'Secure hatch, Raisha,' Zainal said and looked at the arrangement of those standing in the cramped space of the small bridge. He nodded and gestured for them to stay where they were.

Kris inched closer to Mitford who was just behind Zainal.

'You watch good?' Zainal said to Bert, who nodded as Zainal's fingers moved in slow sequence over toggles and switches. 'Got that?'

'Yes, yes . . .'

A quick glance around and Kris saw that Bert was not the only one memorizing the sequence. Beverly and the test pilot were the most eager, but Scott's expression was less critical.

'Ve-ry smooth,' Beverly said. He was the first to be conscious of the vertical take-off.

'It is extremely manoeuvrable craft,' Zainal said in an instructional tone, two fingers of his right hand on the grip. 'One of its biggest . . .' He tipped his head back towards Kris, for her to give him the word he needed.

'Assets,' Kris supplied.

'Ass-ETS, not asses?' Zainal asked, blank-faced.

'You pick up too much bad language, man,' she muttered as everyone else grinned.

'In space as well?' asked Beverly.

'Better in space,' Zainal answered, as he depressed a button on the panel in front of him and began a horizontal forward movement, skimming safely above the heads of those moving back to Camp Narrow.

'That satellite won't see the movement?' Scott asked.

Kris wondered if the Admiral would ever give Zainal any slack.

'Not that kind. Very basic and geo-synchronous,' Zainal replied, twitching one shoulder. 'I use only . . . guide . . .' He craned his head about, for Kris's help.

'Guidance,' Beverly supplied. 'Thrusters? Or rockets?'

Zainal made a gesture with his free hand as if pressing the Earth away from him.

'We'd call 'em thrusters, I think,' Beverly said. 'Do they move?' and he rocked his hand to indicate different positions. Zainal, flashing a look at the signals, nodded. He was watching the landscape closely.

'Is there much fuel left?' the test pilot asked, looking over the gauges and dials. 'Which one?'

'This one,' Bert said and tapped it. A needle pointed just a shade over the halfway mark.

'Reason two for Phase Two. Transport will have fuel,' Zainal said.

'How far will what there is take us?'

Zainal shrugged. 'Not back to your Earth.'

'What sort of fuel do you use?' asked the test pilot.

Zainal rattled out some Catteni sounds and then grinned at the pilot.

'Can't make here.' He made another correction, moved a toggle and the pilot gasped.

'You're gliding in?'

'No need to waste fuel,' Zainal said, and pointed his finger just as the entrance to Camp Narrow appeared in the hillside.

There were a lot of people watching now, waving their hands, mouths open though no sound penetrated the scout.

'Fraggit,' Mitford muttered, his face pale, as he grabbed for something to hang on to as the scout seemed to slide down a corridor that had once seemed much wider.

'Easy as pie, sergeant,' Beverly said, grinning broadly as they headed inexorably towards the target barn's wide-open doors.

'It'll fit?' asked Mitford, taking a firmer hold on the ceiling handle he had found.

'No problem,' Bert said.

Kris sympathized with Mitford. She tried not to hold her breath. The flight vanes on the rear of the fuselage must be just clearing the sides of the alley. Then she noticed someone encouraging the forward motion with hand gestures as he backed towards the barn. Zainal held up one hand, caught the man's attention and gestured him to stand aside. With the slightest possible touches on the thrust handlers, Zainal lifted the ship above the cliff side and, with equally delicate movements, turned the scout around, lowered it and began backing it into the barn. The ground crew leaped in front and now made pushing gestures, as he stood to one side so he could judge when to wave-off.

'No rear mirrors on this thing, huh?' Mitford murmured in Kris's ear, but he had colour back in his face now that they were nearly parked.

The wave-off came and, with one final adjustment, they felt the scout ship settle to the floor.

To Kris's surprise, the observers clapped their hands, even Scott.

'You'd've been a great Atlantis pilot,' Marrucci said.

Zainal stood up, squeezing up against Mitford and Kris in the cramped space. 'Bert, show Marrucci how to shut her down.'

'Can we watch?' asked John Beverly.

Zainal shrugged, looking at Mitford.

'Sure, why not,' the sergeant said, easing himself towards the passageway to give the others more space. But he looked over his shoulder to observe that Scott stayed as well.

'Did it go well?' Raisha asked from her position in the passageway. 'I couldn't see a thing with all the bodies in the way, but I felt it turn around.'

Zainal undogged the hatch and stepped out into the barn, giving Kris a hand down first, and then Raisha.

'Can this be locked, Zainal?' Mitford asked in a low voice, because the man who had acted as ground crew was loping up to them.

'There are six of these,' Zainal said, showing Mitford the small greyish-brown rectangle in his hand. 'I have hidden three. Bert and Raisha each have one. Is that right?'

Mitford looked thoughtful, almost sad. 'For now, but I think the fly boys and the brass will decide who gets to use this baby.'

'Baby?' Zainal asked, turning to Kris. 'Is that like boy-o-boy, and man-o-man?'

'Ships are generally referred to as "she", female,' she said, grinning. 'And special ships are babies. Specially good ships!'

'That's a lot of baby,' Zainal said with suspicious laughter glinting in his eyes as he looked down the length of the scout.

'Hey, Zainal, that was some sweet job of piloting,' the crew man said, running up with his hand out for Zainal to shake. 'I used to be flight deck officer on the *George Washington* . . .'

'Aircraft carrier,' Kris explained.

'Boy, you landed that baby as sweet as if you'd been backing her into this hangar all your life!'

Zainal gave yet another of his shruggings. 'I had to learn. And pay for holes made.'

'Didja?' and somehow that pleased the man. 'Need any more help with her, I'm your man. Vic Yowell's the name.' He gave Zainal's hand another shake and then went to prowl around the vessel.

'All that brass aren't going to take the ship away from us, are they?' Raisha asked, keeping her voice down and her eye anxiously on Mitford.

'Listen up, you lot,' Mitford said, catching them with a stern glance, 'that ship makes this a whole new ball-game. I know General Rastancil by

106

reputation – he has a good one. I heard good things about General Beverly . . . don't know about the navy, but I do know', and he waggled his finger at them, 'that there'll be some changes and we gotta be flexible. So let's go with the flow. Right?'

'Where I flow, you go,' said Zainal, poking Mitford in the shoulder with one finger with each word. 'Right?'

Mitford gave a short laugh, but Kris knew that he appreciated Zainal's statement of loyalty.

'I don't know about you lot, but I need some chow about this time of day.' He walked out of the hangar.

'Me, too,' said Raisha. 'I didn't like Catteni ship-board rations. They tasted like cardboard wadding.'

'Healthy,' Zainal said as he took Kris by the arm to follow the lead.

'*Will* we get to Phase Two?' Raisha asked over her shoulder.

'For fuel we must,' Zainal said.

'So if I get a chance to learn to pilot the scout, I could pilot a transport vessel?'

'You can now,' Zainal said, grinning at her surprise. 'Drassi need very simple controls.'

'Say, Zainal,' Mitford asked, 'how many ships do you think we can hijack before they stop landing here or your destroyers come to have a look?'

Zainal just grinned.

They had finished with the noontime meal when Bert and the others who had stayed on in Baby, as the ship was unimaginatively called, joined them at their table. Marrucci and Beverly were full of questions for Zainal about the performance levels of the ship, its cruising range, cargo capacity, weaponry and maintenance requirements. Kris translated terms as well as she could, with help from both Bert and Raisha when she bogged down over unfamiliar words and meanings. Mitford sent someone for paper and pencil.

'Would you have such a thing as a manual?' Ray Scott asked at one point.

'What good would a Catteni manual do us?' Kris asked, almost defensively although Scott's attitude had modified considerably since the docking hop.

'Diagrams,' Scott said, as if that was obvious.

So Zainal told Bert where to find the service manuals in the pilot compartment, and the day became a session of terminology and translation. Engineers were sent for to decipher the schematics, while Zainal struggled to explain with his inadequate technical vocabulary. For Kris, guesswork worked as well in some instances, but she came up with appropriate ones more often than the others did. Zainal did know the basic maintenance routines and checks required, since he had often flown this type and had had to make repairs.

Worrell arrived at one point and took Mitford off with him. Reidenbacker left later on and took Fetterman with him, but Kris was far too occupied with spatial and aviation words to do more than register that there were other faces where those men had sat. There was also no question that the capture of Baby was the best thing that could have happened on Botany at that particular moment.

It was full dark before Zainal suddenly shook himself and stood up.

'I can talk no more tonight.'

Then everyone became solicitous and grateful, and said that by all means he should get some rest.

'You, too,' he said to Raisha and Bert. 'No sleep last night. Not good. Minds must be rested to learn how to fly Baby.' He caught Kris with one hand, Raisha with the other, and gestured for Bert to follow them out.

There was a brief lull in the various conversations all over the barn but, by the time they reached the door, these had picked up again, including several arguments, with sheets of Zainal's meticulous diagrams and the manual being passed around.

All four walked wearily to one of the less crowded end barns. A 'people' door had been cut into the larger one and a narrow entry area established before three aisles sectioned off the floor space. Screens of woven reeds divided areas into living spaces, affording a certain degree of privacy. Single pallets stuffed with fluff weed, spare blankets, a rough box to hold possessions and two stools comprised the furnishings of the one Zainal and Kris took. He moved two pallets together. Kris got her boots off, emptied her pockets of the comunit and items she hadn't realized she still had with her and lay down. Zainal covered her with a blanket before removing his boots and settling down beside her, reaching out to grasp her hand before he took one deep breath and fell asleep at the end of it. She wasn't far behind him.

Still unaccustomed to Botany's longer diurnal period even after nine months, and despite the excitements and exertions of the previous day and night, Kris found herself waking before sunrise. Zainal was awake, too, lying on his back with hands behind his head.

'What's up?' she asked in a low voice.

He released one hand, curled his arm around her head to stroke her cheek.

'Thinking.'

'Good thoughts?'

He nodded.

'Share them?'

He rubbed his knuckles against her cheek: she could see his teeth in a smile in the dim light. 'I must out-think Catteni.'

She caught his hand, holding it against her cheek as she turned into him, her lips closer to his ear. 'Then there could be trouble over the scout.'

'Not here yet.' She could feel his cheek muscles lifting as his grin broadened. 'Lenvec may not be . . . fooled. Or is it joke this time?'

'Fooled. Why?' She tried not to stiffen against him in concern but he sensed it, far too aware of her body language now, and his hand flattened soothingly against her head.

'He does not wish to do Eosi duty.'

'Is he the other male you meant yesterday?'

She felt Zainal's shoulder twitch and the rumble of amusement in his chest. 'He is next, but may not be chosen.' That seemed to amuse him even more. 'He has life-mate and several childs already,' Zainal added, as if that should be a consolation.

'Children,' she corrected automatically. 'Don't you?' she heard herself ask.

'No chosen has life-mate, but I have two males. Too young to be chosen.'

'So if Lenvec is chosen, we don't have to worry?'

'He did not say how soon the chosen must go. If there is time, maybe. He will be commanded where to search first.' Then Zainal paused, and she sensed he deliberated on whether or not to continue as he stroked her head slowly. 'Maybe . . . he gets better satellite over Botany.'

'Higher tech? More sophisticated?'

Zainal nodded. 'But even that will take time.' And she felt his laugh. Felt him stop, too. 'I must be very careful.'

'Shouldn't we tell Mitford all this?'

Zainal gave his head one shake. 'Not now. He has enough troubles with – what did you call them – the brass? Beverly, Scott, Rastancil, them?'

'Yeah, they're all brass, admirals, generals: Marrucci was a colonel, I think. Watch out for Scott.'

Zainal grunted agreement and surprised her by smiling. 'I like a good fight.'

'You mean, convincing Scott you're all right for a Catteni? Or getting Phase Two and more fuel for the scout?'

'Both.' He gave her hand a warm squeeze. 'This gets interesting.'

'Don't get smug, Emassi Zainal.'

'Me? Never. This Catteni bastard watches his step.'

'Zainal! Where did you pick up that language?'

'Is it not correct?'

She knew he was teasing and laughed. 'I'm damned glad you know as much as you do, particularly right now . . .'

'For the brass-heads.'

She giggled, ducking her head into his chest to muffle the sound. 'Brass-heads' – she must remember to tell that to the sergeant.

At Lenvec's insistence, which was beginning to annoy Perizec both as patriarch and commander, he listened to the record tape and replayed the satellite's recording of the scout's take-off, the suddenly erratic course which straightened into a dive towards the subject planet's second moon, disappearing beyond the satellite's visual limitation.

'But analysis proves that is *not* Zainal's voice. None of them are. What has Personnel said about Arvonk?'

That was the one flaw in Lenvec's arguments. 'There is none of Arvonk, who was only a woman and not in service as Emassi. She was used because Zainal had chosen her several times for intercourse.'

'There are no other Catteni down there. Who else but another scout could have responded?'

'Some of the Terrans have learned our language.'

Perizec snorted. 'But not how to operate comunits.'

'Zainal could teach them.' Lenvec spoke through his teeth with aggravation, an unwise attitude to show his senior and parent but he had absolutely no doubt that Zainal had somehow escaped capture: had probably piloted the scout off the planet. And then, for reasons Lenvec could not understand in a Catteni Emassi who had been chosen to serve the Eosi, Zainal had returned to the planet. He had not taken refuge anywhere in Catteni space because everywhere he would be hunted; nowhere would he find asylum.

Zainal's taunt – 'I drop, I stay' – was like a pulse in the back of Lenvec's brain. What good did it do Zainal to go back to the planet, no matter what technology had been found there? Could Zainal know the origin of the original occupants of that planet? Was that why he took the scout? What good would such a move do?

'He has somehow made friends with the Terran dissidents,' Lenvec went on, desperate to persuade his father to believe him. 'Now he has transportation. He has some plan in mind.'

Perizec dismissed that consideration as he rose. 'For all the good it will do him.'

'Sir, for the honour of the family, insist on a second orbital satellite. Geo-synchronous does not have sufficient capability to keep a watch on his next moves.'

113

'Next moves?' Perizec regarded his son steadily and with such malice that it was all Lenvec could do not to recoil from such scrutiny. 'Your next move is to attend the Eosi Selection. No further delay is possible. Is that understood?'

'Maybe the Eosi will not be so blind,' Lenvec said in a bitter tone, and when the nerve-whip suddenly appeared in his father's hand he braced himself for the blow. Despite that, the agony rocked him to his knees.

He had to be helped to his quarters by his life-mate, where she disobeyed the protocol that required the recipient to endure a whip-lash by administering a nerve block. Clern stayed by his side until the medication took effect. Which was more than she ought to have done but it did not, as she had probably hoped, appease his bitter resentment sufficiently for one final sexual interlude. Lenvec could think only what he had been deprived of because Zainal had been the chosen of their bloodline: the opportunities and promotions that Zainal had enjoyed because he had been the chosen. Eosi liked their 'subjects' to have rich experiences to bring for them to enjoy, to use as guides in their manipulation of their subject species. Lenvec had had to be satisfied with a circumspect life, learning to manage the family estates and accepting simpler rewards than Zainal gathered. Lenvec had even had to rear Zainal's children with his own, since being chosen kept Zainal from having a mate. That was the one privilege which Lenvec had had which Zainal did not.

And now Clern had to be set aside because Zainal had escaped.

During those long last hours of his single being, Lenvec toyed with suicide, but the dishonour would have deprived Clern of wealth and protection and his sons of their inheritance, which would be considerable. If he could have also deprived his father of honour by taking his own life, Lenvec might well have murdered himself.

His hatred of Zainal, his sense of betrayal, his keen awareness of the injustice done consumed Lenvec even when, supported by a blood pride he had not known he possessed in such depth, he was accompanied by Perizec to the vast complex reserved for Eosi. He entered with the three other Catteni being presented by their fathers, and Lenvec's resentment flared and deepened. *They* had been chosen: *they* had had the privileges Zainal had enjoyed and he had been denied. But he had as large a measure of Emassi pride as any of them and so he went, seething with hatred and the now deeply embedded ambition to somehow get even with Zainal.

That kept his back straight, his knees stiff as he faced the Eosi mentat who would engulf him, making him no more Lenvec but all Eosi. A fearsome entity even to an Emassi who had seen what Catteni became when subsumed by Eosian mentats: that shining immensity in a giganticized Catteni form. That one thought, of eventual triumph, sufficed Lenvec as the subsummation occurred. It kept him from screaming as two of the others, previously willing and proud young men, did as they were engulfed.

Certainly the intense emotion intrigued the Eosian as it settled into the strong new body as the shell that it had been using drifted like the dead thing it had been for centuries onto the highly polished floor of the chamber. Quite unusual, in fact, for the Eosian had made such transfers frequently and was delighted by a novel experience as the last of the personality which had once been Lenvec totally dissolved within the mentat.

The shell, crumbling into dust, was swept into a receptacle and returned with proper ceremony to Perizec, who waited with other fathers to receive the husks of their great-grandfathers. Of them all, Perizec was the most relieved. He had greatly feared that Lenvec would be found unacceptable and the dishonour to their bloodline would have been catastrophic. But honour had been served, and their family would continue to supply young men to the Eosi and reap more worldly rewards than other, less favoured families.

However, Perizec must still discover where the cowardly Zainal was hiding and make sure he paid the price of his evasion. Perizec smiled at the thought of a suitable execution. Private, of course, but the event could be enjoyed by Clern who had been deprived of her mate, and should be seen by Zainal's sons so that they would have to live with his dishonour as their lifelong penance.

Perizec took the receptacle containing his great-grandfather's dust to the family crypt and placed it in the niche prepared for it. He looked at the array of ancestors who had done their duty. Then did his final one: listing first Zainal and then Lenvec as dead. Too bad he could do nothing punitive to the sons, but that would give a lie to the reason why Lenvec had had to stand in for his brother. But there were other, subtler ways to make them pay for their father's defection.

Quite a considerable galactic distance from the Eosi home planet and its expanding sphere of influence, the homing device arrived in the slot designed to receive it on the huge moon installation where such devices were processed. When no message was displayed, the container was routinely overhauled for the malfunction. Such homing missiles were rarely despatched without cause. No malfunction was discovered. The device had been well engineered and had always operated within its design parameters. But the lack of any message was unusual and the container was sent to Processing to identify its point of origin. Since that planet was not one in any sense critical, or even very important, the errant device was shunted to the agency that, from time to time, investigated anomalies. The appropriate galactic co-ordinates were tagged for investigation during the next regular maintenance circuit.

Chapter Four

If those intimately connected with Phase One slept, it became obvious to Zainal and Kris when they quietly exited their quarters at dawn that others had not.

A weary duty-cook had propped her chair back against the wall, her head lolling to one side as she caught what rest she could while the knot of men and women at the table furthest from her murmured urgent conversations and passed papers back and forth.

Though Kris and Zainal had entered quietly, their arrival immediately curtailed the discussions. Almost every head turned to see who entered.

'Zainal! Kris!' Peter Easley half-rose from his seat and beckoned them over. 'Grab something to eat and drink, will you? And join us?'

The cook slept on, snoring slightly, so Kris and Zainal helped themselves to the food kept warm in the pans and the tea in the kettle.

Kris identified not only Scott and most of yesterday's 'brass' but others, obviously called in from the other camps for this session.

'You started something, Zainal,' Peter said, rising and gesturing for Zainal to take his place, while he hooked over chairs from the next table for Kris and himself.

'Phase Two?' Zainal asked, settling himself and eyeing the mass of papers, charts and lists that littered the table. He sipped.

'You bet,' said Easley, while several men at the other end of the table resumed their interrupted debate. 'I sent Mitford off to bed at third moonrise. He couldn't keep his eyes open.'

'How can you, then?' Kris asked.

'Oh, I caught a coupla hours before we changed guard,' and Easley winked at her conspiratorially.

She was somewhat reassured, although she had not previously considered Easley, for all the help he gave Mitford during Drops, as a surrogate for the sergeant.

'We have discovered a lot of dropees have had military training, and more than enough have commando, SAS, or similar training in their own countries, so that we can have our pick of the force to make Phase Two successful,' Easley explained in a low voice. 'What is needed now is information from you on—'

'What weapons there are aboard the scout,' and now Scott interrupted, 'some idea of the interior of a transport ship and what weapons they'd have so we can properly train our personnel.'

Zainal took a sip of the hot beverage and gestured that he be given paper and a writing implement.

'Breakfast first?' Kris said in a caustic tone, lifting a spoonful from her bowl of porridge. 'Army . . . and navy, I'm sure . . . still function better when fed.'

'Miss Bjornsen,' Scott began ever so politely.

'Knock it off,' Zainal said in a very quiet voice, but he gave Scott a brief, warning look before he began to sketch the long ovoid of a transport ship outline, sipping as he did so. 'Twenty crew, only Drassi armed with weapons. Others have nerve-whips...' Zainal gave Scott a long look. 'You know about nerve-whips?'

Scott nodded slowly, and it pleased Kris no end to realize that he had had at least one incident of intimate knowledge with that persuader.

'Crew carry on back,' and Zainal demonstrated tying the whip-lash to a handle and slinging the imaginary item onto his back. 'People unconscious no problem.' He outlined the bridge area, the main crew quarters where they seemed to sleep stacked nearly as closely together as their passengers would be, and then indicated the engine room, air plant and other essential elements of the transport, including cargo areas that did not have oxygen. That left an empty mid-section across which Zainal now drew a series of parallel lines.

'Sleepers don't need much space. Empty one deck, remove, shift upwards, empty two deck...'

'We were crammed in like sardines then,' Easley remarked with a bit of a shudder. 'What do they use to keep us in suspended animation?'

'Asleep' Kris whispered, because she knew Zainal would not recognize those words 'suspended animation'.

'Eosi make. Not even Emassi know in-gred-ee-ents,' Zainal said with one of his indifferent shrugs.

120

'So we would have to get the guards, storm through here to secure the bridge . . .'

Kris didn't recognize the voice, nor identify the slight accent, much less the long, non-white finger that had done the walking, and looked up. The slender man had angled in beside Scott and Fetterman. He grinned at her and touched a non-existent hat brim.

'Hassan Moussa, late of the Israeli forces,' he said.

'No,' and Zainal shook his head. 'First, they unload, then we do not risk lives. They will not expect attack. With dropping done, they are also tired. We stun those outside, maybe all will be. THEN we . . .' Zainal grinned at Moussa, 'storm through to bridge and surprise Drassi.'

Moussa wasn't the only one who chuckled at Zainal's suggestion to let the Catteni unload.

'I'm reliably informed that not everyone is unloaded with any caution,' said the British Ainger.

'I will be there, of course, to see,' Zainal remarked.

'Hey, wait a minute,' Kris said, and she wasn't the only one to see the folly of that.

'Not when the Catteni tried to kidnap you . . .' Rastancil said, frowning.

'Drassi will not know that,' Zainal said, 'but they obey Emassi orders any time.'

Open disagreement broke out and, after listening a few moments, Zainal began to eat his porridge, ignoring the dispute.

'He tells us he's a kidnap victim . . .'

'A transport was slated to pick him up the first time, wasn't it?'

'Can we really trust him?'

'If it's that easy to take the transport, why hasn't anyone tried?'

'You haven't seen bare hands against nerve-whips, have you?'

'So, if Drassi and Emassi never mix, who would recognize him?'

'And the risk is better than the twenty-five per cent casualties.'

Kris identified Leon Dane's voice. 'Leon can make like an Emassi from the shadows,' she said, broadcasting her suggestion over the other voices. That stopped them. 'It's the tone they respond to, not the figure.'

'Good idea,' Zainal said, licking his lips. 'He sounds Emassi. Could . . . fool . . . me.' And he cast a mischievous side glance at Kris as he continued to eat his breakfast.

'We can decide on that stratagem later,' Scott said firmly. 'If you've finished,' he addressed Zainal, who had indeed just emptied both bowl and cup, 'let's go through the numbers . . . of the crew . . . again.'

'One Drassi captain,' and Zainal dutifully ticked off on his fingers, 'one Drassi navigator, one Drassi com, one Drassi engineer, four more to take turns, and twelve to unload.'

'That makes twenty. Do all unload?'

Zainal nodded. 'Off-duty help so sixteen unload. Others relax here,' and he pointed to the bridge.

'Not much security,' he added. 'Stand from here,' and he put his finger on the portal, 'and stun all.'

'Stun?' The look on Scott's face was ludicrous.

'Why not? Killing weapons messy.'

'And wasn't it decided', Kris got in, 'that they'd at least have a chance to run for it?'

'Why?' The mood around the table turned ugly.

'Because then we're not the same as Catteni,' John Beverly said, raising his voice above the vengeful babble.

'General, I don't think the population here will appreciate leniency,' Bull Fetterman said.

'I don't see why not,' said Hassan Moussa with a vulpine grin. 'It could provide some sport.'

'Now, wait a bloody minute,' and Kris felt her breakfast roiling about in her stomach. 'We are not Catteni. We are human beings . . .'

'They can be tried as war criminals,' Moussa said, still grinning, and he looked down at Zainal to see his reaction, but the Catteni was adding details to the sketch, apparently oblivious to the moral issue.

'Take a camp vote,' Yuri Palit said, standing up at the end of the table.

'That's always assuming that we take the damned transport in the first place,' Beverly put in.

'Now wait a minute, general . . .'

'Beverly, if we can't overpower twenty . . .'

'Referendum!'

'Everyone needs to know . . .'

'Those guys murdered . . .'

'We don't have to do the same . . .'

Kris got up from the table, taking her dishes and Zainal's before she heaved up breakfast, listening to such vengeful talk. She *did*, she told herself as she stalked to the clean-up area, understand why they wanted to take it out on any Catteni they could, but the slaughter still made humans no better than Catteni and polluted this new world, and this fresh start, with all the old hatreds and prejudices that bubbled just skin-deep and could be sublimated by attacking a new species-victim. So who hit the goat now?

She almost threw the dishes down, but spotted the still-sleeping cook and slipped them quietly in the warm dishwater to soak. Possibly, if she had to, she could kill a Catteni in cold blood. She hadn't minded when Fek and Slav had killed the kidnappers, but her blood certainly hadn't been cold then – it had been frozen with fear that the ruse would be uncovered and Zainal taken. All the arguments were specious. It was the principle that was important. And more important here on Botany than at any other time in her life . . . even when she had feared rape by the brutish Catteni steward on Barevi.

'Kris!' Zainal's voice had not been pitched loudly but he stood at the exit and beckoned to her. The 'strategists' were so involved in arguing points of honour, law, principle and integrity that his departure had not been noticed. Except by Easley and Rastancil, who hurried towards him.

'Zainal?' Easley's quiet voice held a note of apology and Rastancil's expression was entreating.

'We will see what weapons and other useful junk is on scout,' Zainal said. 'That is next step to take to prepare for Phase Two.' He exited first, turned to wait for Kris, Rastancil and Easley and added, 'You are men of sense.'

Then he strode off at such a pace that even the long-legged Easley had trouble keeping up. Abruptly he stopped, staring ahead as the pre-dawn sky outlined the hangar which Kris realized had acquired the most peculiar outline. Zainal snorted and walked on.

'What'd they do to it?' Kris asked, though she thought she knew the answer.

'Mitford suggested we disguise the contents,' Easley said. 'Just enough in case someone should scan. All they'd see is metal hunks. Roof 'll take the weight. The engineers checked.'

The moment they cracked the inset door, a shadowy figure got to its feet and challenged them: in Vic Yowell's unmistakable tones. He even had a lance at the ready. 'Who's there?'

'Zainal, Kris, Easley and Rastancil,' Zainal said, taking him literally.

'Oh,' and Vic let out a relieved sigh. 'More damned people poking their noses in,' and he changed his voice to a whine, '. . . I didn't get to see it when it landed . . .' He altered tone again. 'I want a lock on that damned door.'

'No-one could get into the ship, Vic,' Kris said.

'I told 'em that, but they wanted to see the outside at least if they couldn't see in.'

'Go get some proper sleep, Vic,' Easley

suggested. 'We'll need you later on, and I appreciate your taking charge here.'

Vic gathered up his blanket and pallet and grinned as he passed them.

'Never thought I'd have a chance to land anything ever again. Don't want it messed up.'

Rastancil gave him a genial slap on the back as he went and, when Vic had closed the door behind him, the hangar was dark again. Rastancil cursed, but Easley turned on a hand beam, which Kris recognized as one that had been lifted from the kidnappers' bodies.

'You're quick,' she said with a grin up at Easley.

'Spoils of war are meant to be used,' he said.

Kris wondered was the man ever out of sorts? He'd been up all night arguing with brass-headed types and his equanimity seemed not the least bit strained.

'You always this way?' she asked.

'Which way?'

She could see his so-innocent grin in the light.

'Zainal calls them brass-heads,' she added since he wasn't answering her question.

'Brass-heads?' He chuckled. 'Indeed, indeed.'

'Lord, I can't even get you to commit yourself to a joke.'

'Oh, I commit myself, Miss Bjornsen. Believe me, I do.'

The hatch opened and lights inside came up, surprising an exclamation out of both Easley and Rastancil.

'Do *not*', Easley murmured, lowering his head to

Kris's ear, 'let them get Zainal's control away from him.'

'He isn't planning to let them,' she whispered back under the noise of Rastancil stumbling up into the ship. So Easley had committed himself – and to the right people – she thought, hauling herself up inside the ship. It had been easier from the air-cushion vehicle.

A low noise started, and Kris felt fresh air drawn in past her.

'You can vent to the outside?' Rastancil asked.

'Air is . . . old,' Zainal said; he made a gesture of a spinning blade. Then he indicated for them to go towards the stern rather than the pilot's compartment. They'd only taken a half dozen steps when he stopped and pulled at handles set flush in the wall.

The closet he had opened was stocked with an assortment of ordnance, much of it unfamiliar to Kris, but Rastancil sighed with unadulterated delight and, looking to Zainal for permission, picked up a rifle-type affair with a thick cartridge-case and a stumpy muzzle. Zainal pointed and named what each knob or toggle did. 'Safety, power up is red, white is empty. Make thin or fat spray of . . .' He turned to Kris.

'Bullets?' She made a space between thumb and forefinger. 'Metal? Kill?' Zainal closed the distance to almost very thin. 'Needle?'

He nodded.

'Oh, I heard about them on Earth. They started using toxic tips just before I was rounded up.

Nasty.' Rastancil carefully returned the weapon. 'Any single-shot, revolver-type weapons?'

Zainal frowned. Kris made her hand into a gun shape and enunciated a single 'pow!'

'Stunner,' Zainal said and touched the rack of eight. Then he laid his hand on their neighbour, a thick, long barrel. 'Ground-to-air.' Then nodded towards the bow. 'Space stuff up front.'

'What sort of armament do you have?' Rastancil asked eagerly.

Zainal gave a little laugh. 'Space, air-to-ground, small satellite to mark places. Not much. This is fast, and moves well.'

'So you count on its speed and manoeuvrability more than its ordnance?'

Kris wondered which words needed translating, but Zainal was looking at Rastancil and then gave a brief nod. 'Yes, speed and . . . other word . . .' He did look at Kris now, flipping his hand and fingers.

'Flexibility,' she supplied.

'Any telepathy in your family, Kris?' Easley asked.

'None, but I've been partnered with Zainal since we were dropped. I know what words he has learned . . . and he's got a very good vocabulary,' and Kris stressed that, 'so it's less guess and more acting as synonym finder.'

Easley chuckled. 'I suspect he understands far more English than people think.'

'I don't suspect,' Kris replied, and she meant that as a tacit warning. 'I *know*.'

'I shall keep that remark under my . . . hair, since my wardrobe does not run to a hat.'

Whether or not Easley might just be jollying her along, Kris sensed that Peter Easley was on Zainal's side and wanted to be considered a friend.

By the time Zainal had revealed the other goodies the scout contained, like very high-powered binoculars with thermal readings and nocturnal settings, a variety of comunits, emergency lights, beacons, maps, and the completed photos that he had taken on the way in, as well as hand cameras, Catteni-style, exploratory equipment, compasses, ropes, backpacks, winter and summer gear, thermal suits, and a lot of other gear that would see the scouting teams far better equipped, her head was reeling with such riches. Mitford would go bananas! There was even diving equipment and two water craft, dismantled and packed for transport.

'Sail? Or powered?' Easley asked, coming alive with interest at their appearance. He diagrammed a sail in the air and made a put–put noise for the power.

Zainal grinned. 'Both.'

'It's Christmas!' Kris said, wanting to clap her hands together.

'Well, to a degree,' Easley amended, but he was grinning too. 'You've done so well with so little, don't let all this stifle ingenuity. There isn't even eight of everything.'

'There's eight of everything we'd need for Phase Two,' Rastancil said in a sober tone, eyeing the weapons cache.

Zainal nodded, but he was far more interested in

Kris's reaction to the photos he offered her. She wasn't quite sure why she should be interested in mountains and valleys, until his index finger touched first one and then another point.

'Oh, more dead ends, like the valley we found?'

And he nodded. 'Many.'

'All empty?' she asked.

Zainal shrugged one shoulder and grinned. 'We go see?'

'What?' Easley wanted to know, peering over her shoulder.

'Our scouting project,' Kris said, not wanting to go into much detail.

'Oh, blind valleys like the one your team discovered which Mitford told me about?' said Easley and his face wore a hopeful expression, soliciting their confidence in him.

'Is a thing kept in? Or out?' Zainal said, giving it.

'Out would be my educated guess, considering the nocturnal horrors Botany has,' and Easley gave a little shudder.

'You've seen them?'

He pretended a repugnance that was probably sincere. 'Don't care to, either, but then I never go . . . went . . . to horror pictures either.'

Rastancil craned his neck, nodding approval at the prints. 'Very clear! What sort of camera equipment do you have on board?'

Zainal chuckled. 'I let experts tell me. Baxter says he was cameraman on flims . . . no, fillums.'

'Films,' Kris said as clearly as possible.

Zainal grinned. 'Whatever. I push button and

later,' he nodded to the slot in the wall, 'picture comes out. Show these to Mitford, Kris, please.'

'We can both show him,' she said.

Zainal shook his head. 'My duty is here today, showing off.'

'Show me around a couple more times, Zainal, and I'll spell you,' Rastancil offered.

'Many will want grand tour,' Zainal said, his eyes sparkling with such open amusement that Rastancil regarded him with surprise. 'I learn much from Kris,' he said, dropping a proprietary arm across her shoulders.

'Ah, yes, well,' Rastancil said, ducking his head in what Kris thought was as close to embarrassment as a brass-head was likely to get. 'There wouldn't be an inventory of what's on board Baby, would there? I know it'd be in your language, but we've got a couple of personnel down here now who learned to read Catten.'

'Come,' and Zainal beckoned Rastancil to walk forward to the pilot's compartment. 'You take a good look around, Kris, Peter,' he added, pointing to the other doors along the narrow hall. 'Familiarize yourselves.'

Easley was shaking his head respectfully as Zainal followed Rastancil.

'He's quite a guy. I'd never have thought a Catteni had an active sense of humour.'

'Maybe they just never have the opportunity,' Kris said and slid back the first door. 'Phew! This needs an airing. What slobs!' Clothing was thrown about floor and bunks, while used cups and plates attached to the surface of the table had not been collected for washing. There was a blank screen and a hand control unit which Easley picked up, examined and replaced as the markings meant nothing to him. There were four bunks, wide enough for Catteni bulk, and all unmade and messy.

Easley did look into the nearest locker, pinched his nose and shut it up. But he glanced in at the others. 'Some of the gear can be useful. Especially the uniforms for Phase Two . . . once they've been washed.'

There were two more compartments, one with three bunks and one – the captain's, Kris thought – with one, which contained command equipment. A viewer plate like the one she'd seen the steward on Barevi use, and racks of the disks used in it. Easley homed in on that. He was familiar with such things, neatly inserting a disk and turning on the viewer. A Catteni voice in monotone added comments to whatever was printed in the glyphs.

'Well, very interesting, I'm sure,' he said, clicking it off and absently returning the disk to its rack. 'Now where did they eat and wash – if they did?'

One of the doors in the captain's unit slid back to disclose what had to be a shower compartment, complete with what Kris thought resembled a urinal and another odd opening. Well, Catteni had much the same alimentary requirements as Humankind. Easley gave a mild grunt when he peered in over her shoulder.

There was another unit next in line down the passageway which would accommodate two at once. The galley was just beyond it, almost the last door in the passage.

'One-butt, at that,' she said, looking at the 'kitchen' side and its equipment. A table with padded seating around it was evidently where the crew ate, if not in their rooms. But the place was neat and tidy. Even clean. Ah, but Raisha had said that they'd eaten aboard the ship so she had probably also cleaned it up.

'Wonder what's back here, though,' Easley said after the briefest glance in the wardroom, turning his attention to the final, large door that took up the end of the passageway. It was dogged tight with large Catteni glyphs in white.

'If empty is white on Catteni guns, would it be caution on equipment?' Kris asked.

The moment Easley put his hands on the toggles, an alarm sounded.

'Don't enter.' Zainal's voice issued from an intercom right above their heads. 'Please,' he added.

'He's not totally assimilated, is he?' Easley remarked. 'Let's see what they're up to. Unless you want to clear out those lockers. We might need clean Catteni uniforms.'

Kris gave him a stern look. 'We might, but I think it would count as a morale booster for others to see just what slobs the Catteni can be.'

'Point!'

'What I really want to do is itemize all that lovely gear I hope we scouts have first pick of,' she said, rubbing her hands together. 'Damn, I've no paper.'

'Voilà!' Easley said, taking a wad of small sheets

out of one thigh pocket and a pencil from his chest pocket.

'Hey, the comforts of home. Mitford can't operate without a pad and pencil, either.'

'Where do you think I got them?'

Sharing a grin over that, Kris and Easley began to take stock. They were interrupted by a clanging on the open hatch.

'Who's on board?' an irritated voice demanded.

'Scott?' Easley called back.

'With Fetterman, Reidenbacker and Marrucci,' and the four men climbed on board, crowding the passageway. 'Didn't see you leave, Easley.'

Easley smiled, ignoring the implied accusation. 'Decided to inventory what's here before the crowd gathers. Rastancil's forward with Zainal, doing print-outs or something operational. I have six only of what looks like pack frames,' he went on to Kris and put the first one back in its slot.

When they heard the newcomers moving forward, Easley grinned at Kris.

'Took 'em long enough to miss us, didn't it?'

'I wonder', she replied, grinning back at him, 'if they ever reached any conclusion.'

'Oh, probably not until they've gone over Baby with a fine-toothed comb. The Catteni don't seem to stock such items, do they? Not even toothbrushes or soap.'

'I found what looks like liquid soap, remember?'

'Oh yes, drawer nine.'

The inventory turned out to be the pleasantest part of the day.

Chapter Five

Once that was finished, Kris went to find Mitford. Easley, who had initially gone forward to see how Zainal was faring, ran to catch up with her halfway to the barn where Mitford held office in Camp Narrow.

'The compartment's jam-packed with those who need-to-know. I'll wait for a quieter time,' Peter said.

Kris gave a snort. 'No matter what he explains, they'll still need him to fly the thing.'

'I expect so,' Peter replied equably.

Chuck Mitford's eyes bugged out when he spread out the pages of available equipment. He was flabbergasted when he saw the aerial photos.

'Clearest recon photos I ever saw,' he said, amazed, picking up one after another and scanning them.

'Look, here . . . here . . . and here,' Kris said, pointing out spots on the various photos. One was quite close to Camp Narrow, although it was in an area that had been lightly explored. 'More of those dead-end valleys. Zainal thinks they have, or had, a purpose.'

'If they didn't before, they may now. Especially as

we've got enough personnel – AND the equipment,' and Mitford's voice rang with satisfaction, 'so a team could hang around, safe enough, and see what comes up.' He tapped the near valley with his index finger. 'If we can secure this area—' He broke off as his shoulders convulsed in a shudder. 'I want us *out* of the Farmers' facilities. I got a hunch about 'em.'

He gathered the inventory sheets into one neat pile and the photos into another one. 'Anyone seen these yet?'

'No,' Easley replied, 'you're in charge of exploration. And were I you, I would secure these supplies for your teams and start sending them out.'

Mitford grinned crookedly. 'Appreciate the advice, Pete.' He turned to Kris. 'The rest of your team's doing KP, but they should be finished by now. I'll just rev up the load-bed trundler and secure those supplies. Any weapons?'

'Some, but I'd leave them where they are until Zainal drills us in their use,' Peter said. 'Some of 'em'll make right nasty holes in people. You know,' and he scratched his head, contorting his features as the sort of prelude that Kris decided was his way of leading up to an utterance of a diplomatic suggestion, 'we might take a page from the Catteni book of colonial administration and drop the next bunch of Turs into one of those valleys. Come back in a few weeks and see how they've got on.' He paused. 'Oh, better still, dump any Catteni prisoners we take in them. A bit of turnabout's fair play.'

Mitford stared, frowning at Peter Easley. 'You a bleeding-heart or something?'

'It was Yuri Palit's notion, actually,' Easley replied, slightly abashed. 'I mentioned that you'd discovered the one. I don't see the need for gratuitous violence or killing. There's been quite enough of that. I'd rather we Humans fell on the side of the Angels than the Eosi. Besides, it rounds things out,' and he made a cage of the fingers in both hands, rotating one around the other, 'and they get back a little of what they've been dealing out besides supplying us with guinea-pigs for what-ever might lurk in one of those valleys.'

Mitford was unconvinced. 'They want this refer-endum first, don't they?'

'I think you'll have trouble getting the notion of lenience across to anyone who's tangled with a nerve-whip,' Kris said.

'I can see it for the Turs, Easley,' Mitford allowed. 'I've never liked just turning them loose. They're dangerous and, if there's enough of them, they constitute a menace.' He rubbed his jaw. 'Actually, we could use them as a detention fa-cility. That's less messy than staking a guy out at night for the crawlers.' Then, with a shrug, he dis-missed that topic and split his attention between the photos and the inventory.

'The print won't fade,' Kris said, pulling his sleeve. 'Let's go get what we need before someone else requisitions it.'

'Damn well said,' and Easley and Kris had to run to keep up with Mitford.

Vic Yowell was back on duty, standing squarely in the inset door, his expression inscrutable until Mitford leaned out of the driver's side.

'Open up, will ya, Vic? I've requisitioned some of the gear on board to outfit my scouting teams.'

Vic took no exception to that and pushed the main door back. So Mitford reversed the vehicle right up to the hatch, the load-bed almost level with it. With Joe, Sarah, Whitby, Leila, Pete and Mitford working quickly and quietly, Kris checked off the items they were taking from the inventory list. Soon they had emptied the passageway lockers. While the others were stowing the last acquisitions, Mitford took a quick look at the arsenal and closed that compartment firmly.

Temptation, step behind me, Kris thought.

Just then Scott appeared in the forward end of the passageway.

'What're you doing, Sergeant?'

'Looking at the arsenal, sir. Could be useful.'

'Pete and I have just finished the inventory of the lockers, Admiral,' Kris added, holding up the pad.

'Good idea, Bjornsen. Carry on.'

'We will,' she said jauntily and, stifling a giggle at her deception, she followed Mitford out.

'Get what you needed?' Vic asked as the flatbed silently moved out of the hangar.

'I think so,' Mitford said and elbowed Sarah before she laughed loud enough for Vic to hear.

*　　*　　*

They had their loot all neatly stored at the back of Mitford's office, covered with Catteni issue blankets. The rest of Kris's team went to get some lunch while Mitford called in Judy Blane, who'd been a cartographer; he wanted to match the photos to their appropriate areas on the map. Meanwhile, Mitford called in the recon squads he wanted, ordered travel food from the kitchen and was ready to equip them as soon as they reported in.

'Before the brass-heads find out where it's all gone to,' Kris said when the sergeant paused briefly.

'Brass-*heads*?' He chuckled. 'Zainal?' She nodded.

'Are you going to lead a group this time, sarge, and get out of their way?'

He shook his head with a rueful smile and grimace. 'Naw, not this time. I figure I better hang around.'

'I can't say I'm not happy you will, Chuck,' she said, tilting her head towards the hangar and the 'brass-heads' occupying it. 'But you deserve to get out of here for a while and clear your head. You've done more than your share. You need some R&R.'

'I'll go after Phase Two's complete. And don't you worry, Kris. No matter what they decide in their conferences and brass-headed strategy meetings, they need Zainal more than he needs them. Or us.' Then he levelled a cocky grin at her. 'With the exception of you . . . Bjornsen.'

'Scott doesn't trust him at all,' Kris said, perching on the edge of the worktop.

'The Admiral doesn't trust anyone,' Mitford said with a snort, folding his arms across his chest. 'For starters, he's stuck on dry land which isn't really where he functions best. But distrust's not altogether a bad habit.'

A knock on the door which was opened without his permission disclosed the first of the teams he'd called in, Ninety Doyle's. The Scandinavians arrived, breathlessly eager, before Mitford could brief Ninety's squad on the current situation. Kris left him to it and eased herself out of the now crowded office and went to get some lunch.

Part of the original strategy and tactics group were still busy at the end table, and those coming in to eat left a sort of no-man's land of unused tables around the area to maintain their privacy. She picked up her lunch of soup and fresh bread and made her way to where Sarah, Joe, Leila and Whitby were sitting.

'Are we going to get to use some of that beaut gear?' Joe asked.

'We won't be going out—'

'Until the brass start believing Zainal?' Sarah asked in a caustic voice.

'Oh, I think they believe him,' Kris said.

'It's trust that's lacking,' Whitby added when she paused.

'I would rather wait until Zainal comes with us,' Leila remarked in her quiet but firm way, and sipped soup.

'Besides which, I wouldn't want to miss Phase Two for anything,' Joe added. 'Got any update on that, Kris?'

She shook her head and gave a little snort, jerking her thumb towards the earnest knot of men at the end table. 'They have to make up their minds first.'

'Whaddya bet they'll end up doing what Zainal suggested in the first place?' Joe asked, looking around the table.

'Just so long as they make up their minds before the next transport gets here,' Sarah said. 'It could come any day now, too, judging by the frequency we've been getting Drops lately.'

'You'd think they were planning World War III,' Whitby said, entering the conversation, 'instead of a minor commando action.'

They had just finished their meal when the rumble of male voices was audible, heralding the arrival of Scott, Fetterman, Rastancil, Beverly, Marrucci and Zainal. He halted at the door, surveying the room, spotting Kris and, cocking his finger at her, indicating she was to join them at the Strategy table.

'I've been paged,' she said, cleaning the corners of her mouth of any traces of soup with one hand and brushing breadcrumbs off her front with the other as she rose. 'Hang about, will you?'

'Over at Mitford's, dear,' Sarah said, also rising. 'I don't want to get sucked into another session of KP just because we're all sitting here, looking as if we're doing nothing.'

'Which we are,' said Joe, but he got up, too, and, as Kris joined Zainal, they all left the mess hall. Peter Easley passed them on his way in, sauntering in that easy bent-knee gait, pausing to exchange a few words and a laugh.

As he came up, he winked at Kris.

'There you are, Easley,' Scott said. 'When can the next transport be expected?'

'Any time now,' Easley replied indifferently.

Everyone turned around to stare at him.

'They come when they have a full load, evidently,' he said and looked to Zainal who shrugged.

'Last one was eight days ago. Sometimes there's twenty-one days between Drops.' He dismissed that concern with a flick of his fingers. 'Deskis hear the best. Deskis spread out . . .' and now he waved his big hand, splayfingered, over the map that occupied one end of the long table. 'They hear. They report.'

'And they have been using the same field they dropped us in?' Scott asked.

'Lately at any rate,' Easley said, grinning at Zainal, 'ever since Zainal had a little word with them.'

'Can the Deskis be trusted?' Rastancil asked.

'With what?' Kris asked. 'Hearing or reporting?'

'Do they *know* how to use comunits?' Scott asked, ignoring her remark.

'The ones we have, even your grandmother could manage,' Kris snapped back, 'begging your grandmother's pardon,' she added, making herself grin at Scott's indignant reaction.

'Are they capable of giving a detailed enough report, though?' Beverly asked, slightly more respectfully. 'I mean, I've never heard them use more than one word.'

'What more is needed? Hear ship. Comes down near. Comes down far. Your way,' Zainal said, and Kris was delighted to hear him effect the odd tonality of the Deski voice.

'A Deski did all right warning us about the scout,' she added, 'and telling Worrell exactly where it had landed.'

'Point,' Beverly said. 'So we can count on their ears . . .'

'And eyes,' Easley added. 'Deskis and Rugarians are also blessed with exceedingly acute night vision.'

'Send a human along if you're worried,' Kris suggested.

'No need,' Zainal said, and then took out of his coverall a sheaf of pictures, evidently second copies of the ones now being examined in Mitford's office. He spread them on the table, while some of the other tacticians exclaimed and reached out for one to examine. Zainal found the one he wanted. 'This is line I flew in.'

It had been taken at an altitude of the descent well above the cliffs in which Camp Narrow was located, but showed the fields leading to what was now called the Drop Field. The scope of the photo included the Third Drop area, and the boggy swamp where Zainal had lain, wounded by the toxic thorns.

'Drop made here, too.' And he put his finger squarely on the little patch of field.

'But all the others have been made here,' and Easley pointed to Drop Field.

'Good cover for troops in those hedges. We can improve on it, though,' Fetterman said, indicating the three upper sides.

'And move forward when enough crates have been positioned,' and Rastancil tapped a pencil on where the supplies were usually unloaded.

'There are some spare Catteni uniforms on the scout . . .' Kris said. 'They'll have to be washed first, but I saw them in the lockers. So guys stocky enough could actually get on board easily.'

'Catteni don't talk much when unloading,' Easley said, having watched the procedure often enough in his official capacity as In-flow Officer. 'Most don't even carry whip or stunner.'

The whole procedure was then gone over and over until Kris felt her stomach roiling. She hated meetings where the obvious got repeated and repeated and no conclusions made. Once, when she shifted impatiently, she felt Zainal, who was sitting next to her, press his leg against hers and she settled for a little while longer.

Then orders were issued, for Deski teams – Easley, Beverly and Rastancil backed Zainal's assurance that the aliens would manage such a duty without a human counterpart – to spread out in a wide circle around the sprawling human settlement, equipped with comunits, to report the first rumble of an approaching transport ship.

They were given extra rations and blankets and a translation in Deski by Zainal of their orders, in case they hadn't understood Beverly's. They had grinned broadly enough when they had listened intently to the black general, but they hiccuped with amusement after Zainal's remarks. Kris saw that he was grinning back at them, a grin which left his face as he turned back to the brass-heads.

'Now, we wait,' he said.

'No, now we train the assault forces,' said Scott, and he marched off with those who were assisting him in that. The others drifted away, gathering up their notes, maps and papers and leaving, probably to get some sleep.

'You cleared equipment?' Zainal asked Kris as he guided her to the buffet table to get some lunch.

'Everything that looked useful – except the dirty uniforms.'

She asked for a cup of the herbal tea and joined him at the table he took, set at the opposite end of the mess hall from the conference area, in an un-occupied corner. All day and night people drifted in and out of the mess hall, eating whenever their duties permitted. Kris noticed Aarens coming in, arguing with a man she recognized as a senior design engineer. However, Aarens had lost a lot of his arrogance though he still maintained a unique position as a clever adapter of useful gadgets from the Farmers' materials.

'By now the sergeant probably has sent most of it out with the scout teams he called in.'

Zainal grinned slightly. 'Did he go?'

Kris shook her head. 'He's got the right to be in on Phase Two.'

Zainal nodded. 'He is.'

'Oh, was that decided in the scout?'

'I believe so.' Something else about his morning amused Zainal and although she tried to get him to tell her, he shook his head.

'Not to worry,' he said. 'He is in his office?'

'Probably.' She stood as Zainal did. When they had carried their dishes to the proper place and the weary young woman who was handling that chore, they made for Mitford's office.

Although he called a cheery 'come in' when they knocked at the door, he was not alone. A rather officious young man with a receding hairline, holding a clipboard fashioned from a piece of supply crate, was jotting down notes as fast as he could write. Glancing to the back of the office, Kris noticed that the equipment – which had reached nearly to the ceiling when they had finished unpacking it that morning – was now down to a single level in most places.

'I'm in charge of recon groups and I sent all of them out, properly equipped for the first time. You tell Admiral Scott that we took nothing else.' He flipped an indolent finger at the neatly stacked inventory sheets Kris had made. 'All signed out or accounted for. Not a damned thing *he'd* need for an assault force or training. Ah, Zainal, come to brief me on the overall picture? Well, this in-die-vid-jual's just leaving. Aren't you, son?'

'As I told you earlier, *sergeant*,' the man said in

an icy tone, stressing the rank, 'I was Admiral Scott's aide in the resistance—'

'And still no doubt an admirable aide in this one,' Mitford said, 'but, lieutenant, we're all dropees here on Botany, ain't we, Zainal?'

'We dropped. We stay.' And Zainal held the door politely open for the lieutenant to leave by.

As soon as he was gone, Mitford dropped his chair on all four legs and whistled softly. 'Damn fool! Scott, too. Not a fragging thing he'd need, and my teams do.'

'Good on you, sarge,' Kris said, chuckling as she settled down on a stool. Zainal pulled one up closer to the desk and she let him tell Mitford what had happened so far.

As it occasionally happens with well-laid plans, and just about the time everyone in Camp Narrow started to get real antsy from the waiting, a Deski called into the command post in the dim light of false dawn five days later. Mitford happened to be duty officer on that shift.

'Comes now. Bad noise. Bad smell,' she said. 'Wrong noise.'

'What could she mean by that?' Beverly asked. He'd jumped out of his cot in the duty office and was hunched over the hand-unit which Mitford had politely tilted so that he could hear the report which Mitford asked Tul to repeat.

'Let's ask Zainal.' He rose and shook awake the runners who'd been stationed in the office for this contingency. Each of the youngsters knew who they were to waken and where they were bunked. Then he turned to the diagram on the wall which showed the position of each Deski. 'Hmmm. Tul's here,' and he pointed. 'If it was coming in properly, we should have heard from Fek.' He moved his finger, and drew it in a straight line down to the Drop Field. 'Off course?'

Beverly ran a straight line from Tul's position and wound up klicks away from the usual area. 'We'd better get vehicles ready.'

He was gone before Mitford could remind Beverly that they had plenty of leeway to get to a different position, and still mount the rehearsed assault.

Narrow was not the only camp alerted. The Deskis followed Zainal's orders to contact Narrow first, and then their Camps. Worrell called in to ask for instructions. Even Bella Vista Camp, up in the hills, had been included in the contingency plans that the brass-heads had made. Well, it had been something to do to keep busy until Phase Two actually started. It had!

Fek's report came in a moment before Zainal, Kris and the rest of their team arrived.

'It comes. Noisy,' Fek said.

'Where is it headed, Fek?' Mitford asked.

'You,' she answered.

'Thanks, Fek. Keep listening. Tul said the noise is wrong.'

'Is,' Fek agreed and Zainal nodded to indicate he had heard and understood.

'Kris, find Beverly and tell him it's headed here after all,' Mitford said. 'He'll be at the main garage. Why would a transport be making a "wrong noise", Zainal?'

Zainal cocked his head. 'I told you ships not in good condition. I must hear noise to make a guess. I go up!' And he pointed to the roof of the office.

A ladder had been affixed in one of the alleys between barns to reach the cliffs against which they were backed.

Mitford swore, but stayed on the comunit desk for any further reports.

Two more Deski listeners reported in, also remarking on 'wrong noise'. A runner came back and Mitford beckoned him to the desk and the comunit while he went outside to listen. There was so much noise now, with men and women running up and down, seeking their assigned vehicles and getting their gear on, that he gave up and went back inside.

His comunit went off again. This time it was Zainal.

'I hear wrong noise, too. Ship in trouble. Drive is bad.'

'Fraggit. We need an operational ship,' Mitford said, hopes blasted by the news.

'Not to worry. Attack plan may need change.'

'Not if Scott has anything to say about it, and he *is* in charge of Phase Two.'

'Phase Two is my idea,' Zainal said, and the comunit went dead.

*   *   *

It wasn't long before everyone could hear the transport, wheezing and rumbling and giving off hoarse metallic shrieks, landing lights blazing and on-board sirens audible. The surface force made it to the Drop Field, and into their assigned positions, before the ailing transport came into view, barely skimming the ridge-pole trees and skidding to a stop rather than landing. As many landings as Mitford had already seen, some bouncing several times, others skidding to a stop, this was the worst. He dreaded to think of the unconscious bodies being thrown around inside the shallow decks.

Steam poured out of the base of the transport. The main hatch opened and Catteni – coughing, sneezing, staggering – made a disorderly descent from the vessel. All of them. Mitford counted twenty, which Zainal had estimated was the usual crew complement. And they were running as fast as they could, away from the ship.

Zainal ran into the light, waving a stunner and barking orders. He pointed to one of the faster runners.

'Get him!' he called in English and roared louder in Catteni.

The vanguard did not slow and Zainal let off a stun bolt, hitting the Catteni in the head – a mortal shot. The next two he got in the legs and they fell, moaning in frustration. That was enough to halt the others and make them turn around, hands in the air. He barked another order and they

150

reluctantly retraced their steps, their eyes wide and frightened, darting anxiously from Zainal to the hulk they had somehow managed to land.

Zainal called out a question. He got a response and immediately gestured for those hidden in the shadows to come out.

'Ship's circuitry in overload. May blow. We must get people out. Dane, Chavell, Rastancil, take control of them. Scott, we need every man you have.' He raced up the ramp, Kris and the rest of their team right behind. He went to controls set just inside the main hatch, throwing open the lid which was hot. He was muttering or cursing in Catteni. 'Schkelk!' Kris felt herself go rigid with attention at his Catteni 'listen'. 'They will not breathe, Kris. No air. You pull down this type', he said, pulling the flat lever, 'to open hatch. Push up to close. This one to change decks. Got it? Good! BERT! MARRUCCI! YOWELL! DOWDALL! Come with me! I go to bridge. Things can be done. I need engineers, any mechanics, pilots. AARENS!'

Looking over her shoulder, she saw the deck part its horizontal doors and lights came up to reveal the pitiful mounds of people who had been thrown about in the landing. She didn't need to shriek for rescuers: they were already running up the ramp and ducking into the fetid level. The frightened Catteni crewmen were back, too, each encouraged by a settler holding a stunner on him to unload the passengers.

The evacuation began. Catteni managed to lift

two or three bodies, while their captors managed one in a fireman's hold. More help arrived as the ship trembled and shuddered and made the most hideous and frightening of metallic noises while steam hissed out from unlikely places. Kris's right hand was caught in a gush just behind the control board. Whimpering from the pain, she licked and then blew on it.

'Got them all out,' someone yelled at her.

'No, you haven't,' she yelled back. And switched decks. The smell that issued was appalling. Those going in to rescue coughed and gagged, but they kept at their grim task.

Men carrying tool kits hurried past her, kits bearing Baby's markings. Then a group raced aft, Zainal shouting instructions at them about gauges and controls. The heat and the smell were almost more than Kris could manage, even as close as she was to the outside, and her stomach heaved in rebellion. Her hand was really hurting, and blowing didn't much help. Leaning around the open door, inhaling the fresher air outside, she managed to filter some of the stench by drawing the front of her coverall over her mouth and nose, hunching down in a cramped position to do so.

'Got that lot.' Yuri stopped by her side, his face a dirty mask, his coverall blood-smeared. 'How many more to go?'

'Two more decks.' She worked the controls, although with the noise the machinery made she wasn't sure if the mechanism would shift decks at all. The metal must have warped in the heat. But slowly the third deck level was accessible. 'Have many survived?'

'Others tend them.'

'We should salvage the cargo, too,' Kris said.

'Cargo? The living first.' Yuri dismissed her suggestion with a wave and ran into the newly exposed deck, ducking under the half-raised hatch.

Suddenly the levels of noise from around the ship seemed to abate, and some were silenced. More men and women ran around, both aft and forward, some holding tools, carrying hoses and other equipment she realized they must have found in the transport.

One more tremendous gout of steam erupted from the deck plates beneath her feet and she jumped and skipped about, trying to find some place not burning hot. As soon as she could get the machinery to turn to the last deck, she darted in to help unload. The heat was almost unbearable. How long had these unconscious people endured such temperatures? Or had they?

She slung an arm over her shoulder and hoisted a body, a woman's, and staggered out and down the ramp.

'That way. Make it to the next field,' she was told, a hand turning her in the proper direction. The sun was up and at least she could see where she was going. There were only two bodies in this field – one Catteni, one unidentifiable, and both dead. She staggered along, more conscious now of the sting in her steam-burned hand and very tender feet. The hedgerow had been cut down and boards put on either side over the ditches. This field was covered with bodies. Many of them, she thankfully saw, were moving and being attended to: water poured over them or cups held to their mouths so they could drink. The field was one cacophonous moan, with weeping woven in. She staggered until she could find a free spot to lay her burden down. And seeing the awful stillness in the grey face, she felt for a pulse in the neck. There was none and with a cry of despair she curved in on herself, weeping.

'Easy, Kris,' a familiar voice said, and she looked up at Sandy Areson, who was holding out a cup of water to her. 'Drink.' Sandy's gentle hand soothed the hair back from her sweating face and patted her shoulder. 'We've saved a great many. Thanks to Zainal.'

Kris started to rise. Maybe they weren't all dead on that level. But Sandy's hand held her down.

'Oh no, you don't,' Sandy said and pushed her back. 'Hey, what happened to your hand? It's blistered.'

'It is?' and Kris held it out and looked stupidly down at it. 'So it is,' she heard herself say as she slipped sideways into unconsciousness.

It took several days for the events of the momentous morning to be sorted out. Of the 728 left alive, many were injured: broken bones being the least of the problems for the triage teams that checked over each survivor. All were dehydrated, and that was almost the first need addressed. Internal injuries as well as concussions were more serious, due to a rough landing which had pitched the inert bodies of the passengers around the shallow decks, piling up and injuring those beneath them. Severe heat prostration had caused twenty major and minor heart attacks, which had probably been the cause of many more of the deaths.

Of those from the lowest deck, only 45 survived: 4 humans, 9 Deski, 12 Turs, 6 Ilginishi oozing green goo, and 14 Rugarians who had almost all their body hair singed off.

Even those who had suffered no major injuries needed reassurance, proper food and counselling in that order to recover from their ordeal. The only true advantage the consolers had was that they had been through much the same experiences and really did understand how it affected people. Easley worked tirelessly in directing his teams, asking only for their names and their origin before turning them over to Yuri Palit's resettlement people, transporting the 'walking wounded' to calmer surroundings as soon as possible.

The injured were transported by the air-cushion machines to Narrow for emergency treatment. 'Great ambulance service,' Leon Dane commented, 'nothing to bump or jar 'em!'

The Tur contingent were unusually docile from their recent horrific experience and pathetically grateful for the water and soup passed out to them. The uninjured ones – forty in all – were given such dire and terse warnings by Zainal in their own

155

language about the dangers of the avian predators and night-crawlers that they remained subdued as they were driven off to their new quarters. Joe and Whitby headed the expedition with a well-armed guard contingent. The first night out, Whitby also arranged a demonstration of what night-crawlers did to a dead loo-cow, and that had kept them cowed the rest of the trip. They did not even struggle when they were lowered, with cups, blankets, knives and generous supplies of the Catteni food bars, into the valley.

Zainal also won a second victory, aided and abetted by Easley, Yuri Palit and, surprisingly, Mitford. The nineteen surviving Catteni crewmen were sequestered in the nearer blind valley which Ninety Doyle's team had explored. They had also had an object lesson before their departure, when Zainal forced them to watch the night-crawlers ingesting the bodies of those who had not survived the crash landing. He had also required Scott, Fetterman, Rastancil and Reidenbacker to attend. It was a salutary lesson for each group.

'They expected to be thrown into the field last night, didn't they?' Doyle asked Zainal when the biggest air-cushion vehicle was finally free of its ambulance duty and the Catteni crewmen were loaded aboard.

'They expected death,' Zainal replied. 'They did not expect an Emassi to be in charge.'

'Catteni better learn not to underestimate us humans,' Doyle replied as he waved his stunner to speed up the loading process. The two crewmen

Zainal had stunned were still not very steady on their feet, but none of their companions lent any assistance. 'Mean sonsabitches even to their own, ain't they?'

'One of their most endearing traits,' Zainal said in such a facetious tone that Doyle nearly missed the sarcasm.

As the vehicle glided silently off, the Drassi captain gave Zainal a look, compounded of hatred, fear, and indignation that one of his own species was responsible for this total humiliation.

'He wanted to sear Zainal's skin off him,' Sarah told Kris, and gave her shoulders a shake to rid herself of that memory. 'Hope it doesn't turn out later that it would have been wiser to stake 'em out.'

'No, we'd be no better than they are, doing an eye-for-an-eye bit,' Kris said and then inhaled sharply in pain. Sarah was checking the blisters on her steam-burned hand. There was nothing to treat it, nor the very tender soles of her feet. The soles of her Catteni boots had melted on the hot deck-plates and, had she waited much longer, the injuries might have been even more severe. Leon had seen her, rueful that he had nothing, even from the medical stores of the scout, with which to treat the burns.

'I think there won't be any lasting damage, Kris,' he said, gently laying her hand back in the sling. 'Once that main blister has popped, it'll ease off and your body will take over the healing process. We do have that salve Patti made up which the cooks all swear by, to keep the skin supple. Might ease the soles of your feet, too.'

'I'm not complaining,' she said. 'Sarah was a little officious, taking you away from the ones who really need you.'

'Oh, never fear, m'dear,' Leon said, grinning. 'We've got quite a list of specialists these days, you know. And a supply of the gas they use; it makes an effective anaesthetic.' He gave a little shudder. 'Thank God. Some of the repair work would have been barbaric without it.'

Kris had refused to go back to the Rock – wanting to stay near the hub of activity, and Zainal, and very eager to hear how they had kept the ship from blowing. Sarah and Leila kept her informed and helped her down to the main mess hall where she could listen to the 'hourly bulletins' as Sarah called them, updating those not involved with various aspects of what was going on.

Zainal and the engineers had managed to jury-rig the control board, venting the build-up to an explosion. A pump was found, disconnected from the ship, and dropped into the nearby stream. By combining all the hose on the Catteni ship, the fuel tanks had been kept from exploding and the reduction in temperature had saved other systems from reacting to the intense heat.

'If they hadn't managed, the explosion would have altered the landscape considerably,' Sarah went on, talking to distract Kris from her tender ministrations to the raw sole of her right foot. 'But the fuel got saved and there's plenty for Baby now.'

'So that's why the Catteni were running away as fast as they could,' said Kris through clenched teeth. 'Was the ship badly damaged inside? Can we make use of anything?' Granted all she had seen was just inside the cargo area, with bursting conduits and pipes and hot deck-plates, but surely something was salvageable.

Sarah grinned up from bandaging her feet with sufficient fluff to form a protective layer. 'You better believe it! The entire bridge!'

'Really?'

Sarah chuckled in a mock-malicious way. 'Well, what there actually is of it. Anyone who's ever flown anything is wondering how the damned thing stayed in the air, much less made journeys out into space. However, Scott wanted it where it can be used. And the interior of the transport still stinks to high heaven, so it was dismantled and it's been reconstructed in the hangar. They've even got the communications up and running. And solar panels on the hangar to power it.

'Everyone's over the transport like ants, taking it apart. It's nothing but a shell now – which still stinks. The mechanics and engineers are having a field day with all these new treasures, even if most of the loot is secondhand, slightly damaged goods. But it's more than we've ever had to work with.

'Then there's real competition over who can sound more Catteni than another. More learned the language than you might think.'

'I suppose a knowledge that didn't make you all that popular on Earth,' Kris mused. 'But why is there a competition? You said the crew was sequestered in a valley.' She tried to concentrate on what Sarah was saying, rather than the painful dressing of her feet.

'Sorry, love, I keep thinking you've been in on all the briefings. The Drassi captain sent out a may-day, or whatever Catteni call an emergency, to another transport which said, and I quote, they'd "get around to picking up the crew when they were on their way back to Base". That is, if they survived the crash landing.'

'So that's why Scott wanted the bridge opera-tional,' Kris grinned, for it was easy to see what was likely to happen next. 'So, have they reported they survived?'

Sarah nodded, grinning from ear to ear. 'Leon did it. He's still the best, but not for long.'

'When do they expect this rescue vessel?'

Sarah shrugged. 'From what Zainal discovered in questioning the crew – the captain wouldn't say doodly to him – it's a bigger, newer ship, with a longer range, and so we have to wait for another message from them when to expect them. So there's plenty of time to prepare, rehearse and drill for their arrival.'

'A bigger, newer ship?' Kris repeated. Then she chuckled to herself, thinking of Admiral Scott's bridge being run from a hangar. 'And we'll have three ships!' She was so proud of Zainal that she wriggled in the bed.

Sarah grinned fatuously at her. 'Scott's even acting as if Zainal's not so bad after all. And he's got a committee working to find out something that will add the necessary grey tinge to human skin. Those loose uniforms they wear will camouflage who's in them, but they gotta have grey skin. Leon's dying to take part, but he's really too tall to play a Drassi.'

'So is Zainal.' Kris began to worry again. Zainal was taking so many risks. A bigger, newer ship would be better captained and crewed. But then surprise was still on their side.

The dressings now complete, she glared down at her feet. They'd better be completely healed; she had to be able to be at this second enactment of Phase Two.

Chapter Six

When Zainal spent more time explaining to the mechanics and engineers what the salvageable material had been used for, they could more knowledgeably adapt it to their needs. Once the bridge was sited and up and working again, Scott preempted him to translate the data on the transport's log files.

'Much is routine,' Zainal said, scrolling at a fast pace through the entries.

'But we need to know where they have been, how long it takes, the protocols they use . . .' Scott said, scowling.

'I think I've found someone from the latest Drop who can manage to translate routine reports,' Easley said, once again diplomatically inserting his presence. 'In fact, several someones who have a good working knowledge of the glyphs. Learned to help decipher Catteni documents captured during raids.'

Beth Isbell was the only uninjured member of the three 'someones' who were summoned. Sally Stofers, a petite brunette with an extremely innocent expression, arrived on crutches for a broken leg, while Francois Chavell had his left arm in a sling. Scott insisted on interviewing them first as to their Earth-side activities. Once satisfied, he turned them over to Zainal who tested their skills by having them read out loud from log entries.

'They read Catten well,' Zainal said, passing all three.

Later, Easley asked if he'd spoken truthfully or merely to get himself out of a very boring task.

'I said true. They can copy what they do not understand and I will translate . . . if I can,' and Zainal grinned from Easley to Kris.

Scott next had him interview every male who had listed some understanding and speaking knowledge of Catteni in their Drop interviews. With Kris's help, Zainal made a list in order of fluency and vocabulary of over seventy men. Scott then had his choice of those he felt would be most useful in the commando unit he was training to stand in for the transport's stranded crew.

'You're certain they're coming back for the crew?' Beverly asked Zainal at the very beginning of this new venture.

'That was the message,' and Zainal had shrugged. 'They will not hurry to do so. The crew would be safe in ship, away from us who are dropped.'

Scott might not have been certain of Catteni altruism in collecting a stranded crew, but he was also counting on it as a replacement for the useless hulk in the Drop Field.

Zainal gave Kris a list of the most frequent commands, which she wrote down with phonetic translations, so that all could learn them and learn the proper responses of both Drassi and ordinary crew to commands. Rank had some privileges.

'Catteni crew don't talk much,' Zainal said. 'Just obey.'

'They must also know what is being said so they can act on their initiative if that becomes necessary,' was Scott's reply.

'Not Catteni,' Zainal replied, shaking his head.

'So long as the real Catteni obey, there's no problem,' Scott said, a stubborn look coming into his eye.

'So the surprise will be even greater,' said Easley, smiling at Scott, 'and that will work in our favour, won't it?'

Scott gritted out a surly 'Yes' and went back to the diagrams Zainal had contrived of what he 'thought' the interior of the new transport should be. He hadn't had an opportunity to inspect any himself.

'Designed to carry more with fewer deaths,' he said in summary. 'Just being newer is improvement.'

The engineers and mechanics at the meeting agreed to that.

'Some of the controls were wired together, and I dunno what they used to keep the drive units operating,' Peter Snyder said.

He'd been a jet-engine propulsion engineer and was fascinated by the Catteni drives: especially how they kept working in the state they were in. By using the schematics in the manuals, he and the other aviation and space shuttle personnel were trying to reconstruct one working system from the remainders of four.

'To know how it should work, mainly,' Snyder had said with a grin. He was an amiable fellow, medium in build and height, and usually either whistling or humming, on key, as he and the team worked to rebuild the engine. 'We're in a sort of no-man's land here, with bits and pieces we know worked in a high-tech society and should work if we re-assemble them right, but we are working with the equivalent of early Iron Age tools. Aarens is miraculous; sometimes, if you tell him what you want a tool to do, he manages to provide one which does it. The problem is knowing what tool you need next and how long you'll have to wait until he can contrive it.'

Kris, now hobbling on crutches with well-wrapped feet and a bandaged hand, accompanied Zainal to the various meetings as she still seemed to be the necessary verbal bridge for vocabulary for him. Half the time she was floundering for technical jargon even worse than he was, but she was not about to admit that failing to anyone. Probably Easley had guessed, but he was on their side. Kris would be very glad when she, Zainal and their team could get back to what they were best at: exploring.

Sometimes it seemed to her that Scott resented what Zainal had had no reason to learn – as far as details of his own species' space-drive technology included – and yet was forced to include the Catteni in all major meetings because of the little he did

165

know and the insights he could provide on other details.

'Scott's got an incredible mind for detail,' Easley murmured to Kris one evening during a long session.

'He comes across ultra-suspicious and snide to me,' she whispered back.

'Suspicion is detail, too, you know, but I happen to know that he is impressed by Zainal.'

'You could have fooled me,' Kris replied, glaring at the end of the table where Scott, Rastancil, Ainger, Marrucci and Beverly were crouched, heads together, in inaudible conversation.

'But I don't,' Easley said, his low voice vibrant with sincerity. 'He knows a man of integrity when he sees one, and he sees Zainal as one. I don't think many of us had any idea of the role the Eosi play in what the Catteni do. So he's abandoned the position of detesting the Catteni for what was done on Earth to come halfway to absolving the tool for the work it's been put to. Zainal's responsible for that adjustment, without losing either dignity or respect in Scott's eyes.'

Kris absorbed that speech, feeling a little better about what seemed like Scott's persecution of her lover. But she was only halfway there herself.

Once again, when the extra-acute hearing of the Deski sentries caught the first sound of the approaching vessel, they alerted the camps before the landing ship announced its imminent arrival on the communication band.

The 'bridge' accepted the message with typical Catteni stolidity as Zainal had drilled them, re-affirming the co-ordinates of their downed ship's position. Though Leon had prepared a report of what had disabled the ship, he wasn't asked for it. Zainal had told him it wouldn't be required, but had helped him to learn the terms.

The camps in the line of the ship's descent – Bella Vista, Ayres Rock and Shutdown – cleared away any signs of orderly living. All the air-cushion vehicles were stowed out of sight and there was some concern over people, scouts and hunters, who might be seen out and about. Narrow, particularly, must appear deserted from the air.

'They will know from heat signs people are on the surface,' Zainal had said, 'but not what they are doing or what they live in. Wiser for them to see men out hunting.'

'You mean they'll be counting noses?' someone had asked.

Zainal laughed at the notion. 'No, just the presence of sufficient life signs to suggest survivors down here.'

'So they can send us more?' Mitford had asked in a sour tone.

'At this point, it's the more the merrier,' Easley had said, grinning so infectiously that Mitford had smiled back.

'Guess you're right.'

The instrumentation on the bridge in the hangar was now working with an efficiency it had lacked for many voyages, and the descent of the rescue vessel was easily estimated. The assault team, in position from the moment the first Deski alarm had come in, lounged about the downed transport: some were outside, others sitting on the ramp, while the 'Drassi' would not appear until their counterparts called for them.

Camouflaged in the hedgerows and up the trees in strategic positions were sharpshooters with cross-bows and lances. Zainal had had no information about the crew complement of the new transports. The Catteni to be rescued were armed with stunners, which might be all that was needed. Surprise was on their side.

It was, and the take-over of the transport ship was even smoother than the one hijacking the scout. The supercilious Drassi of the rescue vessel had been so eager to mock the stranded captain that he had been first down the ramp, the other Drassi staff following, while the crewmen began to unload what passengers they had remaining. They were laughing and chatting, pleased to be on the last leg of this journey and going home. They were also looking forward to making the rescued Catteni work while they loafed.

Flat on her stomach in the next field – Zainal by her, chuckling softly to himself – Kris watched as the

Catteni Drassi strolled arrogantly across to the damaged transport.

The mock-Catteni crew had, of course, jumped to an appropriate alert stance, calling out – in an excellent accent, Kris thought proudly – to those inside that the Drassi captain was coming aboard. They followed in, a respectful distance behind, and one remained at the open hatch, leaning against it as the rescuers finished unloading the latest unconscious dropees. They had no sooner finished than they were called to come aboard the wreck.

'Now what do we have to do?' one Catteni demanded of another as they made their way across the field – or so Zainal translated for Kris.

'Probably dismantle equipment the beasts might use,' the other replied.

'Beasts, huh?' Joe muttered on the other side of Zainal. 'We'll beast them.'

Zainal translated the first part of the Catteni response: 'Let's hope it doesn't take too long, then. I need my . . .' And he refused to translate that rather long sentence to Kris. Considering the nasty way the two Catteni chuckled, she was glad he hadn't.

While the observers waited, nervous and anxious, for what seemed an interminable time, suddenly the mock-Drassi captain – actually Vic Yowell, who was not only the right size but had known enough Catteni to handle the necessary interchanges – appeared and, with his men, strode purposefully across to the newly arrived ship and up its ramp.

There was a brief interval before he reappeared,

waving his cap and showing the difference between his Catteni make-up and his own skin colour.

'It's ours now!'

The hedges sprouted humans, cheering and dancing with glee at the success of the second Phase Two assault. Then they hurried to attend to the newly arrived, 114, all from Earth and in far better condition than many of the most recent arrivals. The Catteni prisoners were sent off to join their compatriots in the valley.

Yuri Palit, another mock Catteni with his skin now back to its original shade, headed the guards who accompanied the prisoners. On the way they were given an example of night-crawler activity and so descriptively warned of other dangers of Botany that they were thoroughly cowed by the time they arrived.

When the new transport had been gone over, Scott was actually smiling at everyone. This had been the maiden voyage of the KDT, according to its log and the look and smell of still-new equipment. Zainal, Kris, Bert Put, Peter Snyder, Rastancil and Beverly were up all night, translating manuals and understanding the improvements incorporated in its systems.

Best by far was the discovery of two small airships, capable of short-range planetary flight, and one large well-equipped ground vehicle, suitable for rough terrain, with exterior plating to resist many corrosive-type atmospheres. Looking at its specs on its control board, Zainal said that it was also probably 'water-going'.

'Amphibious,' Kris had murmured, and they had locked eyes and smiled. They would not have to risk using the scout being seen in order to get to the other continents. This craft would hold twelve passengers and three crew, and would transport safely to at least the closest land-mass. They'd better pick a day when the channel waters were calm because she didn't like to think of being seasick in such confines.

But that sort of exploration was not in their immediate future. The next scenario to be played out was to take off in the brand-new transport and head back towards Barevi, its base.

As many as could fit aboard the KDL-45A – which is how the glyphs on its side translated – took off, and that took in just about everyone who had worked in NASA or on air-force jets from various countries. The decks could be arranged in a variety of heights and ways, according to cargo or passengers, awake or unconscious. Rather an ingenious arrangement, Marrucci and Beverly agreed, when Zainal showed them how to achieve various combinations. So the KDL could actually accommodate the many who had some reason, or claim, to make the journey. Some were going to have a chance in space; others because they had to learn how to manage the transport; and all would help jettison the traces of the sudden and complete destruction of a brand-new ship. Zainal had found log references to several minor incidents with the propulsion unit on the outward bound journey: one severe enough for the captain to shut down the engines and send an EVA team to clear the tubes. That had been reported to their Base since it had delayed their touch-down at Botany to collect the transport crew.

Pete Snyder headed a team to figure out just what malfunction could now result in a fatal accident. They had plenty of debris from the damaged ship – fortunately the components were all constructed of similar alloys. With a little ingenuity in their messages to their Base, each describing further problems, and then . . . a delayed action explosion, sufficient detritus would be left floating in space to convince anyone who cared to examine it that the KDL had, indeed, exploded on her way home. An appropriate outer panel had been taken from the old transport, and paint found in the KDL's supply bay to duplicate her glyphs.

The bogus outward-bound voyage was scheduled for a week, since Zainal wished to get beyond the system's heliopause, beyond the satellite's range, before conducting the explosion.

Kris had remained behind, her hand insufficiently healed for her to be useful on the voyage . . . especially when so many, like Raisha and other space-trained women pilots, deserved the chance. Truth to tell, she was tired from late nights and long sessions of translating. And then Mitford had asked for and got the land vehicle for his scouting teams. She'd be much more use familiarizing herself with that piece of machinery than being a supernumerary on a space flight.

'They should be back by now, shouldn't they?' she asked Mitford, as they were storing their equipment on the land-sea vehicle, nicknamed the Tub. When Zainal returned Mitford was planning a trip, with himself as leader, to cross the channel that separated this continent from its nearest neighbour. He was combining two teams for the project, and happier than Kris had seen him since he handed debriefing newcomers to Peter Easley.

'Yeah, in fact they're three days overdue. But the destruction went off okay. You know that.'

The link between the old transport's bridge and the KDL was open and all the mounting hysteria – orders and counter-orders, as the propulsion system 'failed' – had been duly followed by those on the ground . . . including the final bang. So that part had gone well.

The Deski sentries were ordered to keep their ears wide open since their senses were trusted far more than the obsolete and erratic detection system on the 'bridge' in the hangar.

Kris accompanied Mitford when they did a check on the Catteni prison valley and found them alive, but certainly not making any move to 'settle' in.

'No initiative,' Mitford muttered to Kris. 'Just like Zainal said. Not even that pair of Drassi captains.' These seemed to be concentrating on a small space of dirt in front of them, but neither moved.

'Chess?' Kris asked, for they had that sort of concentration about them.

'Chess?' Mitford regarded her with surprise. 'They haven't the wits for checkers, much less chess.'

'Well, there's someone trying to fish,' Kris said, pointing to the one man poised over the stream with a thin lance in his hand.

'So he is. Even Catteni get tired of those dry rations,' he said and turned away.

Yuri Palit, in his authority as head of Resettlement, had gone to check the Turs and came back with the information that they had already made a few shelters, chopping down the lodge-pole trees. There also seemed to be several wounded lying in the sun: broken legs and arms, and one with raw wounds visible down his side.

'Trying to climb out?' asked Astrid.

'How stubborn can Turs be?' Yuri Palit asked of Mitford.

The sergeant shrugged. 'Damned stubborn. Leave 'em alone.'

'And let them ruin that lovely valley?' Kris demanded.

Mitford jerked his head towards the photos that adorned his back wall, those showing the other closed valleys Zainal had seen on his way in. 'There are others as well as the other continents.'

'Now, about them . . .' Astrid began.

Mitford held up one hand, grinning at the tall attractive Swede. 'Gotta wait until Zainal checks us out on the amphibian.'

Which reminded everyone that the KDL was now six days overdue. Kris tried to appear unconcerned but possible disaster scenarios kept her awake most nights.

'What could have happened?' Astrid asked the morning of the seventh day. 'Surely they should be returning now?'

'That bang wasn't for real,' said Mitford, avoiding Kris's eyes, but speaking as positively as if he had consummate faith in Zainal's return.

'There'll be a good reason, I'm positive,' Kris said so firmly that Mitford shot her a quick look.

'Yeah, there would be, kid. I just can't imagine what.'

'Asteroids, some technical difficulty, or operational problem, there could be dozens of good reasons.'

'Yeah.'

'It wouldn't be a good idea for him to get in touch, either, and give it all away since the ship's been destroyed and that damned satellite would catch any message he sent.'

'You're right there,' Mitford acknowledged and then went to do something else.

'New satellite,' Zainal told them as soon as the hatch opened to the crowd waiting so anxiously. 'We go . . .' and he gestured a circuitous course. He looked for and found Kris at the side of the hatch. 'Lenvec's work.' He dropped down beside her, touching her cheek just briefly as the rest of the space-farers exited, exultant in their shouts to the welcoming committee.

The biggest smile was on Scott's face as he came

down the ramp with Beverly, Rastancil and what were now being called the High Command following closely.

'Mitford, Easley,' Scott called out, and added other names, 'meeting at 19.30 at Narrow. Beggs,' and now the officious lieutenant Kris disliked so came running up to meet him, clipboard in hand. 'I want all these men and women to make that meeting if humanly possible . . .' And he continued giving orders while proceeding to the nearest air-cushion vehicle and gesturing for it to take off towards Camp Narrow.

Zainal, taking Kris by the arm, steered her off to one side, away from the general jubilation around the hatch.

'Lenvec got them to put up a more powerful satellite spy?' she asked.

'Someone did. We had to time its orbits to sneak back in. KDL is very good at glide.'

'You glided? From where?'

Zainal grinned at her astonishment. 'Not hard. Your space shuttles did it. Catteni still better space jockeys.'

'Jockeys?' Kris had to admit to herself that she didn't like him picking up slang from other sources. And she severely curbed her reaction.

'Bert brought her down. Good man, Bert. Now, where can she hide?' And Zainal frowned over that problem.

Kris looked up the field at the hulk still sitting there. 'Put it there. They expect a wreck in that place. How much detail will the satellite be able to make out down here on the surface? The name glyphs?'

Zainal began to chuckle. 'Why not? The KDL masses more, but not that much more.'

'Hiding it right out in sight always confuses a searcher,' Kris said.

'Scott will agree?'

Kris shrugged. 'That thing's too big to fit in any garage – except maybe the one we can't get into at the seaside. Who will come looking for it? You had us all excited, listening to orders and counter-orders and all the hysterics . . .'

Zainal chuckled louder now, his yellowy eyes reflecting his laughter, most un-Catteni-ish.

'And if you guys avoided the satellite's eyes on the way in, surely we've succeeded in deceiving them.'

'Some one of your wise men said once,' and he tipped his head back a moment, recalling the exact words which he carefully enunciated, 'that you can fool most of the people part of the time, but not all of the people all of the time.'

She had to smile at him, he looked so pleased with remembering the apt quote. And she was so pleased he was back, safe. 'You think Lenvec is that vindictive?'

'Not think. I *know*. When I was chosen . . .' He paused briefly and then went on, 'I was given privileges the chosen have, Lenvec was . . . jealous. If he is now to take my place as chosen, he will feel like he got robbed.' He gave her a sideways glance, to see her reaction to his slang, and she grinned at him. He was also speaking with a less guttural tone

177

to the English words. Soon his accent would be indistinguishable from a native-born speaker.

'Hmmm, yes, if he's the jealous type he would feel robbed. But maybe he's been . . . chosen already. How much of *him* is left in the Eosi?'

Zainal nodded his head slowly over that point. 'I do not know that. Fortunately,' and now he put his cheek down against hers, holding her tightly, 'I was dropped and I stay.'

Kris was not the only one who thought of leaving the KDL right out in the open. An artistically scorched glyph took the bright new KDL-45's place, but there were actually no other options, even if they could find a Farmer facility big enough to house it. The ship was not just a trophy, gathering dust, although how it would be used was yet to be decided. Scott had approved Phase Two but who knew if the admiral, who seemed to have taken charge of the military aspect of the High Command, felt they should attempt Phase Three.

The KDL settled itself on the wreck, compressing its empty shell. The Deski sentries would give enough advance warning of any landings . . . should other transports be sent here . . . so that she could lift and settle down a few fields over, and camouflaged from casual inspection. The Catteni rarely looked around during the process of hauling out their passengers and what supplies accompanied them. A certain risk was taken, but Scott had come to agree with Zainal's assessment of the Drassi: do as little work as possible and get back to base.

'You know someone might just think it was odd that there have been three ships blown up in this area,' Leon Dane remarked at the end of the final debriefing, 'and decide it isn't worth visiting this sector of the vast Eosi-Catteni empire, and leave us alone.'

'I doubt that,' Easley said with a sad grin. 'According to the latest arrivals, Earth's resistance is growing and the Catteni are still taking anybody they think might be saboteurs and ringleaders into custody. We had a troop of Sea Scouts in the last group, and all they were doing was holding their monthly meeting. We may end up with more of Earth's population here . . . and wherever else they've been dumped . . . than on good old Terra Firma.'

'If we can maintain a good fresh start approach on Botany and ditch the attitudes that made trouble back on good old Terra Firma,' Mitford said, with good reason to doubt the ability of people to forget ingrained intolerance and bigotry. Serving time in the stocks right now were three men and a woman who had revived an old prejudice in an hour-long brawl. The injured would serve their sentences when they had sufficiently recovered. 'The more people we get in, the more trouble we acquire.'

'We've got four continents . . . well, two, if we

leave the Farmers theirs,' Leon said. 'There's enough space for everyone, isn't there?'

'For some types, there's never enough space,' Sarah said.

'Too right,' Dane agreed, exhaling tiredly.

Chapter Seven

Once the excitement of procuring and hiding the KDL calmed down, Scott and others of the High Command military branch spent hours debriefing the latest arrivals from Earth, trying to figure out what had happened from reports which were necessarily incomplete. Not much news was broadcast any more in a world which had had twenty-four-hour news bulletin coverage.

'Disasters every time of the day or night,' Kris had said.

'Do they do that on Catten or Barevi?' Sarah had asked Zainal when they were all sitting around their table after the evening meal in Narrow.

'Tell everyone everything? No,' and Zainal chuckled at the notion. His grey hair had grown so long now that he was wearing it in a pony-tail, a style that suited him better than most. Kris had offered to braid it – Amerind fashion, as she did her now much longer hair – but he had declined. 'Only need-to-know is told.' Then he gave a shrug. 'And evenings of lies about new worlds and brave Catten.'

'Recruiting?'

Zainal considered the word, squeezing Kris's

hand to indicate he was going to figure that one out himself. 'Yes, to join space-army.'

He got a thumbs-up for accuracy from the others at the table, their scouting partners and those from Astrid's six-strong team. They spent a lot of time together, learning how to drive the amphibious machine so that anyone could. The mechanics had been all over it, too, familiarizing themselves with its equipment, engines, communications and life-support systems. While Mitford was ranked a senior in the High Command Committee now governing the settlers, he still had to get 'proper clearance' to take such a valuable piece of machinery. He also needed Scott's clearance to take Zainal away when he might just be needed.

'For something, any damned thing, rather than let us function as a team,' Mitford had ranted the previous night. 'They've got both bridges manned, and the KDL working off solar power, and we still have the Deski perimeter listeners, so little can sneak up on us down here. If they really needed him, Marrucci could fly over in one of those atmosphere planes now that he's learned how not to kill himself in it. And it doesn't leave the sort of trail visible to the spy sat.'

Zainal wasn't exactly reassuring on that count because he didn't know exactly how sophisticated the new satellite was, just that it was on a full global orbit, checking the surface of the world once every thirty-four hours. He was positive that the recondi-tioned air-cushion Farmer vehicles would not show up on the satellite since they ran on solar power.

The amphibious vehicle might possibly be visible – since it was no longer supposed to exist – so he had plotted a course and they would move only when the satellite was at another point around Botany's globe. It might take slightly longer to reach the coast but once in the water, he thought that the Tub would be undetectable since water would not only cool its exterior but mask its emissions.

Kris's hand was still slightly red but her feet had healed, even if she was careful to keep a layer of fluff as an insole. And she dearly wanted to leave Camp Narrow for Mitford's sake as well as Zainal's. She tried to convince herself it was just the wander-itch that made her restless because she didn't think she had a trace of precognition in her, but she did very much want to leave. To go explore the neighbour continent.

Fully accustomed now to its new form, Eosi Mentat Ix was bored. It had returned to pleasures that its weakening husk had been unable to perform, and now these no longer satisfied its seeking for unusual experiences. The form had been relatively circum-scribed, not having had the training of the young originally chosen from that Bloodline.

That was when it remembered the animosity and bitterness of the Catteni mind when it had been subsumed. And Ix accessed the memories. A brief exploration would discover if the entity's suspicions had been valid. Ix was somewhat startled to discover that a more powerful satellite had been put in position around the subject planet. The entity's traces grew alarmed within the Mentat as the most recent report was mentally gleaned from those on duty.

The scoutship had disappeared, and no trace of it found anywhere in Eosi space: it had not re-fuelled at any station, planetary or space. Nor could the satellite find that sort of metal shape on the subject planet. The matter of the wreck of the transport was resolved by the interchange of communications between the KDL and the downed ship. The KDL, the newest of the transport fleet, had taken off after discharging its cargo and been tracked out of that solar system . . . by both satellites. And the tape of its final emergency and explosion was on record.

Ix carefully reviewed that tape, the details of the final moments of the ship's life and the efforts of the crew to remedy the fault. It also reviewed the fault in the light of the KDL's sister ships now coming on line, and found that such a back-surge in the propulsion was indeed a possibility, however improbable.

The Eosi Mentat ordered a search for the log of the KDL which should be found in the space debris. It was. Within the tiny fraction of Ix's great mentality, an infinitesimal scream insisted that such events were suspicious.

Ix screened the orbiting satellite's records and found only the wreck that had been left where it had landed. Then Eosi Mentat Ix was called to a meeting of its peers, to determine what must be done with the increasing problems experienced by Catteni occupying forces on the latest planet they had subjugated. Such continued resistance was unique, even bizarre, and the Ix was caught up in deciding what punitive measures to take that would completely solve this problem. However, all Eosi found themselves rather fascinated by the scope and originality of the opposition to their benign rule.

The general maintenance orb reached the target planet and found its near space occupied by two technological items: one orbiting in a thirty-hour, total global pattern, and the other geo-synchronous. These objects were thoroughly examined before the orb descended to a level at which it could investigate why a homing missile had been despatched from the command facility without a message. The orb discovered some life forms resident in the facility, for what purpose it was not programmed to discover, but their presence was noted. It proceeded on its orderly inspection of the agricultural facilities placed around the more arable continents and discovered anomalies throughout a large area, suggesting malfunction of the indigenous equipment on an unprecedented scale. Checking inventory against what should have been idle at this time of the planet's growing season, it could discover parts of the equipment but not in the usual form. This abnormality was duly noted. There did appear to be more life forms than the natural propagation of the indigenous species would ordinarily produce. There was no possible way in which such a bovine species could damage, much less alter, the machinery that husbanded it. The orb was programmed only for mechanical devices, inventory and supply: it did not examine life forms; that was another department.

It completed the necessary circuits at the altitude programmed into it for the maximum efficiency of required investigations, sent its findings back to its home world and continued on its scheduled maintenance cycle.

The Deski were covering their ears, cowering, but still managed to report in to their bases that there was the most fearful noise in the air. The boards on both bridges reported a spatial object, travelling at an impossible speed, spinning about Botany at what Marrucci stammered had to be damned near the speed of light. Its manifestation on the bridge boards was of a continuous pattern of light, encompassing Botany.

'Then it can't be Catteni,' replied Rastancil, watching behind Marrucci. 'They don't have that capability . . .'

'Yet,' Marrucci added, *sotto voce*.

The team at the Command Post reported a terrifying moment.

'I felt like X-files and being scanned by E.T.s.' reported the generally sanguine Colonel Salvinato in a voice that noticeably shook.

'Well, you're not alone. Something's giving us a

real going-over,' Rastancil replied, which he hoped would reassure the colonel; his body still tingled from whatever it was that had touched him.

Salvinato reported in later that there were now two homing devices where recently there had been only one.

'Replacements by matter transmitter?' Rastancil suggested, condescendingly.

'"Beam me up, Scotty,"' Marrucci said, and this time he didn't lower his voice. 'The Catteni also don't have anything that can do that.'

'That *would* account for how the Farmers' ships managed to load up so fast,' said Mitford when he was called in to give his interpretation of the curious incident. 'I felt it, too, like someone going over me with a mild electrical current.' And then he smiled. 'The Farmers have finally noticed us.'

'Do we really want them to?'

Mitford thought that over for a long moment and then shrugged. 'Beats me, general,' but he grinned because this was not his problem any more. And yet, it was. Anything to do with Botany was. 'It was the only option I had at the time. Still seems a good one. Only no-one hung around long enough to speak to us. So, what happens next?'

Scott called an immediate meeting of as many of those from Camp Rock as had witnessed the fly-past of the Mech Makers'/Farmers' spaceship. Rumours circulated, and each lap doubled in improbability, stupidity and frightfulness, especially about the scan. It was now variously supposed to have infected everyone with a deadly disease, and the entire population would die in twenty-four hours. Others included the fabrications that the Farmers had counted them and would shortly come and round them up, process them in the abattoir and ship them back as delicacies. All of them were 'marked' now and would be enslaved or converted into the six-legged loo-cows or sentenced to turn into night-crawlers.

There was certainly tension as the First Drop folk gathered in the mess hall at Narrow, late that afternoon. Benches (made of old machine parts, and these were the last places where the arrivals sat) and stools formed a semicircle around a table at which sat Jim Rastancil, Geoffrey Ainger, Bill Fetterman, Bob Reidenbacker, John Beverly, Pete Easley, Yuri Palit and the former judge, Iri Bempechat, who had recently taken over the disciplinary duties for work evasion or inadequacy. Ray Scott, with his insufferable aide, Beggs, taking notes and counting noses, rose when it was evident that all who intended to come had arrived.

'I hope none of you have suffered any repercussions from those ludicrous rumours started after our recent visitation,' Scott began, with a rueful expression.

He looked directly at Chuck Mitford, who sat with Zainal on his right and Kris to his left, with Dowdall, Cumber, Esker, Murphy and Tesco – his original assistants during the retreat from the First Drop field – ranged along the row: defenders who had made very certain that no hystericals got near the sergeant. Patti Sue sat just behind him with Jay

Greene, Sandy Areson, Bart, Coo, Pess, Slav, Bass, Matt Su and Mack Dargle. More from the First Drop spread out behind them: Janet, Anna Bollinger, the Doyles, Joe Latore and Dick Aarens.

Mitford, arms crossed over his chest, grinned. 'You and me both know the problem with rumours, admiral, but I'm not going into decline over 'em, scanned or not. Especially when everyone'll wake up tomorrow in the same shape they went to sleep in.'

'Yes, that will solve that problem, but not the bigger ones we must seriously consider,' Scott said. He looked at Zainal. 'I take it that phenomenal display had nothing to do with either Eosi or Catteni spacecraft?'

'Absolutely nothing. The satellites' reports are going to cause a big stir, I know that much,' and Zainal grinned broadly. 'The Eosi won't like to see what came. They will be very worried. Finally.'

'You were a scout, weren't you, Zainal?' Bill Fetterman asked. 'You ever encountered any traces of them in this galaxy?'

Zainal shook his head. 'This is new solar system for Eosi and Catteni. Which is why *we*', and he emphasized the plural as he glanced around to include everyone there in the pronoun, 'are colonizing it. What I know is that their technology is far superior to Eosi. I also do not fear them as I do Eosi.'

'You don't?' Scott was not the only one surprised by that admission. 'How do you arrive at that conclusion considering what just happened?'

'*Because* of what just happened,' Zainal said, as if

189

that should be obvious. 'No-one was injured by scanning. The homer was replaced. No, I do not fear the Farmers. A . . .' and he put his hand flat against his stomach, 'a . . . gut feeling.'

'Does anyone else share this . . . gut feeling?' Scott asked, more amused than patronizing.

'After seeing that valley, I'm inclined to agree,' Kris said. There was something about the ambience in the valley that she thought the entire team shared: its tranquillity, carefully saved and preserved by the blocked entrance. 'These are not killers, like Eosi. They nourish this planet carefully.'

'Why don't they get rid of the night-crawlers, then, I'd like to know?' Dowdall asked sourly.

'Very efficient in clearing up waste and garbage,' said Kris.

'They made safe places to keep something in, or something out. Eosi do not do such things. The Farmers are very different from Eosi . . . and Catteni,' said Zainal.

Lenny Doyle raised his hand, grinning. 'I'd be a bit more apt to believe him if the Mechs . . . the Farmers . . . hadn't nearly chopped us up for the crates. But Zainal got us out before they could – and besides, the machines weren't programmed to know the difference between us and loo-cows.'

Dick Aarens made a low disclaimer.

'Would that suggest the Farmers aren't bipedal?' Scott asked.

'No, it only suggests that the Farmers' machines were not programmed to differentiate between warm-blooded species,' said Kris.

'Could the Mechs have been made in the form of their makers?' Janet asked, her eyes flicking around for reassurance.

Lenny began to guffaw at the notion, laughter he tried to stifle when he saw he'd offended Janet.

'C'mon, Janet,' Aarens said rudely, 'spare us that religious tripe . . . made in their image? Shit, no! Every single piece of equipment on this planet is a masterpiece of design, using renewable power sources and with easy access for self-repair and maintenance. No-one's been able to figure out what sort of alloy was used, but the machinery is practically indestructible.'

'Until you came along,' Janet said angrily, stung by Aarens' snide manner.

'That does not, however,' and Ray Scott jumped in quickly, waving for both of them to sit down, 'give us any insights into what course of action the Farmers might take when that orbiting whizz-ball of theirs reports that all the machinery in a good-sized section of their farmlands is no longer in operating condition.'

Kris covered her mouth to hide her grin. She wouldn't have expected that sort of wry assessment from the admiral.

'Let us not digress into useless speculation,' Scott went on. 'Will the Eosi do anything to Botany while they're studying the reports? Like a blockade?'

'Or at least stop shipping us more colonists?' asked Pete Easley in a plaintive tone.

'That is more likely,' Zainal said.

'What I had more in mind is sending a team to

191

investigate a planet that has been the last point of call for a scoutship and two transports.'

'What about blaming the E.T.s for disappearing those ships?' asked Lenny Doyle with a bright grin.

'That would be too much to hope for,' Jim Rastancil said, but he grinned back at Lenny.

'The Eosi do not care what happens to a colony like this one,' Zainal said. 'But they will not like what happened today when they see the reports. The Eosi believe that their technology is best.'

'And they'll find it hard to swallow that it isn't,' Rastancil put in, quite satisfied with that turn.

'So, it's the Eosi who are your inventors?' Ainger asked.

'Yes. They supply the plans. Catteni build.'

'You're sure they won't come after Botany because it has attracted such extra . . .' Rastancil asked, pausing for the appropriate term, 'stellar visitations?'

Zainal considered this.

'How the hell can Zainal answer that, General?' Mitford asked with some acrimony. 'The Eosi have been supreme in space so far – at least to hear Catteni tell it, and I heard all their tales when I was stuck in Barevi.'

'There will be much worry and many meetings,' Zainal said, obviously enjoying Eosian consternation. 'You', and he gestured to those around the table, mostly the newest to arrive on Botany, 'do not realize how low Earthmen are in their great minds and . . . selfs.' He looked at Kris to see if he had the right word. 'They will spend much effort and time trying to find out who sent that very, very fast space machine. *Not*', and he paused for emphasis, 'why it should appear here around their penal colony.'

'That's a relief,' murmured Anna in the row behind.

'That's some relief,' echoed Rastancil, sitting back.

'So we can put the Eosi response to this in the slow lane, then,' Scott said, 'but I doubt we can ignore the response of the Farmers.'

'He thinks by calling them "Farmers", they won't scare us as much,' Janet remarked to Anna.

Kris grinned over her shoulder at Janet, but the woman was whistling in the dark: her eyes were scared and her chin trembled slightly. Anna Bollinger, who had left her baby son with someone for this meeting, looked even more frightened.

'I hoped to get their attention, Admiral, as the one chance I saw – then – of getting off this planet and back home. Best scenario would be to make *them* notice the Eosi/Catteni combine,' Mitford said.

'A bit naïve of you, wasn't it, sergeant?' asked Geoffrey Ainger.

'Now, wait just a minute, Ainger,' said Kris, sitting up straight with the anger that bit of condescension roused in her. She was not placated by Easley leaning over to murmur something to the British naval officer.

'My apologies, Miss Bjornsen, I forget how little you had at your disposal in the early days,' Ainger said, elevating his butt off the chair. 'Sergeant Mitford, no offence intended.'

'None taken,' Mitford said equably and waved his hand, accepting the apology. The hand came down on Kris's leg, a reminder that he was well able to defend himself.

'It was at the very least what any noncom should do,' Bull Fetterman said. 'Establish what escape route is possible to return to his regiment.'

'We established a lot more than that,' said Dick Aarens, jumping to his feet. 'And we've done a damned good job of converting the Mech Makers' stuff to human needs. Give us some credit, damn it!'

'We do, I assure you, Mr Aarens, especially since you contrived so many of the improvements . . .' Reidenbacker began.

'We'd better stop congratulating ourselves,' Mitford put in, 'begging your pardon, sir, but I'd like to hear what Admiral Scott now has in mind.'

Kris covered her mouth quickly because it was obvious from Scott's expression that he *had* nothing in mind . . . yet.

'What I'd like to hear again . . . friends,' and Scott was having trouble finding an appropriately inoffensive group noun, 'is exactly your impressions of the arrival of the Leviathan you saw, collecting this planet's harvests.'

'If you mean, were we scanned then?' Kris asked. 'No, we weren't.'

'Hell, Admiral, the ship didn't even know we were there,' Jay Greene said. 'It just sailed overhead like some sort of . . .' and he waved his hand above his head, 'monstrous dinosaur.'

'It didn't land?'

'Not that we saw,' Mitford replied.

'Zainal led a group of us back here, because we thought that's where it hovered,' Ninety Doyle said. 'We weren't that far behind it when it took off again. There wasn't a bloody thing left of the acres of crates we had to climb to get out of here.'

'So there was nothing in it of the speed and flexibility of what buzzed us?' Beverly asked.

'Nuh-huh,' and Ninety shook his head emphatically. 'Different yoke entirely.'

'We sort of thought at the time', said Jay Greene, 'that it was pre-programmed to do its job. That there wasn't any life form aboard it.'

Rastancil whistled, impressed. 'Totally automated?'

'And a culture which has patently invented matter transmitters . . .' Scott said, clearing his throat.

'That would have been the only way all that stuff could have been loaded in the time it hovered,' Ninety agreed. 'Just like on Star Trek.'

'Then it is entirely likely that today's scanner is also totally automated,' Easley said, quickly changing the subject from that awesome concept.

'We couldn't get any idea of the mass of the scanner,' Rastancil said. 'I was on the bridge when it began its orbit and the transport doesn't have much in the way of fancy detection devices . . .' He looked over at Marrucci, who had been in the scout.

The pilot shook his head, holding up his hands. 'I couldn't figure out what to activate on the board.' He looked at Zainal.

'The scout will not track such speed,' the Catteni said.

'So, essentially, we must wait until the device sends its reports to the Farmers,' Scott said, 'and then await results.'

'Isn't there anything we can *do* to save us?' Anna Bollinger's voice had a slightly hysterical note in it.

'We can't just sit still and do nothing.' Janet added her protest.

A slightly supercilious expression crossed Admiral Scott's face and Kris, who had started to like the man, changed her opinion again.

'If he asks her what she thinks we should do . . .' she murmured to Mitford, who once again clamped his hand on her leg in restraint as he turned round to Janet.

'There's a lot we can do, Janet, and that's why we're here. Now, we've done pretty well so far, haven't we?' he asked, and waited until she gave her head an unwilling nod. 'So just hold tight a bit longer, huh?' Then Mitford turned back to the front table. 'Since it's a fair bet that the scanner saw that we've altered all the machines that are supposed to be in the various garages and barns we've been using, why don't we start by clearing them out? I'd also recommend that we explore that nearer continent with the view of taking up our residence there . . . that is, if we find the Farmers haven't set up shop there, too.'

Scott was nodding acceptance of these suggestions; even Ainger looked less dour.

'There're all those closed valleys on this

continent, blocked to keep something in, or something out. How many did we discover, Zainal?' Mitford turned to his right.

'Several dozens. We must ask the map woman, Sheila, for details.'

'The caves are ours,' Patti Sue said firmly, the last person Kris would have thought would speak up in such a meeting. 'We've made them livable.'

'But we have trespassed,' Janet said to her.

Kris didn't dare look round at Janet; what she was saying was so weird from a woman who was considered basically quite sensible. Maybe the scan had done something to some folks after all. She shuddered, deciding she wasn't going to think there could be the least bit of truth in those asinine rumours. All products of insecurity and lack of self-confidence: certainly nothing with any factual basis.

'If we give them back what we took . . .' Janet went on and then, hearing Dick Aarens' contemptuous snort at that idea, she whirled round on him, pointing her finger. 'You're the one who started taking their machines apart—'

'Janet!' Once again Mitford called her to order, twisting round to face her. 'You're not thinking this through, and you're not a silly woman. You've been such a strength to so many who got here confused and scared.'

Sandy Areson had discreetly moved to sit on Janet's other side and now put a comforting arm around her shoulders, nodding once to Mitford to indicate she would take over now.

'What was done, is done, and I doubt even the

best of our mechanical geniuses could put all the parts back together again,' Scott said in a conciliatory tone, 'not that that would be even remotely feasible since we'll need every single thing we've contrived from their machinery to effect an evacuation of their premises. If that is one of our options.'

'I think retreat in the face of overwhelming strength is usually considered a sensible course of action,' Bull Fetterman said at his driest.

He got scattered laughter for his attempt to reduce the tension in the mess hall.

'Furthermore we can prepare places for everyone,' Beverly said with a big smile, 'if what I've seen of some of those valleys is any indication.'

'The other continent's a better idea, General,' Mitford said, rising from his chair. 'Especially as we now have the Tub to do reconnaissance. Which I had planned to do anyway.'

'Positive action is always admirable, Sergeant,' said Scott, 'and I suggest you complete your plans and get them under way as soon as possible.'

'Will Yuri's group start immediate evacuations, too?' And Mitford swung half-way round, indicating Janet.

'You better believe it,' but it was Reidenbacker who answered the question and he gave Janet an encouraging smile and a thumbs-up gesture. She made a pathetic little sound in her throat but managed a brief smile, still twisting her hands nervously in her lap.

'They'd better consider that there'll be a lot more

newcomers reacting like Janet,' Kris murmured to Mitford, who nodded.

'Shouldn't we clear out all the things we've made?' Dick Aarens asked.

'We *need* everything to function with. And the scout? Where can we stash that now if we've got to clear the barns?'

Scott held up his hands. 'Give us a few hours here,' and he gestured to the specialists sitting behind him, 'and we'll formulate the necessary plans and set up teams to implement them. Now, I know some of you have been upset by the whizz-ball we had this morning . . .' His label for the orbital caught everyone's attention, and he grinned to see its effect. 'But we don't want to start another batch of rumours with those who still feel insecure here on Botany. Let's be careful how we discuss this meeting outside the mess hall, shall we? I ask all of you, by whatever you hold sacred, not to start a second wave of ridiculous rumours. We'll do as much as humanly possible to rectify our mis-appropriation of housing and effects. Certainly our first priority is getting people out of our landlords' buildings and to safer places, like the valleys. Equally important is preserving the equipment we need to conduct an orderly evacuation.'

Chuck Mitford turned round to those behind him. 'Keep in mind, folks, it's taken the Farmers more than nine months to discover we're here. I'd say we have plenty of time to get elsewhere and at least sweep the garages and barns clean before we leave. Right, Janet? Anna?'

'That should be long enough,' Patti Sue said so staunchly that Kris, remembering how fearful the girl had once been, nearly cheered out loud at that vote of confidence.

Both Janet and Anna obviously responded to her remark and looked less despondent.

'Of course,' Patti threw them all by adding ingenuously, 'they might not come until the growing season starts and we don't even know when winter ends, if this *is* winter.'

Zainal got to his feet again. 'I like the idea of moving us all to the other continent if it is okay,' he said. 'I think we should go soon. The airships can look at the other land-mass. It may not be as barren as it looks from space. If it is, they can help us search.'

Ninety got to his feet as soon as Zainal sat down. 'There are a lot of those closed valleys, too, which obviously weren't used by the Farmers. Maybe we can put people in them.' When he heard protests arise, he added, 'With stairs to get out when you have to. The valleys grow trees and bushes. We could transfer a lot of the stuff we've been growing to feed us to the valleys. And aren't the Turs and Catteni trying 'em out for us?' He grinned broadly, with a teasing glance at Zainal.

Mitford rose. 'I agree with Zainal, for what it's worth,' he said with an unusual touch of humility.

'Sarge, you had the only idea feasible. Don't have a guilt trip over it now,' Kris said staunchly, and her remark was quickly seconded by many in the hall.

'We all helped,' said Joe Latore, and turning

around in his seat, looked straight at Dick Aarens. 'Didn't we?'

Aarens noticeably ignored him.

'Yes, but what happens if we move to the other continent?' Anna Bollinger asked, her face crumbling with fear, 'and they come after us there?' Janet immediately put a reassuring arm around her shoulders and glared around.

'Hell's bells, missus,' Ninety said, 'there're caves all over the planet they'd never find you in. And probably caves across the channel, too, wouldn't you say, Zainal?'

Kris turned round, one hand going to Anna's knee. 'We know it's your son you're really worried about, Anna, but why borrow any more trouble than we've already got?'

'Which brings me to the subject of the Catteni contribution to our present crisis,' Scott said. 'Zainal, what will your High Eosi do when the satellite reports that whizz-ball?'

'Worry,' Zainal answered succinctly, his yellow eyes glinting with mischief.

Scott allowed a slight smile at Zainal's facetiousness. 'Would they come back to inspect Botany or set up a blockade of warships or something similar?'

'First, it will be discussed. Second, the satellite checked for faults that what it reported is true. Third, they may send someone to see what happened to us.' Zainal obviously doubted his third point was likely.

'Fourth, what if they send us more colonists?' Sandy Areson asked.

Zainal considered that for a moment, dropping his chin to his chest. 'I think no more colonists come for a while now, Sandy.'

'Especially since it's been unlucky for them to land on this planet,' Aarens put in, chuckling.

Zainal went on as if Aarens hadn't aired his wit. 'They will not believe the speed of the whizz-ball.'

'And they will know that it did not originate in this solar system?' Scott asked.

Zainal nodded. 'They will think a long time before they do anything.'

'Good,' Scott said, rubbing his hands together. 'Then that will give us time to remove ourselves completely. As I understand Catteni colonial policy, Zainal, they might even abandon the planet as unsuitable. Is that right?'

Zainal nodded.

'So we might be all right after all?' Anna Bollinger asked, her tear-streaked face brightening.

'It is entirely possible,' Scott said with considerable and sincere aplomb.

The upshot of the discussion was not a referendum after all, but the organization of scouting parties to check out every single one of what Ninety Doyle tagged 'lonesome valleys'. Small groups would quarter in the valleys to discover any unusual denizens, though none had been seen in either of the other two inhabited places. Once Mitford had organized the basics of those explorations, he left a sheaf of instructions with Easley as 'the manual' and roused the members of his combined team.

They set off before second moonrise since the amphibious vehicle had lights. It also had excellent suspension, because Mitford slept his usual six hours as Zainal drove it over surfaces rough and smooth.

The driver sat in the centre of this vehicle, with seating for two on either side and control panels across the width of the 'command' position. Zainal gave demonstrations to his relief drivers, Joe Marley and Astrid, conducting a running lesson on the vehicle's potential and what each control was supposed to show, what the various icons on the panel board meant.

'Have we got a periscope?' Marley wanted to know in a facetious mood.

'Third button on right, sun icon,' said Zainal.

'Why didn't I guess?'

'We can drive deep, cannot use scope. Says the manual,' Zainal replied.

'A man who will read manuals!' Sarah gave a sigh of exaggerated respect.

Joe gingerly tapped the 'glass' of the slit window beside him. 'How much pressure will this stand?'

'Enough. We will not go deep. Is more built for cor-ro-sive atmospheres,' Zainal added. 'Which is to close vents, Astrid?' he asked, testing her memory of the functions on the panel in front of her.

'This one,' she said, promptly pointing to it.

'Got it in one,' said Zainal and Kris, seated behind him, chuckled. He leaned back. 'I learn new ones every day, don't I?'

'I, too,' said Astrid proudly.

'You sure do, Astrid,' Joe agreed, grinning at her.

Sarah, seated behind him, tapped his shoulder. 'And what have you learned today, Francis Marley?' she asked, teasing him with his hated Christian name.

'I'll tell ya later,' Joe said, giving her a mock leer.

'Any time, cobber,' she replied.

The point at which they were headed was close to 500 miles from Camp Narrow, and the intention was to drive straight through to their destination with only brief halts to let air circulate through the Tub. It was such a new piece of equipment that it reeked of paint, oil and other strong odours and needed to have its air system flushed out, especially before they submerged. So they stopped from time to time, to brew tea and relieve themselves.

By mid-morning the next day, the sea sparkled ahead of them. Visible without benefit of the binoculars was the irregular lavender coastline of the neighbour land-mass. The water before them was calm, with gentle ripples curling over onto the beach.

'Further away than Dover from Calais,' Astrid said, for she had travelled extensively in Europe in her college days.

Zainal said something in Catteni, flicked up his left hand when the number he wanted refused to come to mind. 'Six or seven plus seven tens,' he said.

'Seventy-six,' said Kris. 'And how fast will the Tub go underwater?'

'Not as fast as on land,' he replied. 'Half the speed.'

'That's far from slow,' said Joe, impressed, and he peered at the sloping shoreline. 'Shallow?' he wondered.

'We'll find out soon enough,' Mitford said. 'All aboard,' and he called in Astrid, Bjorn and Jan who had been searching for clams on the pebbly shoreline.

They had no sooner reached the flotation point for the Tub than a quick ping began to echo from Joe's panel. 'Sonar?' he asked and then saw the gauge that was lighting up. 'Or something like it. Are you taking us down, skipper?'

Zainal shook his head. 'Distance to bottom.'

Water was reaching the slit windows now and covering two-thirds of the main one, and the slight movement of the waves could be felt.

'I forgot to ask,' Mitford said, 'does anyone on board get seasick . . . besides me?'

'Sarge? You can't,' Kris said in mock-alarm.

Leila, who had watched as was her custom, now rose from her seat and went aft. She returned with a large basin which she offered to Mitford. He gave her such a disgusted look that she started to apologize.

'I was only trying to be helpful.'

'He's teasing you, Leila,' said Kris.

'Maybe I'm not,' Mitford said, staring down at the basin.

'Are you claustrophobic?' Kris murmured.

He nodded.

'Oh,' she said, in as sympathetic a tone as she could manage. No wonder he hadn't been so keen to fly in Baby.

'The way the Tub is moving, sarge,' Joe said in a very cheerful tone, 'we'll be there in no time at all. No time at all!'

'Just think of it, Chuck—'

Mitford put a hasty hand on Kris's shoulder. 'Don't . . . use that particular word, will you?'

'Ooops, but you are first to cross this channel, or strait, or whatever it is. Can we name it after you?'

'Huh?' The sergeant regarded her with startled eyes; then he realized she was trying to divert him and managed a grin. 'I'll be all right. There's still some view left . . .' But the waves washed up over the windscreen and he hastily looked away from their activity.

The crossing was completed in just under two Catteni-style hours as marked by the timepiece set in the control panel. The Tub trundled out onto a sandy beach, dotted with the same sort of shrubs that grew on its neighbour.

'Clams, too,' said Astrid, pointing to the air holes as they all emerged from the Tub, once again flushing out the 'newness' smells. 'We get some?' she asked Mitford.

'There's plenty of time,' he said, shading his eyes to glance up the slope that led inland. Then he glanced down at the map he had taken from his pocket and unfolded it. 'We're about here,' he said, pointing and then cocking his finger due west. 'Should be higher ground this way. Zainal,

Kris, Astrid, Bjorn, Whitby – let's have a bit of a recon.' And he strode forward. 'Joe, you're in charge of the Tub,' he added.

When they reached the first height and had an overview, there were green-covered stretches in either direction and right back to the distant hills.

'Like loo-cow pastures,' Bjorn said, pausing to dig a toe through the vegetation to the soil beneath. Little many-legged things burrowed deeper, away from the air. 'Good dirt,' he added, pinching some between his fingers and letting it sift back down. Neatly, he stepped on the divot he had made.

'Think the Farmers'd notice if we rustled some of their steers?' Kris asked, wondering what else was hidden in the soil here.

'No such insects in loo-cow pastures,' Bjorn added. 'Maybe no night-crawls, too.'

Kris looked around her. 'We should be so lucky.' She tried to remember what she'd learned in geography about terrain. 'This looks exactly like the landscape over there,' and she pointed over her shoulder at the distant mainland. 'Could there have been some sort of subsidence to separate the two . . . or maybe the gap just hasn't closed as it did on Earth in prehistoric days. Continents used not to be the way they are now, you know. Maybe this is a young land—'

'No, this is an old planet,' said Whitby. 'No volcanoes on those space maps at all, and a lot of the hills are worn down. But this place does look like the same sort of terrain that we just left.'

'Then why is it not farmed?' Astrid asked, her

usually serene expression marred by a frown.

Mitford shrugged his shoulders and cleared his throat. 'Who knows, but we'll keep in mind that, if it looks alike, it could be alike and we might have night-crawlers here, too. We'll bunk in the Tub tonight.' Then he swung his arm in a wide arc. 'Let's move out and see if we can find a good place to park.'

In the four hours they searched, they caught only a glimpse or two of small aerial life forms but no rock-squats.

'They wouldn't be down here where there's no rocks, for starters,' Mitford said when Astrid grew worried about their absence. 'Not even any trees for the avians either; just bushes. Let's split up into two groups. You head north, Zainal with Kris, Coo and Bjorn. You, Slav, and the rest, we'll go south.'

Several times, Bjorn stopped to check the soil again. It was good, black and moist, but not too moist, full of small creatures to keep it loose. 'Plenty good for farms.'

'Then why aren't there farms here?' Kris asked, almost aggrieved.

'We will find the reason,' Zainal reassured her, touching her elbow briefly.

'They farm well enough on the main continent. Don't need this one,' Bjorn said but he didn't sound all that convinced.

'And the closed valleys?' Kris asked. 'They're even more enigmatic.'

'Perhaps', and Bjorn considered his words, 'they used them to keep animals in. Safe from the night-crawlers.'

'Where are the animals now, then?' Kris demanded.

'Eaten?' Bjorn asked, his eyes twinkling.

'We will ask that questtion also,' Zainal said.

They had gone north and now swung wide on their return to the Tub. Zainal had seen low foothills at a good day's travel to the north, but otherwise this coastal plain was covered in low vegetation and bush. Good smells wafted on the evening breeze as they neared the Tub's position.

Joe had wasted no time in digging for clams; Leila and Oskar had caught several varieties of fish and, having tested them in the Tub's small but efficient laboratory unit, found them safe for humans to eat. Sarah contributed some familiar edible roots and greens found near a stream. Among the Tub's supplies were small cooking units which were occupied by boiling pots of clams. A grill had been laid across stones for the fish, and there was bread from Narrow among their supplies, so when Mitford broke out the beer everyone was in an expansive mood.

The report of the unusual orbiting device was forwarded to the Eosi Mentat Ix, who had registered an interest in everything to do with the colony planet.

Ix snarled each time it replayed the record of the

object, for the speed alone suggested a technology worryingly more advanced than the Eosi had. Ix demanded all records, especially those made by its new entity, for within the entity's fading mind was a memory of a visit to the planet. Ix drew forth all the relevant facts, including the presence of the Catteni it had chosen from the bloodline of its present, but not selected, entity. It examined what the entity had dismissed, the gadget that had been presented for inspection as proof that the planet perhaps had been or was occupied by another species.

Ix worried over all the little memories, having them repeated and repeated until every nuance was dragged out for inspection. The Mentat was pleased that Catten had set up a second, more flexible satellite around the subject planet. Unfortunately this satellite only emphasized the incredibly fast global search that had been conducted by the alien orb, and the anger of Ix increased at the implications of technical superiority over the Eosi.

Logic suggested that the original discoverers of that planet were re-evaluating the world. What had it been programmed to discover? And why had this object, too, disappeared just beyond the heliopause of this solar system?

Ix summoned a meeting of those of its fellow Mentats who were sufficiently cognizant of their responsibilities to be useful in formulating a course of action. In lightning exchanges of information – as unlike the torturous communications with their subject Catteni as the orbiting object of the

Unknown was unlike their own satellite units – it was decided the matter must be investigated in greater detail. All further shipments to the colony planet were suspended, and the great number of recalcitrant Earth people would be sent to the secondary colonial venture.

Since it was the Ix Mentat's idea that the matter must be investigated, its peers decided that it must undertake the onerous journey, forgoing its usual pleasures and routines. Fortunately it could pass the tedium of the voyage in a suspended state, but that amenity required some alterations to the newest and fastest Catteni warship. The delay annoyed the Ix still further and it amused itself thinking of ways to punish those beings which had been instrumental in causing this discommodation.

The Ix Mentat had just been awakened by the high-ranking naval commander of this jewel of the Catteni fleet when proximity alarms jangled fiercely all over the ship, which went into attack alert. The mass approaching the Catteni vessel was so large, it was too large to be contained on the detection screen. Suddenly waves of force rocked the AAI as if it were a pod in a pond. The Ix, in a manner inconsonant with its dignity and size, grabbed for support until the buffeting subsided.

'Report!' it said in its cold and vicious verbal communication form.

'Most High Eosi, an unknown vessel has appeared—'

'You keep no watch?'

'It appeared on screen just as we passed the

heliopause,' the commander said, not daring to raise his eyes to the towering Eosi, 'where other such devices have been seen to disappear.' The commander had been well briefed on the problems of and connected with this colony planet, not to mention the extraordinary fact that the Mentat had not received its chosen of record but another in the bloodline.

'What is it?' the Ix demanded. 'Can you not show it?'

The commander hastily called up on the nearest screen what had stunned his entire bridge crew. The monstrous ship was ten times the size of the AA1, which itself was three times the size of the next largest spaceship in the Catteni navy. The immense ship was obviously headed inward and at a rate of speed which would bring it to its destination thirty time units before the AA1, for all its vaunted improved propulsion system and cruising speed.

'Can you not attach a tracer to its hull before it gets out of range?' Even as it spoke, Ix realized that the ship was probably out of range.

'It is already out of range for such an attachment, Great Eosi.'

Ix fumed that the commander would waste its time stating the obvious. How *could* another species have developed such technology without the Eosi being aware of their existence? The Eosi had not bothered lately with anything more complicated than the improvement in propulsion and cruising range, its present navy having been deemed sufficient for all practical purposes. Such an attitude of complacency was no longer permissible.

'Watch it and record it. Do not fail for an instant.'

'No, Most High Eosi, not for an instant,' and the commander, relieved to have escaped with his life, strode as quickly as courtesy permitted away from the Eosi and back to the relative safety of his own bridge.

No-one commented on his arrival, or moved an eye muscle from whatever panel their duties bound them to.

Several hours later, the captain was awakened from an inadvertent doze by a stir of excitement, palpable on the bridge.

'Sir, the ship is . . .'

Wide awake, and staring at the view screen, the commander watched, awed, as the strange ship – magnified many times to keep it on the slower warship's view screens – dipped briefly into the atmosphere of the subject planet, then bobbed up again and continued on its way to the other side of the solar system. Where, upon reaching the helio-pause, it disappeared from even the most sensitive instrumentation.

The commander reported to the Eosi, who was ensconced on a huge chair in the cargo compart-ment which had been altered to provide it with the maximum comfort. The chair faced a large screen which had already shown the Ix everything the captain would have to report.

'The planet is of no importance in the face of this,' and the Eosi paused. 'Return to Catten. At all possible speed,' and its tone was contemptuous of such a torpid rate now that it had seen a velocity that transcended the best of Eosi capabilities. 'This must be reported – and countered.'

If, as the AA1 passed through the heliopause of the system, a faint shock, like a low voltage of electricity, was felt by those awake, only a nanosecond blip registered the shock on the bridge and it was dismissed as an anomaly.

Deski ears felt the noise in the air long before the huge vessel was visible. But, while frightened people ran for the nearest cover in the caves they still occupied and the valleys they were presently making homely, the noise did not increase. To those with binoculars, it was visible more as a scintillating lozenge very high overhead. On the view-screens on the bridges, the monster seemed to do no more than skim the very top of the stratosphere, skipping like a flat stone across a calm lake, before altering its course and flying off into space, taking its skull-shattering noise with it.

Scott blinked, cleared his throat and managed to unclench his fists. He had been on the KDL's bridge, his eyes glued to the incredible astronautic event delineated on the detection screen.

No-one cared to break the silence, for no-one quite believed what they had just seen until a comunit beeped, an almost impudent noise considering the enormity of the recent event.

'That's about the size of the first one, Admiral,' said Su. 'I think we're lucky it was so high up . . .

214

What's that? 'Scuse me, sir . . .' and the connection was broken.

Dick Aarens came running full clip down the passageway to the bridge, catching himself on the door frame to stop, his face ashen and the expression in his eyes as close to awe as he was ever likely to come.

'They did it, Scott. They did it. They've replaced every last fri . . .'

'Watch your language on my bridge, Aarens.' Scott recovered enough to reprimand him. 'What has been replaced?'

'All the Mech-Makers' stuff, the farm machinery we disassembled. It's all back. Back in the abattoir and everywhere . . .'

Peter Easley, who had been just as flabbergasted as everyone else on the bridge, absorbed that news before Ray Scott or John Beverly did. 'Good thing we got the main garage cleaned out then, isn't it?'

'It would have been very messy if we hadn't,' John Beverly remarked, then he and Peter burst out laughing.

'Yes, but did they take the *parts* back?' Scott demanded.

'The parts?' Aarens was confused.

'I don't think so, Ray,' Beverly said, holding up the comunit usually attached to his belt.

Aarens ran to the hatch but sauntered back to the bridge, a smug grin on his face. 'The air cushion's still there. Maybe the Farmers didn't recognize what I'd done to their material.'

The newly devised com board of the KDL lit up

with other incoming calls from Shutdown, Bella Vista and the other three garage sites that had so recently been cleared of human occupation; then the caves and the valleys that were now human habitations.

'They don't know we're here, then,' was Worrell's reaction.

'And couldn't care less,' added Jay Greene. 'Hope the satellite caught that visitation!'

'You do?' and Worry began to fret over what trouble that could cause back in Barevi or Catten or wherever the Eosi hung out.

The machinery was back, replicas of every single model that had been disassembled by the colonists, in pristine condition and arranged in the appropriate order in each garage, barn or building. The solar panels that had been taken down and installed elsewhere for the camps' needs were also replaced and seemingly operational.

'Why aren't the machines moving?'

'It isn't spring here yet. Not the time to farm.'

'Weren't we lucky to have moved out in time?'

'No messages with the unpacking?'

'As if we could have read them?'

'Was Kilroy here, or his E.T. counterpart?'

'WHAT do we do now?'

Chuck Mitford, having seen the huge spaceship on the Tub's screen as they made their way back to the Headquarters at New Narrow Valley to report, had one answer to that when John Beverly informed him of the arrival of complete replacements.

'Get into those garages and remove the anaesthetic darts from the launchers before those machines are fully charged.'

'Won't such interference be noticed?' Beverly asked.

'I sure hope not. We took the first ones out when they were "down", but you'd want to do it before they get fully operational. Fill the reservoirs with water – that anaesthesia damned near put paid to a lot of us on the First Drop. Lenny Doyle or Pess'll show you how; they've done it before.'

'Any other suggestions, sergeant?' Beverly asked at his most respectful.

'Watch out for avian predators. Those machines can call them down on anything that moves where it shouldn't.'

'Anything else?'

'If I think of something, I'll let you know. But check with Cumber, Esker, the Doyle brothers, Matt Su, any of the First Drop who scouted for me.'

Mitford had been sending back daily reports on their explorations. Now he turned back to his team.

'I thought for sure we'd have more than three weeks before anything happened,' he said, scratching his head in a measure of anxiety. 'Can we make a bit more speed on this thing, Sarah?' he asked, since she was the driver.

'Sure, but it's about to get bumpy again.'

'We are not far now,' said Zainal, peering out of the front windows.

'How long would it take the Eosi to do something,

217

Zainal?' Mitford asked, now drumming restless fingers on his knee with his free hand as he clung to a safety strap with the other.

Zainal shrugged. 'I do not think they can move as fast as Farmers. Eosi are not automated. Nor do they have matter transmission.' He chuckled.

'I sure hope it galls their souls to hell'n'back,' Mitford said, grinning. 'I sure hope it makes 'em squirm with envy and dismay.'

'Just so long as they keep out of our hair,' Kris added. She knew that, despite Zainal's assurances, she wasn't the only one fretting over the possibility of Eosi reprisals on the colony. He would know better than she, of course, but it didn't keep her from worrying. She daren't even *think* how the Farmers might react in a direct confrontation with their uninvited tenants, though Zainal's point about the valleys' protection barriers was comforting – as far as it went with an unknown species.

New Camp Narrow was located in one of the closed valleys, south and east of the original cliff installation and itself suitably narrow but longer than most. It had been opened up by the simple expedient of blowing the barrier down with ingredients taken from Baby's arsenal. Zainal had instructed several miners and an ex-ordnance officer on the explosive capability of the different substances in her lockers. The original notion had been to use such combustibles for mining operations. The Farmers had ignored the mineral and metal resources of the planet. Inside the appropriately long, narrow valley, Baby and the KDL were parked one beside the other; despite Baby's size in comparison to the larger, oblong transport vessel, she looked sleek, powerful and far more dangerous. Parts of the wrecked transport had been utilized to make a fair-sized shelter nearby, and the returning explorers had no trouble identifying it as 'headquarters' from the flow of people in and out.

Small tents of loo-cow skins dotted the other side of the usual valley stream, and the carcass of a loo-cow was turning on a spit over a firepit. The rubble from the opening had been lugged across the stream for use in constructing homes; several were as high as window height, with masons busy around them. A much larger building was already in use, its heavy stone pillars supporting a roof of slate that overhung to provide shelter from rains, while half-built sides of rough timber gave the edifice the look of a forestry preserve facility. Tables, benches, stools, a few chairs and a neat pile of blanket rolls suggested it was providing several functions, unfinished as it was.

As the explorers swung round to park and dismount from their vehicle, they were hailed by many but no-one stopped working for more than a few moments.

'I wonder where they stashed the airplanes and all the air-cushions,' Kris wondered, noting their absence.

'This wouldn't be the only valley in use,' said Mitford, stretching his legs. 'Okay, Kris, Zainal, Bjorn, Whitby, Coo, we'll make the initial report. You got all the maps, Whitby? Yeah . . .'

'I have pictures,' Zainal volunteered, showing the mass in one big hand.

'I have soil samples,' and Bjorn showed the little case he had made for them.

'And I have the log printout,' Kris added, wondering why Mitford was so antsy suddenly.

'Sarah,' the sergeant said, turning towards her and Joe, 'go see what the drill is here. Astrid, see if we can get some food. Slav, put water in the tank. Oskar, Jan, Leila, air the Tub out good, and maybe even give it a good wash.' He waved towards the stream.

If the refinements of headquarters left a lot to be desired as they entered and looked around it, the essentials – including the yet again reconstructed bridge of the wrecked transport – showed it to be in good working order and array. There were even 'offices', cubicles with woven reed walls to afford some privacy. Old mech parts still doubled for stools, cupboards, shelving and benches.

'D'you suppose the Farmers didn't *recognize* their own stuff?' Kris murmured to Zainal.

'Bring your group over this way, sergeant,' called Scott, standing in the opening of one of the larger reed-walled compartments on the far side of the bridge.

'Even has a ready room,' Kris murmured, this time to Mitford.

'You're getting far too impudent, ma'am,' Mitford replied, though he was also peering at the equipment. The crew which had once been operated from this bridge had never kept it in such good order.

'Mitford, Kris, Zainal, Bjorn, Whitby,' and Scott was solemnly shaking hands as he ushered them in. 'Saw you coming,' he added, 'so John, Bill and Jim asked to be in on the debriefing.'

He sat at a desk that was really no more than several planks fitted together, rubbed smooth with some sort of polish to prevent splinters: two woven baskets sat on the surface. For 'in' and 'out', Kris though irreverently but their presence was oddly comforting. 'Business as usual.' The other brass-heads sat on Scott's side of the desk.

'It'd be a super place to settle a lot, if not all, of our people, Admiral,' Mitford said, pulling the stool closer to his legs before he settled on it. Whitby was unfolding the map, indicating the scope of their explorations as Zainal arranged the photos of the sites that looked suitable for habitation. 'Though you look like you've settled in here well.'

'Thanks, sergeant. It is indeed a pleasant place, and there've been no indications of undesirable elements in any of the valleys we're utilizing.' Scott had taken up one photo, and Kris nudged Zainal because she'd had a bet on with him that it'd be the one that took his eyes. 'Now this is a magnificent setting,' he said, and passed the picture to John Beverly on his right.

'Thought you'd like the view of the harbour,' Kris said. 'It's deep enough for an aircraft carrier.'

'What would you know about draught, Kris?'

Scott asked, but he was clearly in a good mood.

'The water's real dark down there,' she said, grinning. 'Too bad we don't have any big ships. Yet.'

Mitford nodded to Bjorn to report now. 'The ground is fertile, though it has not been tilled in many years.'

'You mean it was? Once?' Scott sat forward, dropping the second picture he had taken up.

Mitford pulled the telltale picture away from those overlapping it. 'The Farmers always put their facilities on unusable real estate, rocky or sandy, or plain non-arable. Look at the way this cliff has been hollowed out. We could damned near hide the KDL in here. For sure, it'd take Baby and all our converted equipment. This whole area shows signs of previous usage. And we found another section further along that ridge that reminds me of the way the abattoir was set up.'

The four bent their heads to examine the suspect photos, and it was obvious they agreed with him.

'We found two more garage-type installations further up here,' and Mitford indicated the positions on the map. 'We didn't concentrate on finding any more because they had so obviously been vacant a very long time.'

'We think we saw some likely spots on the other side of the bay,' Whitby said, 'but the terrain was too steep for the Tub, so we didn't cross the bay.'

'Is it possible that the Farmers have just allowed the land to remain fallow because they have enough here?' asked Scott.

'It has been fallow many, many years,' Bjorn said.

'But the soil is rich and would grow everything we needed. Especially if we used the land as wisely as the Farmers do,' and he ended on an admonitory note.

'All we need is another shipment of replacements,' Beverly said with a grin.

'Hell's bells, General,' and Mitford grinned, 'we saved everything we didn't use, so we've still got the ploughs and other farming junk. I'd heard none of the scraps were vacuumed up or beamed or whatever. We only have to mount ploughs and stuff back on the air cushions and use 'em for their original function. No big problem!'

'That's true, though some will not want to give up their runabouts', and he winked at Mitford, 'for ploughing. What about the scavengers?'

'Nary a sign of them,' said Mitford.

'And that's a puzzle,' Whitby said. 'We left out our garbage every night we were there – and found it still there the next morning. But the terrain is very similar to what we have here.'

'No night-crawlers on that continent?'

'None we could find, at any rate.' Mitford took up the recital. 'We did find rocksquats, whole colonies of them up in the hills – and just as dumb as the ones over here. There were avians where the lodge-poles have grown up into forests. Perhaps the damned crawlers died of starvation.' He grinned. 'We can always rustle a few loo-cows from here and see what happens. There're none there that we could find.'

'Many of the same root vegetables and berry

223

bushes already grow there, and other vegetation is similar,' put in Bjorn, his expression glowing with pleasure. 'And fish and clams . . .'

'Roasted corn would have gone so well with them,' Kris said suddenly, and sighed. 'I'm sorry.'

Scott bent an understanding look on her and his lips twitched in a slight smile. 'You're not alone.'

'We may yet find something similar,' said Bjorn, his wide face eager to please her. 'We don't really have a complete catalogue of the planet's flora.'

'By the way, Mitford,' Beverly said, 'we disarmed the darts as you recommended. That's quite a powerful anaesthetic!'

'Indeed,' Zainal and Kris said in unison.

'That's right,' and Scott turned to them, 'you were caught and subsequently saved another, less fortunate group.' He paused a moment. 'If there are truly no night-crawlers . . . There are many valid reasons for shifting our operations to that continent.'

Mitford leaned forward, circumscribing the area they had searched with his index finger. 'It's great country, sir. It'd take quite a few trips in the transport, but it might be the smartest move we've done since we got dropped here.'

'If we could be sure the Eosi aren't watching . . .' Scott murmured and looked at Zainal.

'They will still be "considering", Scott,' Zainal replied to the unasked question. 'Eosi consider long and hard before acting. Here, we use transport at correct times so the orbital does not see – short trip. If thrusters are used carefully, in short bursts, the geo-synchronous one will not show enough to read.'

'Besides which,' Mitford said with great satisfaction, 'they don't even know we've got those ships. And if they've any smarts at all, once they've seen reports of that monster, they'll stay the hell away from Botany.'

Everyone looked at Zainal, who looked right back around the table and then shrugged.

Not every valley being utilized as new accommodation was as far along in supplying shelter and other amenities as the headquarters establishment. Nevertheless, the thought of picking up *again* and resettling was met with a certain amount of resistance, especially from the technical and engineering groups who intensely disliked a second displacement because they were already involved in various projects and didn't want to drop tools – even the ones they were making. However, the availability of the massive caverns, when they were having to put together sheds from primitive substances, did cause them to reconsider. Then, all of a sudden, they wanted to be the first to get over there and resettled.

The miners were less happy – especially Walter Duxie, the mining engineer in charge – since they'd already reached a good iron lode and wanted to continue working it. While the Catteni space mapping did show mineral deposits on the target continent, they were loath to leave one that was already showing results. So it was decided that they could continue where they were: they had an adequate workforce which could take turns hunting and supplying their needs, and the nearby caves were already habitable. Judicious use of the KDL would bring ore to where smelting and fabrication processes would be handled.

'What about the fuel situation?' Beverly asked Zainal at one meeting. 'What happens if we run out? We've scarcely the technology to make it even if the natural resources are available.'

Zainal grinned. 'I know where more supplies are kept.'

'You pirate,' Beverly said with a laugh, and then had to explain the term.

'I will make a very good pirate,' Zainal decided, pleased with the definition. 'Not the only one, too.'

'Hey, what else could you lift at the same time?' Su asked. He was head of one engineering group that found themselves constantly having to invent the tools that had once been always available.

'Depends on what you want,' Zainal said.

'Hey, can I go with you and see what's on display at the store?' Su asked, and Zainal pointed at Beverly.

'Ask him. We will not need to go soon. Not much fuel is needed for short hops.'

Nevertheless, Zainal kept a close watch on the gauge on the first trip and, having decided on the minimum amount of fuel he could use and still reach a safe trajectory, tried to shave minutes off thruster use to preserve every ounce possible.

Mitford had taken a full load of passengers in the

Tub to start up the new location, leaving Zainal and Kris behind, helping to organize who and what would go in up-coming KDL transfers. The farming community wanted to be among the next wave, as it was essential to plant as soon as the danger of frost was over. So far 'winter' on Botany had consisted of cold, damp days interspersed with sunny cold days and a lot of early-morning frosts. No real storms, no snow despite cloudy days when the sky suggested blizzards to many who came from cold climates. The temperature dipped very low occasionally, hampering work outside, but there was always something to be done in what shelter from the cold was available. The people who suffered most were those used to tropical conditions, and they were given extra clothing and first priority when rugs and long vests of rocksquat pelts were available.

Not long after Mitford had left on the first of many Tub trips, Sandy Areson – who ran Headquarters Valley Camp – came over to Kris where she sat, eating a quick lunch in the Big Building.

'Been trying to catch you alone ever since you got back from the other continent,' Sandy said.

'Alone? That sounds ominous,' said Kris.

'It is and it isn't,' Sandy told her, 'and I have to agree with the basic logic of it as far as spreading the wealth is concerned.'

'What wealth?' Kris asked, puzzled. Wealth on Botany meant hours of work applied to what 'extras' might be available, above and beyond essentials like food and shelter. Even she and Zainal had done stints of kitchen duty.

Although they were the only ones at the long table, Sandy leaned closer to Kris and said, 'Us,' pointing to her chest.

'Us?' Then Kris shook her head as she caught on. 'Us as in women . . . of child-bearing age?'

'You got it,' Sandy said, leaning back again and grinning wryly. 'There are far more men than women on Botany, and as there hasn't been a Drop in four weeks, we're not likely to get more. So, if we want to keep up a decent genetic pool . . .'

'You mean, we're operating as if we'll never get off Botany?'

Sandy gave her an astonished stare. 'We're dropped, we stay,' she said, 'or don't you listen to what Zainal says?'

Kris gulped. 'I guess I've been naïve after all . . . I mean, we have the KDL. We could get off.'

'And go back to Earth?' Sandy looked even more disgusted with her. 'You been away from the camps too much, gal, and involved with that hunk of Catteni. Not', and she hastily put up one hand, 'that I blame you. I didn't know they came in any variation of "nice" . . .'

'People are considering him "nice", then?'

'Hey, spare me the sarcasm, Kris Bjornsen – and yes, lots of people have got it through their thick and intolerant skulls that Zainal is a lot more Botanical than Cattenical now. "I drop, I stay".' Sandy snorted in amusement. 'Especially the brass-heads. But you two can't procreate. You do know that?'

When Kris nodded, she went on, 'And you're of an age to do so.'

Feeling a total rejection of what she knew would come next, Kris leaned away from Sandy. She couldn't, she really couldn't go with anyone else, even to increase the genetic pool of a colony she was working very hard to make secure.

'Now don't get all silly about it,' Sandy said. 'We've got enough doctors here now, so you can just get inseminated with sperm at the appropriate time in your cycle. I did. I was one of the first,' and now Sandy patted her abdomen. 'Mind you, I chose the father.'

Kris gulped again, feeling distinctly queasy at the prospect.

'Anna Bollinger's preggers, too, but she got formally hand-fasted to Matt before she did. Janet's too old. Patti Sue also did it the old-fashioned way, but I just wanted to warn you that you're on the list. It won't be like being unfaithful to Zainal at all.'

'That isn't my problem,' Kris said in a weak voice. 'How can I possibly get pregnant until we're all settled and we know what the Eosi and the Farmers are going to do? What'd happen if—'

'Calm down, Kris,' and Sandy captured one of her waving hands and held it firmly in both hers. 'You're one of the last on the list, I should say, because your talents are more valuable elsewhere than in the lullaby line.'

Kris couldn't suppress her agitation. She hadn't planned on having kids for years! She was barely twenty-two, or thereabouts, since she'd lost a lot of subjective time on the way to Botany and hadn't a clue what sort of month, day or year it was. Then she didn't think she'd make a good mother anyhow. She'd never liked baby-sitting jobs in high school or college, unless the kid was asleep. When any of them woke up and screamed at her, she never went back to that family. She didn't think she had an ounce of maternal instinct in her.

'Anyway, we're going to set up crèches and minders who are maternally inclined so once a baby's here, you can ignore it completely if that's the way you feel about motherhood.'

'That is *just* the way I feel,' Kris said, trapped. Which she didn't add. 'When did this get decided? This is the first I've heard of it.' She was starting to get uptight now. She hadn't minded or complained about any of the duties she'd been asked to perform on this alien planet; she'd welcomed the opportunities to show her flexibility and stamina and develop skills she'd never have used in a normal life on Earth.

Sandy kept grinning at her. 'In case you're interested, you're going through the same phases that others have – including Astrid – before accepting the inevitable.'

That jolted Kris; she hated reacting in a predictable way. Sandy chuckled now and patted her shoulder.

'It won't be soon and it won't be as bad as you expect. But I figured you mightn't have been told. You've been out on scouting parties, so you missed the great debate and no-one's had the courage to tell you about it.'

'Who stuck you with the duty? Did Mitford know?'

'I volunteered. Mitford was too chicken,' Sandy said, grinning. 'Look at it this way, Kris. We've *made* Botany our own and we're going to keep it ours, and that means having a next generation to bequeath all our hard work to. I like this planet—'

'Now!' Kris reminded her wryly, feeling a bit sheepish over her outburst.

Sandy shook her head. 'No, I did from the start, because I could be myself here and what I knew was damned helpful, whereas back on Earth,' and she jerked her thumb over her shoulder, 'I was considered "fringe", or "weird" and "anti-social", nonconformist and definitely an oddball. Hell, here I'm running generals and admirals through my hoops as a town manager. Sure beats the hell out of being "tolerated". And I'm not the only one who has found a real home on Botany. I think you have, too, even if it means giving up nine months to producing a baby.'

'I hadn't thought of it all quite like that . . . I mean, *your* situation. I mean, back there as opposed to all the things you've done here. There's one matter that hasn't been taken into consideration, though,' Kris went on. 'The Farmers.'

'Yeah,' Sandy said in a thoughtful drawl. 'But we'll worry about that when we need to. Right now . . . oops,' and she stopped, looking in the direction of the entrance.

Zainal was there, looking around, and he spotted Kris and Sandy. Sandy got up. 'Good luck,' and she left with a wink and a grin.

Kris wasn't sure she was ready for Zainal to join her just then. Sandy's disclosure had really shaken her, and she'd have to sort all this out in her head. Disregarding the unsolved and unknown Farmers, she had to admit that having kids on Botany would give the colony stability, not to mention a morale boost. Especially if someone who'd experienced the abuse Patti Sue had had could now contemplate getting pregnant.

Kris found very little consolation in knowing that she wouldn't have to have physical contact with the male parent, although that route struck her as cowardly, if not downright cheating some guy out of . . . could she call it a 'good time'? Isolated from what 'society' was available on Botany because of the scouting expeditions, she'd had little contact with other guys. Mostly she and Zainal had worked with other pairs, like Sarah and Joe, and Whitby who had attached to Leila although they seemed an odd couple.

She had known, kind of peripherally, that the Sixth Drop had contained a group of women who had at first been totally ostracized by the other women in the camps to which they were assigned. She had noticed and commented on it to Sarah, who took some relish in telling her that these were 'ladies of the night' who had been picked up in one of the German cities along with the actual demonstrators. Apparently, Germany tolerated brothels but insisted that the occupants have periodic medical examinations to be sure they did not transmit sexual diseases, so these 'girls' were 'clean'. With a larger ratio of males to females on Botany, there'd been endless requests of the available women for sexual favours, on any terms. Some of those terms put the offenders up in the stocks to cool off. The arrival of the professionals had been greeted with considerable enthusiasm by Camp managers, so the women had been given the option of continuing their previous profession if they so chose. When assured such practices would be considered 'work hours' for community benefit, all but two had decided to continue. It was stipulated that they would still have to take their turn at the less glamorous chores of the camps, like KP and latrine, though they were excused from sentry duties. But they in turn had laid down strict regulations about how they could be treated by clients and the number they would be willing to accommodate. Proper respect was the first requirement – from the female population as well as the male.

The puritanical among the Botany women refused to admit that the oldest profession had a place on this planet. But they could not refuse to admit that a lot of guys went around camp in much better humour and with fewer snide remarks directed at the so-called 'prudes'. There were a few intolerant women, like Janet and Anna Bollinger who studiously avoided them, but the rest did as requested and treated them with due civility.

'You look worried, Kris,' Zainal said as he

straddled the bench before settling down beside her. 'Isn't the soup good today?' he asked, noticing her unfinished bowl.

'Yes, it's good,' and she hastily picked up her spoon, though it was now only lukewarm.

'Sandy says something to worry you?' He looked concerned.

'Woman things,' she said, avoiding an explanation.

'Mitford says you will have to bear a child for the colony. Maybe two.'

'What!' Kris dropped the spoon in the soup, splashing it, and then becoming furious at such sloppiness, mopping hastily with a wad of fluff.

Zainal regarded her with a very level gaze, one corner of his mouth twitching as he leaned closer to her. 'Was that what Sandy was saying to you?'

She hid her face from him. 'So Mitford had nerve enough to tell *you*? And not me?'

'Man-o'-man stuff,' Zainal said, and she could just see him grinning at her out of the corner of her eye. 'You know you cannot have a child by me. Is that why you stay with me? So you do not have a child?'

She glared at him. 'I stay with you because I'm in love with you, you . . . you . . . brass-head,' she replied in a low and intense voice.

He covered her hand briefly with his, squeezing her fingers. 'You are young and strong. You will be a good mother.'

Kris gulped. 'No, I won't. I'm not in the least bit maternal – motherly!' She blurted out the denial, daring him to object. 'I'd make a lousy mother. I'm not ready to have kids, I'm too young.'

He gave her a long look. 'It is not something all Earth women do? Have babies?'

'Not all, by any long shot,' she told him grimly.

'I see,' he said slowly. 'It is not because you don't want to offend me?'

'I'm the faithful type, I don't want any man but you. Even if we can't have children,' she replied in a tight voice, looking down at the soup which now had a thin haze of congealing fat on it.

'You do not need to sex another man. Mitford explained it to me.'

'That's even worse,' she told him with gritted teeth, rolling her eyes.

'I wish to see a child from you. Choose Mitford. You like him!'

'WHAT?'

Kris half-rose from the bench in agitation, and those by the hearth looked over at them. She dropped back to her seat, one hand over her face, as close to tears as she had ever been since coming to Botany. The trouble was she did like Chuck Mitford, very much, and if she hadn't gotten so incredibly tangled up with Zainal, she might have tried to come on to the sergeant. She had never once done so, nor had Mitford come on to her at any time. Of course, he had kept her so constantly in Zainal's company that finally sexual tension had been inevitable.

Zainal put an arm around her. 'Do not be this way, Kris. It is no big deal.'

'*No big deal*?' She whirled on him, pushing his arm away, and had the satisfaction of seeing him recoil slightly from her expression. 'No big deal!' She started to get off the bench but he held her down, exhibiting far more of his strength than he had ever used with her before.

'You are not a silly woman, Kris Bjornsen. When it is time, you will have the child and I will help you. Do not make it such a big deal.'

Then he got up and so startled her that she grabbed for his hand. Had she lost face in his eyes because she was, indeed, being somewhat silly? If he didn't mind, why should she?

'Your soup is cold. I get you hot.'

Kris was nearly lightheaded with relief and nodded acceptance of the courtesy. She was relieved, too, that she had a little time without him beside her to sort out incoherent reactions and irrational emotions. When she put her hands to her face, they were icy cold. Or were her cheeks burning hot with outrage and embarrassment? Whichever, she needed to cool down and stop acting so stupidly. She started at the point where Zainal had said that he did not mind her having sex with another man; he even wanted her to have a child. All Catteni women had children whether they wanted to or not? Then she coped with him choosing for her the man she respected above all the others. That suggested a sensitivity in the big Catteni most unusual for his species. Or was Humanity contagious? She knew he admired

Mitford, too. Or had he and Mitford discussed a putative father of Kris Bjornsen's compulsory child? Which she doubted. Mitford wasn't that sort of man. And she couldn't really see the sergeant and Zainal exchanging man-o'-man topics.

He returned with a bowl of steaming soup and a watchful expression on his face and, oddly enough, sympathy in his yellow eyes.

'Thanks, Zainal,' she said, spooning up soup and blowing to cool it. 'I did over-react there, I think.'

'I love you, you know,' he said in a sort of off-handed manner which would have exacerbated her already jangling nerves if her remnant of common sense hadn't realized that such an admission was also very un-Cattenish. He covered her free hand with his. 'It is not an emotion I thought I would live as a man to have.'

And that caught her hard, right in the guts. She dropped her head to his shoulder, weeping as quietly as she could. She knew he had had two children; even the chosen had the right to produce heirs on Catten. But he'd never said a word about the woman, or women, who had borne them. So he had not allowed himself to love? Because he knew he was chosen and would not live long 'as a man'?

'Why do you cry . . . now?' He was utterly puzzled.

'For you. Because you can love me.'

'It is not hard to do.'

She could hear the ripple of amusement in his

237

voice and, dashing the tears from her eyes, looked up at him with as good a smile as she could present.

'Eat your soup. We have work to do soon,' he said very gently, and she loved him even more deeply than ever.

Chapter Eight

The Eosi Mentats had deliberated; had examined the reports from both satellites with infinitesimal attention to detail. With each fresh review, their agitation grew. Two separate concerns were identified: firstly, the Eosi were not, as they had assumed, the only highly intelligent species in the galaxy, and why had they never encountered the Others when they had been assiduously exploring this arm of the Milky Way? Secondly, how did the Others arrive at a technology so far superior to their achievements, and how soon could they match and then surpass it?

Mentat Ix called to their attention the brief glimpse it had had of a comunit. Logically, an investigation should be made of the extant equipment for insights into the construction of the machinery situated on the colony planet.

Mentat Ix was assigned, with two younger Mentats which had technological skills and inventiveness, to inspect and analyse the installations. The warship AA1 would take them there and also provide guards against any demonstrations by the indigenous population, who were known to be volatile.

As the superb new warship reached the ionosphere of the subject planet, its new propulsion system developed a fault, an oddity indeed, which resulted in a shock wave passing over the vessel from bow to stern. Gauges on detection equipment went off-scale for a nanosecond, then returned to normal positions, and the engines resumed operation as if they had never faltered. System analyses were run and damage reports undertaken, but no fault was found in any department of the AA1. Even the Ix Mentat was confounded. It liked that no better than the other shocks this wretched back-water system had given it.

The captain activated every safeguard provided by this latest example of Eosi/Catten engineering and technology as he continued into the atmosphere of the third planet. There were no more life-forms detected than there should be, according to the numbers of prisoners sent there and the numbers of lesser creatures previously assessed. There were 2003 fewer humans than the records of removal, but there would have been some casualties both in transport and since landing.

The Eosi had stipulated that they land at the point where most of the Drops had been made, easily identified by the wrecked transport vessel.

Teams of guards trotted out of the AA1, to make a quick surveillance of the immediate area and the wreck, and were half-way across the field when they were suddenly attacked by aerial creatures. Shot down with the accuracy for which such crack troops are famed, these were identified as indigenous life-forms, previously recorded by the original survey team.

Reaching the wreck, they reported signs of intense heat and fire damage in the propulsion section. That, of course, was consistent to the reports from both the Drassi in command of the transporter and the rescuers who had subsequently lost their lives in the second accident.

'Third,' Mentat Ix corrected the captain.

'Lord?' the captain asked nervously.

'The scout ship also disappeared after landing on this planet.'

'My pardon. I didn't know of that incident, Lord.'

'*I* do.' And that was that.

'Odd for three . . .' and the young Mentat Co paused thoughtfully.

'Yes, three is odd.' Mentat Ix nodded for the captain to continue his investigations.

The team commander then added that only the shell of the wreck remained. It had been gutted.

The Mentat Ix irritably remarked that protocol had not been observed in this instance; even a transport should have been blown up so that nothing could have been salvaged from it. It was unfortunate that both Drassi captains had lost their lives in the subsequent explosion.

'There may well have been little of any value left,' it finally remarked, dismissing the problem.

'There is a concentration of metals not far from here,' the captain said, for that report had been hurriedly brought to him.

Ix nodded, and a flick of one finger informed the

captain that he was to despatch a reconnaissance team.

The team returned with pictorial evidence of a large installation – barns, sheds, piles of rectangles that appeared to be crates in collapsed form. And many different machines.

'Farming machines,' the captain said, for he had some familiarity with agricultural procedures.

'What season is it on this place?' the Mentat Se asked.

'The weather is cold but not excessively so. A winter, perhaps?' Co suggested.

'Farm machines are dormant in winter,' the captain remarked.

'Bring one here.'

'Perhaps the Mentats might prefer to see them in their . . . ah . . . normal surroundings?' the captain suggested. That made more sense than hauling large and cumbersome units about.

'The air is pure?'

'Yes, Lord,' the captain said. He was hoping to get a few lungsful himself and, if he could get the Mentats off the AA1, he had ordered the life-support officers to flush out the ship with the cleaner planetary air.

The Mentats were conveyed effortlessly there in the captain's skiff, which was commodious enough for three Mentats and necessary crew. They saw nothing impressive in the facilities built into the cliffs, or in the machines that dutifully awaited the timely resumption of their pre-programmed duties. In fact, the machinery was almost depressingly simple in design and function when compared with the orbital and the massive ship that had stunned the Ix on its first trip to this solar system.

'None of this suits our purpose or forwards an understanding of the mentality of the makers,' Mentat Ix said, although it found no fault with the sun nor the freshness of the air. 'When the colony is established, I may even take control of this planet.'

Mentats Co and Se exchanged discreet glances and followed their senior back into the ship. Despite the failure to find anything of technological significance, Ix did not issue any immediate orders, but retired to its own quarters to meditate.

Eventually Ix sent orders to the captain that the skiff must be readied for a second exploratory trip. It took the other Mentats with it, showing the pilot where it wished to land. It also required the pilot to hover when the glyphs carved into the hillside were noticed.

'The message is in Catten,' Mentat Co said.

'Yes, the renegade Zainal was here.' The Ix Mentat gnashed the teeth in its host's mouth in a most unusual fashion, then peremptorily gestured for the skiff to be landed where once, as Lenvec, it had settled to remind a brother of duty owed.

There was nothing on the site, merely more fields with hedgerows; nothing certainly that would have accounted for the chosen's escape. And only faded traces of where the scoutship had landed. The Ix Mentat turned its head in the direction from which the humans and Zainal had come.

'Take us there!' and it pointed.

The skiff took off and shortly came to the deep ravine which, at a low hover, showed not only visible evidence of human occupation but easily detected a considerable number of life-forms in the intricate cave system. Several emerged to observe the aircraft. The skiff's detection equipment picked up the use of comunits, but on a frequency which could not be directionalized before the signal cut off abruptly.

'They have more of those hand units,' the Ix Mentat said superciliously.

'Does the Mentat wish to land and speak to the humans?' the pilot asked, as more emerged from the caves.

'I have no interest in pests.' But the Ix had been more closely observing the signature of the humans than anyone realized. Primarily it searched for the unmistakable signature of a Catteni life-reading, and that was not visible outside or inside the caves. Deep inside the Ix's mind, one pathetic whimper trembled.

'The humans appear to have moved about a great deal,' said Mentat Co, 'if these', and it flicked a long nail at the screen where more clusters showed at different locations, 'are indeed human pulses.'

Ix Mentat regarded Co with some interest. 'Moved where?'

'To the smaller continent adjacent to this one. Many human life-signs registered there as we overflew it.'

'Return,' Ix Mentat said and sat back, impatient

to reach the ship and order it to the second continent, where the Catteni signature might be found among the other concentration of humans.

As the AA1 lifted, having left a substantial declivity across most of the field with the weight of its visit, the Ix Mentat entered the bridge and stood behind the officer responsible for the life-form detection.

'Set for Catteni sign,' the Ix said, clicking its long nails together in a tattoo that had the Catteni officer cringing with nervousness.

The AA1 made the next continent in a shallow curve. It had not yet reached even the intended altitude when the screen gave off a brief blip – registering the presence of a Catteni. It vanished so quickly that the duty officer wondered if it had been a legitimate sighting, but the Mentat was taking no chances and ordered the vessel to circle the point, a prong of land extending into the narrow channel between the two land-masses. But nothing registered on the screen.

'An anomaly, perhaps,' the Co suggested blandly after sufficient time had elapsed to have done several orbits about this wretched planet.

'Perhaps,' the Ix replied irritably and signalled to continue across the water.

The greatest concentration of the lesser, human signatures was found around the northern bay. 'They've infested the place,' the Co remarked as the 'babble' was screened for any sign of Catteni.

The Ix pondered a long while as the AA1 held its position, using great quantities of fuel to do so.

Then, with an abrupt gesture, the Mentat Ix ordered the captain to return with all possible speed to Catten.

The captain wished to do so as well, anxious to be rid of his Eosi passengers, and he gave the necessary orders . . . and was nearly bounced from his command chair as the forward motion abruptly ceased. The engines were still running, their pulse beginning to reach up to a whine of frustration as the ship met an impenetrable obstacle.

'There's some sort of barrier, captain,' the helmsman said, looking at the opacity which held them motionless. 'It's all around the planet.'

'Destroy it,' the Ix ordered with an agitated wave of its long arm.

The captain ordered a full barrage of all forward weapons, certain his firepower was sufficient for the task. The ship rocked and crewmen covered their eyes at the resultant flashback.

'I see a lessening in the opacity directly ahead,' the navigator said, trying hard not to think how futile this brand-new ship's much-vaunted artillery had been.

The captain called for more power and the ship moved slowly, slowly, slowly, pushing through the barrier it had been unable to destroy. Then, all of a sudden, the ship plunged forward through the obstacle, knocking to the deck many who were not holding on to something, including all three Mentats.

Although several officers sprang forward in an instinctive effort to assist, the Mentats snarled away any help and slowly got to their feet, glaring around them.

'Turn!' the Ix ordered the captain. 'I want to know what that barrier is and how it could impede this ship.'

The captain gave the order to the com-board to switch to the stern view-screen. Nothing happened.

'I asked for the view astern,' he roared but, while the communications officer cringed from his captain's anger, all his attempts to access the rear views came to nothing.

'There is no response,' he said.

'Damage report', said the engineering officer, 'indicates problems with the arrays, sir. It is an external problem.'

'Fix it!' the captain said, bringing his fists down on the armrests.

Orders were forwarded, and the Ix rattled its long nails with far more irritation than the captain dared show.

'Well, then, turn the ship around so that the forward view-screens can enlighten us. I must examine that obstacle,' Ix said, making a small tight circle with one finger.

In getting free, the full power of the AA1's engines had carried them a considerable distance before that manoeuvre was completed. The captain muttered unhappily when he saw how far they were from the misbegotten bubble, and an unhappy silence ensued on the bridge until they had returned close enough to examine the phenomenon. During that time, a damage report suggested that every protuberance of more than twenty centimetres and all the more delicate arrays had been snapped off. And indeed, as they neared the opaque bubble, it was obvious in the forward view-screen that every last one of the missing parts was embedded in the bubble, outlining the less fragile silhouette of the AA1. And the bubble completely enclosed the planet, just short of the two satellites. The orbital continued its programmed circuits, but there would be nothing on its tapes but an endless view of the bubble.

'It admits sunlight,' said the science officer, relieved to find something positive to report for he had to add that its composition was totally unfamiliar.

'Examine it thoroughly,' the Ix said, looming over the technician, expecting answers.

The Catteni, one of the top men in his branch of the service, used every technique available to him at a station that was supposed to be the latest improvement for its duties, but could find nothing further to report. Finally he spread his hands to admit defeat. He dared not look above his head at the Mentat, so he did not see the blow that crushed his skull like a melon.

The Ix stormed from the bridge with its juniors behind it, and the captain told the helmsman to return to the original course back to Catten. Then he gestured for the corpse to be removed from the science station.

★ ★ ★

'Hell, I don't know what it was,' Marrucci told the others gathered on the bridge of the KDL. 'Never seen anything like it – pushed all the gauges off-line and it looked . . .' he paused, 'for a split second, as if deep space got lit up.'

'Now let's not lose perspective here,' Scott began and then stopped.

Beverly whistled under his breath. 'I *know* it can't be technologically possible,' he began slowly, 'but then a lot of stuff we've been seeing recently is so far beyond what we'd generally consider science-fictional that maybe we can stretch that little bit further and think that it's possible to put a barrier around an entire planet.'

'There's something out there now that wasn't there earlier,' Scott said, leaning on the edge of the scanner board and staring at it. 'Even if it only shows up like a mist or a veil or an opacity.'

'There *was* a Star Trek episode I saw as a kid,' Marrucci remarked almost apologetically, 'called the "Tholian Web", and it was building a lattice to keep the *Enterprise* in.'

'So how did the *Enterprise* get free?' Beverly asked without a trace of irony.

Marrucci thought for a long moment and then shrugged. 'I can't remember. But I can see the web being spun around it, and they knew they only had so much time . . .' he trailed off.

'So, are the Farmers keeping us in? And why did they let the Eosi ship in and then out?'

'It blew a hole in the web and got out?' Marrucci asked, looking around the bridge for any other explanation. 'That might explain that flash, the Eosi blowing it open.'

'There's no hole in it now,' Scott said, standing up again but not taking his eyes from the screen. 'And why was the Eosi ship here in the first place?'

'Looking us over?' Fetterman suggested. They'd all been alerted by the Deski sentries here at Retreat Bay when the ship had overflown them. Then the group at old Camp Narrow had informed them that the ship had landed in the Drop Field. Discreet observation had followed, and reported, every move, including the skiff arriving at the abattoir and the subsequent removal to the field near Camp Rock, and Worrell had reported the skiff hovering over Camp Rock. And, in detail, what he had seen *in* the skiff.

'I saw three . . . giants . . . in the skiff,' Worry said, his voice shaky. 'They were staring down at us, and I've never seen such nightmares. They were . . . sort of Catteni, but no Catteni is that big and glows. The heads are all distorted and the features sort of caricatures of Catteni. Not even Catteni deserve that sort of fate. I'm glad Zainal missed out if that's what he was avoiding!'

'I concur with what Worry says,' Leon Dane came on line. 'I've never seen anything like that, not in Sydney nor in any of the material that we commandeered during our operations in Australia. There's a disease – elephantiasis – that causes something that looks similar. But the gross enlargement of the head isn't at all like an encephalic abnormality . . . No wonder ordinary Catteni are frightened by the Eosi. They scared the shit out of me just now.'

Shortly after that report, the warship was seen to pause just over the channel, where it circled for a long time. But time enough for those at Retreat Bay to complete the camouflage around the KDL and Baby, which were now housed in the big cave.

'You don't think they've been looking for Zainal, do you?' Mitford asked. 'He'd've been about there,' and the sergeant pointed to the area that had attracted the Catteni hover, 'in the Tub.'

'What effect does several fathoms of water have on Catteni detection scans?' Marrucci asked those around him.

'Zainal might know, but let's not call and ask him, huh?' Mitford said.

No-one could, anyhow, since that was when the Eosi warship met the immovable opacity and the brand-new worry about whether they were sealed in or others sealed out.

Having completed its programmed task, the bubble-drone assumed its monitor facet and observed the approach of a small spaceship which had just taken off from the subject planet. It had, of course, observed the arrival and landing of the same craft earlier but, as it was not programmed to take any action at that point, it continued its primary assignment, extruding the material that would form the protective barrier.

However, when the spaceship did not heed the initial resistance of the barrier, it accessed its emergency instructions. In that brief period of time of adding scope to its activities, the spacecraft displayed force which had to be disseminated quickly through the barrier to diffuse the effect. The further efforts of the spacecraft to pass its confines weakened the barrier. Then the instructions were available and the barrier assisted the expulsion of the hostile craft. The substance of the barrier caught on and held protuberances and smaller exterior parts of the exiting body. But the overall integrity of the bubble remained intact and the subject planet was now safe from external dangers, of which the spacecraft could now be considered one.

Since there had been an attack, the orbiting mechanism initialized its message segment and programmed it with a full report of the proceedings. Once the message segment reached the point at which its hyperspace drive could safely function without a backlash affecting the integrity of a solar system, it made its quick passage back to its home base.

This time its purport was quickly examined by entities able to deal with the subject matter.

By the time Zainal and Kris drove out of the water at Retreat Bay, they were aware of the excitement of those they passed, who waved vigorously at them as they made their way to Headquarters in the big cave. That's where they found Mitford waiting for them in his little runabout.

'The consensus of opinion is that they might have been looking for you,' Mitford told Zainal. 'Get in, the pair of you. Let the others unpack the Tub.'

'We just made it into the channel when the ship passed overhead,' Kris said, taking a seat. 'We were well started when we heard the reports about the landing in the Drop Field, and Zainal here', she gave him a little grin, 'put the pedal to the metal and headed towards the channel as fast as the Tub would go. It wouldn't have done for them to spot it when it's supposed to be shards in space with the rest of the KDL.' She glanced at Zainal.

She'd said nothing to him about her other suspicion, which Mitford had voiced, that the ship might be looking for him. At least, not until the skiff was reported landing where Lenvec had and where they had hijacked the scout vehicle. That's when Zainal started driving faster than was safe over the terrain they were on. He was racing to the channel, to get as deep as the Tub could safely go. That's when she knew he was really worried. But now he seemed amused by the incident and shrugged off Mitford's report.

'Worry saw three Eosi?' Zainal asked, his yellow eyes sparkling with an almost demonic glitter.

'Yeah, and they scared the shit out of him and Leon Dane.'

Zainal's smile widened with irony. 'They are frightful. It was only with great effort that I did not embarrass my father and all my line by losing water.' Then he gave his big shoulders one of his characteristic shrugs. 'But only the first time.'

'Is that what you would have become if you'd gone back?' Mitford asked, not quite meeting Zainal's eyes.

The Catteni nodded once, slowly. 'So they came back? And looked at the machinery in Narrow, and at the field and at Camp Rock, and didn't find Catteni life-signs. But they have gone. There was nothing on the screen when we got out at the Bay. What happened? I wish to hear more.'

'There is more to tell, too, that you wouldn't have seen underwater. The brass-heads are waiting for you,' Mitford said with a big grin, stopping the air-cushion by the stairs at the KDL's open hatch.

They climbed in.

'Good news, sarge?' Kris asked, remembering those last few klicks before the Tub immersed itself. Zainal's expression had been so grim, so . . . frightened . . . she didn't like to think of anything frightening Zainal, even if she knew very well that the Eosi did. Did he suspect the ship might be searching for him . . . still? Especially if the others did. Could his brother, Lenvec, be still conscious enough to make an Eosi search him out and take revenge?

'Well, sort of good news,' Mitford said with an odd twist to his smile. 'Tell me, Zainal, could that warship scan underwater?'

'I hope not,' Zainal replied and Kris, watching him closely, saw his jaw muscles tighten.

'If it's any consolation, I don't think they can because otherwise they would have found you – if you're what they were looking for,' Mitford said.

'They did spend a lot of time circling the channel on the other side, about where you would have submerged.'

'We cut it pretty close, I think,' said Kris, her eyes on Zainal.

'But they have gone away,' Zainal said with a satisfied nod.

'They've gone. With a bang,' Mitford agreed, grinning broadly, but neither Kris nor Zainal had time to question that because they had reached the bridge where Scott, Beverly and Marrucci waited for them.

'Glad you made it here safely, after all,' Scott said in welcome, but he gestured for Zainal and Kris to join him at the big screen. 'Gino, replay the Catteni ship's departure, will you?'

Marrucci, grinning from ear to ear, tapped in the necessary keys as if he'd handled Catteni equipment all his professional life.

Zainal echoed the gasp Kris gave when she saw the blip of the Catteni vessel stop short.

'How could it hit a wall in space?' she asked. Only then did she notice the barely visible skin of the bubble. 'That's what stopped it?' She turned first to Beverly, then Scott and Mitford, and finally to Zainal.

He was shaking his head, but his eyes were gleaming with intense satisfaction. 'It circles the planet?' he asked.

'We have reason to believe so. But watch,' said Scott, holding up one hand, fingers wide to give his eyes some protection from the flash.

'Wow!' Kris exclaimed, blinking to clear the after-image from her eyes. 'What was that?'

'The forward blasters of the ship firing at once,' Zainal said in a very odd tone of voice. 'And it isn't enough.' He continued to watch, but a half-smile turned the corner of his mouth and he began to chuckle. Now he folded his arms across his chest and, still chuckling, watched as the Catteni warship slowly pushed its way through the obstacle and became invisible. 'Ah!' He dropped his arms. 'That is very interesting indeed,' he said, turning to Scott.

'Yes, we think so,' and Scott settled himself on the edge of the screen control panel. 'We think they were looking for you . . .'

'I told them,' Mitford said, seating himself at the next work station.

Scott shot him a glance. 'Could they have been?'

'For what purpose?' Zainal lifted one shoulder negligently. 'I speeded the Tub so they would not see it out in the open. They might have seen it submerging, if they had the scanners in the right direction. If they came, it was to see what their orbital saw. It was in place when the whizz-ball came over, and it was also there when the big one sent down all the new machines. The Eosi looked at those, did they not?'

Mitford's expression was one of relief and Scott regarded Zainal with a look close to embarrassment.

'They come to see what's new on Botany,' Zainal repeated, showing his teeth in a full grin. 'Not for me.'

Kris allowed herself to relax a trifle. She'd

forgotten all about the fact that the Catteni orbital would have sent reports back. Of course that's what they had come to see! Zainal didn't enter into the matter. He was dropped and he stayed.

'So, do you think the Farmers erected that space barrier?' Scott asked, his eyes fixed intently on Zainal's face.

'Who else? Since the warship had to blast its way out,' Zainal said. 'The watch did not report anything happening in space?'

'Just that the Catteni orbital seemed to have developed a shadow,' Marrucci said. 'I was watch officer when the Catteni arrived. There was nothing, nothing there then.'

'Is the shadow still with the orbital?'

Marrucci grinned. 'Can't see that far any more.' But he did call up the log for that period and showed them the tiny shadow behind the orbital.

'If that's the gadget that did the trick, why didn't it move fast enough,' Mitford said in a low grumble, 'to keep the Eosi from getting in at all?'

'Maybe it just took time to spread out,' Beverly suggested. Then he turned to Marrucci and added, 'Even that Tholian Web took time, didn't it, to enclose the *Enterprise*?'

'The *Enterprise*?' Kris exclaimed in surprise. 'The Tholian Web? Oh, I remember that episode.'

'D'you remember how the *Enterprise* got free?' Marrucci asked hopefully.

'No,' she replied sheepishly.

'You're no help.'

'Enough,' said Scott, making a cutting gesture to

257

stop their levity. 'This episode has no happy ending. This planet is now enclosed.'

'To keep us in?' Kris asked softly, and knew the others had the same question in their minds. Then, because she couldn't bear the tension, she added facetiously, 'Maybe they want to be sure their machinery stays intact. If they can't differentiate between us and loo-cows, they surely will look at a warship that big with some uneasiness.'

'But the Catteni ships were coming in and out of here like yo-yos,' Mitford said.

'But the Farmers weren't alerted to the change in . . . tenants, shall I say?' and Scott gave a mirthless smile, 'until that homing device was sent off.'

'By the way, whose bright idea was that?' Beverly asked, frowning.

'It got a reaction, which is what we wanted,' Mitford said, declining to name a name. Which, Kris felt, was more forbearance than Dick Aarens deserved.

'Not for – how many months was it . . .' Beverly asked, 'before the whizz-ball arrived?'

'Seven,' Zainal said, 'and then only three weeks until the big ship arrives to replace the machines.'

'What I can't understand,' said Kris, 'is why that scan of theirs hasn't apparently taken any notice of the existence of a new type of life-form on their planet? Loo-cows have six legs, noticeably, and we have only two. Surely that was noted somewhere?' She raised her hands in a puzzled gesture.

'And the barrier did let the Catteni warship out,' Beverly said in a puzzled tone.

'For which I, and I'm certain Zainal, too, is very grateful,' Kris said in an undertone. Beverly shot her an understanding smile, his eyes flicking over Zainal beside her.

'Indeed,' Scott said, clearing his throat nervously.

'Very grateful,' Zainal added in a low, fervent tone, leaning back in his chair, stretching out his long legs and giving a sigh of relief.

'But why did it?' Scott asked, pursuing the puzzle.

'Because the ship used weapons against it?' Zainal asked.

'That is a possibility, of course, if the Farmers are pacific by nature,' Scott went on. 'But we don't know that, do we?'

'We know by the valleys,' Zainal said, 'which were to keep something in or something out. But not to kill it. Only now we are kept in and danger is kept out.' He pointed to the screen where the Catteni ship's departure was on replay. 'I think the Eosi have been given much to think about.'

'But where does that leave us', and Scott glanced around those on the KDL's bridge, 'in relation to the Farmers?'

'Remember that we all felt that we'd been scanned?' Mitford began, making sure he had everyone's attention. 'Okay, so the whizz-ball orbital did an inventory and the supply ship dropped off what was needed to fill in the gaps. Let's say that, like all the Farmers' stuff, it was programmed to expect certain life-forms and recorded a great many more of an unidentifiable sort. Maybe that's why there's a bubble around us, until the Farmers can come have a closer look at something that isn't programmed.'

'You're just hoping that's the case, Mitford,' Scott said. 'It would vindicate everything you originally aimed to do. Attract their attention and their help.' When Mitford nodded, he went on, 'Only your plan's gone agley, as the Scotsman said.'

'Not much agley, sir. Not yet, at any rate.'

'It would if the Farmers decide that we're some sort of malignant life-form which has contaminated their planet.'

Kris glared up at Scott, appalled that he'd say such a thing. Then she paused and amended her thinking: that he'd say what possibly everyone else feared – but his expression gave no apology for his blunt speech.

'No,' Zainal said into the dismayed silence his observation caused. 'No,' he added in a stronger tone and sat forward, clapping his big hands to his knees to emphasize that denial. 'The Farmers are cultivators, a race that protects; the valleys prove that to me. The scan could have killed a malignant life-form but did not. The barrier could have destroyed the warship. It did not. But it let it out. We will prove we are cultivators, savers, protectors, too. When the Farmers come . . .'

'You think they will?' Marrucci asked, his thick eyebrows raised in hope of a negative response.

'I think they will, but I will not wait until they do,' said Zainal with a wry grin on his face. 'I will not worry until they do. I will live well until they do.'

'I think I agree with you on that, Zainal,' Beverly said.

'Me, too,' echoed Marrucci.

'I may have reservations, Zainal,' Scott said, 'but worry is futile, especially,' and now he flung out both arms in a gesture of resignation, 'when faced with a far, far superior force.'

'This planet has a great potential,' Beverly said in a quiet, affirmative voice. 'Let us make as much of it as we can, and hope that the Farmers see us as cultivators and, perhaps, useful tenants.'

'Amen to that,' Marrucci added and made the sign of the cross.

Kris ducked her head respectfully even as she reached for Zainal's hand. He did not mention Phase Three but, by the way he returned the pressure of her fingers, she knew that he had not forgotten it.

Chapter Nine

While the brass-heads, with Peter Easley, Yuri Palit and Chuck Mitford, visited the various communal mess halls set up around Retreat Bay and further inland to counteract rumours and explain what had happened, Zainal and the fly-boys discussed a quick run in the scout to examine the bubble. Bert Put, Marrucci, Raisha, Beverly and Vic Yowell were dying to see the phenomenon. The argument had been that, if the satellites could no longer see what they were doing on the surface, there was no harm in making use of the aircraft for exploratory purposes. And one of the first things to be explored was the bubble: 'As close as one could get to it.'

'Or in it,' Kris had added, staying in the background but determined to go along for the ride for a variety of reasons. She'd learned all she could about the new equipment, and had driven the Tub often enough to have got the hang of the Catteni-size finger pads on the control boards. She might never learn to pilot, but there were always other duties during a flight for which she felt herself well able.

She also had a feeling that Zainal had no intention of giving up his plan to 'hitch a ride' on the next

Farmers' vehicle that darkened Botany's skies. How he could achieve that goal she hadn't a clue, and he was giving her none, though there were times when he stared blindly out at nothing, with unfocused eyes, and she knew him well enough to be aware that he was turning over ways and means of achieving a hitch. Considering how quickly the supply ship had made its deliveries, would he have time enough to reach it before it took off again at its incredible speed? What if he got knocked off when the Farmers' ship accelerated or activated whatever it used to travel the immense distances they were now convinced it traversed?

She kept hoping that when his plans were completed, she'd be part of them. For all the good friends she now had on Botany, she did not wish to be left here by herself. Especially since Zainal's presence protected her from importunities. Already she'd had several distressing interviews with men who wanted to be on her 'paternity' list. They professed themselves willing to forgo a natural conception, but they would like to have her bear their child.

She had managed to thank them for their interest – when she really wanted to clout them as hard as she could – and told them she would consider their offer. And made sure to stick closer than ever to Zainal's side, even though it meant stopping work on the quarters they were building. She did what she could without his help – until guys started showing up with offers of assistance . . . and the 'paternity' requests.

Then Raisha discovered she was pregnant, and deferred to whoever wished to take her spot.

'I've been up and it was wonderful,' she said, her eyes shining with the memory, 'but I don't want to whoopsie in free fall, thank you.'

That condition was becoming widespread, Astrid, Sarah and the three girls who had been Catteni decoders all announcing pregnancies. Kris kept as close to Zainal as she possibly could, even sitting through repeated instructions at the scout's control board to avoid the 'infection'. No wonder so many individual quarters were being built in the Bay area.

There was no problem filling in Raisha's place, and Bert magnanimously offered to step down too. Beverly and Marrucci went over the credentials of all those who volunteered for the flight and selected Antonio Gedes for Raisha's spot, but Zainal insisted that Bert remain – having had some experience with the craft and in space – while two other pilots, Sev Balenquah and Sidi Ahmed, were added to the flight list.

'Not that we're ever likely to go far,' Balenquah said gloomily.

He was swarthy, with deep-set black eyes that surveyed his surroundings with reserve. Kris wasn't sure she liked his non-committal posture, when here he was being offered what half-a-dozen less qualified men and women would have killed to get. Well, not 'killed', but definitely envied.

'Look at it this way, mate,' said Bert Put, also displeased by the man's attitude, 'you never know, do you? Did you ever think you'd drive a ship in space again? Well, you're doing it now, and here.'

'I guess . . .' and Balenquah altered his attitude. He was actually the quickest of the three new men to become easy with the unusual equipment and the finger-pad boards.

The flight had been planned in spite of severe reservations from Reidenbacker and Ainger. They were ground personnel, Marrucci had remarked privately to Kris, and suspicious of air and space manoeuvres. If the satellites were no longer visible on the screens of the KDL and the scout, then it was two to one that the SATs couldn't see inside the bubble. It was therefore not only safe, but a wise precaution to see what the barrier was like up close.

'Not to mention the fact that you're dying to go up again,' Kris said and he grinned, more boyish than ever despite having reached the rank of colonel in the Air Force.

'You got it, Bjornsen,' and he cocked a double-jointed thumb at her, making the rest of his hand into a mock pistol before dropping the thumb. He also had a habit of cracking his knuckles when he was nervous, a routine which fascinated Zainal who could not, to Kris's relief, duplicate the action. Having one person do it in the confines of a pilot compartment was enough!

Zainal also wanted to see if he could locate a Farmers' satellite, or whatever was controlling the bubble.

'If they spy on us, it is good. They want to know more before they come.'

'That's *your* interpretation,' Kris said.

He regarded her with his yellow eyes and a slight smile on his lips. 'And what is yours?'

She thought for a moment and then laughed. 'Yeah, we could very well be a mouse run.'

'A what?' Zainal asked, puzzled, so she suggested they take a break from house-building while she explained about laboratory mice and labyrinths to test intelligence and learning ability.

'To add to whatever that scan of theirs discovered about us.'

'But we do what we want,' Zainal said, still puzzled.

'Maybe we just *think* we do,' she replied, just now identifying that possibility.

'Scott would not like to think someone else commands him,' and he chuckled as he got back to his feet and reached for another brick.

'No, he sure as hell wouldn't,' Kris agreed, and laughed as she rose to join him. 'We've got just enough mortar mixed for another course,' she said, scooping up a trowel-full. 'I'm getting quite adept at this.'

Then she remembered Sandy Areson's remark about plastering being like feeding an infant, and that she'd use the same skills when she had one of her own. She tapped the next brick in place with such force that it split in half.

'That's the fourth one tonight,' she said irritably. 'Maybe they need to bake them longer or something.'

Sandy was in fact in charge of the brick-firing, so

266

Kris knew it was no fault of the manufacture. Brick-making was another chore shared throughout the community. But there was something soothing about shovelling the wet muck into the moulds and knowing you were building your own place from scratch – including the ones on your arms, hands and legs, collected from the process of building.

Still, it would be a nice place when it was finished. She and Zainal had picked the spot together, on that first trip. They had a splendid view of the Bay, with enough clear ground around to plant vegetables and berry shrubs, and a stand of 'young' lodge-pole trees behind them. After months of barracks living, nearly everyone on Botany wanted privacy and the Bay area certainly afforded that.

The Narrow Valley mess hall had been disassembled, loaded aboard the KDL and reassembled on a height above the Bay. Smaller 'offices' clustered around it on the natural terraces and levels below and above. The hospital was the only other large single structure, and Leon Dane announced that the medical staff did not have time to build a separate maternity wing. He was, however, training midwives for home births since he was certain all the babies would decide to be born at the same time.

Private accommodations spread out around the Bay in all directions, at first built from the lodge-pole tree timber before the brick manufactory got production up to a useful level. Those involved in cutting timber made the interesting discovery that even the smallest of the lodge-pole trees which had grown down into the plateau were at least a thousand years old.

'They have rings, just like trees on Earth,' said Vigdin Elsasdochter, the environmental specialist in charge of responsible logging, ready to show the section she carried around with her. 'And tight rings to indicate the climate has not changed much throughout the millenium: no drought, no bad winters, no hot summers. Some of the larger trees may be ten thousand years old.'

Once again the question of how long the Farmers had been in possession of the planet was brought up. Especially since the 'new forest' of 'young trees' had been seeded by the much older ones. Even Worrell refused to worry about it.

'I got other more important things to worry about,' he'd said one night in the mess hall. 'Like allocating glass to people who want to have picture windows and stall showers! Of all things,' and he'd flung a hand towards the Bay, 'as if we don't have a great big bath-tub out there!'

Those who had been in the building trades on Earth, like the Doyle brothers, were kept busy – offering advice, showing novices how to do things. Some of the Asians had the most trouble, since they had been accustomed to different building materials. After assigned chores were done and the evenings gradually lengthened, everyone worked on their homes, and lent a hand to neighbours for jobs that required a gang.

While some of the brass-heads were living in the cliff hangar, and bunking down on pallets in their offices, all of them had picked out sites, but keeping track of work assignments for nearly ten thousand people and aliens took most of their time.

'Someone has to do it,' Mitford remarked when Kris complained that the admiral seemed to be the unelected head of everything. 'And, hell, Kris, I might have run the battalion to all intents and purposes, and managed to whip us into some sort of order there at the first, but he had an aircraft carrier and they carry ten thousand; he's used to dealing with those kind of numbers, I'm not. I was only too glad to hand him the can, you know.'

Mitford remained in charge of exploration and mapping, attempting to fill in the spatial map with the details necessary for further expansion of the farming and ranching. 'If you can call loo-cows ranch animals.'

Knowing that the sergeant was truly happier on reconnaissance in the Tub, Kris decided not to harbour any ill-feelings towards Ray Scott. There was no question that he wasn't working all the hours God gave the day here on Botany. And some days he seemed almost agreeable, as if Botany was mellowing him. At other times, she was certain he disliked and distrusted Zainal – and her, by virtue of her association with the former Emassi officer. He vacillated between extreme cordiality when deferring to Zainal's knowledge of some matters and total dismissal of Zainal's opinions. He didn't have command all his own way, which somewhat mollified Kris; and she supposed that, having run an aircraft carrier, he had the requisite experience. She had occasion to be grateful it was Scott who issued most of the orders rather than Geoffrey Ainger, whom she didn't like at all. He was *so* Brit that he was almost as much a caricature of the serving officer as Colonel Blimp had been, and she knew he considered Zainal a dangerous commodity. She got along well with Rastancil, Fetterman and Reidenbacker; John Beverly was the nicest of the lot, because he always looked straight at her when he asked or answered questions. And Easley, but then he was as his name – easy to get along with. In fact, when he was involved, meetings seemed less tense and often more productive. He had such a knack for gently redirecting tensions and making suggestions that kept discussions going around, instead of stopping at Ray Scott all the time.

Which brought her back to the present and the meeting Scott and Rastancil had called them in for. They wanted Zainal to check the more mountainous terrain that had not yet been explored during the flight. The number of orbits had expanded from a quick flight up to the bubble and back down, to five days of circumnavigating the planet.

'See if there are any blind valleys here on our continent, or deposits of minerals. We could use more lead, copper, zinc and tin, if this continent has them.'

'I believe it does,' Zainal said. 'The miner, Walter Duxie, has copies of the original spatial survey maps.'

'Duxie? Do I know him?' Scott asked over his shoulder at his ever-present aide.

'Yes, he agreed to leave the other place and supervise mining here,' Beggs murmured. 'Stocky man, balding, forties, English.'

'Ah, yes, get them for me to see,' and Scott turned back to Zainal and Kris.

She wondered what Beggs's description of Zainal was – and herself. He never seemed to meet anyone's eye, but then he was so seldom asked questions: he just answered Scott's. Then she decided she didn't want to know.

Two days later, Zainal was satisfied that those accompanying him on the Bubble Mission, as its participants named it, were sufficiently trained to put what they had been learning into practice. He announced a dawn take-off and dismissed them, suggesting that they all relax for the rest of the evening. Not that he intended to follow his own advice, because they were ready to put the shakes on the roof of their two-roomed cabin. Kris decided she needed to be so thoroughly tired she couldn't stay awake, because she was far more excited about the trip than she let on.

Zainal had just finished setting the piles of shakes in order and was steadying the ladder against the gable end when Mitford, Worry, Tesco, Sandy

271

Areson, Sally Stoffers and the two Doyles arrived, hammers in hand and with a second ladder.

'Can't have you breaking something the day before the Bubble,' Mitford had said gruffly.

Kris grinned gratefully, because Zainal might have patiently learned the rudiments of construction but she was terrified that he'd fall through the rafters, or break them, and he wouldn't let her go up on the roof by herself to nail the shakes.

'You can't help,' Kris said flatly to the two women.

'Heard about your design with my buff bricks,' Sandy said. She was puffing a bit from the walk up the hill, and had brought along her own stool; she put it down facing the front of the cabin and nodded approval. 'Didn't realize we had so much colour variation . . . Maybe it's all you novices mixing your own batches.'

'I liked the buff so that's what I made, and then added more buff to the red ones,' Kris said, observing the effect objectively. They'd put the darker bricks around the door, window-ledges, corners, the chimney and the hearth surround. They had a back door, too, out of the smaller room, so they had easier access to the latrine. And a sleeping loft which had become a popular idea, especially with those families which were increasing. 'I think it looks well.'

'Does at that. I can help hand out nails, too. Brought you my handy-dandy nail apron, as well.' She handed over the object and, laughing, Kris tied it about her waist while Sandy started filling the three commodious pockets with the nails. 'Is Zainal going to fill that big mouth of his with nails?'

Kris chuckled. 'No, Lenny already warned him about swallowing nails; even a Catteni gut couldn't handle a mouthful. He's got a pail.'

Zainal had the ladder in place now and, before he could pick his pail off the ground, she was up the ladder, a bundle of shakes and the hammer in one hand and the other helping her up the rungs.

'Hey?' Zainal protested.

'You'd never know he was a Catteni,' Sandy said conversationally to Sally, 'unless you had to look at him.'

Sally smothered a giggle as Zainal made as graceful a climb up the ladder as Kris had. Mitford and Lenny Doyle appeared on the roof from the other side and then the hammering began, echoing in the little dell, and picked up by the rat-tat-tat of other hammers on other roofs.

With so many to help, passing shakes and replenishing the supply of nails, the cabin was roofed by the time the sun went down. Then Zainal passed around 'beer' while Kris served up tea from the kettle in the fireplace.

'Looks bigger somehow, with the roof on,' Kris remarked, glancing up at the rafters and taking a deep breath of the fragrance of the new wood of the shakes. They could have had slate, but Mitford thought shakes were nicer and easier to put up.

They lounged about outside until first moonrise and then the guests left.

'We'd better hike to the hangar and get to bed in

the scout,' Kris said, moving towards the doorway. They had no door yet.

Zainal stopped her. 'I want to stay under my own roof, which I have built—'

'Helped build,' she said, teasingly.

'Tonight,' he finished, and gestured towards the pile of blankets which she hadn't noticed in the rush to get the roof done.

'That would make the evening complete.'

'Not quite,' Zainal said in a low voice, drawing her into his arms. 'It is good to have our own place. Very good, indeed.'

And that should have been an idyllic time for them. Except that when she got up in the night, between moons, she didn't want to disturb the soundly sleeping Zainal and, on her way back from the latrine, tripped over the left-over bundle of shakes and broke her right arm.

She was furious with herself for being so clumsy and for losing her chance for going on the mission. 'Why couldn't I have broken the left one? I'm right-handed,' she said, weeping more from disappointment than pain as Zainal carried her to the nearest available air cushion, one of the flat-beds, and drove her the rest of the way to the hospital. Both bones had been broken, although Leon Dane comforted her with the thought that it hadn't been a compound fracture which would have been nasty with their limited facilities.

Then he poured her a tot of the grain alcohol that

was currently in use as a pain-killer. They hadn't quite got a decent smoky taste to it, but she wouldn't complain.

'This is quite nasty enough,' she said as Zainal held her against him while Leon manoeuvred the bones back into place. She fainted after, not during, and regained consciousness while he was fixing the last of the bandages into place around the splints.

'I would like to have immobilized it in plaster, only we haven't got that kind yet,' Leon told her. He poured her a smaller tot, 'to help you sleep,' he said.

Then he led Zainal, who carried her, to an otherwise empty ward. Zainal set her gently down next to the window and then moved the next bed against hers.

'Let's not make a practice of that,' Leon said, caught between severity and amusement at Zainal's pre-emptive rearrangement. But he put out the solar-powered light and closed the door quietly behind him.

Kris could almost have wished that Zainal had let her suffer on her own, but the whisky had dulled the ache in her arm and the warmth of his body, and his concern, comforted her so that soon enough she was asleep.

He was gone in the morning when the noise of the scout's take-off woke her, and the bed had been put back in its proper position. It was dawn and he had blasted off on time. She wondered who had taken

275

her place, and then didn't want to know. She tried to go back to sleep but couldn't with the ache, so she got out of bed and, with a blanket wrapped around her, went in search of someone and preferably a cup of hot herbal tea. Maybe that would help the ache in her arm.

What actually helped her arm was a more judicious shot of the grain whisky in the tea.

'I can't spend the next few weeks drunk as a lord,' she said to the attendant in the hospital's kitchen.

'Ah, the ache'll ease off,' Mavis, the duty nurse, told her, grinning. 'At least we've got a decent tipple to help. Now, let's get back to your room and I'll help you dress. Can I bring your old coverall up to your cabin when it's clean? And have a look round it while I'm there? Cumber and I are building, too, and I like to get a notion of what others have done. Did you use bricks or timber?'

Mavis was deft in the dressing and kept Kris's mind off her awkward and painful arm as she helped.

'Stop at the pharmacy and they'll give you a bottle – for medicinal purposes,' Mavis said with a grin, pointing towards the right door. 'I'll call for a ride, but you may have to wait . . .'

'I can perfectly well walk . . .'

'You can perfectly well not,' said Pete Easley, coming in the hospital at that moment. 'I promised Leon I'd collect you. Got your bottle of medicinal? Sit there while I grab one. I know where they stash it,' and he went into the pharmacy and was out again before Kris could take a seat. Then, with his hand under her left elbow, he escorted her out to the runabout.

'Mitford lent it to you?'

'For you, crippled as you are, Mitford is ready to do a great many things. Besides,' and Easley looked down at her with a devilish grin, 'he promised Zainal he'd look out for you.'

'Hmmm, how kind,' she said in an acid tone, knowing just what might be going through Zainal's mind in asking Mitford to be on hand.

'You could take another day in the hospital, you know,' Easley suggested, his eyes intent on her face.

'I'm not sick,' she said peevishly, and walked ahead of him to climb into the runabout.

The space on the driver's seat was not very wide, though it usually accommodated two people easily – but not one with an unwieldy splint and a brown bottle of hooch. Easley ended up sitting slightly canted so he wouldn't inadvertently bump her. She felt clumsier than ever and definitely out of sorts. She couldn't be hung over from what she'd had last night, but she'd have given her eye-teeth for an aspirin. Then she remembered how Zainal laughed at all the eye-teeth she'd given away, and somehow her mood improved.

'He got off all right?' she asked.

'Right on time. Laughrey took your place.'

'Laughrey, the former Concorde pilot?' Her good humour increased. She liked Laughrey and he'd be in heaven, literally as well as figuratively. 'At least it wasn't Scott's little pip-squeak . . .' She would have hated it if Beggs had got the empty chair.

Pete Easley laughed. 'The guy's good at what he does, but Scott only tolerates him because it keeps him out of other people's hair. He's a natural yes-man, but he's got an eidetic memory.'

Early risers waved a greeting at Kris and Pete, some of them pointing to her arm and signalling 'tough luck'. Not sure how to respond to the sympathy, she waved back, smiling. She glanced skyward, knowing that Baby was probably over the other hemisphere about now.

'Could I sneak onto one of the bridges, d'you think?'

'Only when you've had some breakfast. You're white as a sheet,' he said, pulling in to park at the mess hall.

So she had breakfast, which Pete Easley brought over to the table at which he had seated her, one not visible from the door.

'Don't think you need condolences right now,' he said, sitting so that he blocked her from casual glances.

'Is news of my accident all over the Bay?' she demanded, swinging back to annoyance again.

'Well, there had to be an explanation when Zainal showed up with Laughrey, and we all know how keen you were to go on the mission,' he said, adding, 'and you know how news goes through Retreat.'

'Hmmm, yes, indeed I do.' She grimaced then because even to her she sounded cranky.

'Don't worry about it, Kris,' Pete said. 'I'd be a lot crankier.' And he escorted her back to the runabout without too many people commiserating with her.

'I think I'll take you home, Kris,' he said, making the turn towards her cabin where he should have turned towards the hangar. 'You still don't look like yourself.'

'I'm not,' she agreed. 'I am definitely *not* myself.'

But also she didn't want to go to a cabin that was empty of Zainal. She tried to think of the things she could do one-handed and came up with very few. Even dish-washing required two.

'Look, Kris, they won't reach the Bubble for a couple more hours. How about I drop you off at your cabin and come get you in time for that? Okay?'

'Yeah, that sounds pretty good,' she said as he slowed the runabout right at her front door. She was getting out when she realized the doorway was no longer open. 'Hey, how did that get there?' and she pointed to the brand-new addition.

Pete grinned. 'Lenny Doyle brought it down at first light. He thought you might prefer to be miserable in privacy.'

Delighted with the surprise, she worked the latch up and down.

'If you pull the string to the inside, it's like locking it,' he told her, and demonstrated.

'Like the pioneers used to do,' and she grinned as she experimented, pulling the latch-string in and out.

Pete gave her a gentle push inward. 'Get some rest now. And I'll be back for you.' He shut the door and she pulled the string in again.

'Thanks, Pete,' she called and heard his cheerful 'No problemo' and then the whispering sound of the air cushion driving off.

Someone had also tidied up the bedding and increased the fluff content of the mattress. Kris blessed whoever had done her that service. She nudged one of the stools across the flagstone floor with her feet, knocked it over and kicked it into place by the bed, uprighted it, placed the bottle on it within handy reach, and sat down on the bed to take off her boots. She wouldn't sleep, she knew that, but she took a pull on the bottle before she lay down.

A determined knocking and someone calling her name roused her and she sat up, knocking her arm painfully.

'I'm coming, I'm coming,' she called, discovering it's not as easy to get to one's feet with an arm in a sling. When she opened the door, Pete Easley was leaning on the frame, smiling broadly.

'You did sleep and you look one hundred per cent better,' he said, but he took out of his pocket a comb, one of those carved out of loo-cow bones, and ran it through her hair. 'That's even better. C'mon. We've just time to get to the hangar before they make the Bubble.'

When they entered the KDL's bridge, it was crowded with an avid audience, but Scott made peremptory gestures for her to be let through and then installed her in one of the seats.

'You'll be interested to know', Beverly was saying from Baby's piloting compartment, 'that the Bubble does not register on any detection equipment. But it's visible . . . as you can see.'

Which they did, as from Baby's perspective. They could also see the scoutship on the KDL's screen, with its nose a scant ten metres from the barrier.

'We will poke it,' Zainal's voice said, and Baby drifted into the opacity of the Bubble and bounced slowly backwards.

'Here, let me adjust the screen a bit so they can see what the warship left behind,' said Marrucci, laughter rippling through his voice.

'We'll need a touch of reverse for a proper view,' and that was in Laughrey's amused baritone. He chuckled openly as the view-screen of Baby slowly swung to starboard and then equally slowly reversed.

'See what we mean?' Bert Put asked, and Kris could just imagine the grin on the Aussie's face. 'Lost every array they had, and every mast they had.'

'Outlined for ever in Bubble,' said Balenquah. 'Madre de Dios, the Farmers make some clever stuff!'

'Can you make any analysis of it?' Scott asked.

'Can't if sensors can't pick up anything,' Bert Put said. 'Not unless we go out and see if we can cut a patch of it.'

'No,' said Zainal. 'If you wish, someone will go outside, but we will not take sample.'

'Affirmative to defacing it, Zainal,' Scott said. 'But I'd like an EVA inspection of it.'

'I go,' Zainal said, and immediately there was protest from both Baby and KDL observers.

Kris discovered her left hand on her lips, to keep from adding her protest. Then she conquered her fear.

'He's the one to go, Ray,' she said firmly. 'He knows the gear and the ship. No-one else has checked out for a spacewalk, have they?'

'I have,' said Bert Put, 'but not with this equipment. Zainal'll be just fine, Kris. He's already suiting up.'

Zainal's EVA suit also had its own camera so, after a nervous wait, the view was transferred to his helmet eye and they saw the shimmering veil of the Bubble as he slowly approached it. They could see his hands reaching out to prod it gently, and the reaction of even that light touch as he floated away from it.

'Can you put your helmet on it, Zainal?' Scott asked, receiving a note from the engineers watching the spacewalk.

Slowly the Bubble filled the camera screen and was placed right up against the material. Nothing of the black space beyond could be seen through the fabric, and it was smooth.

'Like a balloon's skin,' Kris murmured under her breath.

'That's how I'd describe it,' Scott agreed.

Then Zainal pulled back. 'There are no flaws, even around the debris from the warship.'

'Could you make it to that spot?' Scott asked.

'He's at the end of the tether right now, Ray,'

Beverly said. 'We've got all the photographic material you need for examination of that flotsam. No need to risk Zainal for it.'

'Agreed,' Scott said indifferently. 'Thank you for your effort, Zainal.'

'No problemo,' said Zainal's deep voice as his helmet turned and took in Baby's bow and the windows into the pilot's compartment.

Kris's mouth went dry. He was a long way from the ship, even if he was slowly returning to it. Feeling someone's hand close reassuringly on her shoulder, she glanced up at Pete Easley. She gave a sigh and controlled the flutter in her stomach. The break began to throb again, but she decided to ignore it: the pain wasn't there, she had no time for it.

Then Zainal was back inside the scout and his camera turned off. She breathed a sigh of relief, oddly echoed around the crowded bridge. Which, she realized, was just a bit too crowded for her and she rose from her seat, glancing appealingly at Pete.

'Thanks, Admiral,' she said, nodding to the others she knew out of those on the bridge.

A way parted for her as Easley conducted her off the bridge and then off the KDL. Her knees were near to buckling as she stepped down the ladder, hanging on with her left hand. And her arm ached despite her efforts to make it stop.

'There're sandwiches and tea,' Pete said, showing where a trestle table was burdened with lunch items. 'And I know where they keep the hangar's hooch,' he added.

'This isn't like me,' she protested, peevish again.

'No, it isn't,' Pete said equably. 'But you're allowed. Sit. I'll be right back.'

He doctored a cup of tea and brought more sandwiches than she thought was fair, but she polished off two and had two cups of hooched-up tea. The ache in her bones subsided.

'D'you want to go back in and see the next show?' Easley asked.

He was really being very nice, Kris thought, but she shook her head.

'Then I'll take you back to the cabin,' and he cupped her left elbow, though he'd parked the runabout very close to where they'd been sitting.

He was really quite a nice guy, she thought, wondering who'd snap him up as the father of a child, or children. He was a good head taller than she was, and rather more athletic than you'd think with that pose of indolence he usually affected. Not bad-looking, either, though nothing as toy-boy handsome as Dick Aarens was. Or Yuri, with his Slavic cheekbones and snapping black eyes. Neither of them was a patch on Zainal though.

The comunit buzzed and Pete answered it. 'Oh, you have? That's great. I'm taking Kris home. She needs to rest. Okay? Fine. See you. No, they don't know what the Bubble's made of . . . except it's the biggest damned balloon ever made. Over.'

'Yeah,' and she giggled, 'it is the biggest damned balloon ever made, and we don't know who blew it up.'

Pete grinned at her and she knew she was

acting silly, but it was better than being peevish.

'I love that door,' she said as the runabout stopped in front of it. 'It's the best front door I've ever seen. Zainal will be so pleased. Say, how much hooch did you pour in my tea?'

'Only enough to stop the ache in your arm. It *has* stopped, hasn't it?'

She looked down at the clumsy white extrusion. 'You know, it has.'

Pete swung the door inward and she had taken the first step before she realized that the inside was different.

'My God, what's been happening with my back turned?' she demanded, swaying a bit as she turned towards Pete.

He took her good arm and led her inside. 'Well, we were going to wait with the shivaree until Zainal could be here, too, but with you *hors de combat*, as it were, Sandy, Lenny, Ninety, Chuck, Sarah, Whitby and Leila thought maybe now would be the right time to bring the stuff in.'

'Stuff?' She blinked, trying to focus on first the table, with six glasses almost symmetrical in manufacture, and a pottery set – which looked like Sandy's best designs – two pots, one large, one small, and a cast-iron skillet. There were benches around the table, and at one end a chair big enough to fit Zainal. She put her hand to her mouth in surprise. But when her startled gaze flicked past the opening to the smaller room and saw the wooden bedstead with carved posts and the huge puffy fluff mattress that covered it, she burst into tears.

'Now, now, Kris,' Pete said in consternation and, pulling her against him, began to stroke her soothingly, saying a lot of things that she didn't really hear because the generosity of her friends and the team was so overwhelming.

Then he was holding one of the glasses to her lips and urging her to drink. She did, because she hated to be such a baby when everyone was being so nice to her. And then her knees seemed to give way and Pete picked her up – as easily as Zainal could – and deposited her on the bed, arranging the pillows behind her and urging her to finish the drink.

'The bed – it's so marvellous. . .and they all know I've wanted a really, really, truly thick mattress . . .' and she clung more firmly to Pete, as the only steady thing in a rapidly whirling world.

She felt arms around her and, out of habit and forgetting that Zainal was off in space, she put her face up to be kissed. And it was. And so were her cheeks, and her neck, just where she liked it, and she was kissing the masculine face, slightly stubbled, which surprised her because Zainal didn't grow a beard but she needed comfort right now, and the kisses were very nice indeed, and she couldn't resist returning them . . . nor protest, even with her right arm feeling so heavy and not quite hers, when the coverall was slipped off and she felt the warm skin next to hers. This was all somehow inevitable and, in the end, quite enjoyable.

★   ★   ★

Kris woke up with a terrible hangover and discovered – the hard way, by accidentally banging her right arm as she tried to sit up – that it was still in a splint, though the throbbing was muted. The struggle just to sit only made her head worse.

She remembered being on the KDL's bridge, and coming back and seeing all the lovely gifts and crying, and sitting down on the bed and Pete Easley . . . She sat bolt upright, collapsing almost immediately with the headache and trying to remember more.

And she'd enjoyed it far more than she should have. In fact, she could almost – not quite but almost – regret that her scruples required her to honour the bond that had grown between herself and Zainal as if it were a legal one. And that meant no jumping in the sack with anyone. Well, there were extenuating circumstances involved last night that would never recur. Furthermore she'd keep far away from any of that 'medicinal', inhibition-destroying alcohol. As much because of the headache she had as to what it did to her self-control.

Well, she thought philosophically and chuckled. At least I remember enjoying it. Then she sighed. She hoped their next meeting wouldn't be awkward. Or that she'd have to explain to Pete that last night was it! She wasn't about to two-time Zainal. Even with someone as good in bed as Pete Easley. Some girl was going to be very lucky! She made another injudicious movement and thought longingly of a cool compress on her forehead and maybe the back of her neck.

Maybe a hair of the dog? She pushed back the blankets, and noticed that Pete had neatly laid her coverall on the stool in easy reach, her boots beside it.

Yes, the bottle of medicinal spirits was on the table, and the glass he poured for her, with a good inch in it. Had he had some before he left? Whenever he had left, and she did briefly worry that his departure might have been noticed. Well, if it had, it had. She lifted the glass and knocked it back, shuddering at the taste. It was remarkable she'd been able to drink any of it.

She made a slow way to the hearth and, holding her head very still, lowered herself, spine-straight, to light the fire laid there. Another considerate touch by Mr Easley. And the kettle was full of water.

One of these days, they'd have water piped in to houses, but that was in the future . . .

She went back to the table to inspect the gifts she remembered vaguely having seen earlier, now sunlight came from the small side window above the bed. Its slightly wavy glass sent a prism of rainbow light onto the table. Then she realized how the sun was shining in, from the east. For they had faced the cabin south! Good Lord! She'd slept the rest of yesterday and an entire Botany night? No wonder her arm didn't ache as much.

The headache had begun to ease off by the time the kettle had boiled. She took herbs from the little pot on the mantel and made a cup which she took to Zainal's chair to drink. It was a comfortable chair, and her butt eased into the contours. It'd need a cushion or two . . . no, she couldn't see Zainal sitting on a cushion but the wood, when she felt it with her left hand, had been rubbed smooth, smelling only vaguely of the vegetable oil that had been used to give it lustre. She wondered who had made it.

Then she absorbed the construction of the table – a three-inch slab of the slate which was quarried nearby, set on sturdy, slightly tapering rounds of lodge-pole trees, with notches which spiked through the slate at the corners, keeping the top firmly in place.

There was a tentative knock on the door.

'Coming,' she called and saw that the latch-string was inside. So she must have come to long enough to do that when Pete left. She opened the door to Mavis Belton from the hospital, a clean coverall in her hand.

'Oh, do come in,' said Kris. 'Kettle's just boiled. I was having a cup to get over my hangover.'

'How's the arm?' asked Mavis, with a grin.

'Not as bad as yesterday, that's for sure. Come in, come in.'

Mavis did, but only after a careful look into the main room of the cabin. Then she saw the furnishings and exclaimed with surprise, running her finger over the surface of the slate slab and admiring the sturdy lodge-pole legs that held up such a weight.

'Not something you could tip over easily,' she remarked, stroking the chest and then Zainal's chair. 'Big enough even for him, I'd say.'

'He'll be delighted with it. He looks so uncomfortable on stools, with his legs sticking up like

Arnie Schwarzenegger on a kindergarten chair. Here's your tea, and I'll just steal Zainal's chair. I can rest the splint on the arm.'

'I just ended my shift, but I thought you'd like to hear that Baby's doing fine in her orbitals.'

'I saw them reach the Bubble, and Zainal's space-walk,' Kris said. 'That was before Pete Easley plied me with so much liquor I must have passed out.'

'I think we're going to have to alter the recipe. That particular distillation is double potency. I told Leon and Mayock they'd better cut it more.'

'They should,' Kris agreed, rubbing the back of her neck. 'My hangover's hung-over for fair.'

'Sit out in the sun; it's a lovely day.' Mavis rose. 'May I look around? Inside and out?'

'Sure, but watch that pile of shakes on the way to the latrine, will you?'

By dinnertime, when Mitford came by in the runabout to take her down to the mess hall, Kris had completely recovered. But she took him to task and demanded to know who had done the furniture she'd found in the cabin on her return from the hangar.

'Whose idea was that table? Not even Zainal could tip it over – and how'd you get it down here?' she asked.

'We were going to do it while you and Zainal were gone, surprise you on your return,' Chuck Mitford said with a sly grin at her. 'But with you on the sick list, seemed a good idea to put up the bed . . . and then what was a bed without a table and the chairs!'

'Well, it was very, very much appreciated. Especially that thick mattress on that wide bed! Drunk as I was, I appreciated that!' Then she caught Mitford's odd expression. 'Oh yes, Pete Easley got me high as a kite just in case you hear rumours that I was drunk. I *was*. I slept through an entire Botany night without so much as moving. Mavis came by this morning and said they were going to cut the last batch. I said they'd better . . . it was damned near lethal. Who made the bed?'

'Oh, the Doyles and me. I cut the timber, and Lenny did the posts and showed me how to make the joints and stuff. He and Ninety did the table and the chair. Said it was the least they could do for the guy who kept them from becoming frozen steaks in a Farmers' freezer. Joe and Sarah did the mattress and pillows; Sandy Areson the pottery and glass-ware, of course; Whitby the benches. Coo traded for the pots and the skillet. No big deal.'

'No big deal?' she exclaimed, and a faint reminder of her hangover made her head ring with the loud-ness of her voice. 'You furnish our cabin and it's no big deal. It's a real big deal to me,' and she leaned over and kissed the sergeant on the cheek before she knew she was doing it. 'There! And don't blush like that, Chuck Mitford. I do appreciate what you all did and, besides, no-one saw me kiss you.'

She giggled when the sergeant lifted one hand halfway to his cheek and then dropped it quickly back to his lap. He was still red-faced.

'You finished your cabin first, so you'll have a chance to help others furnish theirs when they're built,' he said in a gruff voice. 'By the way, stood a tour on the KDL, and the mission's going a-okay. Not a wrinkle on the balloon as far as they've gone. Seamless. All the tech heads are scratching their arses over what was used.'

'What's the general feeling? Or is it too far away to bother the claustrophobics?' she asked, trying not to resent her absence . . . and Zainal's.

'I think people are glad. The Deskis evidently had a wild night of dancing, singing . . . if you can call that warble singing . . . and Coo says there are giants protecting us.'

'Did he see the Eosi?'

'No,' and Mitford shook his head. 'And frankly, I'm just as glad I didn't. Worry's still having nightmares, and I think that's why Leon made the latest hooch so strong. Hoooo-eee!' He let out a long whistle. 'You can blame them for getting you drunk, not Pete Easley. Which reminds me. Officially you're on sick leave, Bjornsen, so don't get any ideas about doing anything with that busted wing until Leon gives you the okay. Got me?'

'Yes sir, sergeant, sir,' she said, saluting repeatedly with her left hand.

The makers and donors of the furniture were saving spaces for them at a table in the mess hall. Kris lavished praise and gratitude on all for making a cabin into a real home, promising to do as well by them, when their cabins were up. Then the conversation devolved to Baby's mission and Mitford, sipping what he assured Kris was a well-watered jolt of hooch, brought them up to speed.

The monitor also tracked the small vessel in its exploration, especially the examination at the barrier, and followed its progress until it landed safely again on the western continent.

Chapter Ten

Baby returned safely and with sufficient masses of information to keep all the brass-heads, engineers, miners and Aggies busy. The mission crew took a longer time to get themselves back down to the surface, they were so high on the experience. Zainal's course had used a minimum of fuel and won the plaudits of the aviators and astronauts. Everyone on board had had instruction from him on how to fly Baby and a little chance at manoeuvring.

'We may not have flight simulators, but what're they against the real thing?' Balenquah demanded. 'Too damned bad we can't go anywhere in the KDL. Zainal says it's much easier to pilot – had to be since Drassis flew that series. That whole caper of capturing the KDL was a waste of time.'

'No,' said Bert Put, evidently rather fed up with Balenquah's opinions, 'it got us extra fuel, a new bridge console and a lot of tools we'd have a hard time duplicating.'

'Oh, yeah, forgot about them,' Balenquah replied. 'Well, if we have to shift population, it'll be handy enough.'

'There'll be flying in the KDL,' Marrucci said,

'maybe only mine and grain runs, but we're not totally grounded, you know.'

'We are for any *real* space work,' the man went on, talking himself into a morose state.

Zainal rose then, muttered something about having to see the admiral and took Kris from the table. Glancing back just as she and Zainal left the mess hall, she saw that others were departing from the table, leaving Balenquah on his own.

Zainal had been gobsmacked, as Lenny Doyle would say, when Kris – who had kept quiet about the surprise until he got into their cabin – saw the gifts. The door – which he admired even before he opened it, with Kris barely able to contain her excitement at what lay beyond it – had required his attention, admiring the detail, the latch-string, which gave him great amusement pulling it in and out.

Then he entered the room and saw the table and the chair, the pottery and glasses which Kris had put on the mantel, having no other place to store things – yet. Lenny had promised to teach her how to do mortise-and-tenon joints in wood and make herself proper chests and drawers. But the table and the chair shocked him, and with one knee raised for the next step, he stared and stared and then inarticulately tried to ask her who, how, where these things had come from.

As she replied, interspersing the explanation with giggles for the surprise yet in store for him, he examined everything, even to trying to lift the slate-topped table. He sat in the chair, got up, turned it upside down to see how the legs had been fitted in, and the stringers, and then righted it to sit in it again, stroking the arm-rests with his big hands.

Maybe Catteni didn't have tear ducts, or never cried, but Zainal's eyes were certainly full of fluid and, though he tried to speak, he kept shaking his head, speechless.

'I've saved the best for last,' she told him and, taking a hand that was attached to a body reluctant to leave the chair made to fit him, she led him to where he couldn't miss the bed.

He had an immediate response to that: the very devil of a look in his full eyes as he swooped her up into his arms and carried her, for all the world the way John Wayne had treated Maureen O'Hara in *The Quiet Man*, and demonstrated how much better he could perform on a resilient surface.

Mitford took her off the sick-list when he wanted their team to find a pass through the western hills to the far shore; he let her go along. He knew very well that she'd be better employed marking klicks, which she could do with her left hand, than left at Retreat fretting that she was useless.

While that was being organized, she spent some time making bricks since she could fill the moulds left-handed. She owed Sarah and Joe for their hand in the 'Great Furniture Surprise'. When some loggers were injured – two badly – she sat in the ward with them, checking pulse and temperature; there were no blood-pressure devices and no thermometers, so it was all hands-on. She also fed Boris Slavinkovin, who had broken both arms and most of his ribs when the rolling log had gone over his body for a short-cut. Being fed by a one-handed aide didn't embarrass him half as much, he told her, because it didn't tie up a whole human who could do other jobs than feeding him. Then he asked her if she could teach him better English, since he was now stuck in bed and had to do something.

Ex-teachers had got together with an ex-cartoonist and created a language primer for those who wished to learn English. There were fifty copies in print, thanks to supplies on the KDL, and they were well-worn by the time Kris snagged a copy for Boris.

Leon and Mayock managed to dilute the potency of their distillations so that it not only had the faint aftertaste of a Botany nut variety, but did not cause such speedy and legless inebriation.

The only person whose metabolism could cope with the previous grain whisky was Zainal so, rather than water down what was left (which Leon felt was a crime), the remaining keg was given to him. The first time he sampled it, Kris told him about Pete Easley getting her drunk on barely two half-glasses of it, and the hangover she'd had the next day. That reminded her that she hadn't seen as much of Pete as usual. But she thought nothing of it, going to her stints at the hospital or the brick factory.

Then they were ready to leave on their exploratory mission, and it was a great relief to all the team to be back together again and out on their own.

'One can get too accustomed to the comforts of home,' Sarah announced, settling back in her seat on the big air-cushion truck. 'Though I wish we could have started the cabin before we left. And thanks again, Kris, for all those bricks. Worry's put his name in for a hundred, and so did Jay Greene. We should have enough by the time we get back.'

'We do appreciate the ones you did for us, too,' said Leila in her often inaudible voice. She was holding hands with Whitby, while hanging on to a strap with the other.

Leila looked a bit white, Kris thought, and wondered if she too was pregnant. Sarah was, and very cocky about it, taking it in her stride like any modern woman.

'Sure thing, Leila. Kept me out of mischief,' said Kris.

And actually, kept mischief away from her, for any of the importunate men who tried to charm her found themselves also making bricks, if that's where they caught up with her, or feeding a bed-bound patient, which was scarcely a romantic setting for the sort of offers they hoped to make.

Boris Slavinkovin put in his bid and she had to threaten him with her absence at mealtimes if he kept it up.

'You'll have to some time, you know,' Sarah said bluntly.

'Oh, I will, I will,' Kris said airily, and did not meet Zainal's eye when he glanced at her beside him. 'Ah, that's another klick, isn't it? We've gone one thousand plegs again.' She added a slash to her sheet.

They found a way through the hills, through twisting but connecting ravines, separated by banks which the air cushion could manage easily. They marked the more accessible routes with 0s in the blue, almost luminous paint that was a recent innovation. (Red and yellow had already been produced from local vegetable dyes.) The culs-de-sac were marked with an X. For some reason, Zainal found the procedure very amusing but wouldn't tell her why. They did not find any blind valleys or night-crawlers, but they did find a new variety of rocksquat and some avians that were almost as good eating as chickens, though some caught closer to the sea left a fishy aftertaste in the mouth.

They made their way down the coast until the rocky terrain was impassable even for the remarkably manoeuvrable vehicle. They were headed back up the eastern coast two weeks later when Kris experienced some fleeting nausea first thing in the morning. For a couple of days she was sure it was caused by the ripe soft fruits that flourished in the almost tropical weather this far south, and she ignored the minor discomfort until one morning when Joe was replacing the splints and bandages on her arm. The bandage material came from the legs and arms of Catteni coveralls, cut in strips, softened slightly by much washing and use and adequate for their purpose. Her arm was sweating so much in the heat that she was glad to change the wrappings with the extra roll of bandage that Joe had in his medical kit.

'Arm's healing well,' he said, feeling the breaks with careful fingers. 'I can feel the thickening of the bones where they've knitted.'

'Doesn't hurt any more either,' she told him, though she sighed as he replaced splints and bandage strips.

He gave her an odd sideways glance. 'Trip's done you good. You were looking a little off-colour before we left.'

'Which reminds me? Anyone else having trouble digesting that pink-fleshed fruit we had last night?' she asked.

Joe was not only medic but botanist.

'No, but we didn't gorge on it either. Why? Got the runs?'

'No, a touch of indigestion, I guess,' and she shrugged it off, but Sarah had overheard her query and joined them, peering into her face with an intensely disturbing grin on her face. 'So?' Kris demanded when Sarah didn't explain.

'Breasts hurt? Had your period? How long have you noticed the nausea?'

Defensively, Kris crossed her arms over her breasts, and as if Sarah's comment had been a curse they were tender. She didn't dare change the position of her arms as her mind raced to the conclusion Sarah had obviously just reached.

'I can't be pregnant,' she said, jerking her chin up. 'I've never . . .'

'Never what?' asked Sarah with a sly expression on her face.

Kris closed her eyes, remembering the potent hooch she'd had for her arm, remembering Pete Easley offering her more, and more, and enough so that she had . . .

'I'll kill him,' she said, meaning it fervently. No wonder he had kept out of her way. Just wait till she got back to Retreat. She'd . . .

'Is something wrong with Kris's arm?' Zainal asked, and Kris wanted to seep into the ground like a night-crawler.

'Nothing, nothing's wrong with my arm,' and she shot to her feet, glaring at Sarah and Joe.

'No, but she's pregnant,' Sarah said gleefully.

Kris hauled back her left arm to punch Sarah, but Zainal caught her around the waist.

'You had to go blab it!' she shouted, trying to reach Sarah who had nimbly danced out of her way, with the grinning Joe moving into position to protect his mate, with hands out in a placatory move.

'Now, Kris, don't go off half-cocked,' he said as Leila and Whitby came running over to see what could possibly have happened.

'Kris is preggers, too!' Sarah crowed.

Then Zainal was holding her so tightly to his chest, leaving her feet dangling above the ground, that she had to hang on to him for balance.

'Thank you, Kris,' he murmured into her ear and all the fight went out of her. She hung limply against him as his arms around her assumed a kinder hold, a loving one. There couldn't be many males on any world who would thank a woman who got pregnant by another man.

'You're welcome, I think,' she added and squirmed to be released. When he put her back on her feet, she apologized to Sarah and Joe with as good a grace as she could manage. 'I wanted to be sure,' she said mendaciously. 'It could have just been the ripe fruit.'

'So, tell us who the lucky guy was?' Joe asked with the familiarity of an old friend.

Kris chuckled, deciding on an entirely different course of action which meant she couldn't publicly go after one sweet-talking Lothario of a Peter Easley, but neither would she confirm it to him or anyone . . . unless of course the newborn gave some clue to its paternity. That would serve that . . . so-and-so right. Taking advantage of a girl in her condition . . . and yet . . . she suppressed any recollection of what she hadn't been able to remember of an incident that would result in a lasting and visible proof.

'That's for me to know, and you to guess,' she said, delighted to be able to pay Sarah back for blurting out what Kris would rather have kept secret.

The long trek up the eastern coast went well, all other events considered, and everyone settled down to the fact of her pregnancy. At night Zainal held her against him with a tenderness she certainly had not expected of him: enough to make her eyes water and wish, with all her heart, that she might have transcended the barriers of biology and been pregnant by him.

By the time they got back to Retreat Bay, she had never felt better in her life. She had to see Leon about her arm and he was very pleased with its progress, but wanted her to keep the splints on anyway, since she insisted on working, though she could use her right hand now. He also confirmed her pregnancy and had the grace not to enquire further.

'Actually, you're lucky you're here on Botany. Doesn't take as long,' Leon said with a wry grin.

'What do you mean? It doesn't take as long?'

'Average pregnancy is 260–280 days. But it'll only take you 212.8 Botanical days to gestate.' When she blinked in confusion at him, he grinned and added, 'Thirty-hour days don't change the development rate of a foetus, but it sure alters the *days* you stay pregnant.'

'Oh!'

'Most of my o.b. patients find that comforting.'

'I'll remember that.'

Word of her pregnancy got around, and she could find additional comfort in the fact that her 'admirers' went elsewhere with their persuasions. And when she saw Pete Easley across the crowded mess hall one evening, she merely gave him a cheerful wave and left him wondering. She did like the man. He'd been drinking, too. Maybe she was assigning his solicitude that day to exterior motives because he'd been drinking as much of that hooch as she had. How could she fault him for getting drunk and doing what was natural enough? Pregnancy was also mellowing her.

The temperature was definitely warming up and bushes were blossoming, spreading a heady smell that the inland breeze wafted down to the Bay area. The agricultural teams had ploughed during their absence, and sowed the fields with seed purloined from the now deserted Bella Vista camp in a special trip of the KDL. As no ship had come to collect what was left of the grain, the KDL did, for the supplies brought across the channel were low.

The silos were swept clean for this year's storage.

On the continent that had been evacuated, the machines had been ploughing, too, and many of the fields were sown. Some wit among the Aggies set up a competition, one-sided though it was, as to the growth and health of their crops versus the Farmers' and the resultant yield per acre. The Aggies had already elected to use fields the same size the Farmers had, since the arable land seemed to divide into such sections: another clue that this continent might once have been farmed too. The rustled loo-cows grazed the less desirable fields and the hillsides.

About the time the crops were a good six inches high and thriving, a most unpleasant discovery was made: there were night-crawlers again. Not many, but enough to know that there was a resurgence of the menace.

Astrid put forward the theory that it was the loo-cows, excreting internal parasites that had a second cycle as night-crawlers. There were enough to agree with her, but it made for an interesting argument in the evenings and had those with wooden floors in their huts replacing them with thick slate or flagstones. And many of those who had not sited their dwellings moved nearer the better-travelled areas. No-one walked out at night on any field, and the sentinel positions were either made of stone or set high above the ground on stilts.

This was, however, a very minor setback. Compost heaps were hastily shifted to stone tubs, and the disposal of noxious wastes was no longer a problem. Not that anyone wanted night-crawlers in a latrine. Since such facilities no longer had to be dug, it became a punishment chore to do the late evening dumps, far enough from the rapidly expanding community to reduce the hazard of night-crawler infestation to the populated areas.

Spring lasted months, but the fine weather assured the Aggies of excellent crops, as good as or even better than what the Farmers were cultivating. The varieties of tubers and pulses occupied half as many fields as the grain crops, and caves were found to store the harvests rather than having to search ever further afield for the edibles. The night-crawlers were not attracted to vegetable matter unless it was mixed with bloody substances, so these crops were not disturbed. The rocksquat compound flourished, and it was discovered that baby rocksquats were far more delicate in flavour and meat than the adults.

Evening classes in various skills were given, although the nights when Admiral Ray Scott threw his first successful pot, or Bull Fetterman completed a set of six dining-chairs, and Marrucci managed a creditable mortise-and-tenon drawer for his chest, remained landmarks in the assimilation of the disparate ex-professionals into true Botanicals.

There were failures, as Mitford put it: people who refused to do their share of work, or felt themselves put upon by 'authority' to always having to do the less glamorous tasks. Judge Bempechat gave each offender three chances to redeem himself or herself in the eyes of the community. Then the unrepentant had a one-way trip back to the Old Continent where they could fend for themselves, with cup, blanket, knife and hatchet. After the expulsion of the first dozen or so, delinquency reduced significantly.

Once a month, the two valley prisons were visited. The Turs disappeared one by one until the valley was empty. The Catteni eventually put up shelters and, when they asked for supplies – like nails, or meat as a change from a fish diet – these were provided. But nothing that could give them any assistance in escaping, though Zainal doubted they would try.

'They are Drassi and Tudo. They have enough to eat, a place to sleep, and that is sufficient.'

'I can't imagine anyone not wanting to better conditions,' Marrucci had said, for he was often in the pilot's seat in one of the two small airships that did the run. 'I mean, when you consider we're damned near city size with our own distillery . . .' He was hoping to add wine to the spirits and had already been south for the soft fruits as a basis for his 'cordial'.

'They like it the way they have it now,' and Zainal shrugged.

'D'you think the Turs did escape?' Marrucci asked.

'Who cares?'

'You gotta point there.'

The Tub went regularly to the mines with supplies for the men and women working there, to rotate personnel and bring back ore. The judge often gave a month's sentence at hard labour for misdemeanors, and only one ever found mining an enjoyable occupation; he stayed on.

For evening entertainment, those with any talent provided shows, managing to remember enough of a musical comedy or even a play to put on abridged versions or invent dialogue and action to add to what they remembered. Decks of cards were manufactured from the heavy wrappings on stores in the KDL and Baby. The cards didn't shuffle well, but that didn't keep the players from betting an hour's work or a special bit of scrimshaw to make it interesting.

Gold had been found but it was decided – not without heated debate – that barter made a better system for a small community like theirs where everyone was expected to work community-hours, not pay to get out of the labour. Among the diverse trades of the colonists there were several jewellers. They would contract to produce jewellery for those who found gold, and even a few gemstones, and decided among themselves what was fair payment in grams of the metal.

Iri Bempechat had taken on several assistants as legal advisers in disputes, most of which could be settled by compromise. However, the ex-military personnel formed a lower court, but their decisions could be appealed, leaving Judge Bempechat to give the final verdict on an issue.

'We don't need a formal government,' Beverly had said one evening when the topic came up again in a mess hall that was more crowded than usual due to an unusually heavy and long fall of rain. (It was the beginning of many such rainfalls which limited themselves to night-times.) 'Why complicate what has been working rather smoothly?'

'If it ain't broke, don't fix it,' Mitford called out, and got a good laugh out of the old army axiom.

'We have a form of government, actually, though most of you don't realize it. We just don't have elected officials or a nominal head of state. Nor do I believe one is required,' said Iri, his cultivated and mellifluous voice reaching to the furthest corners. 'Those of us with special expertise have taken on the duties required to ensure peace and tranquillity.

Community hours handle public services, such as they are, and the rest of us work where we can be useful and at our previous professions for the most part, even in the limited fashion due to the constraints of supplies. I suppose we should thank our lucky stars that we have so many skills among us. Practically every walk of life is represented. Our alien associates,' and he gestured to the Rugarians sitting in their usual group, and the Deskis who were more apt to mix in with humans, 'have supplemented us in many ingenious ways. I think some of us may have a chuckle, comparing what we used to do with what we're doing now, but frankly, I think it's been beneficial as well as instructive. We're all doing very well indeed. And able, for the most part, to do what we do the way we want to. Certainly without any bureaucratic interference, and certainly without a thread of red tape. You don't know how happy that makes me!'

Good-natured chuckles greeted that sally.

'Why indeed should we fix something that isn't broken?' he added, raising his hands in appeal.

'Yeah, but what happens to our pleasant Utopian dream when the Farmers come?' Balenquah asked, glancing around.

'Leave it to Balenquah,' an anonymous male voice said.

'What does *that* mean?' the pilot asked, rising from his chair and staring round, trying to discover the source.

'It means,' Marrucci said, reaching across the table and hauling Balenquah down, 'you're out of order, off course, and being a pain in the arse again. You're alive, you're sure kicking, you're even flying, and if that isn't better than starving in a Catteni prison for blowing up their freighter, you're gone in the head.'

'Don't say another word,' Beverly put in from a nearby table, 'if you want to fly again.'

'That's just what I mean,' Balenquah complained. 'We need a formal government, so you know who's got the right to give orders.'

'That's enough out of you, Balenquah,' said Scott, seconding Beverly's admonition.

'You're not an admiral of anything here, Scott,' Balenquah said.

'Oh, boorrring,' drawled one of the 'ladies' from two tables over. And she yawned ostentatiously, which made the others at her table howl with laughter.

'You are, you know,' said Marrucci, shaking his head at Balenquah, who had coloured with such open ridicule, 'a real bore with all this gloom and doom and I'm obviously', now he turned to look at the 'ladies' table', 'not the only one who thinks so.'

Balenquah rose, with his right arm cocked but, even before Marrucci could rise to defend himself, Scott had nodded to the man beside him and they had risen, captured Balenquah's arm and were hustling him out of the mess hall and into the rain.

'Add bouncer to my list of new-world occupations,' Scott said to Beverly as the two returned to their seats.

At their table, Kris found herself sharing a bit of

310

Balenquah's pessimism. The problem of the Farmers *was* just beneath the surface of everyone's thoughts, despite the way most people carried on as if there were not that threat hanging over them. Zainal kept insisting that the Farmers were benign. He could give no other reason for that, other than the way this planet had been tended for thousands of years, if the 'new forest' of lodge-pole trees was an indication.

'And it has been months since the Balloon was blown up,' he reminded her as they walked back to their cabin when the rain had stopped. Flagstone pathways had been laid around much of Retreat Bay now, to hinder night-crawlers, although walkers automatically stamped hard every third step.

Kris let Zainal do it for them both as she didn't like jarring the baby she could now feel move, in little flutters, within her: normal activity at five months. Sarah kept complaining that her little dear kicked like a soccer star, but she was eight months along. By now, almost every female of child-bearing age, including the Deski and Rugarians, was expecting – which meant that Retreat Bay would have a baby boom of 2,103 new souls. Anna Bollinger might have given birth to the first human baby on Botany, but there had since been thirty-four born to women who had been captured pregnant. Now the new crop – which had been ploughed on Botany, as someone had remarked in a biblical fashion – were reaching full term. Patti Sue was first, and prideful about producing a son for Jay Greene.

Kris didn't know which she wanted, apart from

being healthy and not too much resembling its sire. Somehow she couldn't ask Zainal what his preference would be. And yet, he would act *in loco parentis* to whatever she produced.

Most of the pregnant women carried on in their speciality as long as possible: and Kris, Sarah and Leila were no exceptions. In fact they had arguments with the sergeant that he was assigning the team the 'easy' trips. So he organized Zainal to take Baby to the smallest continent – really more of a very large island than a continental land-mass – to circumnavigate it, the coastline being the only part that was green.

'Bit like Australian outback,' Sarah remarked as Zainal guided Baby criss-cross the interior. 'Like Nullarbor. Nothing for klicks! Not even mulga or brush . . . sand and rock,' she added in disgust.

'Hmmm, yes, I see,' Joe said, without explaining his cryptic remark as he gazed out the starboard side in the pilot's compartment. 'Real rock!' He pointed now to a rocky ridge that ran obliquely across below them, like vertebrae, with dips and spires. 'Dinosaur bones.'

'Hmmm, that's what they do look like,' Kris agreed.

Whitby insisted that they land and spend one night at the base of that range, where the spatial maps indicated one of the ore deposits.

'We should know where copper and zinc are, and that's what's down there. If the lodes are near the surface, it might be advantageous to take a week or so to work up a cargo.'

So they landed, and it was hot.

'Just like home in the dry,' Sarah said ecstatically, throwing her arms back, with her gravid belly out and turning her face up to the sun.

'Good way to get sunstroke,' Joe said as he slammed her reed-weave hat on her head. 'We are not, I repeat, we are *not* delivering you prematurely in the confines of Baby.'

'Having a baby in the Baby?' Sarah was off in a fit of the giggles.

Whitby, Leila, Joe and Zainal went off to try and locate the ore, laden with bottles for samples and soil. Sarah and Kris, who found the heat especially enervating, found what shade they could in the lee of Baby by digging out enough soil under the landing vanes to sit on blankets. Kris dozed off while Sarah dragged her hands through the scattered rocks, trying to find interesting ones.

Sarah, too, dozed off, and they were both awakened by the laughter of the returning prospectors. Each carried some sort of dead animal, resembling a large rat.

Kris recoiled when Zainal plunked three brace beside her. The pelts caught her attention because they were mottled in soft, sandy shades.

'Camouflage? From what?' she said, venturing to touch the nearest. It was rough with dirt and sand.

'Burrowers,' Joe said succinctly, 'but they test edible. We thought we'd give them a try. They eat the insects of which this continent has a multitude. I saw twenty-five varieties and caught', he held up several bottles tied together to prevent breakage, 'only a few for closer examination. You never know what might be useful.' He grinned wickedly. 'Or tasty. And nutritious.'

'How would you know? You never hunted out back with the aborigines,' Sarah said.

'Neither did you.'

'But I did a paper on the ones the aborigines favour,' she replied hotly and they were off again.

The desert burrowers – Kris declined to think of them as 'rats' – were skinned and, after Joe did further tests with the equipment in Baby, were cooked in the galley and served as part of the evening meal. The flesh was different in texture and taste from anything else that Botany had provided: sort of nutty and sleek. Almost difficult to bite into.

Twilight brought out their natural predators, bat-like creatures who swooped on long triangular wings from rocky eyries to catch the burrowers. The cooler air encouraged a different set of insects to appear, ones that bit and itched and forced everyone to take refuge in the scoutship. But not before they saw the desert burrowers in action, making incredible leaps into the air to catch their meal on tongues that elongated to make the capture and seeming to disappear from sight the moment they heard bat-wings above them.

'We've some like that on ol' Earth,' Joe remarked, watching from the scout.

The men were in general pleased with their prospecting and had marked the areas with the blue paint, though Whitby and Joe argued about its durability in the unremitting sun.

'Well, we'll wear-test it good, then,' Joe said, shrugging. 'And we've the co-ordinates anyway.'

Zainal made for the coast in the dawn-light the next day and, keeping Baby at a low altitude, made a touchdown in those spots that looked different. This tropical area displayed fruits and nuts, not unlike citrus and coconut, and samples were gathered of everything, including a different variety of insect life. Kris found the smell of rotting vegetables and fruit unsettling, but said nothing until the reserved Leila murmured a complaint.

'There're sort of plateaus up ahead,' Whitby pointed out. 'Maybe cooler up there, with an off-shore breeze to keep the gnats and nits away.'

Kris disliked using pregnancy as an excuse to avoid any task, but she was glad enough to let the men rig a shelter of the thick fronded vegetation on a height overlooking a rather lovely white-sanded bay. (On inspection, the white sands contained particularly vicious biting insects, so the charm of the area was considerably diminished and Sarah and Kris could lounge in comfort above that nuisance). There were even smaller fronds to use as fans, and the breezes were cooling and pleasantly scented with whatever was blooming further inland.

Leila took off exploring with Whitby, but she came back with her face and bare arms blotchy with contact to plants they had had to cut their way through.

'The sap which zapped me', Leila said as Kris and Sarah washed her arms and face, 'is very sticky, and Joe is hoping we've found a rubber substitute.'

'The hard way,' said Sarah in a droll tone of voice. 'Is this helping?'

Leila gave a little sigh. 'Only as long as the wet's on me.'

'What wouldn't we give for a decent anti-histamine!' Sarah said fervently.

'We've chemists enough . . .' said Kris.

'And only the one microscope, which evidently isn't strong enough to do much, so it's back to old trial and error.'

So, since trial wet compresses helped, more were made of bandage strips in the first-aid kit and wrapped around Leila's arms and laid on her face and neck.

That was when Sarah's baby decided to arrive. In fact, he did before his father and the others returned, though Kris immediately called a mayday for Joe over the hand unit.

'I must've miscounted,' Sarah said apologetically to her midwives when she realized her labour had begun. 'This business of thirty-hour days and seven-month pregnancies!'

'Nonsense,' Kris and Leila retorted in the same breath. 'It isn't as if we don't know what to do,' Kris added, though her mind was revolving in a panic over all the things they didn't have on board the scout that might be needed.

None were, as Sarah's fine lusty baby took the minimum of time in arriving so that both mother and child were all cleaned up when the father leapt into the clearing, red-faced with exertion and badly scratched in his effort to get back in time. Then

Whitby and Zainal were congratulating him and Sarah, and admiring the baby. Kris had her eyes on Zainal, wondering if human babies were in any way different from Catteni new-borns.

'Small,' Zainal muttered, knowing some comment was needed.

'Small?' exclaimed Joe indignantly as his son squirmed in his arms in reaction to the sudden loud noise.

'He's not small at all,' Leila said emphatically, startling the rest of the team since she rarely contradicted anyone. 'He's eight pounds and a few ounces. And healthy!'

'And I feel fine,' Sarah said, 'and it's so good to do this,' she added, for she was sitting up with arms around her knees, a position she hadn't been able to assume for several months.

'How big are Catteni babies, if you think this one's small?' Kris asked, deciding she'd better straighten him out before he could be disappointed in what she produced.

Zainal measured a distance with his hands.

'I pity the females who have to carry *that* much around,' said Sarah, shaking her head.

'Bigger head, quite likely, and bigger bones,' Joe said sagely.

'He's healthy, that's what matters,' Whitby remarked in a definitive tone.

But young Anthony Marley caused the team to leave the insalubrious area and head back to Retreat Bay. Sarah tried to talk them out of an early return, because she and Anthony were fine and the reconnaissance could continue as far as she was concerned. But Joe was having none of it, wanting both wife and child checked over by the medics.

Leon Dane pronounced Sarah in excellent post-natal condition and Fawzia Johnston, the paediatrician on duty when they returned, said that young Anthony was as healthy and normal as any mother could wish. The Doyle brothers, who now spent more time as carpenters and joiners, instructing others in the art, presented Sarah and Joe with a cradle for the infant.

'Working all the hours God gave Botany to keep up with the demand,' Lenny said, after duly admiring young Anthony and congratulating the parents. 'You know, this place is getting more like home all the time, with the babies arriving.' He looked melancholy.

'You miss your own?' Sarah asked, putting a sympathetic hand on his arm.

Lenny's face brightened into a grin. 'Sort've, but who's got time to think of what we left behind with so much to do where we are?'

Chapter Eleven

Zane Charles Bjornsen arrived on Botany at dawn exactly 222 days after conception. He was a long child – in that he did resemble his father. He came with fingernails that had to be cut soon after his birth, or he'd have scratched his fair face, and a mass of very dark hair.

He was not, as Anthony Marley had been, red, wrinkled and an object only his mother could love.

'Zane is a perfectly good name,' Kris had told Zainal. 'One of my favourite Western writers was Zane Grey. And I admire Chuck Mitford.'

'But he is not the father.' Zainal did no more than raise one eyebrow at her, tacitly asking the question she had refused to answer.

'No, but I see no reason I . . . we . . . can't do him the honour of being godfather.'

'God father?' Zainal's lips twitched. 'O God, o God . . .?'

'Not that sort. The deity that Father Jacob reveres, the real God.'

'There is one?'

Zainal had trouble believing in the Almighty, though the several ministers who had been dropped were trying to establish services. The Protestants had no problems, but Father Jacob did since he had none of the accessories properly required to say Mass, and fretted about their lack and how he should manage without them.

Marrucci proved to be a devout Catholic, and did his best to console the good Father in one of those role reversals which continually happened on Botany.

'If God is everywhere, then He's here, too, padre, and He'll accept the worship of the sincere, dedicated to Him. The earliest Catholics had no altar or relics, and communion was bread and wine. We got them. We got the dedication. You say the words and I'll be altar boy.'

Mitford was both pleased and alarmed to have a child named for him. 'Everyone will think he's mine, and he isn't,' the sergeant said at his gruffest. 'Not that I wish he weren't, Kris,' he added hastily. 'I mean, I'd've been honoured if you'd wanted to, but . . . well, hell, you know what I mean.'

'Yes, I do, Chuck.'

'So who is the lucky guy?'

'Remember that hooch Leon and Mayock made, about the time I broke my arm?'

'Yeah, I do,' and Mitford looked surprised, then he scowled deeply.

'You mean you got raped and never reported it?' His fists clenched as if he held the neck of the offender within them.

Kris patted one such fist gently. 'I don't know about any rape. But I do know I was very, *very* drunk.'

Chuck frowned. 'Pete Easley took you back to your cabin, didn't he?'

'He may have, Chuck, but I don't recall a thing – and perhaps that's as well, don't you think?'

'No, I don't.'

'Can't do anything about it. But maybe when Zane grows up, we'll know for sure. Zainal couldn't care less.'

'No, he couldn't – and you know, the way he's taken this hasn't lost him any points.'

Zainal was at that moment changing his foster son's fluff diapers. The reeds which produced the useful material were being cultivated everywhere they would grow around Retreat Bay.

The sticky sap that had been such a problem on their last reconnaissance trip had been harvested and, poured into a mould, made a reasonable facsimile of waterproof garments for baby use. They could be washed and re-used four or five times but gradually dissolved, often at the wrong time.

Mitford grinned, watching the anomaly of a Catteni Emassi acting the nursemaid.

Of the 2,103 new lives expected, all but five made it: two human babies were stillborn; one of the Rugarian young lived three days and died, but even the one Rugarian who understood his species' needs could not give a reason; a fourth was unfortunately strangled by the umbilical cord during delivery, and the fifth, a Deski, was malformed when it hatched and did not survive.

*   *   *

The promised crèches were opened, and every female had the right to leave their youngling in the general care for her day's work or whatever community service she performed. Sometimes it was crèche duty. Kris started the fad of the papoose board, dredging that up from reading Westerns and historical novels about Indians. It worked well for babies up to three months, and for shorter periods after that.

'I said you will be a good mother,' Zainal said with a touch of smug pride when she showed him how she could carry Zane around.

To Kris's astonishment, she didn't find caring for Zane as onerous as she had expected, and that had little to do with Zainal's enthusiasm for the child. She had never had anything so completely dependent on her, so trusting, and so precious to her. Once or twice, she wondered if she was being unfair to Pete Easley by not telling him. But he and one of the Swedish Aggies had made bricks together, which was equivalent to becoming engaged on Botany. If Kris caught him looking very carefully at her son, she ignored the query in his eyes and babbled on about how good a father Zainal was until even Pete Easley got bored.

The baby boom sparked a lot of investigations and experiments – a fine powder for talcum, an ointment for napkin and other minor rashes, a way to weave some of the vegetable fibres into cloth for proper baby-clothes, and a spinning-wheel to make knitting yarn out of loo-cow hairs. The creatures had grown longer coats for protection during the colder weather. These were collected – before the night-crawlers could – and spun, then washed and/or felted.

The crops grew lush and green on both continents. The Catteni continued to do nothing in their valley. The miners excavated tons of iron, copper, tin, zinc, lead, gold and silver – and occasionally some unusual clear stones which the jewellers thought a variant of tourmaline. But then, no-one was looking for gemstones or in the places where rubies, emeralds, sapphires or diamonds – which would have been useful for their hardness – might be found.

Bone was more useful, and the heavy bones in the four rear-legs of the loo-cows were scrupulously cleaned and dried for carving.

Zane was just five months old when the Deski sentinel startled everyone on the south side of Retreat Bay with a warning warble. For such a slender species, with no great lung space, they could make a god-awful amount of noise. The baby was teething so Kris was awake, trying to soothe him. Zainal's comunit buzzed and he shot straight up in bed, alert, unit to his ear before she could take a single step to intercept.

'WHAT?' He was on his feet and hopping about on one foot, listening as he pulled on his coverall. Even in such a ridiculous pose, Kris admired his physique. If only Zane could have osmosed a single gene from his foster father . . .

'It's down,' Zainal added, as he closed the hand-unit and concentrated on dressing himself as fast as possible.

'What's down?'

'The Balloon.' He had both boots on now and was starting for the door.

'I'm coming, too,' she said.

'Not like that!' He raked her with a disapproving look, for she was draped in a blanket.

She thrust Zane at his father and dressed as quickly as he, retrieved the blanket and two spare reed-pods and was inserting the baby into the sling she usually carried him in even as she settled into a passenger seat of the air-cushion truck. Zainal spun the control wheel and the vehicle charged off into the crepuscular light of dawn towards the hangar. Lights were coming up throughout the settlement and occasionally someone called out, 'What's the matter?' when Zainal was identified at the wheel.

'The Balloon is just down?' she asked as they sped along.

'Deski heard something, not like anything else they have heard,' Zainal was saying, 'and warned the bridge. The bridge watch had already seen something on the screen, but couldn't make out what.'

'The Farmers?' Kris asked, scared to the pit of her stomach as she jiggled her son. Motion always put him to sleep, even upset with teething as he was, and even this short trip worked its magic on him.

Those alerted were arriving on air cushion, running as fast as they could and often faster than

324

the basic push-bikes which had been developed for short-distance transportation. Pneumatic tyres were still to be perfected, but the iron rims did well enough on the flagstone and dirt tracks and were speedier than walking.

All the lights in the hangar were on, and the hatches on the KDL, Baby and the office were open. Runabouts were parked helter-skelter.

Zainal guided Kris to the office which was nearest. The bridge there would show just as much as the ships' would, and there'd be more space for her and the baby. In such little matters, Zainal always considered her and Zane.

Scott, Beggs, Fetterman, Yowell and Coo were in the office and Scott waved Zainal over urgently.

'A full orbit already, and it's not large. Not small enough to be a programmed orb, but moving too fast for us to get an accurate picture of its dimensions or shape.'

'That', and Coo pointed to the trail left by the orbital, 'is not heard. Something landed.' He spoke with more force than a Deski usually did. He'd probably been repeating it to Scott. Now Coo stabbed his spidery finger at the Farmers' Command Post, the one which Kris, Zainal and the others had investigated well over a Botanical year ago: where Dick Aarens had deliberately activated a homing device.

'Then what . . .' and Scott irritably followed the course of the orbital with one finger. Just then its track shifted to a north/south orientation. Even as they watched, it completed several whip-round orbits of the large globe of Botany. '. . . What is that?'

'We will know . . .' Zainal paused, eyes watching the progress of the orbital on the screen '. . . about now.'

They felt the tingling zap of a scan and he chuckled.

'Oh migod,' said Fetterman, sitting down as if his legs had given out.

Kris had felt it course through her and Zane squirmed slightly against her in his sling. She stroked his cheek, wondering if the scan could have been too much for so small a body, and then felt Zainal's reassuring touch to her back.

'I will volunteer to go,' Zainal said.

Kris barely prevented herself from saying, 'Oh, no, you won't,' before Scott lifted both hands in a refusal, his eyes not moving from the screen. The comunit bleeped and he toggled it open.

'We were just scanned?' It was Beverly's voice.

'Coo says they landed at the Command Post.'

'Nothing's showing up there,' said Beverly.

Coo nodded emphatically, reaffirming his report.

'Fek agrees,' Beverly went on. 'Haven't we established they use matter transmission?'

'Oh, oh,' Yowell said, and he stumbled backwards to collapse on the nearest stool, his face a study of conflicting emotions: hope, fear, anxiety and confusion.

Coo's head turned towards the office door and he rose to his feet, lifting one arm to point straight ahead.

'They're here?' Scott asked.

Kris gulped, her arms automatically tightening on Zane. But, as soon as Zainal moved she was right behind him, ahead of the others who had hesitated just that split-second longer before acting. If their destiny was coming to them, she wanted to see it.

As they left the office, she glanced over at the KDL and saw Fek's unmistakable shape in the hatch, then Balenquah's stocky frame silhouetted briefly in the hatch light, followed by Worrell's slightly stooped figure, the tall erect one that was probably Rastancil, the slight frame of a woman whom she didn't recognize, and Slav. From Baby came Mitford, Easley, Yuri and Judge Iri.

They converged, forming a semi-circle facing outwards.

What happened before their eyes did not resemble anything from a Star Trek programme. No coloured lights, beams or columns; nor any other special effect Kris remembered from just about all the science fiction films and videos she'd seen. And yet it was. Something was out there, forming a solid mass which moved towards them, a nimbus around a darker interior. Something which even by the dawn light looked larger than the tallest of the waiting humans.

Then it wasn't taller and seemed to spread out, and she recognized the distinctive spider-legged form of a Deski. Beside her, Coo gurgled once and stiffened. With her free hand, Kris reached for Coo's long fingers and gripped them; she had Zane's face shielded with the other. Zainal had shifted his body so that he overlapped her in

327

partial protection. But most of the forms that coalesced out of the mist – only it wasn't mist – were human in appearance as the details of faces and appendages became obvious.

'They're shape-changers,' she whispered. 'They're changing into us?'

Coo sucked breath in, a slow sound – terror? Apprehension? Defensive? Kris tightened her grip, not knowing if she was giving or seeking support.

'Shape-changers?' Scott hissed, eyes never leaving what was in front of his as he leaned slightly in her direction.

'There's a Deski and a Rugarian, and the rest are humans. But not as many of them as there are of us.'

When the transformation was complete, and there was no doubt that these visitors showed representations of the three species facing them, each group regarded the other.

'There's no Catteni.' Kris's comment was barely audible, but the omission caused a little giggle to escape her which she hastily suppressed. If these were the Farmers – and every evidence pointed to that assumption, for who else could have lifted the Balloon? – then they weren't all-seeing and perfect. Somehow that gave her a lift of confidence.

But no-one was saying anything and the tension was mounting. So, if the visitors weren't showing immediate aggression, maybe they should be treated like visitors, all eight of them. We outnumber them, she thought, though 'outnumber' is all we do, considering what they just did. It was so silly to just stand there, looking at each other.

'Hello,' she said, making the word friendly and inquiring. She stepped around Zainal and inadvertently pulled Coo with her, just as Judge Iri Bempechat took a step forward. She knew she had a silly smirk on her face as she looked at the judge for what to do next.

Whether she was impertinent or not, she never did find out, but the judge grinned fleetingly at her – so she felt she hadn't done anything really wrong – and he held out both hands, the galactic indication (she hoped) of being unarmed.

'We have hoped that we would meet you, and explain our presence on a planet which you have clearly used for many thousands of years,' he said, inclining his upper body slightly forward in a gesture that was as dignified as it was hospitable. 'I realize that you do not understand what I'm saying, but I hope the sincerity with which I speak will be apparent. We do realize that we have trespassed on your property, but we were brought here against our volition and cannot return to our own worlds.'

As the judge spoke, Kris felt the very slightest of pressures against her forehead, and at the back of her neck. Zane gave an odd little movement and she jiggled him gently, stroking his back in a reassurance that usually quieted him.

'We moved to this continent because you are not farming it now. We did not wish to interfere with your installations here. We wish to stay . . . with your permission, if it is at all possible, because we do not have sufficient transportation to leave here.

329

Can we try to make you understand? Somehow?'
He opened his hands towards them again, with
dignity and entreaty.

'It is understood,' said a voice remarkably like the
judge's.

Whoever had spoken had done so so quickly that
Kris hadn't seen any mouth moving. Then she realized that no-one *had* spoken; the voice was right
in her own head. Zane moved restlessly again.

'We have come to meet with you. Do not be
afraid. We do not injure. We do not kill. We do not
inhabit. You are very young, all of you.'

'Young species?' Iri Bempechat asked, amused.

'Yes,' and one of the males used his mouth to
enunciate the word, though Kris still heard it more
in her head than her ears. 'Very young.'

Judge Iri smiled. 'We humans are. I believe the
Deskis', and he gestured towards Coo, 'have lived
much longer than humans,' and he pointed to
himself and then to Kris.

'We have seen the Deski and passed them by.
They do well as they are. Why are so many here?
Why are four . . . no, six species . . . here on this
planet?'

'We were dropped here. We have to stay,'
Judge Iri said in a wry voice, flashing a glance at
Zainal.

'Because the others, like this one,' and now the
spokesperson gestured a well-shaped hand towards
the Catteni, 'have put you here against your will to
make a colony of this world.'

'I see that we will not have to tell you much,' said

330

Judge Iri. 'You read the thoughts in our minds.'

'Such as they are,' and yet there was a kindness rather than a condescension in his tone that was sounding less like an echo of Judge Iri and more obviously reflecting this speaker's personality.

'We try to improve,' Judge Iri said, inclining his upper body respectfully.

'A very long, hard process that is eternal. But you are not.'

'And you are?'

'In essence.'

'Not as the Eosi are,' said Zainal.

The entity turned its head to the new speaker. 'We are not familiar with either the name or your mental image of these Eosi.'

'That's the best way to be,' someone remarked softly and, for a moment, Kris thought it had to be Mitford. It sounded like him. Or maybe Yowell, since the sergeant was in the central group, and Vic much closer.

'We seek your help to escape from the domination of the Eosi over my people, the Catteni, and these other species,' Zainal said, gesturing urgently at those around him.

'Such a process includes injury to species which we do not condone.'

'Even if injuries continue to be perpetrated on innocent species who have no protection against the superior force?' Judge Bempechat asked.

'If force is used, there is no reformation of the desires which caused force to be used,' and the entity's face now reflected a gentle reprimand.

'How do you avoid force, then?' Scott asked, speaking for the first time.

'There are ways. Learn them.'

The figures began to dissolve.

'How are you called?' the judge asked, taking a quick step forward in an effort to prevent their leaving.

'You have named us Farmers. It is appropriate.' The spokesman smiled in the most benign way.

Kris mused that this entity would have been well cast as Jesus Christ.

'He is not among you?' was the thought inserted in her mind.

'Don't leave,' Zainal said, also stepping forward, one hand upheld, 'not yet. How do we avoid force when it is used against us? How do we free ourselves and our friends from Eosian domination?'

'Are we allowed to stay here? On your planet?' And Kris jumped forward, startling Zane awake. He let out a yell.

One of the Farmers glided forward. The legs moved but the female – because she appeared subtly feminine to Kris as she approached – did not make contact with the ground in an actual walk.

'They observe well,' and again a thought was inserted in her head as the being reached her and looked down at Zane. Despite Kris's attempts to soothe him, the first yell segued into soft, fearful crying. Not that she blamed Zane for reacting to the tension, the disappointment and the fear that clogged the air around him. Certainly those were her own feelings.

'We have so much to ask you. So many questions,' Easley said beseechingly.

'This is your child!' the female said, and she turned back to Kris.

Kris could no more have refused to display her son than she could have resisted the contractions that had expelled him from her womb. She turned Zane, his face reddening in baby distress, towards the entity. The entity bent over him, slid one graceful, almost transparent hand over his face and he instantly switched to smiling contentment, burbling charmingly up at his newest admirer.

'There are many new young here,' she said, and Kris thought she sounded envious.

'Then we may stay?' Kris asked earnestly.

'You stay. We will observe but we do not interfere.'

'May we leave?' Zainal asked, making a sphere with his hands.

'It is for your protection,' the first speaker said.

'We are grateful,' said Judge Iri, shooting a warning look at Zainal.

'That is more than the others were,' the thought crept into Kris's mind, and the female reversed her glide to rejoin her group.

The instant they were all together again, they disappeared.

Like zap! Kris thought, as her son gurgled happily in her arms.

Everyone started talking at once then, the main argument being that they had learned very little, and who had made the judge the spokesman, and

333

why hadn't more questions been asked while they had the Farmers' attention? And who did Zainal think he was, demanding assistance from obvious pacifists?

Scott called for quiet. Judge Bempechat said in a humble tone that he had certainly not intended to speak for everyone but he suddenly found he was speaking. Balenquah railed at Kris for her stupid 'hello'.

'Well, we couldn't ask them to take us to their leader, could we?' she responded. 'And keep your voice down around my baby!'

'Were you going to give him to them?' Balenquah demanded.

'Don't be such an idiot. She wanted to look at him,' Kris said and walked away from the egregious pilot. She'd thought Aarens was obnoxious, but Balenquah opened up a whole new category of insufferable.

'NOW LISTEN UP,' Scott said, raising his voice over the babble. 'We are allowed to stay. That was the most important fact we needed to know, wasn't it?'

As he spoke, the sound of excited voices and the hum of air-cushion vehicles nearing the hangar could be more clearly heard.

'Hey, they came. We can stay,' Lenny Doyle was shouting as he jumped from the air cushion and ran into the hangar. 'They just appeared outside the mess hall and . . .' He broke off, being close enough to see expressions. 'We *can* call them Farmers,' he finished, his words trailing off. 'They were here, too?'

Worrell, Leon Dane, Mayock and two nurses were next, piling out of the air-cushion flatbed that doubled as ambulance. Their faces were wreathed with the elated grins of persons big with news, which faded as they too realized that their experience was by no means unique.

'How many shape-changers came?' Kris said into the silence.

Then the main comunit was buzzing as all lines into the office seemed to go off at once.

'Rather unusual mass hallucination then,' Dane said wryly. 'Should we compare notes? We can stay, or so they said, and we can refer to them as the Farmers . . .'

'Since that is appropriate,' the judge added in a tone much like Leon's.

'Did we all ask the same questions?' Leon asked, looking at Scott and then Zainal.

'We'd better compare notes,' said Scott, 'after we've answered those calls. Kris, Yowell, Zainal, help me with these . . .' and he gestured to the busy com board.

'How *many* were there?' Kris asked when there was time to review the astonishing simultaneous manifestation of Farmers to all major groups on Botany. Even the miners had had a visitation of ten.

No group of Farmers had been larger than those

they had confronted. The five people on watch at the Command Post had been approached by three: those at the mess hall where the majority of people had been having breakfast had counted thirty. The hospital had been favoured with fifteen.

'All at the same time?' Leon asked, astounded.

'Fifty at least, and they could not all have fitted in that orbital!' Beverly said.

'That depends on how much space shape-changers need,' Kris remarked.

'If they appeared to all of us, why didn't someone find out more about them?' Scott demanded, exasperated. 'We all had the chance to make the meeting substantive.'

'We all had the same chance,' Rastancil said, grinning, 'but I sure couldn't get my wits to work fast enough, nor did I notice you asking leading questions, Ray.'

Despite the way Rastancil phrased it, Admiral Ray Scott took umbrage.

'Nonsense,' Kris said, 'they've had a lot more practice with third-kind encounters than we have. We're young, we are,' and she giggled. 'Did you really think we'd get direct answers from a species that has the technology they have? We're far too young to deserve more than the few minutes they spent here with us.'

'Let us look at the positive aspects of that confrontation,' Pete Easley said, holding up a restraining hand to Scott who seemed to be the one most offended by the lost opportunity. 'We now have permission to stay. I got the distinct impression', and he turned to Zainal for confirmation, 'that we may even be able to get through the Balloon but others, like the Eosi, won't be able to.'

Zainal nodded.

'I'd like you to organize a flight to test that, Zainal. Today, if at all possible,' Scott said, grasping a point he could understand and react to. 'I don't know if that advances your Phase Three plan but . . .' and he shrugged.

'What did they mean about "that is more than the others"?' Kris asked.

Scott, Zainal and the judge regarded her with surprise.

'When you asked to have the Balloon removed, Zainal, and the judge said we were grateful for the protection, one of them said, "that is more than the others were". Didn't you hear it?' Kris glanced around. 'Was I the only one?'

'What else did you hear, Kris?' Judge Bempechat asked, smiling at her in a way that suggested that he might have had private thoughts inserted in his mind too.

'They envy us having children,' she said, looking around. And caught Pete Easley's eyes. He smiled at her and *then* she remembered the female's remark. 'This is your child!' And the female had been looking at Pete, not at Kris.

The truth will out, won't it, Kris thought to herself and nodded. She had been mean not to tell him before: depriving him of that knowledge out of spite. He smiled back at her, a really happy smile, before pointing at Scott who was repeating a question aimed at her.

'I'm sorry, Ray, what did you ask me?'

'What else did you "hear" that we didn't?'

'I dunno,' she said with a shrug. 'I never thought I was telepathic. I thought we were all hearing the same things. Did anyone else beside the judge and me get special treatment?'

'I heard plainly that they will be examining this quadrant for sentient species which have developed since their last visit,' Zainal said, looking around.

'Last visit?' Pete Easley exclaimed. And whistled.

'They have been at Deski world,' Coo said, rather proudly.

'You come off better than we humans do, then,' Judge Bempechat said, grinning broadly.

Kris noticed that Scott had been about to speak but the judge had forestalled the admiral with a much more diplomatic comment. Scott closed his mouth.

'I think', the judge went on, reaching for pen and paper, 'we had best organize that astonishing interview as best we can recall it. And insert whatever we individually may have heard with the public comments.'

'Good idea,' Leon agreed.

'We might have more in the composite than we got individually,' the judge said. 'We must ask the miners to do the same, and those at the Command Post – everyone who met our shape-changing Farmers.'

* * *

Zainal left mid-morning, with Marrucci, Balenquah and Beverly, to fly to the Balloon and see if it permitted them to pass.

'More importantly, come back,' Kris said stoutly when Zainal told her they were going.

It took most of the day to transcribe the various interviews, and more information *had* been exchanged when it was all written down on paper.

'I wonder. Are they doing this sort of re-hash on their way back home?' Kris said at one point during the painstaking reconstruction of who had said what, when and where.

'I doubt it,' said Rastancil. 'They picked our brains quite easily, so they'd probably all know what went on everywhere else.'

'Probably as it was being done,' Worry said with a sniff. Most uncharacteristically, he had a distinctly unworried expression on his face.

Almost everyone – or at least those who worried about special problems – had been given 'private' information. Leon Dane, fretting over medical problems for which he had no treatment and waiting for a chance to ask for advice, had been told which specific plants to find and, 'like some sort of a super blast into my head', he got the method of refining and the beneficial dosages to use.

'We've already tested most of the plants as either noxious or damned well fatal. But, of course, minute and diluted dosages of dangerous substances have often had therapeutic value if properly administered. I just got a short, hard course in the local botanical resources. Seems there's a shrub, located on that dry continent, that can provide a general anaesthetic, but they would prefer us to use our one lone acupuncturist. She's to teach others her skills.'

'They liked us making bricks,' Sandy Areson said, 'and I now know where to get five different varieties of clay . . .'

'And I was told what other bushes have seed-pods like the fluff which we can use to spin into cloth,' Janet said. 'He was so like Jesus Christ.'

'Who is with us,' Kris added.

'What did you say?' Janet was indignant.

'"He is not among you?" was what I heard,' Kris said.

'And you will note', Janet went on, drawing herself up with great dignity, 'that they appeared to us in human form. So we now have confirmation of the Almighty's appearance. Human!'

'That's because you had neither Rugarians nor Deskis in with you at the time,' Sandy Areson said, but she spoke without her usual irreverence for Janet's overt religiosity. 'We had both Deski and Rugarians, because that's who were having breakfast with us humans.'

The sentries at the Command Post had been kindly informed that their presence there was no longer needed. The miners had been assured that the Farmers did not object to the use of mineral and metallic resources. The loggers had been asked not to cut down the oldest trees, and were given permission to thin the other varieties grown on the second farmed continent as these were softer woods, more suitable for 'the making of useful artifacts'.

Universal had been the permission to remain on the second continent, acceptance of the term 'Farmers', and the fact that they did not condone 'species' injury'.

'They were sad to see us so far from home,' Coo admitted.

'And?' Judge Bempechat prompted, when it was obvious Coo had been told more than that. 'Did they suggest returning you home?'

'Not now,' Coo said. 'We are better here.' Then he had smiled in his fashion. 'Much better here.'

'We too,' Slav added. 'No-one safe with Catteni.' He drew his brows together and managed to suck his lips inside his mouth, indicating great displeasure. 'Farmers not see danger?' he added, looking from the judge to Scott, Worrell and those still left in the office.

'Not if it causes species' injury, which they do not seem willing to commit even on territorially aggressive races like the Catteni . . .' the Judge began and when Kris cleared her throat, 'I stand corrected, my dear . . . like the Eosi . . . who command the Catteni subordinates to do so without compunction.'

'Hey, he's there, and I think he's doing it,' shouted Bert Put.

Everyone in the office crowded around the screen to watch the minute speck that was Baby. The speck disappeared, and most cheered and clapped at this verification of the tacit Farmer permission. Kris, however, held her breath.

'I wouldn't,' said Easley, who was standing next to her. 'He could be out a while.'

Inadvertently Kris met his eyes and exhaled with a weak smile. She had been trying to avoid any conversation with him.

'So much hooch that day, I honestly don't remember what I did, or that I did,' he continued in a low voice. 'He's a good baby for you?'

'Couldn't be better,' she said, looking fatuously down at the sleeping Zane. 'Thank you.' And then she added, to keep him in his place, 'I think.'

Pete Easley gave a wry chuckle at her amendment and gave her shoulder a squeeze before he moved away. She would almost rather that he had stayed because the wait was a long one. She bet anything that Zainal was making sure the Eosi knew he'd been outside the Balloon, probably spinning the scout on its axis around the orbital as well as the geo-synchronous satellite. Just like him! Although what she thought he could accomplish, she wasn't sure. She was certain, however, that he did have some sort of a new Phase Three plan. And cocking a snook at the Eosi was part of it. Of course, that blew the painstaking false trail he had laid to get them to believe he was elsewhere in the galaxy. But wasn't he taking an awful risk for all of them? What if the Balloon would give way to the Eosi warship now?

In her arms, Zane sighed and snuggled closer to

her. No, she thought, he would do nothing to jeopardize his son.

'Ah, he's back inside!' Bert let out another loud crow which caused Zane to stir uneasily. 'Heading home!'

Relieved that Zainal had succeeded, Kris decided that she could now leave discreetly. Zane would need to be fed when he woke this time, and changed, and she'd run out of fluff pods. She was tired, too, with all the excitement of meeting the Farmers, and then the re-hash of who had heard what and where. Once she'd fed her son, she'd have time for a rest before Zainal touched down.

The orbital duly recorded the emergence of a small vehicle from the protective veil: its emergence, its brief run around the fixed satellite and then its insertion. Nothing could be recorded past the obstacle, but this brief flight was enough of a phenomenon for the orbital to send an immediate message to its Home Base.

The report, when it was received, went immediately to the Ix Mentat, who was enraged. Very quickly the vehicle was identified as similar in design to the scoutship in which Zainal was supposed to have exited the system.

'Removing the markings fools no-one,' the Ix said. 'And if a scout with limited power can penetrate that obstacle in both directions, so can we!'

The warship, the AA1, plus its sister ship which had just passed its test flights and been commissioned, were supplied and crewed for the fastest possible return to the system in question. Twice the fire-power of the previous visit would certainly punch a hole through whatever it was that had impeded their exit and then refused to readmit the AA1.

'This time Zainal will return for appropriate punishment,' the Ix Mentat said, turning over in its mind the kinds of physical abuse that would wreak the worst pain and humiliation on the chosen who had failed to present himself at Eosi command. It savoured scenes of dismemberment, of flaying alive, of the application of noxious substances to the few tender portions of Catteni anatomy.

Meanwhile, the impetus to reach new heights of technological development extended to every single Eosi. They had been idle too long, complacent in their mastery of seven solar systems, their exploitation of the riches available to them, but with so many worlds still to be discovered and turned to Eosian advancement and enjoyment. They were on the threshold of a new era in Eosi domination! Let no one curtail their pleasure in achievement. The galaxy would eventually be theirs!

When attacked by the might of Eosian naval strength, the barrier remained impervious to any combination of the missiles, beams and force available. The attack was useless against the barrier, and the bombardment of weapons of all kinds proved insufficient to pierce it. Only those on

le Shuttle

Duty Free Shopper's Pass

EEC Directive & Customs require that this Le Shuttle Duty Free Shopper's Pass be presented to the cashier when purchasing Duty Free Goods.

Only one limit per person is permitted.

Tobacco limits are restricted to persons over 17.

Alcohol limits are restricted to persons over 18.

The following table shows the duty free limits per person.

If you have any questions on your limits, or would like more information on our products, our staff will be happy to help.

This voucher is not transferable. Valid for one visit to the Duty Free shop only. This pass must be handed to the cashier at the time of purchase, where it will be retained.

This pass remains the property of Eurotunnel at all times.

VALID FOR DATE OF ISSUE ONLY.

IT IS A CUSTOMS/DOUANES REQUIREMENT THAT EACH PERSON PURCHASING DUTY FREE MUST BE PRESENT AT THE POINT OF SALE.

ATTENTION !!!!

LES DOUANES BRITANNIQUES/FRANCAISES IMPOSENT QUE TOUT ACHETEUR DE PRODUITS HORS TAXES SE PRESENTE EN PERSONNE A LA CAISSE.

MERCI DE VOTRE COMPREHENSION.

MOORE

Your duty free limits

SPIRITS	
Spirits, strong liqueurs over 22% volume	1 litre
OR fortified wine	2 litres
OR sparkling wine	2 litres
OR other liqueurs	2 litres
WINE	
Wine (still)	2 litres
BEERS	UP TO £75.00
TOBACCO	
Cigarettes	200
OR Cigarillos	100
OR Cigars	50
OR Tobacco	250G

9 999990 011114

31-AOÛ-1998 14:50

Passager tourisme

FR / UK

Num equip :06

the planet remained unaware of the attempt.

Throughout the Eosian-dominated systems, captains and governors were apprised of this unexpected insult. Word filtered down to the suppressed on Rugarian, Deski, Iginish, Turs and Terran home worlds, and on the compulsorily colonized planets. Hope was reborn! Reborn and thwarted by the savagery of Eosian frustration which now focused on extracting some means of penetrating that barrier from whatever source that might come. The Eosi had been unpleasant at any time; now they turned vicious. All effort was aimed at combating the first real test of Eosian supremacy since the Mentats had sloughed off their corporeal forms to find a type of immortality by using the strong Catteni bodies.

And still the barrier remained impregnable.

So the Ix Mentat sent out every available scout, far beyond previously explored sectors, to find any trace of those whose advanced technology prevented it from achieving the revenge it now craved.

Chapter Twelve

'Baby slipped through like an eel,' Marrucci said, grinning broadly as he wiggled his clasped hands in demonstration. 'Mind you, Zainal had us at dead-slow and that might be the trick. Come charging at it and it bounces you back as it did the first time we nosed around.'

'I think we were a little speedier re-entering,' Beverly said on consideration.

'We could have blasted the Eosi orbital. Baby's armed. Blown it out of the skies as a warning,' Balenquah said, sullen as ever. 'We should have, you know! Proven we can do something positive against their surveillance! And we didn't get so much as a whisker sensor stripped off.' He added a 'Ha!' of satisfaction before wandering off to grab some of the sandwiches set out on the table, then left the office.

'Glad you were along, General,' Marrucci said softly, 'That guy grosses me out.'

'He is a good pilot,' said Beverly, but without much enthusiasm.

Scott leaned across his desk, gesturing for the other two to do the same. 'Is what Balenquah said accurate? You weren't beyond the Balloon long enough to be seen by the orbital?'

Beverly grinned. 'Of course we were. Zainal even booted us past the geo-sync sat. That was his main object in seeing if he could breach the Balloon, to get the exit and re-entry noticed.'

'Won't that just make the Eosi madder'n ever?'

'Frankly, I hope so. With Farmers protecting us—'

'Now, wait a minute.' Scott sat bolt upright. 'What makes Zainal think they will if we pull damn-fool stunts like that?'

'If you're on the top of the pile by many light years, you don't need to do injury to species to maintain the position – not with the technology the Farmers have. But the Eosi don't. That'll piss them off, according to Zainal, and I think he's right. If they keep trying to storm Botany, won't the Farmers object?'

'Damn Zainal. He's going to get that Phase Three of his started one way or another,' and there was a touch of admiration in Scott's tone. 'But damnation, he should take us into his confidence on such decisions. We have the good of the entire community. And where is Zainal? I need to do more than debrief him now.'

'Oh, he dropped us off and went on to check the Catteni valley, to see if the Farmers visited them. I thought you knew.'

'Me? I certainly didn't suggest it.' Scott's frown deepened. 'That damned Cat!'

'Frankly, Ray, I'd like to know if the Farmers did appear to them. Mind you, I'm comfortable enough here on Botany, but there were a lot of things left undone on Earth and I'd expected to have a major part in their doing,' Beverly said, giving his head a final nod of emphasis.

'A soldier's first duty is to return to his unit if at all possible?' Scott said with a slightly condescending smile.

'You got it! As far as I'm concerned,' Beverly folded his hands together, 'I'm not stopping until Earth is free of the Eosi. A lot of us here feel the same way, and I suspect more than you'd guess would back Zainal in an attempt to get active Farmer support.'

Scott considered that and sighed. 'If we could . . .' Then, in an altogether different voice and with a rueful smile, he added, 'Not that I haven't learned some very valuable lessons here on Botany.'

'We all have,' Beverly agreed with a wry expression, and he looked down at the callouses on his hands.

When Zainal returned, he immediately reported to Ray Scott that the Farmers had appeared to the Catteni and scared them so badly that two were still in shock. The others refused to believe that they had not been visited by Eosi, and pleaded with him to take them to a safer place.

'I told them these were not Eosi but the true owners of the planet, and if they tried to leave the valley, worse would happen to them.'

'What would be worse than Eosi?' Scott asked with a snort.

'What they do not know is always worse,' Zainal said with a shrug. 'They will never leave the valley.'

'Had they been trying to?'

Zainal gave another of his shrugs. 'No. The Drassi has authority over them only on the ship. They will do nothing.'

'You stayed long enough outside the Balloon to let both satellites have a good look at you?'

'As John told you,' Zainal said.

'Tell me, Zainal,' and Scott made himself lean back, as if totally at ease, 'is it wise to aggravate the Eosi this way? How can we be sure the Farmers will protect us if we taunt our enemy? We know very little of their philosophy and society, or their technology, except that it is superior to everything any of us have seen.'

Zainal grinned, and the look in his eyes was menacing. 'Right now, the Eosi are very worried. Some other group is more advanced than they are – they will not stand for that. They will be doing two things: searching for the Farmers and trying to take as large a technological leap forward as they can.'

'Yes, but are they capable of it? I mean, matter transmission such as the Farmers used is a huge step forward, I would think,' Scott said.

'Wars have a habit of improving technology,' said Beverly. 'We should know that better than most, Ray.'

'A lot of good our improved technology did us

when the Catteni landed,' Scott said with a bitter laugh.

'Did they ever track down the subs?' asked Beverly.

Scott glared at him, tilting his head at Zainal.

'Whose side is he on, Ray?' Beverly said.

'My own,' Zainal said with a grin. 'I go home now.'

Kris was asleep but she roused briefly when she felt him slide under the blankets beside her.

'You've planned Phase Three, haven't you?' she murmured and, before he could admit that he had, she was asleep again.

Zane woke them as night was falling, ready to eat and play awhile.

'Well, you have, haven't you?' she said as she was nursing the baby by the fire while Zainal sat in his big chair, watching the process as he idly stroked one chair-arm.

'I have what?'

'Planned Phase Three.'

He grinned at her. 'It is only logical to complete what Mitford started. To get the Farmers to notice us and come to see what we have done to their world. That Eosi came is very good. We upset *their* plans, and that has needed doing for many generations.'

'Don't tell me other Catteni have wanted to do away with the Eosi?' That surprised her.

'It has been talked of, privately,' he admitted, and

the stroking turned to a drumming of his fingers. 'I was on Barevi to speak to . . . a group about a plan.'

'You were? And I ruined all that for you?' Kris flushed with chagrin. 'Did you mention that to Chuck? Or anyone?'

Zainal shrugged. 'No reason, until now.'

'Is that why you wanted to be able to leave the planet?'

'I am thinking that to have a base for those who resist the Eosi would be a very good thing.'

'More Catteni here?' Kris could think of several hundred people who would object to that. Or maybe they wouldn't, now that it was pretty well established in people's heads that it was the Eosi who were masterminding Catteni activities. The problem with that was that so many Catteni *enjoyed* far too much what they did to subject races.

'That would cause trouble if it was known,' Zainal agreed, instantly following her thought. 'There is that desert continent. No-one goes there.'

'That's true. And if folks didn't know there were Catteni . . . but you can't keep something like this from the brass-heads, Zainal. They trust you now, they wouldn't—'

'Do not worry. I respect their trust. I will tell them if I think I can do what I wish now to do. I would need much assistance from Beverly, Scott, Easley, Yowell, Bert, Raisha. We must rescue more from Earth, too.'

'The transport ship?' She startled Zane and had to comfort him.

Zainal nodded. 'On board the KDL is much

351

we would need. The star maps, the codes—'

'Wouldn't the Eosi change codes? Just in case you get loose?'

Zainal shook his head, his yellow eyes dancing in the firelight.

'Drassi learn too slowly to do that quickly.'

'So you must move more quickly, and soon. Is that right?'

He nodded. And her heart pounded in fear for him.

'You're planning to infiltrate Earth?'

He gave his head a quick shake. 'Barevi is safer for me. Many coming and going, and we can find out much information from new prisoners. And "transport" those we need.'

'You, Emassi Zainal, can just walk in and demand the worst of the prisoners, and they'll be handed over to you?' Anxiety made her sarcastic. 'You with a crew of—'

'Deski and Rugarians, and friends hidden from Emassi and Drassi eyes.'

'I didn't know Deski and Rugarians crewed for Catteni.'

'They will not be the entire crew, only the ones most seen,' said Zainal. Then he rose, in a smooth graceful movement for such a big-boned man, and began to pace. 'We are not transport ship. We are from mines at K'daskt Nik Sot Fil,' he said as he paced. 'We need certain workers, strong, with perhaps some mechanical experience. We get what we need – and certain things Botany needs . . .'

'And no-one will be the wiser?'

'The grey skin stuff? How long will it last on a man's face?'

'I don't know,' she said, though she was beginning to see just how he would be able to cope, 'but you can take as much as you need with you.' She ran over in her mind those who had been fake Catteni when the KDL was captured. 'But won't the Eosi be watching everything? What if they've already seen the scout getting in and out?'

Zainal chuckled, pausing by her chair to stroke her cheek and looking down at the hungry baby.

'I hope that they have.'

'Yes, but you can't meet them sneaking out the back door, can you?'

'Bert Put goes up and takes a quick look to see if . . . the shore is clear?' He lifted his eyebrows in query.

'Coast is clear . . .'

'Good, and I take Catteni speakers, too.' Now he started pacing again, rubbing his hands together as he thought out loud. 'Have you forgotten all Barevi?' he asked in that language.

Startled, she replied in the Barevi negative. Could she go with him? Did she want to go with him? She certainly didn't want to stay behind. But Zane?

'Chuck would be useful,' she added. 'And Jay Greene . . .'

He had paused by her and looked down at Zane who had nursed himself to sleep. 'I need you, too.'

She almost burst into tears, her heart so full of love

for both, her responsibilities pulling her in two directions at once.

'Sandy has more milk than a cow,' she said, not daring to look at Zainal just then. She added more briskly, 'And this is the sort of situation we set up the crèche system for, isn't it?'

She heard Zainal tap out call numbers. 'Chuck? Are you free to talk over an idea this evening?'

Chuck Mitford immediately said they had to talk this over with the brass-heads.

'Only a few of them, at that,' he added, grinning and rubbing his hands together because Zainal had included him as the crew foreman. Chuck hadn't even taken that as a slur, because he was indeed the build and height of many Catteni. Handsomer than most, however, as Kris could not resist saying.

Scott had to be consulted – especially as Chuck wanted him to play Catteni, too. John Beverly, Gino Marrucci, Ninety Doyle, Dowdall, Matt Su for his electronics knowledge, Yuri Palit and several others who had been in the original commando group because they had some knowledge of Catteni.

'I don't see why we can't go straight to Earth,' was Scott's first objection.

'I do not have codes for Earth . . . KDL is Barevi-based. I figure that we speak with latest transports from Earth . . .'

'What about stealing another ship with the right codes?' Marrucci wanted to know, flexing his fingers as if already settled in a cockpit and about to take off. 'I sure would love to get back to good ol' Terra Firma!'

Zainal grinned. 'That is also a possibility. If one just happens to be ready to fly.'

'You can't leave the crew around—' Scott began.

'There are other valleys here,' Zainal said. 'The KDL can get in and out of Barevi without difficulty. That is important. I know I can get supplies that we need with no problem.'

'We get to make a wish list?' Rastancil asked, brightening.

'No, a "need" list.'

'Medical supplies?' Chuck asked hopefully, taking his pad and pencil stub from his pocket.

'If we can find any,' Zainal replied, reminding Mitford that Catteni medicine was rudimentary at best. 'Good steel we can get,' he added, knowing that the fabricators needed better materials to form proper surgical instruments.

Chuck wrote 'steel' and underscored it.

'This time, can we have clean Catteni uniforms to wear?' Yuri Palit asked, wrinkling his nose.

Zainal shook his head. 'You must smell like Catteni, too, and you don't.' Yuri made a grimace and sighed. 'Wear what you have on voyage, *then* change at Barevi,' Zainal added with a grin. 'Now,' and he took out the sheets of the Barevi Spaceport and its environs which he had worked on, to show Chuck. 'We must know where to go, and you must learn what to answer to questions. If you walk fast as if you know where you're going, that you are taking a message, no-one will question. So you must *know*!'

They readily agreed to that but along with the language lessons came questions, especially from those who had not been enslaved on Barevi and were unfamiliar with it. That was where Kris came in, because she had flitted all over the city with her owner.

'Can't we just steal flitters and not walk everywhere?' Dowdall asked.

'You may *rent* flitters,' Zainal corrected him. 'We must fit in or be noticed. If we fit in right, we can come back again.'

'Hey, I like that,' Ninety Doyle said, grinning. 'There're a couple of Tudos . . .'

Zainal pointed his pencil at Ninety. 'You will be good Tudo and follow your Drassi's orders.'

'Yeah, sure, boss, gotcha, boss Drassi,' Ninety said good-naturedly, tugging at an imaginary cap and nodding agreement.

'Chuck, can you remember the exact layout of where slaves were held?'

'Can do, have done,' and Chuck took out a sheet on which he had earlier drawn an outline. 'We better learn some Catteni symbols, too, you know . . . to follow hall markings . . .'

Preparations took ten days, with long learning sessions for those who were chosen to take part. The selection was restricted to those whose physical appearance was closest to Catteni, who had already had some knowledge of the language and some experience with Barevi. Scott, Marrucci and Yuri did not, but they could be paired with those who did like Chuck, Ninety Doyle, Dowdall and Matt Su. Coo, Slav and Pess were a bit nervous about going, but they would be required to contact their own ethnic groups for what news they had. Kris was an essential addition for her knowledge of the city and familiarity with the flitters. The legs of one Catteni uniform had to be lengthened to fit her but, with her hair skinned back with the grey mud that would disguise Terran locks and the grey powder make-up, she passed well enough. She also knew enough Catten and the Barevian lingua to hire flitters and bargain properly. Someone not bargaining with Barevian shopkeepers would immediately be suspect. On both the KDL and the scout, enough Catteni script and coin were found. Zainal then told them that the habit was for ships to charge to their number, and the charges would be sent back to a central bank to make payments.

'And we'll be long gone before the reckoning,' Doyle chuckled, rubbing his hands together in anticipation.

'What happens, Zainal,' John Beverly asked one morning during the planning sessions, 'if someone recognizes *you*?'

All at the table – and Sandy Areson was sitting in that morning to explain about the grey 'make-up' – turned towards him.

'I am dead,' Zainal said, shrugging off that

consideration. 'No-one will expect to see me, especially in Drassi uniform,' he added.

Sandy tilted her head and then, rising and reaching across the table, turned him by the chin from one profile to the other.

'No problem,' she said. 'We add cheek pads so he looks fatter, another in front and some lines down his face to make him look older – and his own mother wouldn't recognize him.'

'What is this? Pads?' Zainal asked, somewhat dismayed.

'I used to do make-up for our theatre group, Zainal. Trust me. You won't recognize yourself. I'll bring some over to the cabin and show you,' and when she saw other sceptical expressions Sandy added, 'You won't know him either. Trust me.'

When she demonstrated to Kris and Zainal later that evening, it was remarkable the change those few alterations made.

'I'd slump were I you,' Sandy remarked. 'Drassi are small men and don't walk proud like an Emassi, you know.'

Zainal grinned as he thanked her, a grin that was substantially altered from his normal one with the pads in place.

'Take them out,' Kris said when Sandy had left. 'I'm not sharing this cabin with a total stranger. A very unattractive total stranger, I might add.' And she gave a shudder of dismay until he had removed the pads and looked himself again.

*   *   *

The arrival of the Ix Mentat and its two juniors at the Catteni main Earth spaceport in Texas, near what had been Houston, caused major security problems. Its reason for coming caused consternation, since the military governor was somehow sure that he would be forced to honourably end his life because he had *not* been able to quell the rebellion of the indigenous population, despite the severe measures he employed. He had scrupulously followed orders sent to him by the Mentats on Catten, but seemed no further towards controlling the tides of revolt and producing the wealth available from the planet than he had been in the first months of occupation.

When High Emassi Bulent learned the sort of equipment the Mentats had brought with them, he turned ashen, until he also heard that the mindprobes were to be used on humans, not ineffective Emassis.

Therefore he listened intently to the Ix Mentat's wishes, organized the search and rounded up as many of the required subjects as could be found. Some could be proven dead; others might well have been already transported, since they had resided in the fifty cities originally depopulated in the first wave of Catteni suppressions.

Bulent could almost feel sorry for the men and women rounded up and crammed into the open slave-pens, for the summer heat was intense, though he himself revelled in such temperatures. There were casualties from the heat and the crowding. He had the unenviable task of explaining to the Ix

Mentat that humans could not endure the solar rays that Catteni hides could, particularly humans in this upper age group as were most of the new prisoners. So they were moved to a huge shed that had been cleared of its exhibits.

Bulent's staff then had to assign numbers to the types of specialists the Ix wished to interrogate in order of rank within the science the humans had practised.

The Ix, Co and Se made trial examinations on lesser-known individuals with varying results. After four deaths with little information retrieved from the bursting brains, the instrument had to be re-calibrated. It had originally been used to upgrade Catteni mentality by expanding cerebral and cortical areas and stimulating certain centres in both lobes. The result had been the intelligent Emassi subset of Catteni who had originally been primitive and little more than upright animals. But what could be enhanced could also be withdrawn; that was the purpose of using the equipment on the humans.

The actual examination could take up to half a day, if the initial information plucked from the more accessible areas of the mind looked interesting. That is, if the subject was worth treating carefully. Otherwise an hour's viewing would suffice, but the subject rarely recovered much personality and memory. Incontinence was a frequent problem, and some retained insufficient intelligence to feed themselves. These were quietly disposed of.

In more judicious use of the mind probe, the Ix

and its juniors gained the codes to private files in research laboratories, but much of the material dealt only with human concerns. The Mentats found top security codes but they weren't interested in the politics, finding them very commonplace and predictable in the extreme; though there were one or two ploys that the Ix might use if the need arose.

Among its victims were the remaining heads of state who had not met with either transportation or execution, revealing the names of more important officials whose brains were full of sometimes amusing if petty details. Some investigations were more fruitful, leading the Mentats to find out what particular scientific studies were in progress and where. This was what the Ix had been searching for and it gave the High Emassi a list.

The High Emassi Bulent sent his minions scurrying to find these people. Often they returned empty-handed, with stories that the named persons had died or had possibly been transported, but certainly could not be found. Several of these, the Ix decided, must be found unless proof of death could be established beyond doubt. So Bulent despatched his best people, including several of the renegade humans, with instructions and promises of titillating rewards for success, to make a thorough sweep of known hiding-places and refuges.

The Ix exhausted all avenues to discover what little the humans had learned about the galaxy, the universe, and their incredibly primitive methods of star travel, as well as theories that, over its millenium of existence, it had already investigated, implemented or discarded.

The resultant human chaff that remained alive after these sessions was loaded on transports and sent to Barevi, to be sold as slaves for whatever use could be found for the near-mindless.

Then the Ix closed itself in its vessel and began to sift carefully through all it had learned, in the hope that perhaps there might be even one theory that would spark its high mentality towards a viable line of research.

On the off-chance that they could hijack another ship, Bert Put and Balenquah would come along as auxiliary pilots. It fell to Raisha, then, to pilot the scout to the Balloon and see if the coast was clear. Beverly and Marrucci had plotted the next five windows available that would avoid the orbital satellite, so it only remained to check on the absence of any Catteni ships in the general area.

Kris found it both hard and easy to leave Zane in Sandy's charge. She had been able to partially wean him, and he was already eating puréed foods. But Sandy promised that she would not stint him, and Kris could trust her. Pete Easley put in an appearance when she brought Zane to the crèche, feeling treacherous and unnatural because part of her was dying to go on this adventure and the other part would miss her darling son terribly.

'He's a good size, isn't he?' Pete remarked to no-one in particular as Kris started to hand him over to

Sandy. He was awake and in one of his giggling moods, the kind that are hard to ignore. 'Here, give him to me,' he said and gave Kris no chance to refuse.

Being the adaptable personality he was, Zane had no problems with being passed around and gurgled up at Pete Easley as happily as he would have done at Zainal.

Kris, watching the transfer, suddenly realized that Pete was telling her he intended to watch out for his natural son during her absence. His proprietorialness was both welcome and disturbing. But should the unthinkable happen, Kris knew that Pete Easley would assume responsibility for Zane – and, she had to admit, he had a right.

With a cheery wave at him and a farewell hug and kiss for Sandy, Kris left the crèche, her conflicting emotions gradually easing as she focused all her attention on the Mission.

Raisha took off in the scout to test the space beyond the Balloon just as Zainal aimed the KDL at the 'back door'. She poked the prow through the obstacle long enough to get a reading that there was nothing immediately visible in space. Zainal eased the KDL through the Balloon just above the southern polar region. He wasn't the only one to expel a gust of relief that the manoeuvre was unrestricted and the KDL allowed to exit. Then he aimed the ship towards the nearest of the five moons and, using that to hide his trajectory surveillance, made all speed to that point. Once there, he plotted the course out of the system and to Barevi's.

Even at the speed the KDL was capable of making, the journey would take three weeks. So there was more time in which to perfect their Catteni roles, and automatically respond to orders and queries. The meagre library of the KDL did contain spaceport plans for those planets under Catteni domination, and these were enlarged for study, especially by Bert and Balenquah if the chance of a second hijack was feasible. Scott was not yet committed to that objective.

'He wants a warship,' Mitford confided to Zainal and Kris. 'Fire-power.'

Zainal considered that. 'It might be possible to steal weapons, but even Catteni keep guards on warships. We don't have enough for crew. Maybe another time.'

Chuck and Kris gawked at him in surprise and he grinned back.

'Who was it said "think big"?'

'Dick Aarens?' Kris suggested.

There were also maps of Barevi which augmented the memories of those who had spent time in it – and how much a flitter should cost to such and such a destination. How to argue with cheaters, how to act if accosted for a fight . . .

'Catteni always fight,' Zainal said. 'Work off anger that way. Avoid at all costs.'

'Hey, it's easy enough to topple a Catteni,' Yuri said, proceeding to demonstrate a jujitsu manoeuvre on the unsuspecting Zainal. One moment the

Emassi was on his feet, the next flat on his back on the deck, looking both surprised and annoyed.

When Yuri offered him a hand up, he ignored it, but he was smiling when he got back on his feet.

'Teach us!'

So jujitsu, karate and other forms of martial arts were included in the daily training sessions.

'It is better we do no . . .' and Zainal grinned, 'species' injuries.'

'As if the Farmers would know or care,' scoffed Balenquah.

'*We* will know and *we* will care that harm has been done,' said Zainal, making his position plain to the surly pilot.

'You're a fine one to talk,' Sev Balenquah replied at his most contentious.

'I am finer than you know,' was Zainal's retort.

At this point Mitford, who was sitting next to the man, jabbed him so roughly in the ribs that he was winded.

'There's a brig on this ship,' Beverly said. 'D'you want to spend the rest of the trip in it?'

'Have it your way,' Balenquah said and, pushing away from the table, stalked off.

When Beverly would have called him back, Scott shook his head.

'We'd better watch that one,' Marrucci murmured to Beverly. Both the general and Scott nodded. 'Can't figure out what's wrong with him. And he's even got to fly again.'

Everyone took turns in the galley, leaving the Catteni food stores alone since they were even worse in taste than the bars supplied to transported prisoners. The KDL had originally had three freezers: two medium-size and one large storage type that was now in the mess hall, while one of the mediums was in the hospital. But the remaining one was adequate for the journey since Zainal expected to restock perishable goods from the markets at Barevi. Surprisingly enough, the Catteni galley had the equivalent of a microwave heating device, so that the pre-packaged soups, bread and meals that the mess hall had contributed to the Mission could be reheated.

By the time the first contact was made with the Barevian planetary authority, they had each perfected their skills to the best of their abilities. Even Balenquah could spit out appropriate answers; despite his more glaring personality defects, he was a natural linguist and Zainal hoped to use him to accompany Kris on her buying missions.

'He glowers just like my old boss,' Kris said, 'typical nasty Tudo. Whoops, not Tudo, Foto,' she said, correcting herself. She had known 'Foto' before she was aware of the distinction between Emassi and Drassi.

When hailed by the Barevian perimeter guards, Zainal, posing as Drassi Kubitai, barked the responses and Kris understood every word he said and every word the duty officer said. The KDL was officially the KDI, since the KDL would be listed as missing. There was no problem in the code.

'Sloppy,' Zainal muttered under his breath,

thankful though he probably was that this was the case.

He elected to overfly the town to give everyone the aerial aspect of it and help orientate them, giving a description of each area on his way to their appointed docking facility.

Matt Su was the putative navigator and Yuri the engineer. They both had immediate work to do, checking in with the port authorities: Matt to handle the 'paper work' and show the log which Zainal had created for them, while Yuri organized refuelling, watering and the usual docking procedures. Zainal paced about the dock area to be sure they encountered no immediate difficulties, while the various teams disembarked for their assignments.

Coo and Slav went off first, pretending pathetic eagerness to be away from the Drassi, while Pess stayed on board with Matt, Bert and Beverly – the latter two not to be seen. Pess and Matt had basic Barevi and some Catteni, so they were the best ones to stay behind and prevent unauthorized entry. Ninety and Dowdall would see if there were any humans in the slave markets. Zainal, Mitford and Scott would go into the centre of Barevi to have a meal and some drinks, and hear what there was in the way of gossip. Then, when Matt and Yuri had finished their details, Yuri and Marrucci would combine with Kris and Balenquah to get supplies in the market. Some could even be charged to the ship, so they could use what Catteni money they had for other things like the 'plursaw' additive the Deski needed. The original shipment was running low and there were new Deski babies in need of it. Zainal had made up a shopping list for them to display, as most Tudo couldn't read or write more than their own names, and signed it 'Drassi Kubitai'. He also made her practise the glyph for 'Kubitai' in case she had to sign chits for orders.

Kris was scared to the nails on her toes in the heavy Catteni boots. They were a bit large for her, although that only made her plod in a more authentic Catteni gait. She'd probably get heel blisters in spite of fluff-padding the toes, but she marched as smartly as the others did out of their berth and onto the main dock staging area. There were a few Catteni lounging about, watching Rugarians and Deski shift crates, load and unload material at other berths. The ship, berthed three places beyond the KDI, looked like another of her class, still so new she had few meteor pock-marks or dinges on her hull, and all of her paint looked fresh.

Marrucci caught Kris in the ribs with his elbow, grinning at the ship as a possible hijack victim. She grinned back and mouthed, 'No way, José!' at him. He kept grinning.

They saw no Terrans at all once they were out of the main facility and looking about for flitters. Zainal had said there were always a few waiting for possible passengers. They approached the first, its driver a wizened old Catteni whose face was badly scarred. Balenquah gave the orders, as sullen as a Catteni, and shoved everyone on board, his fingers lingering a little too long on Kris's hip as he did so, grumbling about wanting to get this duty over with. He squeezed himself next to Kris on the hard wide seat, his thigh pressing against hers in a way that made her want to prang him good. She could do nothing now but sit there and endure his attentions. Had the man no wits about him at all? Didn't he know she'd never let him get away with such nonsense? Wait till they got back to the KDL . . . no, KDI, she must keep that alteration firmly in mind. With the manoeuvres of the flitter in and out of traffic, Balenquah must be enjoying the ride, rubbing constantly against her leg. Marrucci caught her eyes once and gave her a look that meant he had not missed Balenquah's ploy.

Then they were over the open market area, their driver skilfully avoiding ascending arrogant flitters in the fashion that had always caused Kris near heart failure in her slave days. They got down safely enough, the driver grabbed the fare Balenquah offered and then flung his craft aloft, out of the way of incoming craft.

'Don't push me around, Balenquah,' Kris said in an undertone as they moved off.

'Who? Me?'

Marrucci prodded his back, telling him in Catteni to talk right, then asked Kris, also in the language, which direction to take.

'Here is food market for Deski additives. We buy enough, they deliver.'

'We buy plenty,' Marrucci said. 'Where?'

Kris had been looking around and spotted a crowd of Deski. 'There!'

'Deskis! Huh!' and Kris wasn't sure if Balenquah was acting in character or just being his charming self.

On their way, they passed a booth selling the alcoholic beverages only Catteni could stomach, but Balenquah insisted on stopping to sample one, saying he was thirsty.

'Not good,' Kris said, frowning because that was the best way to prove to Balenquah that he *should* try one. All were swill, but let him find that out.

Laughing and jostling her, he pointed to the amber bottle and a large glass. Even the stall-owner looked surprised. Guffawing, Balenquah clapped Kris so hard on the back that she nearly lost her balance but, knowing what was to come, she stood firm and waited.

Balenquah was even stupid enough to try to knock back the entire portion; he should have watched another Catteni, who was sipping cautiously. As the raw liquid began to burn down his throat, his eyes bulged and his greyed skin turned red enough to startle her, but somehow he got most of it down.

'Told you not good,' Kris said, deepening her voice. 'Better over there!' And she pointed to the corner where her master used to take a drink on market days. She left Balenquah to recover from the pilth – ah, she remembered the name of that particular poison – and strode on towards the Deski. She was also keeping on the alert for any bands of Catteni, swaggering around the market area just looking for trouble. Marrucci waited with Balenquah while Yuri moved out in step beside her.

'Good on you,' he muttered in English and she elbowed him. 'Agreed,' he added in Catteni.

They could both hear Balenquah hawking and spitting behind them, and gasping as his system tried to cope with the Catteni equivalent of anti-freeze. It certainly smelled like it. The pilth had also affected Balenquah's vocal cords, and he was reduced to gargling unintelligible words when he and Marrucci joined them at the Deski plursaw stall, for that was all this merchant sold. She argued over delivery charges, but then added more for an imme-diate delivery to the KDI. This was actually the most urgent of the supplies they were after. The next was salt: enough to use to preserve meats. Sugar was not a commodity known to the Catteni, so she was to get enough vinegar for pickling. These were easy, since she'd dealt with kitchen supplies and knew where to find them. At the same stall, she was aston-ished to discover what looked like rolls of cinnamon bark in a sack and a keg of nutmegs: the spicy scent of them was so familiar. She lifted a piece of curled brown bark high enough to her nose to be sure that it was indeed cinnamon – though what it was doing on Barevi was beyond her.

Then, in the gravelly voice she affected for Catteni words, she asked, 'What's this?' of the stall-keeper, dropping the bark curl indolently back into the bag and brushing her hand off on her uniform as any Catteni would.

She understood only half of what he said, catch-ing that it was from Terra and used in cooking; she should try some. She pretended indecision until

371

Marrucci tapped her shoulder and came to her rescue.

'Drassi Kubitai likes new things. Try it.'

That's when they were lucky, because the two commodities were so unusual and suspect that the stall-keeper had been unable to shift any and was feeling he'd made a bad purchase. So the bargaining began in earnest, but in the end she got the spices, the full keg and the sack, and had him throw in a large bag of peppercorns which he also hadn't been able to sell. Kris had no problem getting him to deliver to the KDI and could barely contain her delight in finding the seasonings; the mess hall would bless her for ever. She also got gallons of vinegar of a good quality.

In the next rectangle, Kris found fabrics of all kinds, colours, patterns and materials, some of which she recognized as Terran manufacture which both pleased and upset her. The Catteni must be looting the Earth right, left and centre. She suppressed resentment and went about bidding for whole bolts, in different shades and weights, for children's clothes. The local weaving industry would suffice any females who wanted something to wear that wasn't made over from Catteni coveralls, but the kids' needs were different. Kris bought enough to make the shopkeeper ask if she was a trader.

'Drassi is,' she said as if she thoroughly disapproved, pointing with no real attention to what she was buying. The last shop also sold needles, and indifferently she threw a handful of packets on the counter and made the shop-owner scrawl a receipt for her. 'Drassi requires.' Which was all she needed to say. 'Deliver by sundown and will get extra,' she said, winking as she had seen her steward master do from time to time.

Then she looked around for her shipmates and found them near a fruit-seller's stall as Balenquah tried to restore his throat lining.

'I told you no good,' she said and took a goru pear from the display pile. She turned her head slightly so the stall-keeper would not see that she did not have Catteni-size teeth as she tore off the tough peel as any good Catteni soldier would do and spat it out on the street. One thing for sure, she never thought she'd be eating these lovely winey fruits again. My, she'd come a long distance from that forest. She pointed to a net of the pears, asking the price.

'Four,' she said and then began haggling for a discount, just like in the old days. She got them at a good price – enough for everyone to enjoy on the way back to Botany – and tied the nets together and slung them over one shoulder. Yuri and Marrucci were watching her. 'Tell you later,' she said in Catten. 'This way.'

They went through another arcade, doors open to display the wares of the more permanently sited merchants, to where she thought she'd find ironmongery. The mess hall had also asked for some big stewing pots and cooking sheets. That sort of thing would be there and, sure enough, she acquired five cauldron-sized kettles and some huge baking tins. She also saw other items that were definitely Terran in origin, like the fabrics. If there was so much looting on Terra going on, maybe they'd be lucky enough to find medical equipment; Leon Dane had patiently drawn out the tools he especially needed. If she did, they'd basically filled today's list, and she wanted to be out of the market area soon. Once the guard changed, there'd be all kinds of gangs of them off-duty, drinking and looking for trouble: any trouble. So she wanted to get away from the area before the guards arrived.

Knives of the fine size and shapes Leon Dane had wanted were indeed available in one of the arcade stores, but at a price higher than Zainal had estimated. She bought what they had funds for – bundles of scalpels, lancets and the retractors, small-headed hammers and surgical saws. It looked from the display as if Earth hospitals had been thoroughly looted. Still, she bargained so hard that the trader wanted to know why she needed such Terran things.

'Terran? What's that?' and she pretended to try to find the name on the scalpel's handle.

'Where you been?'

'There and back,' she said with an indifferent shrug.

'Make it fast,' Marrucci said in an irritable tone and jerked his head over his shoulder at a gang of Catteni entering the rectangle at the far end, six abreast and brushing past everyone and everything in their way.

'Pack them. We have other business today,' she said and managed enough saliva to spit into the

374

gutter with. Turning her head, she was able then to gauge the speed at which the gang moved. 'Get Bal to a flitter,' she told Marrucci. 'Yuri stays.'

She didn't trust Balenquah if those Catteni muscled him out of the way.

'What takes you so long, Foto?' she snapped at the storekeeper who was making quite a job of packing the tools, but then the blades were very sharp.

Marrucci did get Balenquah out of the way: thanks to the pilth, he was in no condition to argue much. Kris had just got her hands on the packet from the shopkeeper when Yuri was bowled into her, knocking her into the shopkeeper's cabinet, causing half his stock to tumble about and several pieces – since the cabinet was open on his side – to stick into him. He was howling with pain and rage as he plucked sharp objects from his thighs.

Yuri reacted, ducking under the first swing of a squat Catteni guard and then kicking out at the assailant's kneecaps with a double strike that had the guard howling with pain and dropping to the ground. The shopkeeper shouted for help and grabbed at Kris, almost tearing the precious package from her hand; but she twisted her arm down and up and freed herself. When he came round the cabinet, bleeding from the cuts, she got him square in the guts with a karate kick, thrusting him backwards and into another glass-fronted cabinet. She heard him scream as a shard of glass penetrated his backside, but she didn't stop.

'Out of here,' she yelled in good Catteni, fright thickening her voice as she grabbed at Yuri's uniform just as he flipped another Catteni to his back.

Several of his mates, reacting to his groans and curses, started after them, but Catteni are not good runners and Yuri and Kris had very good reasons to run as fast as they could. They nearly ran over Marrucci who had come back for them, and so they all made tracks to the flitter where Balenquah slumped, victim of the pilth.

However, the state of him – or rather the smell that emanated from him – added to the bruised goru pears that had split open in the nets Kris had been carrying over her shoulder – made the flitter-driver waste no time in getting them back to the dock. When they arrived, the merchandise had too, with Pess, a cloth bolt in each arm, dealing with the loading.

'Did the plursaw come?' Kris asked, racing up the extruded gangway.

Pess grinned and nodded, speaking Barevi. 'First thing. See me, ask questions. I say Drassi orders. Don't know *what* he orders.'

Well, she could hope no-one heard her speak in English. Marrucci and Yuri were angling the un-conscious Balenquah out of the flitter as she went back to pay the driver.

'We the first?' she asked Pess as she helped him stow the cloth away, making sure that the needles had been included.

Pess nodded. 'What's wrong with pilot?'

'He drank pilth,' she replied, then grinned as she added, 'I told him it was no good.'

Pess smiled broadly and she managed to look away from that yawning cavern of greenish gum without giving him offence.

Beverly and Bert Put came out of hiding and, though they seemed somewhat distracted, listened to their adventures, chuckling over Balenquah's mishap. They approved her purchases, especially the spices, salt, vinegar and pepper.

'We had to quit because there was a roving band of Catteni looking for trouble,' Yuri said. 'We'll go for the electronics tomorrow,' he added, looking at Kris for confirmation.

Kris shared out the goru pears and explained how this particular fruit had figured heavily in her first trip to Barevi. They all agreed that the fruit was very tasty indeed.

'We can keep the pips and start our own bushes back on Botany,' she said, and was looking for something to store them in as she asked if there was any word from the other parties.

'Zainal reported in when he and Mitford reached the restaurant. So did Coo and Slav,' Beverly told them. 'But they had upsetting news.'

'How upsetting?'

Beverly and Bert exchanged anxious glances.

'It's not going to get any better waiting,' Kris reminded them, but a sick feeling started in her stomach.

'There are large numbers of Terrans here now, waiting to be shipped out.'

A pause.

'What's new in that?' she asked.

'Coo says they're damaged,' and Beverly tapped his skull. 'They sit or stand and do not speak.'

'WHAT?'

She, Yuri and Gino reacted simultaneously and stared in horrified consternation at Beverly.

'Coo says he heard their minds were taken from them.'

'The Eosi have mind-wipes?' she whispered, appalled.

'Does Zainal know?' Marrucci asked, equally shocked.

'Coo says everyone talks about it – quietly. Even the Catteni. Zainal will also hear.'

Marrucci swore inventively and without repeating himself. Yuri looked pale under his grey face-paint; it was cracking around the natural creases of his face and, absently, she reminded herself to tell him to powder up before he went outside again.

'Zainal won't do anything drastic until he can check with you, will he?' Kris asked Beverly. 'WHAT do the Eosi intend to *get* out of minds? They wouldn't know about us.'

'Coo said they are older men mostly, some women . . .'

'Scientists, I bet,' Kris said and Beverly nodded sadly. 'Oh God, what did we start?'

Beverly covered her hand with a reassuring grip. 'We started a rebellion, Kris, as we wanted to on Earth and couldn't. But Zainal knew how and has.'

'But the cost!' She gripped her hands together, holding in the pain of guilt.

'When was there ever a war without casualties?' Yuri said in a bleak voice, absently doodling with the water spill on the table until it was spread out in a Rorschach blob.

'What about Ninety and Dowdall?'

'They say the pens are full of humans. They also heard about the zombies,' Beverly said. 'They're on their way back, too, before the guard changes.'

'Dowdall remembered that, did he?' Kris said, nodding with satisfaction.

Zainal, Scott and Mitford returned in a silence that spoke more profoundly of the tragedy than words. The first thing Zainal did was remove the cheek and chin pads that disguised him.

'We managed to get into one compound,' Scott said, slumping in a chair and taking the glass of hooch that Kris immediately poured for all three. 'I recognized a few faces from articles and newspapers. You'd probably recognize more, John, Gino. The ones I could identify were top people in quantum physics, organ transplants and laser applications.'

'Lasers can be used as weapons,' Kris murmured.

'Eosi have such already,' Zainal replied, also speaking in a low voice.

'Will they . . . recover?' Kris asked.

Zainal shook his head but added, 'It depends how long they were subjected to the probe. The Eosi have little pity.'

'Other news is good, though,' Scott said, shaking

379

off that dispiriting vision. 'Earth continues to rebel, and Catteni are looting on a massive scale.'

'I wondered about that,' Kris said. 'I bought nutmeg, cinnamon, pepper, salt, bolts of Earth-made fabric and needles, surgical equipment: no doubt part of that loot. I hadn't enough money with me to buy everything Leon said he needed. Do we have more to spend?' she asked Zainal, who nodded.

'No electronics?' Scott asked, perturbed. 'We need them more than surgical tools.'

'If the Catteni have looted as thoroughly as it looks like they have, we'll find all the Terran electronics we could possibly want. But we encountered an off-duty squad,' Kris said and Zainal grunted. 'And left.'

'We did, too,' Dowdall said. 'The spaceport's full. We were lucky to get a berth.'

'Any damage?' Zainal asked.

'Not to us,' Kris grinned. So did Dowdall.

'Where's Balenquah?' Scott asked, looking around.

'Sleeping off a full glass of pilth,' Kris replied, grinning maliciously.

Zainal roared with laughter.

'I told him it was no good,' Kris said, still grinning as Yuri and Marrucci chuckled.

'Serves him right, too,' said Marrucci, but Kris gave him a look and he didn't elaborate.

'Did you get the Deski plursaw?' Zainal asked.

She nodded. 'At a good price, too. I got as much delivered as I could; Pess has most of it already stored away. "Drassi says",' and she grinned at him for the efficacy of that cryptic explanation.

Coo and Slav returned then, Slav with a cut over one eye and Coo with visible abrasions down one side of his slender frame.

'Trouble?' Zainal asked, on his feet.

Coo held up one hand reassuringly. 'Catteni gang. Hate aliens.'

'They hate anyone,' Dowdall said forcefully. 'Here, lemme fix that cut for you, Slav,' and he took him over to the cabinet containing the few medical supplies they had. Slav endured the ministrations though the orange-brown Catteni antiseptic stung like fire, even a Catteni.

'Bad news,' Coo said, joining the others at the table.

Mitford fixed herbal tea when Coo politely refused to drink the hooch already set out.

'They're after your people, too?' Scott asked.

Coo shook his head. 'We do not make machines.'

'My people must work in noisy places,' Slav said, scrubbing his chest hair in agitation. 'We are strong.'

'You Earth no good working,' Coo said, grinning. 'Too much trouble.'

'We make trouble,' Slav said, 'if word is given.' And he looked pointedly at Mitford.

'All suppressed minorities rebelling at one time would be difficult for the Eosi to handle,' Scott said, immediately savouring the notion.

Zainal, however, snorted and shook his head. 'More species' injuries.'

Scott slammed one fist onto the table so hard that

381

the hooch bottle jiggled. 'Damn it, Zainal, there're already species' injuries on my people. You saw the state of them. How many more will be put through the same torture? Then sold off as mindless zombies and die who knows where!'

Kris had never seen Scott so emotional but then, she could only imagine the horror of seeing brilliant people reduced to imbeciles.

'The Eosi look for ideas from your people,' Zainal said, and there was no doubt from the perturbation on his usually inscrutable face that he felt for the victims and agreed with Scott. 'When they find none they can use, they will stop.'

'When . . .' demanded Scott, stretching the 'n' out to stress the urgency, 'will that be?'

'I heard nothing today. Tomorrow we can go elsewhere and listen, and maybe ask.'

'And all those . . . those desecrated people?' Scott asked, grieving so keenly that Kris saw tears in the admiral's eyes.

'We can do something about *that*,' Zainal said firmly. Then he turned to Kris and Marrucci. 'Tomorrow, early, get the wire, the plastic, the electronic supplies needed. Be ready to move if I arrange . . .'

'What are you arranging?' Mitford asked, though the look on his face suggested to Kris that he already had a suspicion.

'What can be done to help. The Farmers do not *like*', and Zainal emphasized that word, 'species injuries. We show them what can happen.'

'We'll bring them back with us?' Scott began, his

expression brightening for a scant second before common sense overruled that possibility. 'How can we possibly care for so many damaged people?'

'We will somehow.' Kris spoke so fiercely that Scott recoiled. 'How many are there?'

'Hundreds,' Scott said, waving a despairing hand about.

'Not all are damaged,' said Zainal. 'But they *will* die in mines and fields with no care given.'

'We can't leave them if we *can* take them,' Dowdall said firmly, glancing around the table for agreement. Even the two Deski and Slav were in accord.

'Zainal, did you notice the other ship of this class a few berths down from us?' Marrucci asked, his eyes sparkling.

Bert Put, who had been silent through most of the discussion, sat up with an expectant look on his face, watching Zainal.

He nodded, a grin turning his mouth up in one corner. 'I maybe go see guard tonight, drink a little pilth.'

'No,' Mitford said with an evil grin, 'he'd be used to that. Take some of the hooch.'

The next morning as they breakfasted, Zainal had good news from his evening's interview. Most of the KDM's crew were on shore leave, having just completed a wide swing which had included Earth. In fact, they had brought two decks full of the brain-wiped humans to the slave marts, and loot that would soon be available in the Barevi markets. Only two crewmen were on board, taking turns on watch; they were not happy about that duty but expected to be relieved in another two days. As was standard practice with Catteni ships, the KDM was already refuelled and stocked. The crewmen said they were slated for another trip to Earth: to collect cargo, as the Catteni invaders were systematically clearing warehouses and storage facilities, whether the items were useful or not.

'Whatever the Eosi hoped to find on Earth, they have not,' Zainal said. 'Not even information. They may even be pulling out.'

'What?'

'Leaving Earth?'

'Hurrah, we socked it to them and they couldn't take it.'

'No rush,' Zainal said, raising his hands to indicate caution. 'Your Earth may never be the same.'

'Then we improve it when we get back home,' Beverly said, a fierce expression on his face.

Zainal pointedly said nothing. 'I also learn that the port manager is very busy with so many ships going in and out.'

'Which means he's not checking on individual ones?' Beverly asked.

Zainal nodded. 'We come at a lucky time.'

'Let's leave lucky, too,' Mitford said gruffly. 'If we get all the stuff we need, can we like leave tonight? I got a gut feeling we're crowding what luck we've already had. On our way back, I spotted just too many of those roving gangs charging about drunk. Glad we weren't on foot.'

Everyone looked at Zainal, who hesitated and then nodded. 'Sooner is better than later, but first,' and he held up one finger, 'we do not go back empty.'

'Hey, if there's only two crewmen aboard the KDM, couldn't we hijack it?' asked Gino eagerly.

Mitford made a disgusted sound, dismissing the notion, but Scott leaned forward eagerly. 'Could we?'

'I think it would be very easy. Gino can be captain. Balenquah . . .' and Zainal looked around for the man.

'He was sick all night,' Mitford said sourly. 'He's no use to us at all. I never did have more than a sip of pilth, and that was enough to make me avoid it.'

'I told him it was no good,' Kris repeated, with an innocent expression on her face.

'Which made him all the more eager to try it, huh?' Mitford asked, giving her a dirty look.

'He deserved it—' Gino Marrucci began, but Kris kicked him under the table. 'Sullen bastard that he is,' the pilot said, in place of what he had started to say.

'All right,' said Scott, getting back to the jobs at hand, 'we find out what we can about the . . . disabled? Right?' He looked at Zainal, who nodded. 'You got yesterday's list, Kris? So today escort Matt Su, Ninety and Marrucci for whatever electronics we can acquire . . .'

'We'll find plenty,' Kris said, scowling. 'I only had

a quick glance, but everywhere I looked I could see things that had to have come from home.'

'Good,' said Matt, 'that means we'll have a good chance of finding what we need. We've done as much as we can with the Farmers' material. But we could do a helluva lot more with familiar components, couldn't we, Dowdall?'

'Also get more hand-units,' and Zainal tapped his Catteni comunit. 'We need all we can get, or make.'

Kris shoved pencil and the thin plastic that the Catteni used for notes towards him. 'Make us out another shopping list, Drassi Kubitai!'

Zainal grimaced. 'I do not know the Catteni shapes,' he admitted wryly.

'No word for spare parts in Catteni?' Matt asked, grinning.

'Ah, yes,' and Zainal deftly created the glyph, adding tails and squiggles to it. 'That means anything to repair electronics.' He peered at it. 'I think.'

'Have we completely contaminated an upright Catteni lad?' Matt asked with one of his displays of whimsy.

'Absolutely,' Zainal agreed heartily. 'Let us make . . . con . . . con-something plans . . .'

'Contingency plans?' Kris asked.

'Them. In case there can be two shipments of humans to mines or colonies or wherever they plan to send them. We are ready to go and take the problems with us,' Zainal said. 'I call in to Chuck, I tell him where to bring KDM. Then, sergeant, you will take more hooch to guard on duty. The other will be sleeping. You will know what to do. Then Gino,

Beverly, Coo, Pess and Slav get aboard as crew. Bert, Gino, be ready to bring the ships where I tell you.' He flipped through the pile of maps and charts and found the one he wanted. 'Here are slave pens, but you must go round the city, not overfly.'

'Don't we have to clear take-off with the port authority?' Gino asked.

Zainal slapped his forehead and sucked in breath between his teeth.

'After we secure the KDM, I can come back and do that, Zainal,' Mitford said. 'Give me the words for slave compound in Catteni. I only know Barevi.'

'Use Barevi if you need to,' Zainal said, rocking one hand to indicate that the port authorities would know both. Then he rose in a decisive manner. 'Good luck.' And he gave the thumbs-up signal, grinning when his eyes fell on Kris.

'Right back atcha,' she said as everyone else got to their feet. 'And watch your face paint if you start to sweat, you guys. And, for godsake, remember to keep your caps down, shading your eyes. No Catteni I've ever seen has blue ones, much less brown.'

'Slav, Pess, Coo, you guard ship,' was Zainal's final order as he made for the hatch.

Kris, with Dowdall, Matt and Ninety, got the last remaining flitter outside the port. The driver grumbled that the market wasn't open yet.

'Shop I go is,' Kris answered in Barevi. 'Drassi says so.'

That ended any further enquiries from the

Catteni. He had no left hand, a hook attachment replacing it, but a flitter was easily driven with only one. Did only disabled Catteni get taxi licences on Barevi?

As the craft made its way to the market area, they all noticed smoke rising from various places.

'Many fights?' Ninety asked in Barevi, grinning but remembering to keep his lips over his teeth.

'Many,' replied the Catteni in his own language and in a sour tone. 'Nine ship gangs. Biggest fights in weeks.'

Which meant the survivors would likely be sleeping off pilth as well as any injuries from the fighting – or hiding out for the requisite twenty-four hours. Luck was again with them, she hoped, but didn't dare hope too loudly.

Much of the first marketplace they overflew – the one they had shopped in the day before – was a wreck of tangled stalls, debris, and shopkeepers sorting for what might still be saleable. As they crossed over the line of apartments separating the two, she saw that streamers of fabric, probably from some of the shops she had visited, festooned the area.

'Boys had lots of fun,' Ninety muttered and got Kris's elbow in his ribs for speaking in English. He rolled his eyes in apology, but the driver had not heard.

There was not quite as much damage in the third rectangle, the one they had directed the flitter to – possibly because there were fewer drink and food stands in this one. But one section seemed to have been levelled. Kris just hoped it wasn't the very one they needed the most.

'Another ticco if you wait,' she told the driver in her gravelly Catteni voice. She was getting so she could do it whenever she needed to, though her throat was a trifle sore from all the rough-voiced bargaining she'd done yesterday.

'Just one ticco?' he complained.

'Wait and see,' she said, leaving it to him. She handed him a smaller coin and pointed to the stand selling hot drinks and the almost indigestible bread Catteni baked.

That sweetened him sufficiently and she walked off with the others to find the 'spare parts'.

Four shops which displayed boxes spilling loose chips in their grilled windows were not open. They came upon a fifth on the long end of the rectangular market area where the shopkeeper was sweeping up components and chips, with total disregard for the damage done. Matt and Dowdall winced and Kris hissed at them for falling out of character.

'You selling?' she asked, acting the stupid Catteni Tudo.

'What does it look like?' the shopkeeper replied angrily, gesturing at the havoc within and without. He ranted on, switching from Barevi to Catteni in his fury.

Kris held up Zainal's glyphed note. 'You got some?'

The shopkeeper paused long enough in his description of what he would do to the gang who had smashed and kicked his stock into garbage and, eyeing her suspiciously, then turned his attention to Matt and Dowdall who were lovingly picking up this and that which had not been damaged.

'Got everything needed for repair. And then some . . . if it hasn't all been smashed.'

He put down the broom and led them through the shop, palmed open a rear door and showed them unopened cardboard boxes, all bar-coded and listing the contents in English, French, German and either Japanese or Chinese . . . Kris couldn't tell the difference.

'Ah, many unhurt,' she cried. 'Drassi wants.'

'All?' The shopkeeper was both delighted and suspicious.

'Drassi Kubitai trades,' said Dowdall, winking as he began removing boxes from the shelves and stacking them in the centre. His eyes were so alight with success that Kris yanked furiously at her own cap to warn him. 'Kubitai pleased with us,' he said in Barevi, turning his face away.

'Not all, but samples to show. How much?' Kris began, tapping the boxes Dowdall had chosen and to which Matt was adding selections, breathing heavily with excitement but remembering to keep his head down. 'You deliver?'

'Ha! When I must clean this and lock up before they come back again?'

'Kubitai wants comunits, Drassi?' Matt asked, returning from a back shelf with a crate.

Kris pretended to look at the list. The shopkeeper pointed to the right glyph. 'Here, stupid,' he said, his yellow eyes turning crafty as he suspected he might be able to do her on the prices.

'I count well,' she said, jerking her cap to shade her eyes but looking fiercely at him. 'I be Drassi soon. You see.'

'Ha!' was his reply, but he began to move the chosen boxes towards the front of the shop. 'You got transport?'

'Flitter,' she said. 'I call it over.'

She had to fetch the flitter driver, who had indeed been treating himself to a meal on her coin. When he saw how much was stacked out in the litter in front of the smashed shop, he shook his head.

'Call another,' she told him, pointing to his control panel. 'Drassi Kubitai very happy with us. We get long shore leave.' She strutted back to the shop to find Dowdall, looking anxious.

'Won't he suspect when we order so much? And check out the KDI?' He spoke in a barely articulated whisper.

'He probably has and, if the port authority has time to answer him, will know which berth the KDI has,' she murmured back and then, seeing the shop-man out of the corner of her eye, punched Dowdall in the arm. 'Work! No work, no leave!'

However, greed – and possibly the call to the dock to verify that a KDI with a Drassi Kubitai was in port – moved the shopkeeper to encourage the large order.

Kris bargained in earnest with him, as part of her character as not-so-stupid-Tudo messenger. She had no idea what the parts would have cost on Earth, but Matt was slightly agog at the range of the merchandise. There were even laptops still in their packing-cases. Now what possible use would the Catteni have for such items? They couldn't even read the manuals, much less figure out what the icons meant. She'd had enough trouble with her 286 IBM clone at college. Noticing a dozen units along with all the other parts, plus toolkits and several cases of floppies, she devoutly hoped she wouldn't have to explain why those were among her purchases. She only knew so much Catteni and Barevi.

Kris haggled, and finally made her mark on the collection of glyphs that spewed out of his electronic equipment. She also added the glyph for 'Kubitai' that Zainal had shown her, grateful for his forethought.

Then they all loaded the boxes into the flitters. Their driver had estimated the cargo space required and called in two, not one.

All the way across the city, Kris forced herself to cheerful thoughts, terrified that something might happen and they'd be caught by an army trap or port patrol or some other unexpected glitch. But they made it safely back to the berth, and started unloading. Mitford, Gino, Slav, Coo and Pess hurried out to speed the process along, Gino whistling under his breath at the range of their purchases.

'Catteni can't whistle,' Kris said inside the safety of the ship.

'Ooops!'

'Any word from Zainal?'

Gino shook his head, trotting back down the ramp, muttering unintelligible noises that could be muffled Catteni curses and adding, 'Drassi says,' in a grumpy tone.

They had nearly finished the unloading when Balenquah staggered into the open hatch, his grey face-paint smeared with rivulets of sweat, his hair mud rubbed off overnight on the pillow, looking not at all like any Catteni.

Mitford recovered first. 'Sick! Get back! Dow, Nin, get him back!' The two hauled the pilot back out of the way and he had time for only one muffled protest before someone knocked him out. Mitford rolled his eyes at Kris, who was facing the stunned flitter drivers.

Taking her cue from Mitford's remark, she shook her head, feeling quite ill suddenly too.

'Very sick. Terran sick,' she said, still shaking her head and making her wobbly legs carry her back down the ramp. There were only a few more boxes to be stored.

'Dockmaster knows?' the one-handed Catteni asked, his murky yellow eyes suspicious.

'Dockmaster says keep him on board and take him back to Terra,' Mitford said, keeping his face away from the Catteni. 'Leave him there.'

'Drassi say we leave today,' Kris added for good measure. 'I take shore leave back here! Told Bal no good there.'

She gave the drivers just enough to satisfy them, not too meagre a sum to annoy them yet not enough to be considered a possible bribe. Mentally she blessed those awful shopping journeys with her Catteni steward for knowing the difference.

With them safely off the dock area, she marched herself straight to the bottle of hooch and poured herself a stiff one. Dowdall and Ninety joined her, silently taking the bottle from her hand.

'We tied him in,' Dowdall said, 'goddamn stinking arrogant bastard nearly blew the whistle on us!'

'He might still have,' Mitford said, holding out his hand for the bottle. 'I'm not sure the one-handed guy bought the explanation.'

'Yeah, but why would he suspect Catteni-dressed soldiers to be anything but Catteni?' Kris said, reaching for reassurance.

'There is that,' Mitford agreed.

'Is it safe?' whispered Beverly and Bert Put from their compartment.

'For now,' Kris told them, sitting down because her legs had never felt so kneeless. She buried her head in her hands. 'I never want to go through another moment like that.'

An urgent buzz from the com board on the bridge startled all of them. Beverly and Mitford tried to get through the door at the same time, with the sergeant twisting his torso edgewise to allow the general through first.

'Schkelk?' Beverly asked in proper Tudo response as he keyed open the ship's unit. 'Oh, thank God,' and, craning her head towards the bridge, Kris could see him visibly relax. For just one moment . . . then he straightened and urgently beckoned the others to come in. 'Yes, yes, I got you. What does forty-seven look like in Catteni, for God's sake? Oh.' He had grabbed up a pad which Mitford now held firmly for him since he had the hand unit. 'Thick upright, two cross bars, three down strokes and a small right-hand square within the end two right-hand down strokes. Got that. That's for the KDI?' Beverly began to smile and heaved a sigh of relief that seemed to permeate his whole frame. 'Thank God,' he whispered. 'Okay, so there's just a change in the final figure, a circle rather than a square between the two right-hand down strokes? Got it. Be there as fast as we can get permission to quit the dock. Watch for us.'

He toggled the line closed.

'Contingency plan is now in operation. Mitford, grab another bottle of hooch and go visiting. Gino, Coo, Slav, Pess, Ninety, lounge outside like you're bored. We're going to rescue us some folks. And God grant there's some spark of mind left to them. We're clearing the prisons.'

'I know how to work the levels,' Kris said and grabbed Ninety by the hand. 'I'd better show you. Let's hope they're the same as the wreck's.'

The controls were sited in the same place by the hatch, although they looked in far better working order.

'And will they be drugged and all?' Ninety asked anxiously.

'I hope so. They'll survive better if they are,' Kris said, deliberately not thinking about that process and the bodies that would shortly inhabit the four levels of shallow deck. 'Take a peek outside, Ninety, just in case we have unexpected visitors,' she said, shoving the comunit from her belt at him.

Chapter Thirteen

For a contingency plan, hastily organized and speedily executed, it went very well. But there were other Catteni around on the dockside now, shifting cargoes or watching the Rugarians do so. Bert Put's height would make him stand out like the proverbial sore thumb. So he got wrapped up in blankets and Dowdall and Slav carried him over to the KDM, grumbling about Drassis and their crazy tradings back and forth. Then they returned to the KDI.

'Piece of cake,' said Mitford when he returned to the KDI. 'Front and centre, Bert, General. We're about to shift ass off this sinkhole.'

'What about Zainal and Scott?' Ninety asked.

'We meet them at platform forty-seven and forty-nine when we pick up our passengers. Now I gotta log on to port authority and get clearance.'

While Bert settled into the captain's chair, Beverly took the engineer's place as Mitford made contact with the port authority. Kris watched as his shoulders stiffened and he rolled his eyes.

What now? That glitch she had been expecting all along that was going to betray them? She fretted, knees getting wobbly again.

'Sick?' Mitford exclaimed in Catteni, and swore

with unexpected fluency in the language for emphasis. 'Yes, Terran sick.' He sounded disgusted. 'We dump him with others. They not see,' and he managed a very evil chuckle. 'Kotik. Ten.'

He whistled when he closed the switch. 'That driver was suspicious. Let's get out of here before anyone comes to look at our Terran-sick soldier. Take her no higher than a thousand plegs, Bert. That's our assigned level.'

He gave Kris a good-luck sign and, grabbing another bottle of hooch, leaving only two left for the journey home, he sauntered back to the recently hijacked vessel.

Bert initiated the undocking procedures, starting the siren to warn the crew back inside, closing the hatch when they reported all in, starting the engines, just as if he'd done it all his professional life. The KDI lifted easily, Bert made the course correction and they could see the spaceport steadily receding. On the small thrusters that were permissible in such crowded air space, it seemed to take a long time to circumnavigate Barevi town, strewn before them, and out into the nearby forests and fields. They could see where big land-moving equipment was knocking down trees and scooping up great mountains of rock and dirt to clear more space – doubtless, Kris thought bitterly, for the masses of products they were importing from a pillaged Earth.

Flitters darted in and around, and each one that seemed to choose a trajectory in front of Kris made her catch her breath.

'They can't see in,' Bert said, to reassure her. 'And I'll turn this seat over to you immediately if we are hailed. Wouldn't you like to drive this beauty for a while?'

His banter made her relax, but she stayed right beside his position in case they had to execute a quick shift.

They did have a little trouble deciding which platform they should dock at, since there were only minor changes in the basic glyph that Zainal had given them. But as they cruised at the slowest possible forward speed, everyone on the bridge identified the number at the same moment, and could even see the KDM's platform just beyond.

Below were the slave pens, similar to the ones Kris had been in when she'd been forced aboard the transport that had landed her on Botany so many months ago. There were acres of pens, spreading out from a huge rectangular building. However, not all the pens were full or in use. Only four. She couldn't see who inhabited the ones beyond platform forty-nine, and hoped she wouldn't ever know who or what they had had to abandon that day.

Bert neatly sidled into the platform, cut the engines and opened the hatch. Kris took her station at the controls and suddenly Zainal strode up the ramp, spitting out the disfiguring pads, muttering under his breath and snarling up at her but winking as he passed on his way to the bridge. Kris managed a very subservient 'Yes, Drassi,' and saw the first of the pathetic transportees.

She nearly burst into tears at the sight of the

expressionless faces, the dead eyes, the automatic motion that no intelligence motivated. She did manage to alter the decks to the lowest one as the loading process began.

Half the time, she had all she could do to keep from bawling out loud, getting some relief by snarling at the Catteni who drove these poor wights up the ramps. Most had their blankets slung over their shoulders, and one hand held the packet of ration bars to their bodies, the other held the treacherous soup cup now emptied of its contents. She told herself over and over that she was rescuing them: they'd soon be safe, they'd soon be cared for – and wondering how on earth they would manage all these walking dead at Botany where there was so much hope and life and a future.

She shifted blindly when the first level was filled. Several of those trudging like sheep up the ramp staggered and fell. It was all she could do to keep herself at the controls and not go to help them up, but that would have been out of character for the Catteni Tudo she was pretending to be. She was *not* going to cause a glitch; she was rescuing these people, she was doing all she could.

She shifted to the third level and then it was filled up. So was the air around her, with little sobs and cries for pity from those in the lower decks. The drugged soup couldn't put them out of their immediate misery – and hers – soon enough.

It was Zainal who carefully removed her hands from the controls when the ramp retracted and the hatch clanged shut. He helped her back to the wardroom and poured her another shot of hooch.

'We're almost out of it,' she protested.

'You need it now, Kris,' he said. 'I hadn't realized what you were in for. I'd have done it myself—'

'No, no,' and she shook her head, 'not a Drassi captain.' Then she put her head on the table and began to weep.

'They're all asleep now,' Zainal said, gathering her up in his arms and against his chest, stroking her hair.

'Zainal?' she cried, raising her tear-marked face. 'Did we get them all?'

'All we can cram on board. A few spare Deski, Rugarians, half a dozen Ilginish and some Turs for good measure.'

'We need Ilginish and Turs so badly, don't we?' she quipped, trying to control her weeping.

Ninety and Beverly stood in the doorway. Zainal nodded at them to enter and both poured a hefty tot from the bottle.

'We don't have much left,' Kris said inanely.

'It's medicinal, my dear,' said Beverly, and she thought he looked awful under his coffee-coloured skin. 'Dowdall says the KDM's on a parallel course. There's incoming traffic, but we're cleared to leave the system and doing it with all possible speed.' He let out a long sigh and knocked back the rest of the hooch. 'You're relieved, Bjornsen. I don't want to see you on deck for two full shifts.'

'Aye, aye, sir,' she said, managing a weak smile and limp salute.

Zainal helped her to stand and guided her back to

her compartment. He had to lift her up into the upper bunk but his hands, as he covered her with the rough Catteni issue blanket, were very gentle.

They answered several challenges over the next two weeks, until they got to the less trafficked area leading to the Botany system. Most were more or less standard ship-talk, which Zainal handled on the bogus KDI and Mitford on the KDM.

They also talked about how they could integrate the people they had rescued into the Botany colony.

Kris found herself regarding Admiral Ray Scott with amazement: under all that naval braid and command training there was a man with un-expected compassion. And a high moral integrity. She wasn't the only one who kept reassuring him that there was no way those folks could have been allowed to depart on Catteni slave ships.

'Hell, Ray,' Beverly said the second evening, 'it isn't as if there are more of them than there are of us! So we'll need to hunt more often and plant a few more fields. If we have to, we'll form a crèche situation for the ones who can do nothing for themselves. We don't even know just how badly some of them were mind-wiped. There may be something there that some of our psych people can revive. For all that, maybe just being among humans again . . . begging your pardon, Zainal . . . and good food and attention will bring some around.'

'Almost everyone's got some kind of house now.

We can give them shelter, food and . . . a lot of caring,' Dowdall said, clearing his throat. He was another one who didn't let emotions overwhelm him.

'And we shall inform the Farmers,' Zainal said.

'You think they can perform some sort of psychic whammy and replace what got wiped?' Dowdall asked.

Zainal shrugged. 'It is possible since their science is so much better than ours. Why not such healing?'

'I think that's asking for too much of a miracle,' Ray Scott said, although the brief flare of hope in his eyes at the mere suggestion of a possible restoration was not lost on anyone at the table.

'We shall inform them,' Zainal repeated.

'Speaking for myself,' Kris said, 'they can't be any more trouble than a baby and we can handle one more in our house, can't we, Zainal?'

He nodded. 'If he or she doesn't get too upset seeing a Catteni around.'

'Well, I think', Kris went on staunchly, 'it's important for everyone to know that there is at least one good Catteni in this universe!'

They were nearing the heliopause when Zainal mentioned – quite casually, Kris thought, that it was just possible that they might have a little trouble getting the second ship through the Balloon.

'Why?' Kris asked. 'They're alike as two peas in a pod.'

'There are two, and only one went out.'

'The KDL was pregnant when she left. The KDM is her daughter,' Kris said, surprising herself with such a whimsy. The others around the wardroom table laughed politely.

'It is a problem,' said Beverly.

'Why?' Scott wanted to know. 'If we proceed slowly as we did getting out, just nudging past the Balloon.'

Zainal was not convinced.

'Too bad we can't call downside and get Raisha up in the scout to poke a hole for us,' Bert said. 'We could go piggy-back, maybe,' he suggested, and then cancelled that notion with a whisk of his hand. 'Too risky.'

Zainal agreed with a sceptical twist of one shoulder.

'Fine thing if we get these folks right up to the door and can't wedge 'em in,' said Dowdall.

'There *has* to be a way,' Scott said, looking at Zainal for inspiration.

'If there is, we find it,' the former Emassi said.

But it was obvious that everyone on board the KDL worried about it for the rest of the journey through the solar system to its third planet.

'Engines,' said Kris as she sat on the bridge watching their approach to Botany.

'What?' Scott demanded. He looked up from the final course plotting that would escape both the satellite and orbital observation.

'Would there be such a thing on board as a tractor beam?' she asked Zainal.

'A what?' He frowned, unable to find those words in his now very large vocabulary.

'Something to pull another ship along, a ship with no power.'

'She's got it!' Scott said. 'Does the KDL have one?'

It took a little time for Zainal to understand exactly what they meant, but when he did his grin was broad.

'Not a tractor beam but is possible to connect,' and he jammed both fists together. 'One ship hull is negative, the other positive. Very easy to do. I tell Bert.'

They had not allowed themselves many inter-ship broadcasts on the off-chance that they might be overheard. But now, so close to Botany, they could risk it. The orbital might pick up some of what was transmitted, but not enough to give any alert. Not unless there were Eosi hiding behind the moons.

'Oh, he means magnetize the hull,' Bert said, catching on. 'Okay, give me the procedure.'

The light bump as the KDM magnetically sealed itself behind the KDL was felt by everyone. There was also a certain tingling in the air. The KDL would be pushed through the Balloon first, propelled by the KDM. All watched nervously as the Balloon's smooth skin got closer and closer and behind it, a luminous half-moon, was Botany. Bert had slowed to the barest possible forward motion while Zainal, in the fore, guided him. The nose of KDL prodded the Balloon, which gaped wide enough to admit the ship. All of the KDL was

shortly inside the Balloon and they felt no resistance, nor sudden disconnection of the KDM.

'We did it!' crowed Bert on the open line. 'We did
it! Now how do I separate us? Just kidding.'

Then Rastancil opened a channel, demanding to
know were they all right? What was the other ship
doing on his screen? 'What have you guys been up
to?'

'Well, we needed it to complete our . . . rescue
mission,' Scott said, suddenly dropping from the
high of successfully penetrating the last obstacle to
home. 'We couldn't just . . .' and his voice faltered
then continued firmly, 'leave them there on Barevi.'

'Rescued? Who? What?'

'You'll see,' Scott said almost angrily. 'Some of
them are pretty bad. Have all the medics on hand
and anyone else we've got with any nursing experience. Especially the psychiatrists. We've some more
Catteni prisoners to go to the valley. So have Raisha
stand by to fly 'em out. Then we'll need another
valley for a bunch of Turs we had to bring along,
too. She ought to have guards with that lot in case
any wake up prematurely.'

'Medics? Psychiatrists? What sort of casualties are
they?' Rastancil sounded alarmed.

'You'll see soon enough,' Scott said in a terse
voice, 'and we'll need a good nutritious soup or
something easy to eat.'

He disconnected, a brooding expression on his
face.

'It'll work out, Ray,' Kris said, laying a hand on
his arm. 'You'll see.'

405

'Botany can take on any challenge,' Dowdall added with the pride of a First Drop survivor.

When the two ships landed in the big field in front of the hangar, Rastancil had mobilized transport, medical staff and enough personnel to assist in unloading the sleepers. Jim Rastancil, Geoffrey Ainger, Bob Reidenbacker, Bull Fetterman – in fact all those who constituted the Council, waited patiently for Scott, Zainal and Mitford to descend from the KDM which landed slightly ahead of its sister ship.

'This should have been a unanimous decision by all Botanists,' Scott began, nervously finger-combing his hair back from his forehead and rubbing the back of his neck.

'It was sure as hell unanimous with all the Botanists there,' Beverly said firmly.

'Hell, yes,' Dowdall, Kris and Mitford added in unison.

'Who? What?' Rastancil asked, surprised to find Scott hesitant.

'The ones the Eosi mind-wiped,' Scott said flatly. 'They were about to be shipped off to God knows where as slaves.'

'Jesus! Of course you had to bring them here,' said Rastancil. 'Leon, Mayock, front and centre and let's get them out of there,' and he charged up the ramp with the medical personnel.

Kris slipped ahead of him to her post at the deck controls.

'All right, now, let's do this efficiently,' she heard Bull Fetterman roaring. 'Move that big sled up, stretcher-bearers up front. Someone get blankets ready as makeshift . . .'

The cargo hold doors parted and, although several people choked over the rancid body smells that wafted out, they walked on and stopped.

'God in heaven . . .' Rastancil whispered, staring at the human debris, crumpled in small heaps, though some had managed to lie flat before the drug overcame them.

'And I thought we had it bad,' Leon murmured, kneeling beside the first unconcious body, feeling the neck for a pulse, his eyes ranging around the deck.

Kris had turned on what lighting there was.

'Stretcher here,' Leon said, pointing to the man and then moving inward, to the next prone body. 'Mayock, we'd better do a triage.'

And the operation began its final stage.

Sixteen hundred humans, fortunately not all of them mind-wiped but many with abused bodies and minor injures, were disembarked from the two ships. And two hundred Deski, one hundred and fourteen Rugarians, ninety Ilginish and twelve Turs.

The Turs were left on a lower deck which confined them should they wake before Raisha returned from taking the Catteni to their new accommodation. The two crewmen from the KDM

407

had been secured in its cheerless brig throughout the trip, seeing only Coo or Mitford in his Catteni role. They were told that their ship had been commandeered. One of them protested such treatment every time food was brought: even protested the good food he was served because it wasn't what he was accustomed to. The other Catteni slept almost the entire time, rousing only long enough to take care of natural needs and eat. They were blindfolded before they left their cell so they would have little to add to what information the other captives might have.

With many hands to help, Leon's triage team separated those who needed the most attention from those who needed only rest, good food and reassurance. By then, quite a few were regaining consciousness and could be offered water and soup, hastily brought from the dining hall. Even without formal orders, there was suddenly a carer with every victim in a response that certainly gladdened Kris's heart. Scott should have had more faith in the community's generosity. It wasn't as if he hadn't seen examples of it with every new Drop the Catteni made.

Some awakened and were utterly passive: their empty faces expressionless. They had to be helped to drink, though they could manage to swallow or eat once food was put to their lips. Others woke, screaming or sobbing helplessly and that was nearly as heartbreaking even if it gave an indication that some vestige of the original personality might remain.

'Just keep talking to them, folks,' Leon called out. 'Let them hear English, see human faces around them. Feed 'em, but don't let them gorge.'

'Who knows when they've had a decent meal,' Anna Bollinger muttered, trying to keep the bruised and battered woman beside her from gulping down the entire can of soup. 'Just sip it. There'll be all you need.'

'Gawd, it's like a disaster scene, an earthquake or something,' Joe Latore said, helping his male victim to his feet since the man was trying so desperately to stand. 'What'n'hell are you doing, Zainal? Taking pictures of people right now.'

'I show the Farmers what Eosi do to people. I show the Farmers what humans do to help,' he said, bringing the taper in close to the vacant eyes of Joe's man.

Then Zainal turned the camera to include the woman Leon was treating for body lacerations that covered every inch of her torso. He went from her to a group of three whose faces were devoid of any expression, eyes dulled and unfocusing.

Those who could be classified as walking wounded were sent to the homes of volunteer carers, with instructions for basic care.

'Like a bath!' someone remarked loudly. 'Wonder what I'll find under all that dirt and . . . yuck.'

Everyone volunteered to help almost to the point of being disappointed when all the victims had been assigned a place.

Leon and other medical staff gave general directions for emergency care. 'Keep them warm, give them plenty of fluid, but limit solid food until their bodies can adjust. Let them sleep all they want. But don't let them go off on their own. We'll set up evaluation conferences and see which might respond to rehabilitation.'

'Can you manage, Leon?' Scott asked earnestly.

'You better believe it, Ray,' Leon replied sharply. 'In fact we can and have managed it,' and he swung his arm in a broad gesture across the all but empty field. 'Who knows? Good food, fresh air, plenty of friendly faces . . .' he added with a wry grin, 'and good trauma skills, we may even effect a significant number of complete recoveries.'

'You really think so?' Scott looked ready to accept any reassurance for the responsibility he had off-loaded on the colony.

'Sure do!' Leon said in such a positive tone that Scott finally relaxed. 'No way you could have left them! Any road, they're better off with us.'

'They are, you know,' Kris said. 'You look beat, Ray.'

'I should take one in with me. My house is finished,' and Scott stared after the last couples leaving the field.

'We'll switch people around, Ray. I'll make sure you take your turn,' Leon said ironically. 'Now, my prescription for you, Ray Scott, is get some rest. You too, Kris. You left your baby in the crèche or does that seem years ago?'

'It does, you know,' she said. She'd been too busy

to give much thought to Zane. But he was happy where he was: one of the crèche girls had told her that he'd been just fine.

'I believe it. Get on up to him, now,' and Leon gave her a little push in the right direction. Then, when he saw Kris glancing about her for Zainal, he added, 'He was following the final load on the sled that last time I saw him.'

To her delighted surprise, she met him just short of the crèche, with Zane in his arms. He shrieked with joy on seeing his mother and, almost over-balancing himself out of Zainal's arms, reached out both hands for her. Zainal let the exchange be made, one hand holding the recording camera tight against his side.

'I saw you filming,' Scott said, altering his direction to join them. He even managed a tired smile at the enthusiastic way Zane was hugging his mother.

Zainal patted the camera, nodding. 'Such evidence is needed to show the Farmers how the Eosi treat humans. You will help me write a report, Ray?' And when Scott nodded wearily, Zainal added, 'What words do not say, the film will.'

'You'll use one of those homing capsules the Farmers have in the Command Post?'

'The Farmers do not approve of species' injury. Once they see what Eosi do, we will hear from them again.'

There was considerable discussion about whether or not the Farmers would be able to play the pictorial record when Zainal, Kris and the former movie cameraman had finished making it. Baxter, however, did still photographs that were indeed worth a thousand words of explanation, and these were carefully inserted in the message tube.

The homing device had no trouble penetrating the Balloon on its way to its destination. Its departure was once again noted by the orbital and the geo-synchronous satellite, as well as its abrupt disappearance just past the heliopause. The event was immediately sent to Eosi headquarters for distribution.

The Ix Mentat, just returned from its almost futile investigations on the rebellious planet, was so contorted with rage that its juniors feared it might lose connection with its host. It had only just received a report from Barevi, citing the disappearance of one of the new transporter vessels as well as over 2,000 slaves, destined for the mining colony at Ble Sot Fac Set which had been expecting replacements for unavoidable casualties in a major shaft collapse. When the report came to the composition of that shipment, the Ix Mentat came closer to self-extinction than any of its peer group in their long history.

Its recovery from such a seizure was slow: its host had suffered bodily injury and had to be repaired, an almost unheard-of complication in an Eosi/Emassi symbiosis.

To calm their senior, Mentats Co and Se issued orders that an installation was to be built on the innermost moon of the subject planet: a second orbital, programmed for a slower rotation, would provide constant surveillance and prevent the recalcitrant population from effecting another covert exit since it was now obvious that they had two or more spaceships.

When the Eosi Ix recovered fully from its incapacity, it began to organize the largest expedition ever mounted by Catteni forces. It would wreak the most horrific vengeance on that recalcitrant planet that had ever been mounted by Eosi Mentat. Afterwards there would be no opposition left in the galaxy that could subject an Eosi to such humiliation. But first, they must find weapons or the method to breach the barrier around the colony planet. A planet, the Ix Mentat stoutly told all its colleagues, which was undoubtedly the cause of all the problems recently encountered by Catteni and Eosi alike. Once it was destroyed, the Eosi could resume their normal activities and enjoy their conquests unopposed.

THE END

FREEDOM'S LANDING
by Anne McCaffrey

When the Catteni ships descended on earth it was one of the most terrifying experiences humankind had ever known. Kris Bjornsen, along with thousands of others, found herself herded by forcewhips into the hold of giant spaceships to be transported to the slave compounds of an alien planet. And even then it wasn't over. For, after a partially successful escape attempt, Kris was once more shipped across space – to an apparently empty and untamed planet. The Catteni just dumped an assorted load of humans and aliens on the strange world and left them to see what would happen.

Brilliantly the refugees began to organize themselves into a pattern of survival. The planet was eerie and not as empty as it seemed. For someone – something – had built giant storage barns – the planet was being used as a huge larder – for an entity they could not comprehend.

As Kris and her patrol set out to explore the enigmatic world she had yet another problem to contend with – the presence of Zainal, the high-ranking patrician Catteni who had been abandoned with the rest of them. Zainal was strong, brilliant, and . . . kind, and Kris was puzzled by his presence, his personality, and above all by the tenuous tie she felt towards this man – who was not a man but one of the hated Catteni.

The first of the brilliant new *Catteni* sequence.

0 552 14271 9

RED STAR RISING
The second Chronicles of Pern
by Anne McCaffrey

For two hundred years there had been peace on Pern –
but now the signs were ominous. Violent winter storms
and erupting volcanoes heralded the coming of the
second Pass of Thread, when the red planet would rain
down its horrifying harvest and destroy every living
organism on the face of Pern. No human or dragon or
animal or plant was safe from the hideous death inflicted
by Thread.

Weyrs and Holds tried to prepare, but they had serious
problems. Over the generations much of the old technology had been lost. AIVAS, the giant information
bank, was buried under tons of volcanic ash, and valuable and skilled men and women had succumbed to
disease and old age, taking with them the knowledge of
a great civilization.

They had to prepare as best they could, training the great
flights of dragons and ensuring that the Lord Holders
did their part by protecting their people in every possible
way. Only Lord Chalkin, Holder of Bitra, refused to co-
operate. He did not believe in Threadfall. It was a plot
of the Weyrs to gain ascendancy over the Holds. He
would do nothing to protect Bitra or its people. The
Lord Holders and Weyrleaders were of one accord.
Chalkin must be impeached and removed from his lands
if the planet was to be made safe.

0 552 14272 7

A LIST OF OTHER ANNE McCAFFREY TITLES AVAILABLE FROM CORGI BOOKS

THE PRICES SHOWN BELOW WERE CORRECT AT THE TIME OF GOING TO PRESS. HOWEVER TRANSWORLD PUBLISHERS RESERVE THE RIGHT TO SHOW NEW RETAIL PRICES ON COVERS WHICH MAY DIFFER FROM THOSE PREVIOUSLY ADVERTISED IN THE TEXT OR ELSEWHERE.

All Transworld titles are available by post from:

Book Service By Post, P.O. Box 29, Douglas, Isle of Man IM99 1BQ

Credit cards accepted. Please telephone 01624 675137, fax 01624 670923, Internet http://www.bookpost.co.uk or e-mail: bookshop@enterprise.net for details.

Free postage and packing in the UK. Overseas customers allow £1 per book (paperbacks) and £3 per book (hardbacks).